STATE OF PRESERVATION

FIRST FAMILY SERIES, BOOK 10

MARIE FORCE

State of Preservation
First Family Series, Book 10
By: Marie Force

Published by HTJB, Inc.
Copyright 2025. HTJB, Inc.
Cover design by Kristina Brinton and Ashley Lopez
Cover photography by Regina Wamba
Models: Robert John and Ellie Dulac
Print Layout: E-book Formatting Fairies
ISBN: 978-1966871187

HTJB, Inc.
PO Box 370
Portsmouth, RI 02871 USA
author@marieforce.com

The First Family Series

Book 1: State of Affairs
Book 2: State of Grace
Book 3: State of the Union
Book 4: State of Shock
Book 5: State of Denial
Book 6: State of Bliss
Book 7: State of Suspense
Book 8: State of Alert
Book 9: State of Retribution
Book 10: State of Preservation
Book 11: State of Unrest
Book 12: State of Mind (2026)

CHAPTER ONE

Ethan *is missing.* Her sister Tracy's words echoed through Sam's mind as her heart slowed to a crawl. Her nephew was eleven, no longer a baby, but not old enough to be in any kind of trouble.

"Sam! What do I do?"

Tracy's frantic question jarred Sam out of the spiral of unsettling thoughts. "I'll be right there."

Sam snapped her phone shut and forced herself to refocus on what she'd been doing before the call. She and Nick had come to their former Ninth Street home to finish cleaning out their personal belongings so her colleague and friend Tommy Gonzales could move his family in.

"What's wrong?" Nick asked from his place on the floor in front of the fire where they'd made a camp to re-create an earlier night in the first home they'd shared as a couple. He was on his side, naked as the day he was born, holding his head up on an upturned hand.

Sam crossed the room, picking up articles of clothing they'd discarded in their haste. "Ethan is missing."

Nick sat up. "What? For how long?"

"Tracy didn't say, but I've got to get over there."

He reached for his boxers and pulled them on. "I'm coming with you."

She paused in her frantic effort to get dressed. "Um, I hate to point out the obvious, but…"

"I'll tell Brant to make it happen."

As the president, any time he went anywhere, a three-ring circus was required. She hesitated to bring their level of chaos to an already-fraught situation at her sister's home. However, she wanted him with her badly enough to let him go tell his lead Secret Service agent, John Brantly Jr., to get them to Tracy's as fast as possible. Luckily, her sister's family lived only a few blocks from Ninth Street.

Nick shut off the gas fireplace and left the room to arrange things.

Sam pulled on the leggings she'd worn with a new silk top for their "date night" to clean out their former home. Nick had surprised her by having the work done by their devoted White House staff so they could enjoy a romantic last evening in their former home before they turned it over to their friends.

She hadn't thought to bring a brush, so she ran her fingers through her hair and twisted it up in the clip she always had with her, hoping she was somewhat presentable. She was anxious to get to her sister and figure out what was going on with Ethan.

Tracy had recently come to Sam for advice on dealing with her son, who'd become quiet and secretive, especially after he'd gotten a cell phone for his eleventh birthday. Sam had connected her sister with the daughter of her colleague Dr. Anthony Trulo. Dr. Trulo's daughter, Christi, specialized in family therapy and had recently begun to work with Ethan.

Sam had so many questions. Where was Ethan supposed to be, and who was he with? When was the last time Tracy or Mike had spoken to or heard from their son? Were they able to track his phone? What did they know about his friends? She raced down the stairs to find Nick surrounded by his detail as they conferred on a plan.

"We have to go," Sam said. "Or at least I have to. You guys can catch up?"

"We need five minutes, ma'am," Brant said. "I promise we'll be quick."

"Thank you."

Nick put his arm around her and kissed the top of her head. "I'm sorry for even a five-minute delay."

She rested her head against his chest. "It's worth it to have you with me."

"I'm sure he's fine. Probably just doing stupid kid shit and not thinking about how worried his parents must be."

"I really hope that's all it is."

Her stomach churned with dread. After everything Tracy had shared about Ethan's recent behavior, Sam no longer knew what to think.

When they'd been loaded into the presidential limousine known as The Beast for the short ride to Tracy's, Sam called her friend and boss at the D.C. Metropolitan Police Department, Captain Jake Malone, to tell him her nephew was missing. "I'm out of my realm on this." She understood the moves in Homicide. Missing Persons was a whole other procedure. "What's our first move?"

"We'll need the family out of the house so Crime Scene can do a full search of the premises, and we'll get IT on the devices."

"Tracy will want to know why Crime Scene is involved when there's no crime that we know of."

"They'll collect evidence that may or may not become relevant to the investigation. Is there somewhere you can move Tracy's family to while we search the house?"

Sam was rattled by the idea of a CSU search of her sister's home. "I'll move them to Celia's house."

"Good idea. They can't take anything with them. No phones,

no devices. All that has to stay there for the investigators, with the codes and passwords written down."

"Right."

"Sam."

"Yeah?"

"You can't be the lead on this. Tell me you know that."

"I do, but I have to help, or I'll go mad. Please don't say I can't help."

"You can provide peripheral support, but we have to play this by the book so we don't fuck up a potential prosecution, if it comes to that, which I hope to God it won't. But you know the drill."

"Yes, okay. I'll stay in the background, but I have to be able to support my sister and her family."

"I have no objection to that as long as you cede to the Missing Persons detectives and let them do their jobs with no territorial shit, you got me?"

"Yes, sir. Who's their commander again?"

"They fall under Captain Ruiz."

Fuck. She'd had a previous encounter with the captain that hadn't gone well, at least as far as Sam was concerned.

"I'll call Missing Persons right now and send them and CSU to Tracy's."

"Thank you."

"Keep me posted if you hear anything."

"I will."

Tracy was frantic with worry. Ethan had been difficult lately, full of attitude and secrecy about his friends and what they were up to when they were out together. Ethan had pleaded with them to let him go with his friends by Metro to the mall, the skate park, the arcade and to get food. She'd thought he was too young to run around the city without adult supervision.

She and her husband, Mike, had argued about it.

"He'll be with his friends," Mike had said. "He'll be fine."

"He's too young to be set loose," Tracy had replied. "I'm not at all comfortable with this."

"Trace, his friends have already been doing it for a while now. If we hold him back from doing things his friends are allowed to do, he'll resent us."

"He's eleven. Not fifteen. It's too soon."

"He'll have his phone, and we can track him. We'll make that nonnegotiable."

"What will you say when Abby wants to be running the streets at eleven? Will that be okay, too?"

For a second, Mike had seemed uncertain. Abby was his angel, his little girl and best pal. "That's different. She's a girl."

"I'm going to pretend you didn't say that."

"Let's face it. A lot worse things can happen to her than could ever happen to him."

Tracy had stared at him incredulously. "Is that what you think? Have you watched the news lately? *No one* is safe in this world, let alone kids."

"Ethan has a good head on his shoulders. He's bright, strong and sensible. We raised him to have street smarts and to be aware of his surroundings. I say he'll be fine to go out with his friends."

Tracy had realized that if Mike was on Ethan's side, she was fighting a losing battle, so she'd reluctantly gone along with giving Ethan some freedom—with conditions. He had to have his phone with him at all times with location services on, and he needed to check in regularly about where he was and who he was with. She'd also asked for his closest friends' phone numbers so she could contact them if needed.

He hadn't liked that request, but he'd traded the numbers for the freedom he craved. And now she couldn't reach him or any of his friends. His phone was going right to voicemail, and the location wasn't available, which her older daughter, Brooke, had told her meant the phone was probably turned off or was in airplane mode.

"Do you want me to come home?" Brooke, who was in college at the University of Virginia in Charlottesville, had asked when Tracy called her in a panic.

"I don't think that's necessary, but thank you for offering."

"Nate's here this weekend. We could be there in a couple of hours. Let me know."

Brooke was seeing the lead Secret Service agent on the detail of Sam and Nick's "bonus" son, Elijah Armstrong. He was stationed in Princeton, New Jersey, where Eli was a junior.

"I'll keep you posted."

"Please do," Brooke had said. "This is so scary. It's not like Ethan to do something like this."

Tracy had wanted to say that it was just like him lately, but she hadn't told her eldest about the issues they'd been having with her brother because she hadn't wanted to burden Brooke with their concerns. She had enough on her plate with her schoolwork and her relationship with Nate, which had gotten serious in recent months. Brooke was planning to transfer to Princeton next year so she could be with Nate.

Tracy checked her phone to see if there was an update from Sam on when she would arrive.

On the way from 9th, Sam had written five minutes ago.

"Anything?" Mike asked when he came in from driving around to check some of Ethan's usual haunts.

Tracy shook her head. She didn't bother asking the same question, because Ethan wasn't with him.

"Did you call Sam?"

"She'll be here in a minute. She was at Ninth, so close by."

"That's good."

Tracy wanted to scream at him that it wasn't good, nothing about this was *good*, and it was all his fault. If only he'd listened to her when she'd said Ethan was too young for the kind of freedom Mike wanted to give him. If only... She bit back the vitriol that burned the tip of her tongue. Saying the words would only make everything worse.

On the way to Tracy's, Sam texted Freddie, Gonzo and Archie to let them know what was going on. *Malone is calling in Missing Persons, who'll take the lead on his orders, but I want to help, and there's not much I can do being a relative. I'm so sorry to ask you to give up a Saturday evening, but there've been some concerns with him recently that have me truly worried. We're going to relocate Tracy's family to Celia's so CSU can process Tracy's house.*

I'm on the way to Celia's, they answered one after the other.

Thank you all so very much.

Anything for you, Freddie said.

The other two put exclamation marks on Freddie's text.

"Freddie, Gonzo and Archie are coming to help," she told Nick.

"That's good of them."

"Yeah, for sure."

They knew there was nothing she wouldn't do for them either. It was how they rolled. Her entire team had recently stood by her side when she was under attack from two colleagues who blamed her for everything that'd ever gone wrong in their lives. Thankfully, former Sergeant Ramsey and former Officer Offenbach were now locked up and facing charges that should keep them in prison for the rest of their lives.

Chief of Police Joe Farnsworth had put out a message informing his entire four-thousand-member department that there'd be zero tolerance for lawlessness going forward and that the union had agreed to work with him to weed out the bad apples. There were a lot of them, and Sam was relieved to see two of the rottenest ones gone for good from their ranks.

Not to mention the death of disgraced former Deputy Chief Paul Conklin, who'd taken his own life when he was implicated in yet another crime, the first being the shooting of Sam's late father, a case that had gone unsolved for four long years while Conklin had known all along who'd shot Skip—and why. This time, they found out he'd tried to discredit Sam and Skip by feeding dirt on her to Offenbach and Ramsey, who'd paid him for it.

It'd been an exhausting few years for the Metropolitan Police Department, and Sam was still processing the fallout from the most recent situation in which Offenbach had sent armed drones toward the Easter Egg Roll at the White House, among other egregious crimes.

And now her young nephew was missing, her sister and brother-in-law were in a panic, and they'd be looking to her to find him and fix this for them. She'd do as much as she possibly could without crossing the lines Captain Malone had drawn. But she was as tired as she'd been in a long, long time.

Nick gave her hand a squeeze. "You know it's okay to defer to others to handle this if you don't have it in you right now."

Of course he knew she was maxed out. He always knew. "Yes, I do."

"You were looking forward to a little break after closing that nightmare of a case with Offenbach and Ramsey."

"I have to help find Ethan. How could I do anything else while he's missing? But I just have to wonder when the hell my family is going to catch a break."

"It's been a lot. No question."

While still in high school, Brooke had been attacked and raped at a party in which other teens had been murdered. Sam's dad had died in October, her brother-in-law Spencer in February and now her nephew was missing. Enough already.

She sent a message to Dr. Trulo, the department psychiatrist. *My nephew Ethan, who recently began seeing your daughter for therapy, is missing. If she has any info that might be helpful, we'd appreciate hearing from her. I'm not sure what the ethics are on this when the patient is a minor. Anything you can do... Thank you.*

Her phone rang a second later with a call from the doctor.

"Hey, I'm sending Christi a text as we speak. I'll let you know what I hear. What else can I do?"

"That's it for now. Thank you for jumping right on it."

"Of course. Call if there's anything else I can do."

"I will. Thanks, Doc."

"I'll be praying for your nephew and family."

"Appreciate it."

Sam closed her flip phone. "Dr. Trulo's daughter is a therapist and was seeing Ethan. He's asking if she has any insight. He said he'd pray for Ethan and our family."

"That's nice of him."

"What does it say about me that praying is the last thing I think to do when things go sideways?"

"Your first impulse is more about taking action yourself than asking the Almighty to handle things."

"I almost envy people who have that kind of faith, how they can turn it all over to God, or whoever they worship, and know it'll work out the way it's meant to."

"You're too service-oriented to leave the details to anyone else."

"Is that your way of saying I'm a heathen?"

"I never used that word."

"I have a knot in my stomach, worrying about where Ethan is and what this'll turn out to be about."

"Let's hope it's all a big misunderstanding."

Sam hoped against hope it was, but her gut was telling her something much bigger than that was going on, and she wouldn't rest until she figured out what it was and helped to get her nephew home safely.

CHAPTER TWO

After a frustrating delay caused by the Secret Service securing the area outside the Hogan home, Sam and Nick were escorted to Tracy and Mike's front door. Her capable eldest sister dissolved into tears the second she saw Sam.

"Thank you for coming. Both of you. Thank you so much."

Sam hugged her sister. "I hate to add to your stress, but we have to relocate you to Celia's house."

"What? Why?"

"Crime Scene needs access to your house. It's standard procedure when someone goes missing."

Tracy's expression shifted to horror. "They think *we* had something to do with it?"

"No, Trace, but they have to cover every base, and that starts at home, where there may be clues we can use to find him."

"Can we pack some things to take?"

"You have to leave everything behind, including your phones. They'll be returned to you after they're processed."

Tracy's eyes flooded with tears. "What if he calls? How will I know? I'll go mad without my phone."

"I'll have mine, and I'll make sure everyone knows to call me if there're any updates."

"I have to tell Brooke... She'll be frantic if she can't reach me."

"You can call her on my phone. Before we go, write down phone numbers from your contacts for anyone who might be able to help us locate Ethan or his friends. Do that while I get Abby and Mike. We have to move you so the Crime Scene detectives can do their work. They may find something that'll lead us to Ethan."

"This is too much on top of my son being missing."

"I'm sorry. They thought it would be easier for you to hear this from me."

"Nothing about this is easy. I'm going crazy coming up with worst-case scenarios."

"Don't do that. We don't know anything yet. Let's take this one minute at a time."

Within twenty minutes, Tracy had made a list of phone numbers while Sam rounded up Mike and Abby, who was wide-eyed with fear as she hugged Sam. She wished she had some comforting words for her niece, but what could she say that would help?

Outside, Sam saw Agent Quigley standing outside one of the black SUVs in the motorcade. She led her family members to that SUV for the short ride to Celia's. Nick would be conveyed in The Beast. "Ninth Street, please," she said. "My stepmother's house."

"Got it."

When they were on the way, Sam called Brooke.

"Did you find him?" Brooke asked.

"Not yet, but we're moving your family to Celia's so we can go through the house looking for anything that might help us find him. They had to leave their phones behind, so call me if you need us."

"So there's nothing new?" Brooke asked anxiously.

"Not yet, honey, but we're on it. Here's your mom."

Tracy took the phone and seemed to answer the same

questions Sam had fielded from Brooke. "No, honey, there's nothing new, but we're moving to Celia's house because the police need access to ours." After a pause, she said, "No, we're not suspects. They're looking for anything that might tell us where he is."

Sam wanted to wail as she thought of the many things that could've happened to Ethan. She didn't even know yet how long he'd been gone or where he was supposed to have been.

"Yes, I'll call you if anything changes, but in the meantime, check in with Auntie Sam. Okay, I will. Love you, too." Tracy closed the phone and handed it back to Sam. "Nate is with her. They might come home."

"I'm glad he's there for her."

"Where's my son, Sam? Where *is he*?"

"I don't know yet, but we're doing everything we can to find him."

Across from her, Mike swiped at a tear as he stared out the window.

Sam's heart broke for them, and for Abby, Brooke and everyone who loved Ethan. The not knowing was horrible.

The SUV came to a stop at the curb outside her stepmother's home, which was dark other than a single light in the living room window that was on a timer. Celia was away on an Alaskan cruise with her sisters and not due home for a few more days, which was a blessing of sorts. Sam wouldn't say anything to Celia until she had to as there was no sense in upsetting her when there was nothing Celia could do from afar.

Sam punched in the code to the front door, deactivated the alarm and turned on lights before sending a quick text to Celia. *Borrowing your house for the night. Will explain later.*

Ah, OK, she responded a few minutes later. *Was wondering why I got the alert on the alarm. My house is your house. Love you. Miss you.*

Same, Sam replied before taking a seat next to a tearful Tracy on the sofa.

"Every time I come here, I expect Dad to come wheeling around the corner, asking what's up."

"Me, too." She took her sister's cold hand as Nick arrived with Brant. "Tell me what you know. How long has he been gone? Where's he supposed to be? Who's he with?"

Tracy pressed a tissue to her swollen eyes. "He left around four with his friend Tomas. They said they were going to meet this other kid they know."

"What's his name?"

"Brecken something. I don't know him. They said they were going to get pizza and then play video games at the Wharf. Our calls to Ethan and Tomas are going to voice mail."

"How were they getting to where they were going?"

"On the Metro."

"By themselves?" Sam asked, surprised to hear Tracy and Mike had allowed that.

"They've been doing it for a while now." Tracy glanced at Mike, who looked at the floor. "I wasn't in favor, but I was overruled."

"All his friends are doing it," Mike said with a defensive edge to his voice.

Palpable—and unusual—tension beat between them. "What do we know about the friends?" Sam asked.

"Tomas is a great kid," Mike said. "Ethan knows him from school, and they play youth football together."

"Do you know his parents?"

"To say hello to," Tracy said. "That's about it."

"So you don't have their numbers or know where they live?"

"No, Tomas is on a different team than Ethan, so we don't have that info," Mike said.

"Last name?"

Tracy and Mike exchanged glances before shaking their heads.

"I can't recall his last name, but I have his phone number if that helps," Tracy said. "It's on my phone."

"What does Ethan have for money?"

"Some cash," Mike said, "and a debit card that we keep a small balance on so he can grab food when he's out."

Sam took notes. "Can I get the info on that? The number on the card or the account number?"

"I'm not sure how to get that for you without my phone or computer. All my passwords are preprogrammed."

"We'll come back to that," Sam said. "When was the last time you had contact with him?"

"I checked his location around four fifteen," Mike said. "He was on the Green Line heading to Waterfront Station."

"What's there?"

"The arcade they like. They go there all the time."

Freddie came in and looked to Sam. "What can I do?"

"Ethan is with a kid he goes to school with at Hardy Middle School. His name is Tomas. We don't have his last name but need to talk to his parents. They were meeting another kid named Brecken at the arcade at the Wharf. Not sure where he goes to school." She looked up at Freddie. "Where have I heard the name Brecken before?"

"Wes Hambly's brother in the Audrey Olsen case," Freddie said.

"Yes! That's it. Thank you. Let me know what you find out about Tomas's parents."

"On it." Freddie turned and left the room as quickly as he'd arrived.

"What else do you know that might be relevant?" Sam asked. "And keep in mind we need to know everything, even things that you might normally be tempted to keep private. This isn't the time to be concerned about that. All cards on the table."

"We've gone over everything before we called you," Mike said. "We can't think of anything out of the ordinary that might've led to this. You knew we've been butting heads with him, but things had been better since we'd agreed to give him a little freedom."

In Sam's opinion, that was the worst thing they could've done when he'd been acting defiant, but she kept that thought to herself. As someone whose kids were surrounded at all times by Secret Service agents, she was in no position to judge the choices other parents made.

"I need a recent photo of him."

"We just got his spring school pictures back." Tracy sounded relieved that there was at least one thing she could do to help.

"I have one in my wallet," Mike said, reaching for his back pocket.

He handed her the wallet-size photo, and Sam took a close look at it. Ethan had light brown hair that became blonder in the summer, golden-brown eyes and an impish grin that produced a dimple on the left side. He'd grown up a lot in recent months and was starting to look more like a young man than a boy.

Sam loved him fiercely, and the sight of his adorable face nearly brought her to tears. She fought back the surge of emotion because it would only upset Tracy even more and handed the photo to Gonzo when he arrived. "Can you put out a BOLO for Ethan Hogan, age eleven, please?"

Gonzo took Ethan's photo from her. "Yep, it'll go out to everyone currently on duty, and we'll post it to the NCIC."

"What's a BOLO and the NCIC?" Mike asked.

"A BOLO is a be-on-the-lookout alert," Gonzo said. "And NCIC is the National Crime Information Center, which puts the notice that Ethan is missing out to law enforcement around the country."

Tracy gasped. "You think he's *somewhere else*?"

"We have no way to know, Trace," Sam said. "We're covering all the bases."

"Will it be all over the news when he puts out the alert?" Tracy asked.

"Yes, but we want people looking for him."

"Will he get in trouble if you find him doing something he shouldn't be doing?" Mike asked.

"Like what?" Sam asked.

"I don't know. The shit kids do."

"I guess that depends on what he's doing."

"Sam, come on…" Mike's voice had a pleading edge to it. "We don't want to ruin his life. We just want him to come home."

"Why in the world would you think he was doing something that could ruin his life when he checked out to get food and play video games?"

Mike shook his head. "He's never gone missing before. I don't know what to think."

Gonzo came back into the room. "The Wharf is closed now, and Patrol is looking for Ethan in that area. Dispatch got a call from Tomas Cambra's father, Joaquin, reporting his son missing."

"Do you have the phone number?" Sam asked.

He handed her a slip of paper.

"Please let Dispatch know our team will be in touch with the Cambras and add Tomas to the BOLO. Get a photo from the parents and work out relocating them so Crime Scene can process their house."

Gonzo left the room to see to her orders.

Sam handed her phone to her sister. "Let's give them a call, Tracy. Put it on speaker."

As Tracy punched in the number, Sam noticed her sister's hands were shaking. Seeing the usually unflappable Tracy so undone was unsettling to Sam, who'd turned to Tracy for reassurance her entire life.

A man answered the phone with a tentative "Hello?"

"Mr. Cambra, this is Tracy Hogan, Ethan's mom. We're trying to find him and heard you'd reported Tomas missing, too."

"Yes, he's been gone since this afternoon and isn't answering his phone, which seems to be off." His voice wavering with emotion. "We can't see his location."

"Same with Ethan. I'm here with Lieutenant Holland from the MPD. She's my sister and is helping us."

"Mr. Cambra," Sam said, "when was the last time you heard from or had contact with Tomas?"

"It was around four thirty. I checked his location and saw he was on the Metro going to the Wharf. The next time I checked, around five forty-five, his location was unavailable, and he didn't reply to calls or texts. We waited a couple of hours before we called the police. We're very concerned. This isn't like him at all."

"We've put out a be-on-the-lookout alert for Ethan and are adding Tomas, too. Do you know the other boy they were with? Ethan's parents said his name is Brecken."

"I don't know him, and my wife doesn't either. We haven't heard his name before."

"Do any of you have the names and numbers of other kids who go to school with Ethan and Tomas who might know Brecken?"

"We can reach out to the parents we know," Mr. Cambra said.

"Call us back if you find out anything about him or hear from Tomas," Sam said. "One of my colleagues will be contacting you to get a recent photo of Tomas. It would help if you could send it over quickly."

"We will."

"Does he have a debit or credit card on him?" Sam asked.

"A debit card," Mrs. Cambra said.

"I'll need that account info ASAP so we can check for activity."

"We'll get that to you."

"Thank you. I hate to say this, but we're also going to need to relocate you so Crime Scene detectives can process your home and devices."

"You think we're involved in his disappearance?" he asked, incredulous.

"As we've said to the Hogans, there could be information in your home that might help us find the boys. This is standard procedure. Do you have somewhere you can go?"

"My wife's sister lives close by. We can go there."

"Please text me her address and phone number so I can reach you."

"How can we leave our phones when our son is missing?" the mom asked tearfully. "What if he calls?"

"The detectives will take any calls that come in while the phones are in our custody."

"Very well."

"Leave everything behind, along with the passcodes. It's very important to follow procedure so we don't miss evidence that could help us find them."

Freddie returned when she was on the phone.

After she ended the call, Sam said to Tracy and Mike, "You need to call anyone who might know where the boys could've gone and figure out who this kid Brecken is."

"Let's go in the kitchen and do that." Mike stood and extended a hand to Tracy. "We can use Celia's landline."

Tracy ignored his outstretched hand and got up on her own to go into the kitchen.

"What're you thinking?" Freddie asked when it was just him, Sam and Nick in the living room.

"I'm not sure yet, but this 'disappearance' feels deliberate," Sam said. "Their phones are off, which they knew would set off alarms at home."

"Unless someone forced them to turn off the phones," Freddie said.

"Which is also possible." Sam rubbed her stomach, which ached with worry over the idea of someone kidnapping her nephew. She glanced at Nick. "We probably can't rule out that this could be related to us somehow."

His grimace said it all. If his presidency had resulted in someone snatching their nephew... It was a stretch, but the Offenbach case had shown them that anything was possible, including sending armed drones toward the White House with the intent to kill innocent people enjoying a fun event.

But to go so far as to *kidnap* their nephew?

That couldn't be it. The very thought of it was bigger than she could wrap her head around.

Gonzo came in with Archie.

"Got here as soon as I could," Archie said. "What's going on?"

Sam filled him in. "I need you on the computers and other devices. Let me ask Tracy and Mike what he had access to and get any passwords they haven't provided yet." She led them into the kitchen, where her sister sat staring at the wall while Mike was on the landline phone.

After Mike finished the call, Sam said, "This is my colleague Lieutenant Archelotta. As the head of our IT department, I want him to review any computers and devices Ethan might've had access to at your house."

"We have a desktop computer for the kids to do homework on in the second-floor hallway, but it's not connected to the internet when he's using it," Mike said.

"Are you sure about that?" Archie asked.

"If he's connected it, Tracy and I aren't aware of that."

"Can you take Archie to your place and get him started?" Sam asked Mike.

"Sure, let's go."

Sam glanced at her friend pleadingly.

He gave a nod, letting her know she'd be the first to hear of anything he found.

After they left, Gonzo signaled for her to join him in the other room. "I want to call in the Juvenile Investigative Response Unit. They're a proactive team that works closely with youth and affiliated agencies, such as schools, courts, faith-based groups, social services, etc. They may have info we're not privy to in Homicide."

"Do it. Do anything you think would help."

"I'll see if I can reach their commander and get her over here ASAP."

"Thank you, Gonzo."

Sam returned to the kitchen. "You learning anything new?"

"Nothing," Tracy said. "No one knows this Brecken kid. I've got everyone I know working on trying to figure out who he might be, which means everyone I know has now heard my kid is missing." Tracy dropped her head into her hands. "I'm terrified, Sam. He knew full well that if we couldn't reach him, we'd clip his wings. That's the last thing he'd ever want to have happen after finally convincing us to let him go out."

"I was surprised to hear he was out alone with his friends."

"Talk to your brother-in-law about that," Tracy said bitterly. "I was completely opposed, but Mike said Ethan's friends were doing it and he'd resent us if he wasn't allowed to do what they could. I said he was far too young to be set loose in this city, that nothing good would come of it. Especially after what we went through with Brooke... I just wanted him here where he was safe." She ran her fingers through her hair as frustration rolled off her in waves. "I hate to say I was right, but..."

Sam took a seat next to Tracy and reached for her sister, holding her close while she sobbed.

"If something has happened to Ethan," Tracy said between hiccupping sobs, "I'll never forgive Mike. *Ever.*"

"Let's not get ahead of ourselves. They could be off on some crazy adventure they don't want anyone to know about."

"He wouldn't do that. He knew if he went off the grid, he'd never leave this house again on his own."

"Peer pressure can be intense," Sam reminded her. "You know how kids can be about that. If one of his friends told him he was a wimp or a baby for not going along with them, then he might risk everything to fit in with the crowd."

"Ethan's not like that. He's more a leader than a follower. He always has been. Remember when he was little, and he used to convince Brooke to play trucks with him when she had no interest whatsoever? He was so persuasive that she couldn't resist."

"I do remember that, but it doesn't mean he's not susceptible to being swayed by a peer he looks up to. If this Brecken kid is older, Ethan might be trying to gain favor with him by following his lead. Who knows?"

"I suppose that's possible. I like that better than thinking some human trafficker grabbed them and we'll never see him again."

"Try not to go to the worst-case scenario. There could be a perfectly innocent explanation for this."

Tracy raised her head off Sam's shoulder and looked her in the eyes. "Do you honestly think that's possible?"

Sam didn't, but she'd never say so to Tracy. "Let's follow the information and see where it leads, okay? Don't let your mind run away with you."

"Too late. It's already long gone."

"We've got to do something," Nick said to Freddie. "We've got to find this Brecken kid and figure out who his parents are."

He was increasingly concerned that this would turn out to be tied to him somehow, and if one hair on Ethan's precious head was harmed because of his relationship to Nick... He'd fucking resign.

That would take him right over the edge.

"I've got a call in to the principal at Hardy Middle School to figure out who he is."

"What about a search of the Master Names Database for kids named Brecken?" Sam asked when she came into the room. "We can do a cross-agency check and make sure you use different spellings of the name. We need to check Ethan's and Tomas's social media for any ties to him. Maybe he's listed in a news article about school sports or an honor roll or something?"

"I'll work on those angles now," Freddie said as she walked toward the front door. To Nick, he added, "The name is fairly popular."

"I'd never heard it before," Nick said.

"Me either until a recent case, but there're quite a few of them around Ethan's age. I'm making a note of each one I find and will follow up to figure out which one is with Ethan."

"Thank you for coming to help. We appreciate it."

"You guys are family. Tracy and her crew are, too."

Nick squeezed their friend's shoulder. "Same goes." Then he got up to consult with Brant, who was hovering in the doorway to the living room. Nick led the agent into the dining room to speak to him privately. "I'm worried this is related to me somehow. If someone took him because he's my nephew, what the hell will I do?"

"I've alerted our entire local team to be on alert that a member of the president's immediate family is missing and presumed to be in danger."

"Oh, thank you for doing that."

"No problem, sir. Anything like this triggers a huge response from the Secret Service, even if the person in question isn't under our protection. He's related to you and the first lady, which makes him ours in a situation such as this."

"That's actually comforting. Pass along my thanks to everyone involved."

"I will, sir. I'll keep you informed."

"Appreciate it, Brant."

After Brant walked out the front door, Nick stood in the entryway, wishing he could do something useful, such as go out and help to look for Ethan rather than having to stay safe inside the gilded cage of presidential protection.

It occurred to him that he needed to call Scotty before he saw news about the cops issuing an alert for Ethan. He hated to make that call, but he couldn't let his son hear about his missing cousin online.

"Hey, Dad, how's it going? Are you and Mom still at Ninth?"

"Buddy, I have to tell you something that's upsetting. While we were at Ninth, we got a call from Tracy that Ethan is missing."

"What? No... How can he be missing?"

"He was out with a friend to play video games at an arcade. His phone seems to be off, which he knows is a deal-breaker for his parents, so Tracy called Mom. We're with them now."

"Can I do anything?"

"You can help Nana with the twins. I'm not sure how long we'll be here."

"Yeah, I can do that. Is Mom scared?"

"We all are. I hate to have to call you with this news, but I didn't want you to see it online. They've issued an alert about him."

"God, Tracy and Mike must be losing it."

"They are. I'll keep you posted, okay?"

"Yeah, okay. Tell Mom and Tracy... Tell them all I love them."

"I will, buddy."

"Thanks for calling."

"Love you."

"Love you, too."

As he ended the call, Nick's heart broke for Scotty and everyone who loved Ethan, but especially Tracy and Mike. After what they'd endured when Brooke was drugged and sexually assaulted at a party where other kids were murdered, they'd already been through every parent's worst nightmare. They didn't deserve more.

Thankfully, Brooke had managed to put her life back together, was excelling in college and enjoying her first serious relationship with Nate. Nick loved that the two of them were a couple.

He could only hope and pray that Ethan would be found safe quickly and that his disappearance had nothing to do with his uncle, the president.

CHAPTER THREE

"I don't know what I should do," Brooke said to Nate two hours after the initial frantic call from her mother about Ethan being missing. Her baby brother... Although, at eleven, Ethan wasn't a baby anymore. However, he'd always be one of her babies, one of the original loves of her life, along with her sister, Abby, who was nine.

The thought of something bad happening to either of them was so unbearable that Brooke could hardly keep it together while she waited to hear something from home.

"What do you want to do?" Nate asked as he massaged her shoulders.

He'd driven down from Princeton the night before for a three-day visit they'd been counting down to for weeks. This was to have been their last time hanging out together in Charlottesville, before she—and Elijah—went home for summer vacation, putting all of them in DC for a few months before she transferred to Princeton in the fall.

"My mom told me not to come running home, but how can I think about anything else as long as my brother is missing?"

Nate turned her so he could see her face. "It could turn out to be a simple case of miscommunication or something."

Brooke shook her head. "That's not it. I'm sure of it. Ethan knew if he messed up, they'd lock him up at home. He'd never have done anything to endanger his newfound freedom."

"I'm kind of surprised to hear he's allowed to run around in DC at eleven."

"He's with his friends."

"Still... That's kind of young."

"I don't know what to say. I'm so scared that something terrible has happened."

"Why don't we get you home to be with your family?"

"I have an exam Wednesday and a paper due and—"

"Will you be able to focus on anything as long as he's missing?"

"No."

"Email your professors. Tell them what's going on and that you're going home to DC to help look for your brother."

"What if I can't make up the exam and get the paper done before the end of the semester? My acceptance to Princeton is contingent on finishing the year here."

"Maybe they'll let you finish remotely. Worry about that when Ethan is home safe."

"Right. Okay."

"Let's go pack what you need for a couple of days at home."

Nate was by her side as she gathered clothes, toiletries, notes for the paper she'd been working on and other items needed to study for her last final exam at UVA.

Twenty minutes later, they were in his Mustang heading north.

"Thank you for this."

"No problem."

"Yes, it is. You just drove more than five hours yesterday, so it's got to be the last thing you feel like doing today."

"This'll be much quicker, and don't worry about it. I understand that you need to be with your family right now. Did you tell your mom you're coming?"

"I will now."

Brooke composed a text to Sam's phone, hoping it would reach her mother. *I decided to come home. Nate is bringing me. Will be there in about 2.5 hours.*

"How much you want to bet he'll be home when we get there?" Brooke asked.

"That'd be good."

"I'll smack him upside the head for messing with our time together." She hoped against hope that he was there to be smacked when she arrived.

Brooke called her brother for the twentieth time since her mom had told her he was missing. Once again, the call went straight to voicemail, so she texted him—again.

Ethan... we're worried sick about you. Please check in with one of us. Whatever is going on, we'll handle it together. We love you.

"What do you know about his friends?" Nate asked.

"I knew his elementary school friends, but my mom says he's hanging out with a new group since he's been in middle school. She's been trying to find out more about them, but he's become secretive and sneaky."

"All the more reason not to let him run around unsupervised."

Brooke sighed. "Yeah, probably."

"I don't mean to be critical of your parents. It's easy for me to say what I'd do when I don't have an eleven-year-old begging me to go out with his friends."

"It's your law enforcement training talking."

"Yes, that. Exactly. Most people don't realize..."

She looked over at him. "What don't they realize?"

"Nothing. It doesn't matter."

"What were you going to say?"

He released a deep sigh. "I don't want to freak you out any more than you already are by telling you things you don't need to know right now."

"Things about kids?"

"Yeah, and what they're up to online, among other things."

"My parents monitor his online activity."

"Kids have figured out a way around that."

"What do you mean?"

"They have codes and stuff that parents would never understand."

"Seriously? How does that even work?"

Nate glanced at her before returning his attention to the road. "You sure you want to hear about this?"

"Not at all, but it might help find Ethan to know more about it."

With obvious reluctance, he said, "Say you want to score weed, for example. Maybe the code word is strawberries, and you text a friend saying you're craving strawberries, which is a super basic example. It's usually much more sophisticated than that. Parents scrolling through a kid's phone would never stop on the word 'strawberries' like they would if the message said 'weed' or 'pot.'"

"That's terrifying."

"I'm sorry. I've said too much."

"No, it's fine. I'm so naïve about these things. Ever since everything happened to me, I've sort of checked out of social media and keep in touch with far fewer friends than I used to. I found out who my real friends are."

"You're not missing anything by staying away from social media and online nonsense."

"Sometimes I feel like I am. My friends from home are still connected through social media, and I'm not. But I talk to the ones who matter, the few who stood by me through the bad times."

"I'm sorry if this situation is resurrecting painful memories for you."

"They're never far from the surface." As she looked to him for reassurances, she noticed for the millionth time how beautiful he was. She never got tired of looking at him. His wavy dark blond hair, blue eyes and dimples had led her roommates to give him the McDreamy nickname, which had stuck, much to his dismay. "Thank you for taking me home."

"I want to know where your brother is, too. I hope it turns out to be no big deal."

Brooke hoped the same thing, but the longer they went without word from Ethan, the more convinced she became that whatever was going on would end up being a very big deal.

Mike called Sam on her cell. "Lieutenant Archelotta wants to see you over here."

"I'll be right there." She went to tell Tracy she was leaving for a short time but would be back and conveyed Brooke's message that she and Nate were on the way home.

"Has something else happened?" Tracy asked.

"Nothing new. I'll let you know if I hear anything. Stay close to the landline."

"I've got nowhere else to be but sitting right here hoping to hear something before I go insane."

Sam squeezed her shoulder, wishing there was something more she could do for Tracy. "I'll be back as soon as I can."

"Okay."

"I've got to go back to Tracy's house," Sam told Nick in the living room.

"Brant told me the Secret Service is assisting in the search. I was coming to tell you that."

"That's great news. We'll take all the help we can get."

"I also called Scotty so he doesn't hear about it on the news."

"Oh cripes. I never even thought of that. Should you reach out to Eli, too?"

"I will. Do you want me to stay with Tracy while you're gone?"

"That would help." She went up on tiptoes to kiss him. "Thank you."

"I want to be out there looking for him."

"I know, but we've got everyone on duty watching for him. You're better off here, providing support to Tracy."

"Sure I am," he said with frustration, "but whatever. It is what it is."

"I'll be back as soon as possible."

"I'll be here."

"Love you."

"Love you, too. Be safe out there."

"Not going far."

When she stepped out of the house, Agent Quigley greeted her. "Where to?"

"Back to Tracy's."

"Got it." He held the door for her and had them on the way in a matter of seconds, with a young female agent she didn't recognize riding shotgun.

Agent Quigley, who went by Q, had been filling in on Sam's detail while one of her regular agents, Jimmy McFarland, recovered from being shot while protecting her. Apparently, Q had drawn the weekend shift.

"Anything new?" Q asked.

"Not yet. Our IT lieutenant is working on the devices at the house and asked me to come there."

"Hopefully, he's found a thread for you to pull."

"I can't pull the threads on this one. But I can help find the threads in the first place."

"They told you not to work the case?"

"In so many words. I don't care about who's in charge. I just want to find my nephew. Before I had kids of my own... They were my kids, you know? Brooke, Ethan, Abby, Jack, Ella. They made the infertility bearable because I had them. I love them like they're my own."

"How's your sister doing?" Q asked.

"Terrible. I can't bear this for her and Mike. It's horrible not to know where he is."

"Yeah, for sure. It was the thing my mother was most afraid of when we were growing up—one of us going missing."

"It's a parent's worst nightmare."

"Definitely. Were you told that our team is assisting the MPD?"

"Yes, Nick just told me that, and I'm so grateful. You know what else I'm grateful for…"

He glanced at her in the mirror. "What's that?"

"That this can never happen to my kids because of you guys. I wish every kid had dedicated Secret Service agents keeping them safe like mine do."

"I wish they did, too. Might get some societal pushback on that, however."

"Yeah, probably. People get itchy about being watched. I'm wondering when Scotty will start chafing. He's probably already wishing he could be running the streets with his friends."

"You wouldn't let him do that, even if his dad wasn't the president."

"No, I wouldn't, and frankly, I'm shocked that Ethan was allowed to at eleven."

"They don't know what we know. If they did, no one would let their kids out of their sight until they were fully grown."

"Which isn't feasible, so where's the line?"

"I don't know, but letting them run loose in this city isn't safe."

"I can't bear to think of the hundreds of things that could've happened."

"Try to stay focused on what you know and not get too far down that road."

"I just gave my sister that same advice."

"You should take your own advice."

"Q is right," the female agent said. "Follow the evidence, and don't get ahead of yourself."

Normally, Sam would want her name and story, but tonight,

she didn't have the bandwidth for anything more than searching for Ethan. "I'll try. Thank you, guys."

"Wish there was more we could do," Q said as he pulled up to Tracy's home, where numerous vehicles from the MPD were parked outside.

She took a calming breath, hoping to settle her out-of-control nerves, and released it before letting Q walk her in to see what Archie had for her. Inside her sister's home, she came face-to-face with Captain Michelle Ruiz, who headed the Emergency Response Team, including Missing Persons.

They'd worked together on a recent case, and Sam had picked up on animosity from the other woman that she still didn't understand, as they'd never worked together before. Ruiz was about five-seven, with a curvy figure and curly brown hair. Her dark eyes were hard, though, which was something Sam recalled from their earlier interactions.

"Captain."

"Lieutenant. What can I do for you?"

Sam thought quickly about what she could say that would keep her from being shown the door by someone who didn't want her there. "I'm here to see Lieutenant Archelotta, who asked me to come by to answer a couple of questions on behalf of the family."

"He's upstairs."

Sam waited for her to step aside. "Thank you."

"I hope I won't have a problem with you on this case."

"Excuse me?"

"I can't help but notice you called in IT and your sergeant is here, as if your squad is working this case."

"They're here as my friends, helping to look for my nephew."

"You've been told you're not allowed to participate in this investigation."

"Yes, ma'am, I'm well aware of what my boss told me, but I sure do appreciate you refreshing my memory. That's very helpful during this difficult situation for my family." Sam pushed by her, prepared to put the captain on her ass if she got in the way, and took the stairs two at a time, propelled by rage. Why did people have to be dicks? What possible thrill did Ruiz get out of busting her balls at a time like this?

She found Archie seated in the hallway in front of the desktop computer.

"What's up?" Sam asked.

"Mike helped me gain access to their bank and cell accounts. The bank card showed only the purchase of the Metro ticket today. I've been reading Ethan's text messages to his friends and thought you'd want to see this."

Sam glanced over her shoulder to make sure Ruiz hadn't followed her.

Archie brought multiple exchanges from that afternoon up on the screen that showed Ethan texting with Tomas and Brecken about a girl who'd called them incels.

"What does that mean?" Sam asked.

"Involuntary celibate," Archie replied. "It means the girls purposely choose not to have sex with them."

"Wait, what? These kids are *eleven!*"

"Read this." Archie pointed to a message from Brecken.

I don't know bout u, but I don't think she shld get away w that. Need to teach her a lesson. Who wit me?

"Oh my God," Sam whispered. "Are you able to see who they're talking about?"

"They're careful not to name her."

"Did Ethan reply to that?"

"No, but Tomas did. He said he wasn't sure about that. 'Maybe she doesn't know what that means.' To which Brecken replied, 'Fuck that shit. She knows.'"

"Is there any way to find out who this Brecken kid is?"

"Not without a warrant to trace his phone to the account, which'll take days because the phone companies are never helpful that way."

"Is there a back-office way to do it if someone's life is at stake?"

"Not that I could do without endangering my career."

"What the hell are we dealing with here, Archie?"

"Could be anything from aiming to have words with this girl to wanting to assault or kill her."

"They're *babies*," she whispered, her heart racing with fear. "How can they be involved in something like this?"

"We don't know for sure Ethan is involved. Maybe he's trying to talk them out of doing something stupid."

"Do you really believe that?"

"I don't know him. What do you think?"

"I haven't seen as much of him in recent months as I used to." Sam felt enormously guilty about that. Since Nick had become president six months ago, their lives had been more complicated than ever. "Tracy told me recently that he'd been giving them some trouble. She said since he got the phone for his eleventh birthday, he's been withdrawn and secretive and dropped most of his friends from elementary school. He's got only phone and texting on the cell phone, but no internet."

"He has access to the internet on this computer, which Mike didn't realize. Mike says he spends hours on it every day doing homework and playing games. He and Tracy were under the impression that the games had been downloaded to the computer, but that's not the case. He plays live online."

"Are you able to look at the history?"

"I'm working on that. The whole family uses this computer, so it's a lot to go through."

"Do you want me to call in someone from HQ to do that so you can go home?"

"I'll give it a couple more hours."

"I owe you one."

"No, you don't."

"We'll fight about that after we find Ethan. Where'd Mike go?"

"Last I knew, he was in the kitchen talking to Ruiz's team."

"That's just great. She hates me."

"How come?"

"Who the fuck knows? Could be anything or nothing. Picked up on a vibe when we were together for the operation with Judge Sawyer, and just now, she reminded me that I'm not allowed to work this case. I told her you needed to ask me questions only the family could answer."

"Ah, okay."

"Can you hang on to this incel thing for a minute? I need to wrap my head around it."

"How long of a minute are we talking? Ruiz is running the investigation. She won't take kindly to me sitting on evidence."

"Give me until the morning?"

"Sam... Listen, I know this is incredibly upsetting for you and your family, but the goal is to find Ethan. Waiting until the morning to share this with the team leading the investigation isn't wise. You'd never do that on another case."

"You're right. I'm just so afraid it'll turn out to be something that'll ruin him."

"We have to take that risk to get him back safely. This incel shit is seriously fucked-up. There's a whole subculture online called the manosphere that's devoted to toxic masculinity and misogyny. I doubt he even knows what those things are. If he's involved in something to do with that stuff, he probably has no clue what he's gotten himself into, and that'll matter when push comes to shove."

"Okay. Pass it on to Ruiz, but keep me posted if you can."

"I will."

"Thank you for being a voice of reason. I've lost all perspective here. He's like my own kid in many ways."

"I get it. I have nieces and nephews, too. I'd be losing it if one of them went missing."

"I'm so afraid that something awful has happened, and whatever it is..."

"Take a breath. It's early days."

She nodded, but her chest was so tight that she wondered if she'd breathe normally again until they found Ethan.

"You gotta stay out of Ruiz's way, as hard as that'll be. She can make life difficult for you if she wants to."

"I know, and I will. Feel free to give me a bitch slap if you think I need it."

"Will do."

"I'll go tell her you've got something for her."

"We'll do everything we can to get him back. I promise."

"I feel better knowing you're on it."

"I'll stay on it for as long as it takes."

Sam was too choked up to speak, so she nodded and went back downstairs.

CHAPTER FOUR

"Archie's got something," Sam said to Ruiz as she headed for the door without waiting to hear what the captain had to say.

Mike was outside, taking deep breaths of the cool spring air. Her brother-in-law's complexion had gone ashen over the last few hours.

"We've got to figure out who this Brecken kid is." She kept her voice down so she wouldn't be overheard and accused of participating in the investigation. If their efforts yielded new information, she'd pass it on to Ruiz.

"Archie told you about the incel stuff?" Mike asked.

"Yeah. What do you know about it?"

"I watched a documentary a while ago, and it's terrifying that my son could have anything to do with that crap. He's certainly never seen me treat women the way those guys say they want to."

"Can you go back to Celia's and help figure out who this kid is?"

"Yeah, I will." He started to walk away but turned back to her with tears in his eyes. "I... I was wrong to let him go out with his friends. If something has happened to him, I'll never forgive myself—and Tracy won't either."

Sam hugged the man she'd loved as a brother for almost twenty years. "Let's hope for the best while doing everything we can to find him."

Nodding, he wiped his face and left for Celia's.

Sam took a call from Dispatch, hoping it was news about Ethan. "Holland."

"Lieutenant, we have a potential homicide at Vacation Inn and Suites on 10th Street Northwest. A body was found in a room where guests go to get ice. Patrol believes the victim was stabbed to death. Are you able to report to the scene?"

"I'm not, but I'll send Sergeant Gonzales."

"Would you like me to contact him?"

"I'll do it. Thank you. Is there any news on the BOLOs for Ethan Hogan and Tomas Cambra?"

"Nothing new. Patrol is on the lookout for them."

"Will you please call me if you hear anything? Ethan is my nephew."

"Yes, ma'am. I'll make sure you get a call if there're any updates."

"Thanks."

Sam spotted Gonzo down the street, on the phone.

He raised a brow in inquiry when he saw her coming toward him.

"Dispatch called. New body."

With a grimace, he nodded. "I'll be back to you," he said into the phone.

"In an ice room at Vacation Inn and Suites on 10th Street Northwest," Sam said. "Can you take it?"

"Yeah, I got it."

"I'm sorry to have to delegate—again."

"Don't sweat it. You would've called me in anyway, and besides, you need to be here."

"Yes, I do."

"Is Archie getting anywhere?"

"Unfortunately, yes." Sam filled him in on what Archie had learned from Ethan's text messages.

"Are you kidding me? These kids are eleven and talking about teaching a girl a lesson because she called one of them an incel? Do any of them even know what that means?"

"I didn't until Archie told me."

"It's unbelievable. *Eleven*, for fuck's sake. I'll get over to the hotel and keep you in the loop—and I'll be back here as soon as I can."

"Thanks, Gonzo."

"Let me know if you hear anything about Ethan."

"I will. My stomach is in knots."

"Mine is, too, and he's not my kid or nephew." He gave her arm a squeeze. "Hang in there. We'll find him."

"I hope we find him before he does something he can never come back from."

"I hope so, too."

AFTER GONZO LEFT to supervise the investigation at the hotel, Sam returned to Celia's. It was getting close to eleven when Q walked her to the door.

Nick was seated on the sofa and stood when she came in. "There you are."

"Here I am."

He put his arms around her. "I was wondering if we should call Avery," he said of their friend FBI Special Agent-in-Charge Avery Hill.

"I'm not leading this investigation. Calling him—in any capacity—could get me in a lot of trouble."

"What if I do it?"

"Well, that's a different scenario, I suppose."

"He's a friend, and if he could help, he'd want to."

"Yes, he would. I suppose you can text him and see what he says."

"I'll do it. Are there any new leads?"

She filled him in on what Archie had found, and he was as shocked as she and Gonzo had been. "Apparently, there's an entire subculture online devoted to the many ways these men believe women have done them wrong. According to Archie, it's some pretty sick shit."

"I've never heard of it."

"I hadn't either and still wish I didn't know about it."

"You don't think Ethan would be involved with hurting a girl, do you?"

"I'd like to think no way, but how well do I know him anymore? He's grown up while I was busy raising my own kids, chasing murderers and being second and then first lady. I hate to say I don't know him the way I did when he was younger."

"And naturally, you're feeling guilty about that."

"Well, kind of."

"Sam, please tell me you know there's no way even you could've stopped him from doing something stupid, if that's what this is. You were a kid once. You remember how it is when your friends talk you into doing something you know you shouldn't do, but you're afraid to say no to them."

"Yes, I remember that pressure."

"It's so much worse for these kids, thanks to cell phones, social media, the internet and a million influences that shape them in ways we're just beginning to understand. I was briefed on this subject a while back and told how young people are becoming radicalized online. Homegrown terrorism has become a greater source of concern than foreign threats."

"We've had some briefings on that at work, too, but it hadn't played into any of my cases, so I didn't pay as much attention to it as I probably should have."

"As much as the internet has revolutionized the way we live and work, it's created a whole host of other issues that're becoming more serious all the time."

"Scary shit." A shiver of apprehension went through her

body. "If this turns out to be something big, I don't know what'll become of Tracy and Mike. They barely survived what happened to Brooke."

"I know. I was thinking the same thing."

"Auntie Sam."

Nick released her so she could turn to see Abby.

Sam held out her arms to her niece, who came to her and held on tight. She had dark blonde hair and hazel eyes and looked like her mother had at the same age. "How're you doing, honey?"

"I'm so worried about Ethan."

"I know, baby. We all are."

"He's been so…"

"What?"

"He's mean to me. He never used to be. It hurts my feelings."

"I'm sure it does, and I'm sorry that he's been like that." Sam's heart broke for Abby, who'd take her brother's harsh treatment hard as such a sensitive soul. "Has he said anything to you that might help us figure out where he might be?"

"I've been trying to think about that, but I can't remember anything that might help, other than him being kind of mean sometimes."

"Thank you for trying to help. I'm sure we'll find him soon."

"What if we don't? What if he's gone forever, like Grandpa and Uncle Spencer?"

"He's not gone forever." Sam fervently hoped that was true. "He's probably off having an adventure with his friends and lost track of time."

She realized they needed to get Abby out of there, which Tracy would've determined herself if she hadn't been so panicked about Ethan. "How about if Uncle Nick takes you back to our house for a sleepover with the kids? Nana is there, too."

"I have Uma's birthday party tomorrow."

"Nana will get you there. What do you think?"

"I guess that would be okay. Will you tell me if you find Ethan?"

"Of course we will. Do you want to go with Uncle Nick?"

"Yes, please."

"Okay, I'll talk to your mom and dad about it."

"Thank you, Sam."

"No problem."

Abby took off to get her coat with a new sense of purpose now that there was a plan in place.

"Good call to get her out of here," Nick said.

"Glad you agree. She doesn't need to be here for this."

"No, she doesn't."

"I don't want to call my mother and tell her Ethan is missing."

"She'll find out soon enough."

"Still…"

"I know, babe, but asking her to help with Abby will give her something to do, so it'll help them both."

"True." Sam placed the call to her mother, hoping she wasn't waking her. When she stayed with the kids, she slept in a room in the residence that they'd assigned to her a while ago.

"Hey, how's date night going?" Brenda asked, sounding sleepy.

"It was great until we got a call from Tracy that Ethan's missing."

"What?" her mom said on a gasp. "*Missing?*"

Sam gave her a brief recap of the evening's events and told her Nick was heading back to the White House with Abby in tow. "I think it'd help for her to see you when she gets there."

"I'll be waiting for her. She can stay in my room if she wants to."

"I'm sure she'd love that, and there's a birthday party tomorrow she's very eager to attend."

"I'll get her there. How's Tracy? I mean… she has to be out of her mind with worry."

"She is, but we're doing what we can to help. She'll be relieved to have you taking care of Abby."

"Tell her I love her, and I'm praying for our Ethan."

"I will."

"You don't think…"

"I don't know much of anything yet. I'll keep you posted."

"Okay, thank you."

Sam closed her phone and glanced at Nick. "Now I need to tell Trace and Mike that I made plans for Abby."

"They won't mind."

He accompanied her to the kitchen, where her brother-in-law was on the house phone while Tracy listened intently to his side of the conversation.

When he finished the call, he shook his head. "Nothing new. No one seems to know who this Brecken kid is."

Sam told them about the plan for Abby.

"That's a good idea," Mike said wearily. "Thank you for thinking of it."

"Do you have contact info for the school principal?" Sam asked.

"Just her email," Tracy said.

"Write down the address. I'll have Freddie send her an email to tell her what's going on and ask her to help us figure out who this kid is and where we can find his parents. We'll tell her it's an emergency."

Tracy swallowed hard at the word *emergency* and wrote down the email address.

Sam walked it out to Freddie and asked him to send the message, even as she wondered whether the principal would see it so late on a weekend night.

While he did that, Sam called her old friend Roberto, who had a job with the city that she helped him get after they both survived their involvement with the Johnson crime family—her as an undercover cop and him as a former member of Johnson's gang. He was now a paraplegic after being shot during the final standoff that had led to the death of young Quentin Johnson. Sam had helped Roberto get the job at DC City Hall.

"Hey, hey, hey, First Lady Cop. Were your ears ringing?"

"Sorry to call so late."

"Never too late for a call from you. I was just telling my Angel that I needed to reach out about getting a wedding invite to you. If we send it to 1600, will you get it?"

"Why don't you send it to my sister Tracy's house just to be sure?" Sam gave him the address. "I'm looking forward to the wedding, but unfortunately, this isn't a social call."

"What can I do?"

"I need the personal cell number of the superintendent of schools. You got any way to get that for me? It's urgent."

"I'm on it. I'll call you back."

"Thanks, friend."

"Anything for you."

Sam closed her phone, feeling more anxious with every minute that went by without any word from or about Ethan.

SHORTLY AFTER SAM sent Abby off with Nick to the White House, a young woman appeared at Celia's front door, introducing herself as Detective Sergeant Allison Brewer, commander of the Juvenile Investigative Response Unit. "Sergeant Gonzales asked me to come by."

Sam welcomed her into Celia's home. "Thank you for coming. I'm Lieutenant Holland."

"I'm aware," Brewer said with a small smile. "It's a pleasure to finally meet you."

"I really appreciate you coming so late on a Saturday, and I need another favor right out of the gate."

"What's that?"

"I'm not the lead on this investigation. Captain Ruiz is, and I'm not supposed to be involved due to a family connection to the case. That said, I want to help, and Sergeant Gonzales, who works with me, suggested calling you in."

"What am I looking at with Ruiz if she finds out I was here?"

"You could say we called you before assignments were made, and we were looking for advice more than investigative help."

"That's a slippery slope."

"You could add, 'When a lieutenant asks me to come, I come. Work out the command shit separate from me.' That way, it's all my fault. Would that work?"

"You're okay with that?"

"I'd never want to get you in trouble for coming when we asked you to. I'll take all the blame for dragging you into it."

"Um, well, okay, then. What's going on?"

Sam briefed her on what they knew so far, which wasn't much, about Ethan and Tomas's disappearance. "Lieutenant Archelotta from IT has been working on the devices and uncovered an exchange in which the word incel was used."

"That's concerning. We've seen a huge uptick in activity regarding incel culture and toxic masculinity and have been increasing our presence in the schools in recent months, trying to educate boys in particular about the dangers of being involved in online spaces devoted to misogyny."

"I'm flying blind on that topic. What do you suggest?"

"Ruiz should call in the FBI. They're much deeper into this space than we are."

Sam retrieved the secure BlackBerry she used to communicate with Nick. *Send the message to Avery. We need their expertise on this. Ask him to call me as a friend, not as the Homicide LT.*

Nick responded right away. *Will do.*

"What're you doing?"

"I'm asking my husband to contact our friend Agent Hill so the request doesn't come from me."

"This is making me very uncomfortable, Lieutenant. You

were ordered to steer clear of the investigation, but you're calling in the FBI?"

"My husband is asking a friend to help."

"Is that how the brass will see it? Is that how Captain Ruiz will see it?"

"I'm not concerned about that right now. I want to find my nephew."

"As do I, but I'm not willing to risk a rap. If it's just the same with you, I'm going home. If Captain Ruiz requests assistance from my team, we'll gladly provide it, and I suggest you loop her in on these matters so she can pursue them. I hope you understand."

Sam held back a frustrated retort that wouldn't accomplish anything in the effort to find Ethan. "I understand."

"I'm sorry."

"It's fine. I get it."

"I want you to know I admire you very much."

"That's nice to hear. Thank you for coming."

"I'll pray for your nephew."

As the woman departed, Sam wanted to scream with frustration and a powerful feeling of impotence. She was used to taking whatever action necessary to serve her victim of the moment, but in this most important of cases, she was being forced to stand down.

CHAPTER FIVE

S am was contemplating her next move when her phone rang
with a call from Avery Hill.

"Hey."

"I heard about your nephew. What can I do?"

"Nothing officially. I've been told to steer clear, and if they think I called you in, I'll be in deep shit."

"You didn't call me in. My boss did."

"The big boss, you mean."

"The biggest one. My friend, the president, told me his nephew is missing and asked if I could help. He told me about the incel texts, and that sends up all sorts of red flags for me. We've got people assigned full time to that area."

"Like, how many people?"

"About twenty agents from the Domestic Terrorism team."

She gasped at such a large effort. "Avery, my God. I've never even heard of it before today."

"It's been an issue since the nineties. They're heterosexual men who blame women and society as a whole for their lack of romantic partners. There's all this crazy vernacular as part of the so-called manosphere. In addition to incels, they're classified as

Pick-Up Artists, Men Going Their Own Way and Men's Rights Activists. Incels seem to have the most violent tendencies when it comes to acting on their grievances against women. We've seen cases where couples have been targeted because the guy is successful in getting a woman to be with him, so they hate him as much as they hate the woman who rejected them. Remember when the husband and daughter of that federal judge in Oregon were murdered at their home?"

"Yes," Sam said, swallowing bile that burned her throat as this became more horrifying by the second.

"That was a guy who called himself a Men's Rights Activist, or MRA, and he was out to punish the judge for siding with women in many of the domestic cases that came before her."

"How would these kids, these *children*, know about this?"

"It's hard to say where they might've heard about it, but if they have access to the internet, this is the kind of shit that's out there waiting to find them. We've got people much better versed on this than I am who might be able to help."

"I feel like I'm going to be sick."

"From what Nick said, it doesn't sound like there's anything Ethan said in the texts that could be considered threatening. He didn't respond to the kid who was trying to start the trouble."

"What do we do, Avery? Tell me what to do."

"Let me call Malone. I'll tell him Nick told me about Ethan being missing and mentioned what Archie found in the texts. I'll strongly suggest to him that he bring in our team sooner rather than later based on the use of the word 'incel' in the texts. Would that work?"

"As long as you don't mention that you talked to me."

"This call never happened. I'll hit up Malone now. I'm sure you'll hear about whatever is decided."

"Don't be so sure. They want me far away from this one."

"I'll keep you in the loop."

"Thanks, Avery."

"Of course."

As she put the phone in her pocket, Freddie came into the room. "How'd it go with the Juvenile Investigative Response commander?"

"It didn't. She's afraid of getting in trouble for talking to me about an investigation I was ordered to stay out of."

"Why're you paler now than you were an hour ago?"

"I talked to Avery and learned more about incel culture than I ever wanted to know, and it's terrifying."

"I've read about it, and it's truly disgusting. Did he tell you how they believe that eighty percent of women are interested in only the top twenty percent of the best-looking, richest, most successful men, leaving the other eighty percent of men without a partner?"

"Ah, no, he didn't mention that."

"They call the twenty percent Chads, and the rest are incels," Freddie said. "Chads date Stacys, the women who won't have anything to do with the incels."

"It boggles my mind that people spend the limited amount of time they have in this life nursing grievances and plotting revenge when they could be out there bettering themselves and making a real contribution."

"Playing devil's advocate... Think about the guys you've said 'no way' to in your life. Then imagine every other woman out there is having the same reaction to them. Nothing these men do or say changes their track record with women, so who do they start to blame for that?"

"Why blame anyone? That's what I don't get."

"That kind of consistent rejection for guys who want a romantic partner but can't get one is what can turn them into bitter, lonely, dangerous people."

Sam's stomach had begun to ache an hour ago, and the ache had only intensified with every new detail she learned about this topic. "It's scary that this exists in the ether, and I had no idea—

most people have no idea. And now, somehow, they've gotten their hooks into my nephew?"

"We don't know that for certain. We know that someone who texted him used that word, and we've fallen into a rabbit hole while trying to understand the meaning. Ninety percent of what we've learned probably won't apply to this situation with Ethan."

"It's the remaining ten percent that has me terrified."

GONZO ARRIVED at the Vacation Inn and Suites hotel and was greeted by Patrol Officers Clare and Youncy. "What've you got?"

"A white male, maybe midthirties, was found in the ice room on the sixth floor by a guest who'd gone to get ice," Clare said. "He'd been stabbed in the chest and was dead by the time he was found."

"Do you have a name?"

"We made the decision not to touch anything until you guys got here. We wanted you to see the scene as we found it."

"Good call."

"We've requested Crime Scene detectives and footage from all the cameras. The manager said corporate will want warrants, so we asked Captain Malone to get them moving."

"Great work. Take me up."

"Uh, Sarge," Youncy said, "the manager is insisting on being present for everything we do."

"Is he now?"

"Yeah, he's been a pain in the ass."

"What his name?"

"Mr. Wright," Clare said.

"No first name?"

"He didn't provide it."

"Where can I find Mr. Wright?"

"This way, Sarge," Youncy said.

They led Gonzo into the lobby, where a nervous-looking man with thinning blond hair and wire-rimmed glasses was surrounded by staff in uniform, all of whom were so focused on him they failed to notice the cops approaching them.

"Mr. Wright?" Gonzo said, loud enough to be heard over the others.

The wiry man nearly jumped out of his light gray suit and bow tie. "Th-that's me. I'm the manager. And you are?"

He showed his badge. "Sergeant Tommy Gonzales with the Metropolitan Police Department Homicide unit. I'd like to see the victim, please."

"We... we can't be sure he was killed in our hotel."

Gonzo tipped his head. "You want to run that by me one more time?"

"What I'm saying is he could've been killed anywhere and left here to cause trouble for us."

"So you think a murder in your hotel is intended to cause trouble for *you*? What about the trouble it's caused him and his family?"

"Of course that's of paramount concern to us."

"Of course." Gonzo hoped the sarcasm landed. "Take me to him. Now."

"There's no need to be hostile," Wright said.

"I wasn't at all hostile until you placed concern for the hotel above that of a murdered man."

"When did I do that? Cindy, Louise, Russell, did any of you hear me do that?"

"No, sir," they said in unison, as if they'd been programmed to do so.

"You're wasting my time," Gonzo told him. "If you'd like to be there when I view the body, I suggest you take me there immediately. Otherwise, I'll go without you."

Gonzo could tell Wright wanted to argue but wisely decided against it.

"Russell, come with us. The rest of you get back to work."

"Don't let anyone touch the main computers at the check-in desk," Gonzo said to the women being dismissed. "We'll be seizing them as part of our investigation. We'll also want passwords and operation manuals for the systems you use. Maybe you can work on that for us?"

Wright almost fainted. "But—"

Gonzo gave him a look that stopped that question in its tracks.

The two women nodded to acknowledge Gonzo's request and scrambled off like they'd been set on fire. Wright and Russell led the way to the elevators.

"What are your first names?" Gonzo asked.

"Why is that relevant?" Wright asked.

Gonzo was ready to arrest this guy for being a dick. If only the charge would stick. "I determine what's relevant. Now what's your first name?"

"Edward," Wright said. "Russell's is William, but everyone calls him Russell."

"Was that so difficult?"

"This whole thing is difficult," Wright said. "We're not the kind of establishment to have a murder on our premises or police officers visiting us."

"I'm sorry for your troubles, but I'm much sorrier for the troubles of the guy who was murdered."

"I feel like you're enjoying this or something."

"Yeah, a murder is the highlight of my entire day. What've you got for cameras on the sixth floor?"

"We have security cameras in all the public spaces."

"Including the ice rooms?"

"No, not there."

Gonzo would've been surprised to hear they had cameras in the ice room. "I'd like the film from the last twenty-four hours on the sixth floor."

"I'll have to check with corporate on that."

"Why?"

"That's the policy."

"The policy is that when a murder occurs in one of your

hotels, you have to get corporate's permission to assist the police investigating it?"

"I don't make the rules. I simply follow and enforce them."

"I bet you enjoy enforcement."

"What does that mean?"

"Nothing. Just an observation."

Russell, a tall, imposing fellow who looked like he was once a linebacker, cleared his throat as if trying not to laugh.

"We've already requested a warrant for the video," Gonzo said, "but you could help us out if you're able to get permission to turn it over to us."

"I'll send an inquiry right away."

"How long will that take?"

"The corporate offices are open twenty-four hours a day. Someone will get back to me soon."

"Excellent. Keep me posted. In the meantime, I'm going to have my captain request the warrant. I should hope it goes without saying that no one is to touch the surveillance equipment between now and when that video is turned over to us. If you haven't yet given that order, do so now."

Oh, Mr. Wright did *not* like being told what to do. Too bad. He'd soon realize he wasn't in charge of this situation.

Russell led the way to the ice room, where another staff member stood outside the door.

Gonzo showed the man his badge. "Sergeant Gonzales, MPD Homicide. Who's had access?"

"Just the female guest who reported finding the body and your officers."

"Great. Thank you."

The man stepped aside before Gonzo had to ask him to. He wondered if he'd been on the job at one point. A bloodbath awaited Gonzo inside the room. It was on the walls, floor, ice machine and all over the man on the floor. Judging by the smell of urine and shit mixed in with the metallic scent of blood, the man had lost control of his bodily functions.

Gonzo pulled on gloves and squatted next to the man, reaching under him for a wallet but coming back with only shit that'd seeped through the man's pants on his gloves. He had a handsome face marked by a scar on his top lip.

Noting the keycard on the floor next to the body, Gonzo said, "Can we get access to the room where he was staying?" He removed the gloves, rolled them into a ball and tossed them aside to dispose of them later.

Wright had put a monogrammed handkerchief over his nose and mouth. "We'll need a warrant for that, too."

"You could make this easier on all of us by letting us in there now so we can figure out who he was, what he was doing here and who might've wanted him dead. Not to mention, his family will need to be notified."

"We can make that phone call."

"You will *not* make that call. We'll take care of that."

"It's corporate policy for us to notify the emergency contact when something happens to a guest at our facility."

"If you or anyone on your staff makes that phone call, you'll be arrested for interfering in a homicide investigation. Do I make myself clear?"

"Crystal," Wright said on a growl.

Gonzo took a look outside the room and saw the hallway extended some distance in both directions. "Does the hallway hook around that corner there?"

"Yes, there are thirty more rooms down there."

Sighing, Gonzo realized this was going to be an all-nighter. He stepped away from the others to call Sam.

"What've you got?"

"A thirtysomething guy stabbed in the chest in the ice room on the sixth floor of a nine-story hotel with... How many rooms?"

"One hundred and eighty-two," Russell said as Wright dry heaved at the smell coming from inside the ice room.

"Shit," Sam said as she, too, realized they'd be processing a massive crime scene.

"I'll need some help over here. Okay to call in the team to canvass?"

"Yeah, go ahead."

"I've got to get with Malone about warrants. I'll ask him to send some additional Patrol officers, too."

"Sounds like a plan. Thank you for handling it."

"I'd say it was no problem, but... Anything new over there?"

"Not yet."

"Jeez, Sam..."

"I know."

"I'll get back to you."

To Wright, he said, "We'll need to wake up the guests."

The horrified look on Wright's face would've amused him under any other circumstances.

"We can't do that."

Gonzo had had just about enough of this guy. "We're doing it. I'll remind you yet again that if you get in my way, I'll arrest you to get you *out* of my way. You got me?"

Wright's only reply was a glare over the handkerchief he held over his nose and mouth.

Gonzo called Captain Malone.

"Hey, I've requested the warrant for the hotel video."

"I also need one to get into the victim's room, if it's actually his room, since the manager won't tell me who he is."

Wright doubled down on the glare.

"Can we wake up a judge for this?" Gonzo asked Malone.

"Already on it. Waiting to hear back."

"Okay, let me know."

"I'll be right back to you."

"I'm calling in our team and will also need additional resources from Patrol to canvass one hundred and eighty-two rooms. Is that approved?"

"Yes," the captain said with a sigh. He was probably

calculating overtime costs that would add up fast in a case like this. "Go ahead. What're you hearing from Sam?"

"Nothing new as of a few minutes ago."

"What the hell is going on there?"

"No idea, but it doesn't seem good."

"It sure doesn't."

CHAPTER SIX

Right at eleven thirty, Sam got a call from Dr. Deborah Monahan, superintendent of DC's public schools, which had been arranged with Roberto's assistance. She put the woman's call on speaker so Tracy, Mike and Freddie could hear.

"We've checked our entire database, and we have no student named Brecken enrolled in the system. We do, however, have one student named Brecken who's homeschooled, but his reporting is out of date."

"Do you have an age, last name and address for him?"

"Brecken Mayfield is fifteen and completed eighth grade before we lost touch with his family. The last known address we have is on O Street Northwest in Truxton Circle."

"This is Lieutenant Holland. What's the process for finding kids who fall off the map?"

After a short pause, the woman said, "We have a team assigned to that, but the numbers are increasing all the time, and a lot of these people don't want to be found."

"Have you had someone looking for Brecken?"

"I don't see anything listed in his file, but I can check with the team in the morning."

"Can you report back to me if you get any new info?" Sam asked.

"Yes, of course."

"I'm getting another call. Please let me know if you uncover any other information that could be relevant."

"I will."

"Thank you very much for your help." Sam pressed the button to end that call and left Celia's kitchen to talk to Dispatch, marveling that she didn't inadvertently cut off the new call. "Holland."

"I was asked to update you on anything that might be related to the BOLO on Ethan Hogan."

"Yes, what've you got?"

"Captain Roback, who's covering Patrol tonight, received a report of a missing thirteen-year-old girl, who left to meet some friends earlier and hasn't returned home."

Sam's stomach sank as the news just kept getting worse. "Can you send the details to Detective Cruz?"

"Yes, ma'am. Shall I tell the captain that you'll respond to the parents' home?" She recited an address in the Truxton Circle neighborhood. Clearly, Dispatch hadn't been told this wasn't her case, and she wasn't about to fill them in. She'd worry about that fallout after she helped to find Ethan.

"Yes, we'll be there shortly."

"Very good, thank you."

Sam closed her phone and signaled for Freddie to leave with her.

"Sam!" Tracy called after her. "What's happened?"

"Nothing new, but we were asked to follow up on a possible lead. I'll tell you more as soon as I can."

"Is it bad?"

"Nothing new to worry about."

"You'd tell me if there was?"

"If I could. Please know... we're doing everything we can, and some of it would be upsetting to you to hear about and may have nothing at all to do with Ethan. It's better that we don't give you the blow-by-blow, okay? You have to trust me on that." Sam took the time to hug her sister. "Hang in there. Every base is being covered. I promise. If there's any news about Ethan, I'll let you know the minute I hear about it."

"Okay."

"I'll be back as soon as I can. Stay by the phone."

Tracy nodded.

On the way out of Celia's house, she asked Freddie, "What the hell is this?"

"I have no idea, but I don't like it. Not one bit."

OUTSIDE, Vernon held the back door to her Secret Service SUV.

"Where'd you come from?" Sam asked.

"I offered to come in when I heard about your nephew. Figured you might be working."

She squeezed his arm. "Thank you."

"No problem."

Of course it was a problem for him to come into work on a Saturday night, but he'd done it for her, and she appreciated it. He was quickly becoming one of her closest friends and advisers.

"Thanks for coming in. Q has been doing an admirable job of running me around."

"No problem, ma'am," Q said.

Normally, she'd tell him not to call her that, but she couldn't be bothered to care about such trivial things while Ethan was missing.

"Where to?" Vernon asked.

Freddie gave him the address for the missing girl's house.

While Vernon drove them, Sam tried to process everything she'd learned so far. Most of it was too horrifying to be believed.

"Sam."

She glanced at her partner.

"What're we doing here?"

"I'm sorry. What?"

"We're going to talk to the parents of a girl whose disappearance may or may not be related to Ethan's when you were told to stay out of the investigation. So, I'm wondering what level of shit storm I'm getting into by going along with you. Not that I'd let you go by yourself, but…"

Sam's emotions were all over the place, the primary one being panic the likes of which she hadn't experienced in quite some time. "I think maybe you should go home."

"That's not what I was saying."

"I know, but still… You're absolutely right that I shouldn't be doing this. I should've consulted with Ruiz about the missing girl. I should've told her what we learned from the superintendent about the kid who might be the Brecken we're looking for. The thing is… I don't trust her to do the right thing, and maybe that's totally unfair, but my gut is telling me to bypass her. It's quite possible I'll get in trouble for doing that, and if you're with me, you could, too. So that's why I want you to go home."

Freddie seemed to be pondering what she'd said.

"We'll drop you at the Metro."

"That's okay. I'm along for the ride."

"Freddie…"

"I'm aware of the potential consequences, and I'm choosing to participate in whatever comes next."

"Are you sure?"

He nodded.

"What's the girl's name?" Sam asked.

He consulted his phone to read the information sent from Dispatch. "Luna Ahern." Then he glanced at her. "What're you thinking?"

"I'm praying her disappearance isn't related to Ethan's."

"I can't believe we need to be concerned about that."

"If it's related to that incel shit…" Her voice caught. "I'm trying to picture our sweet Ethan involved in something sinister."

"We don't know anything about what Ethan may or may not be involved in. Don't go to worst-case until we know more."

"It's hard not to. Where in the hell is he? He has to know his parents are frantic by now."

"Maybe he's being held by someone."

"Please tell me it's not going to turn out to have something to do with him being related to me and Nick. That would wreck us forever."

"As you well know, it could be anything, but if you ask me, that's a long shot. What possible motive could someone have for snatching the nephew of the first lady?"

"So many people hate me, Freddie. You know that. I've made enemies on the job, arrested a lot of people who have families and friends who could seek revenge against me. What better way than to snatch one of the precious kids in my life because they can't get to mine?"

"You're not asking me," Vernon said, glancing at her in the mirror, "but I think that'd be a very unlikely scenario."

"Why do you say that?"

"For one thing, if there was any kind of threat against either of your extended families, we'd probably know about it."

"You would? Even if it involved my sisters' families?"

"Even if. We're not actively protecting them, but we keep an eye on everyone close to you."

"Including me?" Freddie asked, sounding incredulous.

"Everyone."

"Wow, that's kind of crazy," Freddie said.

"It's not in any way as violating as it can be for the people under our protection. It's more of a thirty-thousand-foot view."

"I'm oddly comforted to know that," Sam said.

"Whereas I'm oddly freaked out," Freddie said with a small grin that let her know he was teasing.

Vernon chuckled. "I promise you it's nothing invasive. Just eyes and ears to make sure the people around you aren't being targeted due to their proximity to you and the president."

"Very interesting," Freddie said. "Does it include my wife?"

"Everyone close to the first couple."

"What defines closeness?" Sam asks.

"The people who'd matter most if they were used to get to you."

Sam swallowed hard at the thought of anyone they loved being used in such a way, but she was comforted to know that if someone was targeting her young nephew, the Secret Service might've picked up on it. She wondered how much Nick knew about the wide net the agency cast to protect their loved ones.

When they pulled up to the Ahern home off Bates Street Northwest in the Truxton Circle neighborhood, every light in the house appeared to be on, and cars were double-parked outside.

Vernon pulled up behind one of the cars and put on the hazards. He got out to hold the door for Sam. "Stay with the car, Q."

"Yes, sir."

Escorted by Vernon, Sam and Freddie made their way to the spacious front porch, which was full of people. Sam wanted to groan at how the home being overrun with visitors would make for a more complicated investigation for the Crime Scene detectives.

When a woman on the porch saw them coming, she let out a scream. "*Why'd they send her? Is our baby dead?* Oh God, please *no!*"

"She's not dead that we know of." Sam spoke loudly, trying to be heard over the racket the woman was making. "We're investigating other missing kids and were informed about Luna. Where're her parents?"

"They're inside," the screamer said. "I'm sorry. She's my niece, and when I saw you, I thought the worst."

"It's okay. Will you take me to her parents, please?"

The other people gathered on the porch gawked at Sam as the aunt cut a path to the front door and led them to a room where a man and woman were seated on a love seat, staring at their phones, seemingly willing them to ring.

"Jordy, Court, the police are here. Other kids are missing, too, and the first lady is investigating."

Sam wanted to tell her to fuck off with the first lady shit, but that was the least of her concerns at the moment. Instead, she showed her badge while Freddie did the same. She didn't bother with introductions. "Where'd your daughter tell you she was going?"

"To her friend Crosby's house, which is about six blocks from here," Court said. "We just started letting her walk there two weeks ago." She dropped her head into her hands. "I knew it was too soon. I knew it."

"Have you spoken to Crosby and his or her family about whether they've heard anything from her?"

"I called them right after I noticed her location services were turned off on her phone," Court said. "They said she never arrived, and Crosby hasn't heard from her."

"How soon after she left did you notice her location was turned off?"

"About thirty minutes. My friend called me right after Luna left, and I got distracted. By the time I checked, it was off. She knows better than to shut it off. That's her ticket to a little independence, that I can always see where she is."

When she started to sob, Jordy put his arm around her.

"Something awful has happened to her," Court said. "I just know it."

"Was she having trouble with anyone that you're aware of?"

"She was always having some sort of issue with boys," Jordy said. "They won't leave her alone, even though she tells them she's not interested in them. She's... she's very pretty, and they're relentless."

Sam wanted to ask them why *in the fuck* they'd let their "very pretty" *child* walk around a city *by herself* when boys are *relentlessly* pursuing her.

"Did she give you the names of any of the boys who were bothering her?"

Court shook her head. "She kept that stuff to herself but told us they were annoying. That was the word she used. Right, Jordy?"

"That's one of her favorite words. Everyone is annoying to her, especially the boys at school. They won't take no for an answer."

"Have you reported this to the school?"

He nodded. "They're aware of it and have been helping where they can, but Luna doesn't want a big deal made of it. She feels that would only make it worse."

"Would it be possible for our people to access her text messages via your carrier account?"

They exchanged glances.

"That feels sort of intrusive," he said.

Sam took a deep breath, trying to keep in mind how horrible this was for them while also getting the info she needed. "Mr. Ahern, your thirteen-year-old daughter is *missing*. We may have a matter of hours to find her before something terrible happens. We're trying to do everything in our power to find her. Will you please help us?"

"Yes, of course I will."

"So that's a yes to accessing the messages?"

"Yeah, I guess."

"Give Detective Cruz the login information, along with Luna's number. We'll also need your number to send you a consent form to sign that says you've given us permission to access your account."

Jordy reached for his phone to get the account info, which he relayed to Freddie along with his phone number that the account was under, as well as Luna's number.

Freddie stood. "I'll have the consent form sent to your phone. Please print it, sign it and give it to Lieutenant Holland."

"Okay," Jordy said.

His eyes looked wild, as if he was about to lose his shit at any second.

Not that Sam blamed him. She couldn't imagine many things worse than what he was going through.

"You have to understand," Court said haltingly. "It's not like Luna to make us worry. She's a good girl. She does what she's told and sets a fantastic example for her younger siblings. She's not at all rebellious or difficult in any way—and yes, we know that makes us very lucky. Some of our friends' kids are nightmares, constantly bucking their rules and ignoring their requests. That's not Luna."

"Is there any chance she might've run away?"

"None," Jordy said. "She's actually a homebody by nature. We were relieved when she started asking to go out with her friends."

"Have you ever heard the names Ethan Hogan, Tomas Cambra or Brecken Mayfield?"

Jordy looked to Court.

"None of them are familiar to me," Court said.

"Me either," he added.

"Any chance she might've connected with someone online who lured her out?"

"We monitor everything," Court said.

"Does she have access to the internet?"

"Only through a computer we all share."

"And you've checked her activity on that computer?"

They looked at each other.

"Not recently," Court said. "Please understand, we have no reason not to trust her. She's not sneaky or deceptive."

Or she hasn't been yet, Sam thought. "I'd like to have some of our IT people take a look at the computer. Do I have your permission to do that?"

"Is that really necessary?"

Sam stared at her. "I believe we have the same goal here."

"We do, but we also want to protect her privacy."

"Ma'am, if my daughter has been possibly communicating with a predator online, I'd want to know about that, and I assume you do, too."

"You think that's what happened?" Jordy asked in a whisper, suddenly looking even wilder than he had a few minutes earlier.

"I don't know, and I won't know what we're dealing with until we investigate further. Do I have your permission to call in IT to look at the computer?"

Jordy nodded as Court sobbed next to him. "Do what you have to do."

"We're going to need to relocate you so we can fully process your home for evidence."

"What?" Court gasped. "Nothing happened here."

"We don't know that for certain, ma'am, and if there's something here or on your phones and other devices that might lead us to her, we want to make sure to find it. This is routine procedure in the cases of missing people."

"We have to give up our phones?" Court asked on a gasp.

"Everything. Is there somewhere you can go?"

They exchanged glances. "We can ask our neighbors, two doors down."

"Go ahead and do that. We'll need their names, address and phone numbers where we can reach you."

Sam got up and left the room to make the call to Archie.

"What've you got?" he asked.

She updated him on the situation with Luna. "Do you have someone you can send over here to review a family computer?"

"Have you reported this to Ruiz?"

"No."

His deep sigh said it all.

"The thing is, I know I should be working *with* her, but I

don't entirely trust her. You can feel free to say no. I'll understand."

"I'm not saying no. I'm just... not wanting to get caught up in, you know, bullshit."

"I'm sorry to ask this of you. I never would if it didn't feel as urgent as anything ever has."

"I get it. Text me the address. I'll call in Walters," Archie said, referring to his second-in-command, a sergeant.

"Great, thanks. Anything new at Tracy's?"

"Still wading through the messages and emails and following the browser history."

"Thanks for your help, Archie."

"I wish I could do more."

"You're doing what I need right now."

"I'm on it. I'll call you if anything new pops."

She slapped her phone closed and then opened it again to text him Luna's home address to pass on to Walters.

Freddie came in through the front door as she stood in the hallway.

"I need a permission form for the family computer, too."

"I'll send it to the dad." He used his phone to see to it. "What else?"

"Walters is on his way over to dump the family computer that Luna has access to. The parents haven't checked it in a while because she's given them no reason to be concerned about her activity."

Freddie winced. "I'm keeping my kids offline until they're adults."

"Good luck with that. It's easier said than done."

"I'm sure it is, but I'll hang over them like a mad stalker."

"Also easier said than done." Sam checked her watch to find it was inching closer to midnight. She shuddered to think of where and how Ethan might be spending the night. If he was still alive.

CHAPTER SEVEN

Tracy had never been happier to see her eldest child. She hadn't wanted Brooke to come running home but was glad she had. Her presence—and Nate's—was comforting.

"What's the latest?" Brooke asked.

"Nothing new. Sam and her colleagues are working the case. Her friend Archie from IT has been working on the computer at our house for hours. They've put out an alert to be on the lookout for Ethan and his friend Tomas. We're trying to figure out who this other kid, Brecken, is. We know he doesn't go to school with the boys and could be a homeschooled kid who's a few years older, but we don't know for sure that he's the Brecken we're looking for."

"So you haven't met his new friends?"

"We've asked to meet them, but it hasn't happened yet."

"But he's still been allowed to go out with them?"

"You'll have to take that up with your father. He's the one who allowed it."

Mike came into the room and hugged Brooke. "Yes, I did allow it, Tracy, because every one of his friends is allowed to go out, and I don't want him to hate us for not letting him do what his friends can do."

"God forbid he should hate us, but of course that won't matter much if he's dead."

In all the years they'd been together, she'd never been this angry with Mike. Most of the time, she kept him on a pedestal for the way he'd stepped up as a father to Brooke after her biological father had cut and run when Tracy got pregnant.

"You guys." Brooke glanced nervously between her parents. "This won't help anything."

"It makes me feel better to say it out loud," Tracy replied.

"So if something has happened to Ethan, it's always going to be my fault?" Mike asked. His face had gotten very red.

"Well, it's not *my* fault! I was adamantly opposed to him going out with his friends without an adult with them, and I said so many times. No one wanted to hear my opinion, and once he knew he had you on his side, there was no point in arguing anymore. Whatever happened to our united front?"

"I thought you were being unreasonable."

"And now? Do you still think that?"

Mike turned and stormed out of the room.

"Mom..."

"I'm sorry, honey, but I'm so angry, and I can't contain it."

"If you blame him for this, you might never recover."

"Who else should I blame? If it were up to me, Ethan would be upstairs in his room playing video games, not God knows where with God knows who."

"I'm sure he's going to be just fine," Brooke said, her voice tremulous.

Tracy put her arm around her daughter. "I want to tell you what we all want to hear, but I'm scared he's not okay."

"I am, too."

SAM AND FREDDIE left Walters and yet another group of CSU detectives working at Luna's house and headed for the last known address for Brecken Mayfield. "I feel like we're spinning our wheels."

"Because we are. Ethan could be anywhere by now."

"Our family can't sustain another loss so soon after the other two."

"Don't give up hope. For all we know, he might've found himself involved in something way out of his depth."

"It's hard not to let all the worst-possible scenarios run through my mind."

"I know, but don't do that. Remember what you always tell me... Just because we've seen something horrible on the job doesn't mean it'll happen to someone we love."

"I do say that. I'm very wise that way."

He rolled his eyes and smiled, seeming relieved by the usual banter. "I'm actually comforted by the fact that two other kids have been reported missing. Whatever this is probably doesn't involve only Ethan."

"That's assuming Luna's disappearance is related to Ethan and Tomas."

"How can it not be?"

"Is that a rhetorical question?"

"No, but really, it has to be related."

"We don't know that for sure, and we don't assume things without proof."

"Right, I know, but still..."

"But nothing. Until we have proof they're connected, we're treating them as if they aren't. How would Luna even know them? They're zoned for different schools."

"Are you really asking how she would know them? Through social media, sports, friends of friends, cousins, running into each other at a mall or an arcade or a pizza place. There're a million ways other than school that kids know each other these days."

"Granted, but these kids are young."

"They're young, but they've been allowed out with their

friends to all corners of the city, so it's very possible they know each other."

"I'll concede that point."

"Thank you."

"I'm not on social media. I forget it exists."

"Trust me, it exists, and for kids their ages, it runs their lives. Please tell me you know that Scotty's on Instagram, Snapchat and TikTok. I'm friends with him on all of them."

"I know that, but I'm not monitoring his activity on social media. Should I be?"

"Probably, but you have the Secret Service keeping an eye on him, so it's not as critical for you as it is for other parents."

"I've finally found the single advantage to Nick being president."

"That's a huge advantage, as you're discovering tonight. There's no chance of your kids going missing on their watch."

"Well, there's always a chance, but it's far less likely than it would be for kids who aren't surrounded by federal agents at all times."

"Those agents would die before they'd let anything happen to your kids."

"Yes, they would," Vernon said. "They love the kids like their own."

"I know they do," Sam said. "I can see that every morning when they come to collect them for school. The kids run to them the same way they do to us. I wish every kid had the Secret Service looking out for them."

"Malone just texted me. There're active warrants for Brecken Mayfield and his father, Asher, for failing to report into parole on schedule."

"That tells us they both have records."

"Long ones. Malone sent that info, too."

Connecting Ethan to actual criminals only added to Sam's already considerable anxiety.

Sam noted that it was almost twelve thirty as they pulled up to the last known address for Brecken Mayfield on O Street Northwest, also in Truxton Circle. She was starting to get seriously tired but couldn't stop when there were threads to pull that might lead them to Ethan.

With Vernon escorting them, Sam and Freddie walked up the sidewalk to the front door of the dark house and rang the bell. In deference to the stressful situation, she didn't care to comment on the fact that it was a normal doorbell rather than some of the air-raid sirens they regularly encountered.

No one answered, so she rang it again, pounding on the door this time. "Police. Open up!"

When the door next door opened, Sam, Freddie and Vernon instinctively reached for their weapons.

An older woman poked her head out the door. "No one lives there. The Mayfields moved out months ago."

"Did you know them?" Sam asked.

"Just to say hi to."

"Do you know where they went?"

The woman's expression changed in an instant when she realized who she was talking to. "I, uh, no. They didn't say. They were here one day and gone the next. Haven't seen them since."

"Were they friendly with anyone in the neighborhood?"

"Not that I know of, but I keep to myself."

"Thank you for your help."

"I can't believe the first lady is out working late at night. Thank you for all you do."

"Oh, well… It's my job, but thank you."

"Are we waking up the neighbors?" Freddie asked as they returned to the sidewalk.

Sam looked around, saw that most of the homes on the street were dark and weighed her options. "I don't know what to do."

Freddie's head swiveled in her direction. "I've never heard you say that before."

"I've said it before."

"Not that I can recall."

"Where do we begin to look for him, Freddie? He could be anywhere, including the other side of the country—or out of the country entirely, for that matter."

"We're not going there yet," Freddie said. "It's too soon for doomsday scenarios."

"We both know how critical the first hours are in a situation like this. If we don't find him soon, we might never find him."

"What can I do? I'll do whatever is needed."

"I appreciate it, but you should go home and get some sleep. Let's meet at HQ at seven and start fresh."

"Are you going home, too?"

"After I see Tracy. I'll decide what I'm doing after that."

"You're sure you don't want me to stay with you? I don't mind at all."

"I know you don't, but go get some sleep. We might be in for a long few days if this drags on."

She could see he was torn by the tense expression on his face and the rigid set of his shoulders.

"What about the new case at the hotel? Should I get over there to help with the canvass?"

Sam thought about that for a second. "Go get some sleep so you can relieve Gonzo at the hotel by seven instead of meeting me at HQ."

He hugged her tightly. "Call me if you need me during the night. I don't care what time it is. Call me."

"I will," she said over a lump in her throat.

He gave her a last squeeze and then took off, looking at his phone as he went, probably hailing an Uber.

"Back to Celia's, then?" Vernon asked.

Sam nodded as she got into the SUV.

Vernon stood next to her, one hand hooked over the open door. "Don't let your mind go crazy. Remember, like Freddie said, you experience the worst of everything in your job. That might not apply here."

"You're right. I know you are, but my brain can't help cycling through all the disasters I've seen over the years."

"Which is entirely normal for you, but you'll only make it worse for yourself by applying those disasters to this situation before you know what's going on."

She looked up at him, the man she'd come to love and trust like a surrogate father, and asked the question that scared her the most. "What if we never find him?"

"You will. I'm sure of it. I believe in you."

"That helps. Thank you."

"Keep the faith."

"I'm trying."

He closed the door and drove them to Celia's, through deserted streets that would be teeming with traffic on a workday in the nation's capital. With buildings and trees whizzing past, she kept her gaze trained outside, hoping for a glimpse of her nephew that never materialized.

She took a second to text Gonzo to tell him she'd sent Freddie home to sleep so he could relieve him in the morning. Then she put her phone in her pocket while trying in vain to calm her racing mind.

Feeling defeated in a way she hadn't experienced in quite some time, she walked into Celia's home a few minutes later to find her sister and niece on the sofa, holding hands as they wept.

"Anything?" Tracy asked when she saw Sam.

Sam shook her head.

Tracy further dissolved into heartbroken sobs that devastated Sam.

She wanted so badly to fix this for the sister who'd taken care of her all her life, but some problems couldn't be solved by wishing or hoping.

"*Where could he be?*" Tracy wailed. "*Where in the world is he?*"

Brooke tried to comfort her mom as she sobbed right along with her.

Sam sat on the coffee table and reached for both of them, giving in to her own tears after hours of fruitless searching.

A throat clearing behind Tracy and Brooke had them pulling back from each other and wiping tears from their faces.

Sam looked up to see Archie, seeming embarrassed to have witnessed their emotional breakdown.

"Hey," Sam said to her friend as she brushed at tears. She'd thought he was still at Tracy's. "Where'd you come from?"

"Can I talk to you in the other room?"

She nodded. "I'll be right back," she said to Tracy and Brooke before she followed Archie into the kitchen, closing the door between the rooms.

"We might have something from Luna's phone." He put sheets of paper on the table and pointed to highlighted lines of text. "She's been talking to several boys who were trying to get her to come out to meet them, but she didn't want to go."

Sam scanned the texts, which showed increasingly aggressive efforts on behalf of the boys, which Luna continued to ignore.

Archie pointed to one of the contacts. "That's Ethan's number, and that one is Tomas's."

Sam's gasp said it all. "Archie... what the hell?"

"All this shows is that he was trying to get her to come out."

"For what reason, though?"

"He never spells that out. It's mostly 'come on, let's have some fun, you know you want to' kind of stuff."

"What time were those messages sent?" Sam asked.

"It started around five thirty and went on sporadically until after seven."

"Wait," Sam said. "That would've been more than an hour after they'd stopped responding to their parents."

"What're you thinking?"

"What if someone else had gotten ahold of their phones?" Sam went back to the living room. "Tracy, have you ever heard Ethan talk about a girl named Luna Ahern?"

"No, I've never heard of anyone with that name."

"He said something to me," Brooke said, "when I talked to him last week. I was teasing him about liking girls, and I asked if there's anyone he particularly likes. He said there's a girl named Luna, but she's older than him and even though she was nice to him, he's not sure if she likes him."

"Did he say anything else about her?" Sam asked.

"Not that I can recall. We moved on to talk about the Feds season and if he's going to opening day with Dad this year. He said he isn't sure yet. What does this have to do with him being missing?"

"Luna Ahern is also missing," Sam said. "Ethan and Tomas were texting her, trying to get her to meet them."

"Oh my God," Tracy said. "This just keeps getting worse all the time. Will he be blamed for that girl going missing?"

"The messages were sent after you said he stopped responding to you, so we need to figure out what's going on. Try not to go straight to worst-case. We're still putting pieces together to figure out what's happened."

"I don't know what to do," Tracy said. "I'm completely panicked at the thought of my eleven-year-old son being who knows where—overnight. *Where could he be?*"

"Take it easy, Mom." Brooke tried to comfort her mother. "We'll find him. I'm sure of it."

Tracy's tears and anguished wails were like knives to Sam's heart.

The secure BlackBerry Sam carried so she could speak to Nick rang, startling her out of her thoughts. She left the room to take the call. "Hi."

"How's it going?"

"Some progress, but nothing yet. Tracy's taking it so hard, but having Brooke and Nate here helps."

"I'm glad they're there. So, listen, the BOLO for Ethan led to press inquiries after someone figured out he's our nephew. I was thinking I might make a statement that confirms we're looking for our missing nephew and would appreciate the public's help, or something like that. Would you be okay with that?"

"Let me check with Malone on that. I'll call you back."

"I'll be here. I love you."

"Love you, too. Be right back to you."

Sam called Malone and explained the situation at the White House. "Would it be okay for Nick to announce we're looking for our missing nephew and two of his friends?"

"I can't see why not. I just talked to Ruiz, and we're no closer to finding them now than we were a few hours ago. It might help to have Nick make a statement."

Sam's heart sank at hearing no one else had made any progress either. "All right. I'll let him know to go ahead. Thanks, Cap."

"I'll tell Ruiz what he's doing."

"Okay."

Sam ended that call and picked up the BlackBerry to call Nick back. "Please make the statement. We'll take all the help we can get."

"Can you send me a recent photo of him?"

"Yes, I'll have Brooke do that."

"Great, thank you. I'll get right on it. Will you be home any time soon?"

"Maybe. There's not much more I can do tonight. We'll start fresh in the morning."

Sam's regular cell phone rang with a call from her other sister, Angela. "Ang is calling. I need to grab that. I'll keep you posted on what I'm doing."

"I'll be right here if you need anything."

"That helps. Thanks. See you soon."

Sam juggled phones to take the call from Ang. "Hey."

"What the fuck is going on, Sam? One of my friends just saw a report on the news that Ethan is missing and asked me about it."

"We were hoping he'd be home before we had to worry you and everyone else."

"So he's really missing?"

"Since around four this afternoon."

"That's like almost nine hours!"

"Yes, I know. We're doing everything we can to find him."

"Tracy and Mike must be out of their minds."

"They are. Brooke is here with Nate, and she's been a big help." Sam walked back into the living room. "Brooke, will you please send a recent photo of Ethan to Uncle Nick?" Everyone in their family had the number for the BlackBerry so they could reach him if needed.

"Right away."

"Thanks, hon."

"What's Nick doing?" Tracy asked.

"The press put two and two together from the be-on-the-lookout alert we put out and connected Ethan to us. Nick is making a statement and will ask for help from the public."

"So it's blowing up into a massive story, then," Mike said when he appeared from somewhere.

Sam gave him a helpless look that she hoped conveyed a world of apology for their high profiles elevating Ethan's disappearance into a national story.

"What can I do?" Angela asked.

"Nothing, for right now. I'll let you know if there's any news. I'm sorry we didn't call you before now, but you have enough to deal with over there." Since her husband Spencer's sudden death, her pregnant sister was now a single parent to a seven-year-old son and a two-and-a-half-year-old daughter.

"I'd still want to know my nephew is missing, Sam."

"Understood. I'm sorry. It's been stressful."

"Do you think... I mean... Did someone take him? Because he's related to you and Nick?"

"The thought has crossed our minds, but we're working a number of different angles. The Secret Service assures us that if there'd been any threats against Ethan or any of our close people, they'd probably know about them. They're assisting in the investigation, and the FBI is helping, too."

"Sweet Jesus, Sam, the FBI is involved?"

"We're covering all the bases."

"Are you scared?"

"Yeah."

She whimpered. "Sam…"

"I know, believe me. I know."

"Tell Tracy… Tell her I love her, and I'll be over in the morning."

"I will. Talk to you then."

"Call me if anything happens overnight."

"Okay. Love you."

"Love you, too."

Sam closed her phone and conveyed Angela's message.

"How'd she find out?"

"A friend saw the BOLO on the news."

"Everyone will know. No matter what happens now, everyone knows he was missing, and that'll stick to him—and us—forever, even if it turns out to be nothing."

She wanted to tell Tracy not to worry about that, but how could she? It was true. Something like this didn't just go away when the incident was resolved. All they could do right now was pray that Ethan would come home soon—with an explanation for his absence that would make sense.

With every hour that passed with no news and no word from him, Sam became less optimistic about that outcome.

CHAPTER EIGHT

A small group of reporters was gathered in the press room when Nick walked in at twenty minutes after one that Sunday morning to read the statement he'd crafted.

Everyone sat up straighter when he entered. It still amused him all these months later how people snapped to attention in his presence, as if he didn't put his pants on one leg at a time like everyone else.

"Around eight o'clock last evening, the first lady and I were informed that our eleven-year-old nephew, Ethan Hogan, was missing. The first lady received a call from her sister Tracy Hogan, who told her that Ethan wasn't answering his phone and that the location services had been turned off. Needless to say, in the hours since, we've been doing everything in our power to find Ethan and bring him home safely. Sam is consulting with her colleagues at the Metropolitan Police Department, which issued a be-on-the-lookout alert several hours ago. The BOLO included a recent photo of Ethan as well as photos of Tomas Cambra and Luna Ahern, who are also missing. We'd appreciate your help in distributing the information. I'll take a few questions."

"Has your nephew been in any trouble?"

"Not that we're aware of."

"Where was he supposed to be?"

"He left with Tomas to get pizza and play video games at the arcade at the Wharf. The MPD has released information about Tomas as well."

"Is there any connection between Luna, your nephew and his friend?"

"That'd be a question for the MPD."

"How is the first lady doing?"

"As you can imagine, she's consumed with worry for her nephew and his friend and hoping to get them home safely. The MPD will have more information for you in the morning. Thank you for your help in spreading the word."

He stepped away from the podium, ignoring unrelated questions they tossed at him as he left the room. As if he'd bother to answer random questions about Congress or pending trade agreements when his nephew was missing.

Brant walked with him from the West Wing to the residence. "Is there anything I can do for you tonight, sir?"

Nick realized the young man was asking as a friend and not as an agent. "No, thank you, Brant. Not sure what we can do that's not being done already. Sam said the FBI is coming in tomorrow, which is a relief. We'll take all the help we can get."

"Please give Mrs. Cappuano my regards and tell her I'm thinking of her and the family."

"I will. Thanks, Brant."

"Assume you're in for the night now?"

"I hope so."

He reached up to touch his ear piece. "I'm receiving word that Mrs. Cappuano is on the way home with her detail."

"That's good news."

"Hopefully, you both can get some rest."

Nick suspected rest would be the last thing on Sam's to-do list with Ethan missing. "I hope so, too."

He parted company with Brant as he went upstairs to the residence, where Cory, one of the new agents, stood guard.

"Good morning, Mr. President."

"Morning, Cory."

Nick looked in on the twins and Scotty, all of whom were sound asleep, before heading to the suite he shared with Sam, feeling exhausted and as anxious as he'd been the day they'd learned armed drones had been dispatched toward the Easter Egg Roll.

Their family had been through a lot in recent months. Ethan's disappearance was almost too much to bear. He couldn't imagine how Tracy, Mike, Brooke and Abby must be feeling.

When Sam came in fifteen minutes later, he'd changed into sweats and a T-shirt and was waiting for her with a glass of wine.

"Sit for a minute," he said.

"I'm not sure if I can. If I stop moving, I might be tempted to scream my head off."

"If that's what you need to do..."

"I would if I thought it'd make any difference."

She took the glass as she sat next to him on the sofa. "I looked in on my kids, sleeping peacefully, always under the watch of world-class security. We're so lucky this could never happen to us and that Scotty isn't allowed to run around DC on his own with his friends."

"Thank goodness for the small mercies of the presidency, huh?"

"Yeah. Remind me to never complain about any of it ever again."

"You're still allowed to complain about the shitty parts. Is there anything new?"

"Archie was able to tie Ethan and Tomas to the missing girl through text messages they sent to her quite some time after they went dark to their parents."

"What does that mean?"

"We're not sure yet. He's got people working on the data

overnight, looking for more info. Patrol is currently looking for all of them. Not sure what else we could do that we're not doing. And on top of that, we had a murder at a hotel that's got my whole team recalled for a canvass of nearly two hundred rooms and their occupants."

"Damn."

"Yeah, so…"

"Do you think you could try to get some sleep?"

"I suppose I should try so I can give it my all tomorrow."

"Finish the wine. It'll help you sleep."

They sat in silence for the time it took her to consume the wine. Then she got up to change into pajama pants and a T-shirt. She set her alarm for six before sliding into bed next to him.

"Come here."

She turned toward him, resting her head on his chest as he held her close. "I've dealt with a lot of shit on this job, a lot of things that struck far too close to home, but this… Not knowing where he is… It's making me crazy."

"I know, honey. It's so scary, but Ethan's a good kid who was raised by strong parents and the savviest cop around. He knows how to keep himself safe. Let's have some faith in him."

"He's only eleven," she said tearfully. "*Eleven*, Nick. Why were they letting him go out with his friends? He's too young for that."

"I agree, but you know how kids can be when they want something badly enough. They wear down their parents until they give in on something they know they probably shouldn't."

"I swear I'll never complain about the confines of security again after this."

"Yes, you will, and so will I, but we'll always be grateful for the way they care for our kids."

"I just thought of something." Sam sat up and reached for her phone to send a text to her friend U.S. Marshal Jesse Best. The marshals specialized in finding missing people.

I need your help. Did you see the BOLO for Ethan Hogan issued earlier? He's my nephew. We're going nuts trying to find him and don't know what to do. Can you help?

Jesse wrote back right away. *When and where?*

HQ 8 a.m.?

I'll be there.

Thank you.

She returned her phone to the bedside table and tried to settle her mind so she could attempt to sleep. An hour later, she gave up and got out of bed so her disquiet wouldn't disturb Nick, who struggled for every minute of sleep he could get.

In the office Nick used for after-hours work, Sam fired up the laptop and opened a browser to do a search on incel culture and found much of the information Freddie and Archie had imparted earlier, but with additional terrifying details about incidents in which people who called themselves incels had attacked innocent men and women for being everything they'd never be.

Hours later, she knew more than she'd ever wanted to about a sick, twisted and disgusting subject.

When Nick's hands landed on her shoulders, she startled and then relaxed as her mind regulated to accept it was him and not one of the vile men she'd been reading about.

"What're you doing?"

"Scaring the ever-loving shit out of myself by reading about incel culture. It's terrifying."

"You need to get some rest, babe."

"I can't. Every time I close my eyes, I picture Ethan in some horrible situation. I need to be out there looking for him."

"Everyone on duty is looking for him. Even the Secret Service is assisting."

She ran her fingers through her hair as he continued to knead the tension from her shoulders. "I have to do *something*. I'm going to shower and head to HQ to see what's going on."

"If you make yourself sick, you won't be any help to Ethan or Tracy."

"I know, but it's what I have to do. Tell me you understand."

He kissed the top of her head. "I do, and I wish I could go with you without causing a circus."

"You could come to HQ if you wanted. We could make that work." She turned so she could see him, feeling madly vulnerable. "It would help me to have you there."

"Then that's what we'll do." He helped her up. "Take your shower while I notify the agents."

"What about the kids in the morning?"

"Your mom is still here. She won't mind staying."

Sam nodded, hoping her mom didn't have other plans.

"Give her a call. I bet she's up, worrying about Ethan, too."

"Probably." While he went to talk to the agents on duty in the residence, she made the call to her mother.

"Any news?" Brenda asked when she answered.

"Nothing yet. I'm going into work, and Nick is coming with me. Do you think you can handle the morning with the kids?"

"Of course. Anything I need to know?"

"I usually make an egg sandwich for Scotty and pancakes or French toast for the twins. Sometimes they just want regular toast with peanut butter. You have to make sure the twins brush their teeth, and…" Her voice caught as she thought of Ethan and how he wouldn't be home with his family in the morning.

"This is awful," her mom said. "I can't bear it for Tracy and Mike and the girls. And the rest of us."

"It's unbearable. I've got to go do something to at least try to help."

"I'm glad you're working on it. That brings me comfort, and I'm sure it does for Tracy and Mike, too. I'll take good care of your babies. Go find Ethan."

"Thanks, Mom."

"Love you, Sam. Be safe."

"Love you, too."

Those words from her mother meant everything to her. As she headed to the shower, she was filled with gratitude to have her mom back in her life—and her children's lives—after long years of estrangement following her parents' divorce. Sam had been firmly on Team Dad, but she'd later learned there were two sides to every story and that no one knew what went on inside a marriage besides the two people in it. Now that she understood more about her mother's perspective, she had a deeper appreciation for what she'd endured at the end of the marriage, and that had led to reconciliation.

She raced through the shower, put her wet hair up in a clip and prepared for a long day by getting dressed in jeans, a T-shirt, sweater and running shoes. This time of year, the mornings were chilly, and the afternoons were warm, not that she cared about any of that as she made a mental list of things she wanted to do when she got to HQ.

As soon as possible, she wanted to see Dr. Anthony Trulo, the department psychiatrist, to get his take on incel culture. The FBI would be briefing them, and Jesse Best would be there to help, too. Knowing the marshals would be assisting made her feel slightly better.

But nothing could dissolve the hard knot of fear in her stomach that would be there until Ethan was found safe.

She had unlocked the drawer in the bedside table where she kept her service weapon and cuffs when Nick came into the bedroom, dressed in jeans and a Dewey Beach sweatshirt.

"Ready when you are."

"Thank you for coming with me. I know you had to jump through some hoops."

"Not as many as usual on a Sunday. Besides, I always want to be wherever you are, especially at a time like this."

She took hold of the hand he held out to her as they left their suite and went downstairs to meet the agents who waited for them in the foyer. With their regular teams off duty until the morning, they were met by agents Sam didn't know, but Nick did. He greeted them by name and thanked them for arranging transport.

"Right this way, Mr. President, ma'am."

"It's weird to be going somewhere without Brant or Vernon," Sam said when they were in the back seat of The Beast on the way to HQ.

"I know. I was thinking the same thing."

"What're you missing today to come with me?"

"A couple of meetings that Gretchen will take for me. Nothing to worry about."

"I'm sure it's far more complicated for you to call out of work, even on a weekend, than you're making it sound."

"Our nephew is missing. I'm where I need to be."

Sam closed her eyes against an instant flood of tears. "I feel like I'm spinning in a thousand directions as the fear multiplies with every minute that goes by with no news."

"I know, babe. It's horrible to not know where he is."

Sam's phone rang with a call from the landline at Celia's. "Hey."

"Have you heard anything?" Tracy asked tearfully.

"Nothing new, but I'm on my way to HQ now. I'll let you know of any developments the minute they happen."

"I'm going out of my mind, Sam. *Where is he?*"

"I don't know, but we're bringing in all the best people to look for him."

"I'm glad you're still on the case even though they told you not to be."

"I'll be right here for as long as it takes to bring him home. I promise."

"Thank you. I love you."

"I love you, too. I'll be back to you as soon as I have anything to tell you."

"Okay."

"Hang in there, Trace."

"Hanging by a thread."

They said their goodbyes for now, and Sam closed her phone quietly as tears rolled down her face. She'd said what her sister needed to hear, but the truth was she had no idea whether anything they were doing would lead to Ethan's safe return. At the moment, she felt like they were throwing things at the wall to see what would stick rather than doing something strategic to find the three missing kids.

Her phone rang again, this time from a number she didn't recognize. "Holland."

"This is Joaquin Cambra, Tomas's father, wondering if there's any news. We haven't heard anything in a few hours."

"There's nothing new, but I'm on my way to MPD headquarters to get an update from Patrol and the officers who've been out looking for them tonight. If I hear anything new, I'll be right back to you."

"We don't know what to do. It's... We're sick with worry."

"I'm so sorry. I wish I had more news for you. Hopefully soon."

"Thank you for taking my call. We appreciate what everyone is doing to find them."

"We're bringing in federal agents this morning to assist."

"Oh God... That makes it sound so dire, which it is, but..."

"I understand, but the more help we have, the better. I'll be back to you as soon as I have anything to report."

"Thank you."

Sam closed her phone and held back the urgent need to scream her head off with frustration and fear. She hated feeling out of control of anything, and this situation was so far outside her control...

Her phone rang again, with a call from Gonzo. It was a good thing she hadn't tried to sleep. She hadn't given the murder at the hotel a single thought in hours. "Hey, what's up?"

"We're finishing up the canvass, speaking to every guest and employee. We're still waiting for the warrant to enter the victim's room, but I'm sending everyone home to get a few hours of sleep. Freddie texted that he'll be here shortly to take over."

"I'm getting a call from Dispatch. Hang on." She accepted the new call, hoping she wasn't cutting off Gonzo. "Holland."

"Lieutenant, we've received a call from a woman, Trisha Carver, in Spokane, Washington. She's been trying to reach her husband for hours and has been unable to get through. He was staying at the Vacation Inn and Suites on 10th Avenue Northwest. She said no one at the hotel will tell her if he's in his room or what's going on. What would you like us to do?"

"Can you please give her information to Sergeant Gonzales? He's working the scene at the hotel."

"Will do. Thank you."

Sam returned to the call with Gonzo. "Your vic's wife is looking for him. Dispatch is sending you her name and number."

"Fabulous," he said in a grim tone.

"Sorry."

"It's okay. Maybe she can give us permission to enter the room."

"Wait for the warrant."

"Yeah, okay. I'm exhausted and not firing on all cylinders. Anything new with Ethan?"

"Not yet. We're briefing with the FBI and Marshals at eight."

"I'm praying for him and your family."

"Thanks, Gonzo."

CHAPTER NINE

For several minutes after the contact info for the victim's wife arrived by text, Gonzo stared at the screen, hating that he had to call her and change her life forever with the worst-possible news. Like everyone in their squad, he hated making calls like this one, but it had to be done. Anxious to get it over with, he put through the call.

A woman answered on the first ring. "Hello?"

"Mrs. Carver, this is Detective Sergeant Thomas Gonzales with the Metropolitan Police Department. I received the message you left with our dispatchers about not being able to reach your husband."

"Yes, he's not answering his phone, and he never doesn't answer his phone, especially when it's me calling. We have young kids, and he's there for work, and... I don't know what to do."

"Can you describe him for me?"

"He... He's thirty-four and has dark blond hair. He has a scar on his upper lip from a fishing hook when he was a kid."

"Ma'am, I'm so sorry to have to tell you that a body matching your husband's description was found deceased in the hotel last night."

Her piercing scream had him holding the phone away from his ear as he closed his eyes, wishing he'd chosen a different line of work.

"He can't be dead!" she said between sobs. "*He's my whole world!*"

"Is there anyone with you?"

"M-my sister is here. I... I called her when I couldn't reach Dale."

Gonzo made a note of his first name.

"Wh-what happened to him?"

"He was found in the ice machine room on the hotel's sixth floor. He'd been stabbed in the chest."

"Oh my God! Who would want to kill him? I... I don't understand."

As she broke down into fresh sobs, a rustling sound came as the phone was transferred to someone else.

"Dale is really dead?" a woman asked.

"You are?"

"His sister-in-law, Mercy Roth."

Gonzo wrote down her name and told her what they knew so far, which wasn't much. "Can you confirm he was a guest at the Vacation Inn and Suites on 10th Street?"

"Yes, he was. What should we do? Should we come there?"

He choked back a yawn and rubbed eyes that'd gone gritty during the long night. "Not yet. We'll get back to you about next steps. In the meantime, can you tell me what he was doing in DC?"

"He works for an agricultural company here in Spokane and was there for meetings at USDA."

"Can you get me a point of contact for his company and text it to this number?" He wasn't sure he'd need the information but wanted to have it anyway.

"Yes, we'll take care of that. What happens now?"

"Our medical examiner has taken custody of the body and will perform an autopsy, which is standard procedure in a homicide. Once her work is completed, we can coordinate with a funeral home of your choice to transport him home."

In the background, Gonzo heard a baby crying, and he felt sad for a family torn apart by a senseless murder.

"I can't believe this has happened. They just had their third child... He's such a wonderful husband and father."

"Has he ever been in any kind of trouble?"

After a long pause that had Gonzo standing up a little straighter, she said, "He had some trouble with drugs a few years ago, but he went to rehab and got past that."

Aw, shit. "How many years ago?"

"Um, I think it's been four years."

"What was his drug of choice?"

"Is this really relevant?"

"Everything is relevant in a homicide investigation."

"He was addicted to heroin and worked very hard to get better for his wife and kids. They're his everything." She sniffled. "I can't believe this has happened to him. What in the world will Trisha and the kids do without him?"

"I'm so sorry for your loss and for hers. We'll be back in touch with more information later today."

"Thank you."

"If you think of anything else that might be relevant to our investigation, even the smallest of things, please be sure to get in touch and pass that request along to your sister as well."

"I will. I'll tell her."

Gonzo ended the call, feeling sad for people he'd never met. Murder came out of nowhere to upset lives that'd been somewhat ordinary beforehand and changed every single thing about the future for those left behind. Having to tell family members that their loved ones had been killed was the most devastating part of a heartbreaking job.

Officer Youncy approached him. "We've completed the canvass of all the rooms, Sarge, and haven't found a single witness."

She looked as exhausted as he felt.

"You can let everyone go home with my thanks for staying all night."

"Yes, sir." She glanced toward the closed door to the ice room, which was sealed off with yellow tape. Crime Scene detectives had quickly processed the room overnight and had left until they were able to access the victim's room. "Do we know who he was?"

"Dale Carver from Spokane, Washington. Married father of three. Here for meetings at USDA."

"Damn."

"I know." As a recovering addict himself, Gonzo decided to keep the info about Dale's addiction and recovery to himself until he had a chance to delve deeper into the man's final hours. He hoped this wasn't a case of a relapse gone bad. "Go get some sleep. Appreciate your great work and that of Officer Clare. Tell him to take off, too."

"I will. Sorry we weren't able to get you more information."

"At least we know that no one in the hotel saw anything—or if they did, they're not talking about it."

"Right."

"In an investigation like this, ruling out is as important as ruling in."

"Good point. See you around campus, Sarge."

"Take it easy."

After Youncy walked away, Gonzo called Dr. Lindsey McNamara, the department's chief medical examiner.

"Hey, Sarge. How's it going over there?"

"Slow but steady. I spoke to the vic's wife, Trisha. His name is Dale Carver, here from Spokane, Washington to meet with USDA. I have her number if you want to get in touch when you're finished with the exam." He recited the number for her. "I told her you'd call about funeral homes and transport."

"Will do. What else do we know about him?"

"He's the father of three young kids, including a new baby."

"Shit."

"You said it. What've you found so far?"

"The first blow severed his aorta, and it was game over after that. The other five wounds are extraneous."

"Judging by the amount of blood, I figured there was an artery involved. I'll be handing off to Cruz soon. I'll have him get in touch."

"Got it. Is there any word on Sam's nephew?"

"Just that the Feds and Marshals are coming in this morning."

"God, this is just terrifying."

"Sure is."

"I'll let you get back to it."

"Thanks, Doc."

Gonzo had no sooner stashed his phone in his pocket than it rang with a call from Captain Malone.

"Hey, Cap."

"I've got your warrants for the video and to enter the victim's room. Sent copies to your email."

"Great, thanks."

"Where are you over there?"

Gonzo filled him in on the results of the canvass and the new information he'd gotten from the victim's family.

"What's your gut saying?"

"Not getting a reading just yet. I want to get into his room."

"Go to it and keep me posted."

"Will do."

Gonzo girded his loins before he called Wright to request access to the room now that he had the warrant.

"I'll send Mr. Russell up right away."

He was surprised by the hotel manager's quick action. "I'm sending Detective Carlucci down to retrieve the video. Please hand over everything for the entire hotel from yesterday."

"We have it ready."

Gonzo wondered if the manager had gotten a talking-to from

corporate about the importance of cooperating in a homicide investigation. He put the call on speaker while he texted Dani to ask her to retrieve the video and get it to Archie's team for analysis. Then he asked Detective Cameron Green to join him at the victim's room.

"Do you know how long the police vehicles will remain outside the building?" Wright asked.

"Until we're done."

After a long pause, Wright said, "Very well, then."

Gonzo pressed the red button to end the call. Even when he was cooperating, the guy irritated him.

Russell came off the elevator five minutes later. He nodded to Gonzo when they met up outside room six thirty-two.

Green came from the other end of the hallway and arrived as Russell used his passkey to open the door.

Gonzo and Green gloved up before entering the room.

"Thank you," Gonzo said as he used his body to block Russell's view of the interior. "We'll take it from here."

Russell grunted out a reply that Gonzo couldn't decipher and turned to walk away.

Inside the room, the situation quickly became clear. Gonzo sighed when he saw drug paraphernalia, including hypodermic needles, powder residue and small plastic bags, on the desk.

"Shit," he muttered.

"Heroin?" Green asked.

"That was his drug of choice. According to the wife's sister, he'd been clean for four years. Son of a bitch. I so don't want to have to tell his wife about this."

"I can handle that for you, Gonzo," Green said, knowing the discovery would strike close to home for him.

"It's okay. I'll do it when the time comes. Let's take some photos and get Crime Scene in here." They'd process the evidence that would probably lead to a drug deal gone bad.

While Gonzo took photos on his phone, Green contacted

Lieutenant Haggerty to let his team know they'd gained access to the victim's room.

"Haggerty said they're on the way."

As Gonzo looked around at evidence that told the story of a relapse, he felt chilled to the bone, knowing Dale Carver had thrown away years of sobriety—or at least as far as his family knew—while on a work trip across the country, far away from the family that loved him and depended on him.

Addiction was a bitch that way. Just when you thought you had it beat, opportunity knocked, and you walked through that door as if the monumental effort to kick the habit had never happened.

There but for the grace of God go I. Gonzo felt sick to his stomach.

Freddie Cruz came through the door they'd propped open by engaging the security lock. "Heard you guys were in here."

"Hey, you're early," Gonzo said, relieved to see his close friend and colleague an hour earlier than expected.

Freddie's sharp-eyed gaze took in the drug paraphernalia. "Couldn't sleep thinking about Ethan and the family, so I figured I may as well come in."

"Glad to have you," Gonzo said. "We're running on fumes after an all-nighter." He brought him up to speed on what they knew so far. He handed Freddie the piece of paper with the wife's phone number on it. "Her name is Trisha Carver. I told her sister Mercy that there was no reason for them to come here unless they wanted to. They'll be waiting to hear from Lindsey with next steps. She has their numbers, too."

Gonzo rubbed the back of his neck, which was aching from the long night. "The manager, Wright, was a prick last night, but he's changed his tune this morning, presumably after being told to by corporate. Russell's his assistant and is easier to deal with. Carlucci is getting the film and taking it to Archie's team for analysis."

"Got it. Go on home. I'll take it from here."

"Thanks, man. I'll catch a few hours and come back in later."

"Me, too," Green said as he headed for the door.

"Call if you have any questions," Gonzo added.

Freddie stopped him with a hand on his arm. "Are you okay?"

Gonzo wasn't surprised that his friend understood his torment. "Yeah, just... you know... A drug addict relapsed while away from his family. Somehow that probably led to his death."

"What do you need?"

In a past life, he might've lied to his friend and said he was okay. He'd learned that lying about stuff like that led to the kind of trouble that ruined lives and careers. "I think I need a meeting." He'd attended daily Narcotics Anonymous meetings for months after leaving rehab. These days, he attended only as needed.

"Do you want me to find one nearby for you?"

"I can do it, but thank you for offering."

"I'd go with you if you needed me to."

"I know, and I appreciate that. Stay here and keep working the scene. That's what I need from you right now."

"Will you check in with me after the meeting, so I know you're okay?"

"Yeah, I can do that."

"Don't forget."

"I won't. I promise." Gonzo gave his friend a tired smile as he left the room.

In the elevator, he put his head back against the wall and closed his eyes, beyond exhausted from the sleepless night and emotionally charged case. What had seemed like a "routine" murder, as those things went, had turned into something much more fraught for him as a recovering addict.

At times, he still couldn't believe those words applied to him. *Recovering addict.* But that's what he was and what he'd be for the rest of his life. With a wife and a son counting on him, another baby on the way and coworkers he considered family, Gonzo had many good reasons to protect his hard-won sobriety. He was lucky to still have a job, and he'd never forget the way his colleagues had stood by him through the epic struggle.

With them and his family in mind, he looked up the closest NA meeting and headed for the exit as he called his wife to say good morning.

"Hey," Christina said when she answered. "You never made it home. Good thing I know you don't have time for other women."

"Haha, as if I'd want anyone else when I've got *the* woman."

"Good answer on no sleep. Props. Are you on your way home?"

"I'm going to hit a meeting first. Are you working today?" As Nick's White House spokesperson, it wasn't unusual for her to work weekends.

"For a few hours. I can work from home if you need me."

"I always need you, but I'm okay. Just had a somewhat routine case take an unexpected turn that left me a bit shaky."

"Tommy... Are you sure you're okay?"

"I'm sure, honey. It's safe to go to work."

"I'll stay home anyway. It's fine."

Knowing she'd be waiting for him at home immediately lifted his spirits. "Then I guess I'll see you shortly."

"I love you."

"Love you, too. More than you'll ever know. You're my reason. You and Alex and the baby..."

"And you're ours. Don't ever forget that."

"I never do. See you soon, love."

"I'll be here."

Gonzo was nearly in tears as he got into his car to leave work behind to tend to his sobriety and his family. He was so, so lucky that Christina had stood by him through the darkest time in his life. The murder of his partner—right in front of him—had sent him off a cliff straight into an opioid addiction that'd nearly taken everything that mattered.

For as long as he had breath left in him, he'd continue to fight back.

CHAPTER TEN

Sam and Nick were almost to HQ when Sam's mom called.
"Aubrey woke up crying. She's got a fever and a sore throat."

"Oh shit," Sam said. "I'll text Harry to come see her."

"I hate to say that she's asking for you."

After she sent the text to their friend, the White House medical director, Sam closed her eyes against the start of a headache. "Can I talk to her?"

"Sure. Here she is."

"Hi," Aubrey said in a small voice.

"Hi, honey. Nana says you're not feeling well. I'm so sorry."

"It's not your fault."

Sam smiled. "I wish I was there to hug you and make you feel better. I'll be home as soon as I possibly can, okay?"

"Okay. Is Nick here?"

"He's with me."

"Oh."

Sam winced from the agony of needing to be in two places at the same time. "Dr. Harry will come see you, and he'll fix you right up."

"I like Dr. Harry."

"I know you do. We all do. Call me if you need me, okay?"

"I will."

"I'll come right home the minute I can."

"It's okay. Nana said I can eat Popsicles and watch *Frozen* again."

"That sounds like the perfect sick day to me. I love you, and I hope you feel better very soon."

"Love you, too. Tell Nick, too."

"I will, sweetie."

Sam closed the phone and looked to Nick. "I hate that I'm not there with her."

"She's in very good hands with your mom and Harry."

"I know, but it should be me. I'll be her mother when the adoption is settled. Cleo would've been right there with her."

"Don't do that to yourself, Sam. If Aubrey knew Ethan was missing, she'd want us helping to look for him."

The twins had massive older-kid crushes on Ethan and Abby, so he was probably right about that.

"I guess so."

"Every day requires an ordering of priorities for both of us. Our marriage and our family is always the number one thing on our list, but there're times, such as this, we have to give our full attention to something else because lives are at stake. Public servants make sacrifices all the time that others never see or know about."

"That's a fact. In this case, I'm a terrified aunt who has to put her own child's needs second to her missing nephew."

"And I'm a terrified uncle putting his own child's needs—and those of the entire country—second to our missing nephew."

"I feel a little better when you toss the entire country in there."

His low chuckle made her smile for the first time all day as she rested her head on his sturdy shoulder, thankful for his presence for what promised to be another difficult day.

"Sometimes it's all just too much."

"Only sometimes?"

"Yeah, most of the time."

Her phone rang with a call from Freddie.

"Hey, are you at the hotel already?"

"Yeah, I relieved Gonzo about twenty minutes ago. He learned from the victim's sister-in-law that he was a recovering heroin addict. Evidence in the hotel room shows he'd relapsed. Our goal today is to figure out where he got the stuff and whether the dealer is the one who killed him."

"Shit, that must've been a tough scene for Gonzo."

"It was. He said he'd attend an NA meeting this morning and promised to check in with me after."

"Keep an eye on that."

"I will. I'd ask how you are, but..."

"Yeah, not so good, and now Aubrey is sick, too. Nick and I are almost to HQ to see what we can do to help."

"I'm glad he's with you."

"As am I. It's been a minute since I had a take-my-husband-to-work day."

Nick tightened the arm he had around her.

"Sure has. Let me know if I can do anything for you today."

"Keep working that case. That's what I need."

"I'm on it. I'll check in after a bit."

As Sam closed her phone, The Beast pulled up to the morgue entrance.

"Please stand by for a moment," the lead agent said.

Sam desperately missed Vernon, who had no need to clear the way into the police station for her. This agent would follow protocol to the letter.

She vibrated with tension as she waited for the door to open. Her mind raced with a thousand things she wanted to do before the meetings with the FBI and U.S. Marshals. She sent a text to Dr. Trulo asking him to call her when he could. As far as she knew, they hadn't heard back from his daughter yesterday, which was one of several things she needed to discuss with him.

Sam leaned around Nick for a better view of the goings-on outside. "What's taking so long? It's a police station, for fuck's sake."

"I'm the problem," he said, sounding pained. "You could probably go ahead."

"I'll wait for you."

"Breathe, Samantha. Keep breathing."

"Trying."

Seven minutes later, the door finally opened as agents swarmed the vehicle, creating a barrier around them as they walked the short distance to the morgue door.

"Let's keep it to one agent inside, guys," Nick said. "No need for the full complement."

"We'd need approval from headquarters for that, sir," the young agent said.

"I'm giving you approval. One agent. That's it. I'll take the heat if there is any."

"There'll be heat, sir."

"I'll make sure it doesn't burn you."

"Yes, sir." He signaled to the other agents to stay put while he accompanied them inside, looking around as if he expected a shooter to jump out at them at any second.

Sam acknowledged that it had to be nerve-racking for the agent to bring the president into a building full of armed officers with no advance notice and none of the usual preparation that preceded the president's arrival at any destination.

"Let's stop to check in with Lindsey," she said, taking a right into the morgue, where her friend was completing an autopsy.

"Do you want to wait out here?" she asked Nick.

"That's okay. I can handle it."

"Morning," Sam said to Lindsey when they were inside the room that smelled of antiseptic and other chemicals. "Is that our vic from the hotel?"

"Morning. Oh, and hello to you, too, Mr. President. Yes, it's

Dale Carver, age thirty-four, from Washington state. Stabbed in the chest, which severed his aorta."

Nick winced.

"Did you get the word that Gonzo suspects a drug deal gone south?"

"I did. I'm running a tox screen, as I always do." She glanced at them. "What're you hearing about your nephew?"

"Nothing new yet today. Hoping to make some progress soon."

"Are you on the case, then?"

"Not officially. Just helping out."

"I wondered because I heard there was a screaming match between Ruiz and Malone first thing, and your name came up."

"Great," Sam said with a sigh. "That's just what I need."

"Sorry to be the bearer of bad news, but I thought you should have a heads-up."

"I appreciate it. Better go see what's up." She glanced at Nick. "Aren't you glad you came with me?"

"Any day with you is a good day."

"Aw, good answer, my love. See you later, Linds."

"Praying for Ethan and your family."

"Thank you. We appreciate it."

She took Nick's hand to lead him from the morgue to the pit, which was all but deserted today as most of her team had worked overnight at the hotel. As she was unlocking her office door, Captain Malone approached, looking aggravated. "A moment, please, Lieutenant." He nodded to Nick. "Mr. President."

"Captain."

The three of them went into Sam's office and closed the door.

"Ruiz is furious that you called in the Feds and the marshals without discussing it with her first."

"I didn't technically call in the Feds. I called some of my friends for advice, and they offered to come in to help."

"Fine line, Lieutenant, and Ruiz is rightfully annoyed. This is her case."

"We're looking for *my nephew*, Captain."

"I'm aware, and that's why I told you to stay in the background on this case."

"Which is what I've tried to do."

A loud knock sounded at the door before Ruiz walked in, loaded for bear. She stopped short when she encountered the president of the United States standing in Sam's office.

"Captain Michelle Ruiz, this is my husband, Nick."

Ruiz nodded to him and then turned her ire toward Sam. "What part of 'stay out of my case' did you not understand yesterday?"

Already exhausted with a day that'd barely begun, Sam took a seat behind her desk while Nick leaned against her filing cabinet, directing a steely stare at the captain that would earn him some extra favors at home.

Sam stared at a spot on the wall as she began to speak. "My sister Tracy was twenty-one when she had my niece Brooke. I was seventeen and had no interest whatsoever in kids or babies until Brooke arrived." Sam gave a small smile as she remembered the life-altering birth of her niece. "I was obsessed with everything she did and was so in love with her, I started thinking for the first time that I might someday like to have kids of my own. Prior to that, I would've said kids were the last thing I wanted."

"What does this have to do—"

"I had a miscarriage in college," Sam went on, ignoring the interruption. "I've talked about that so often, I feel like the whole world knows." As she continued to stare at the wall, her eyes became unfocused as she took a painful trip down memory lane toward some of the most devastating events of her life. She hoped she could keep her composure. "I was relieved when that happened, because I was in no way ready to be a mother. Like most people in their early twenties, I thought I had all the time in the world to have kids. The miscarriage was one of the worst things I've ever been through. I ended up having issues for years afterward and was later diagnosed with endometriosis. The theory was that it'd been dormant until I got pregnant, and the hormones triggered it, or some such thing. Who knows?

"I was twenty-four when I was told for the first time that I might not be able to have babies because the endometriosis had left so much scar tissue. That came as a total shock to me. I mean... I knew things weren't great in that area because of the way I'd suffered every month with intense pain, but it never occurred to me I was losing my fertility one month at a time until a doctor said those words out loud. I was so shattered by that news I could barely function. I was out of work for a week because I couldn't get out of bed. For the only time in my entire life, I wondered if it'd be easier to give up than to face a future without the children I'd dreamed of having someday. Who would want to marry a woman who couldn't have children? Who would love me?"

She kept expecting Ruiz to shut her down, but the captain stood by the door with her arms crossed, listening without seeming to blink.

Sam wiped away the tears that always showed up when she revisited this painful era, even after all these years. "I was in a bad way for about three weeks. I went so far as to fantasize about how I might end it all. I had pills for the endometriosis pain. If I took them all, maybe I could escape the hell of this life-altering news. I thought about it nonstop, every waking moment. I dreamed about escaping the agony of physical pain and emotional anguish. I was about to set a date to do it when my brother-in-law Mike called to tell me Tracy was in labor and asking for me.

"I didn't want to go. I thought I was the last person who should be there when my sister was giving birth, knowing that would never be me. I almost didn't go, until I remembered the million and one ways that Tracy has been there for me all my life. There's never been a time when I needed her that she wasn't right there to take care of me. How could I stay away when she wanted me? So I made myself go, and I was there when my nephew Ethan came into the world, making a huge racket, his face red and scrunchy with outrage. He was so, so beautiful, and like with Brooke, I was in love from the first second I saw him. I never again thought about taking those pills or harming myself, because my niece and nephew were there to soothe the ache. They'd always be there. They were my kids as much as they were my sister's."

She finally looked directly at Ruiz through the blur of tears. "That's who I'm looking for, Captain, the boy who saved my life once upon a time. I'm sorry I didn't follow your orders to the letter, but there's nothing I won't do to bring him home safely. I have to save him the same way he once saved me."

Ruiz looked down at the floor, her face pulsing with tension, obviously moved by Sam's story. "I understand what he means to you, but we have to do this by the book so we don't screw up a potential prosecution. You know that as well as I do."

"You're right, and at the meeting, I'll brief you on everything I know. I spoke to Luna Ahern's parents and got Archie's team and CSU started at their house. I've asked my friends Avery Hill and Jesse Best for help. I spent all night reading about the horrors of incel culture. I've done things anyone in my position would do to help find a missing family member."

"What else have you done?" Ruiz asked.

"I tried to find the family of a kid named Brecken Mayfield at their last known address. The neighbor told me they moved quite some time ago, and she doesn't know where they went. If I had to pose a theory at this juncture, I'd guess that Brecken, who was several years older than the three missing kids, was interested in Luna. She wanted nothing to do with him, so he recruited two boys close in age to her to befriend her and try to get her to come out to meet them. I can't prove any of this, but that's my guess from what we know so far. We've learned there're active parole violation warrants for him and his father, Asher.

"From what I read about incel culture, this isn't something people stumble into. Someone in their life leads them to it, perhaps a father, older brother or someone else close to them."

"That's a good thought," Ruiz said. "Why don't you work on that until the meeting at zero eight hundred?"

"I'll do that."

"Let me know what you find out."

"I will. Thank you, Captain. I'm sorry for not keeping you posted on my efforts. I'm running on pure adrenaline."

Ruiz gave a brief nod and left the room, closing the door.

Malone blew out a low whistle. "Well done, Sam. You took the starch right out of her spine."

"But at what cost?" Nick asked, his beautiful hazel eyes full of love as he looked at her.

She'd felt him watching her throughout the entire encounter with Ruiz. "It was worth it to make her understand where I'm coming from."

"She knows where you're coming from," Malone said, "and that's why you were told to stand down."

Sam smiled at him. "Yes, you're right, but now she knows the whole story."

"For what it's worth," Malone said, "I'm glad you called Avery and Jesse. I want to find these missing kids. I don't care what we have to do to make that happen or who else we need to bring in to get it done. That said, please collaborate with Ruiz going forward. I don't need any more screaming matches today."

"I'm sorry you were subjected to the first one because of me."

"I'll get over it. Let's get to work and find these kids."

"Yes, sir."

CHAPTER ELEVEN

After Malone left the office, Nick closed the door. "Come here for one second."

Knowing he needed it as much as she did, Sam stood, went around the desk and stepped into his embrace.

"I hate that you had to open that old wound to make her understand what's at stake here. I hate that you still hurt the way you do, the way you always will, and more than anything, I hate to hear that, for a time, you didn't want to be here anymore."

"You knew that."

"I don't think I did."

"Well, I'm sorry you heard about it like that. It was a few weeks of true darkness that've never been repeated, thankfully. I don't hurt the way I used to. I'll always be sorry we weren't able to have a baby together but look at what we do have. Our kids are everything I could ever want and then some. I don't yearn for things I used to think I wanted more than anything. If I have you and our kids, I have it all."

"And soon, they'll all be legally ours." Their court date for the official adoption of Elijah and the twins was fast approaching.

"I can't wait for that." She kissed him. "Thank you for the hug. It helped."

He released her so she could get back to work trying to find Ethan. "I'm here all day."

"That makes everything better."

She dove into the research on the Mayfield family. "It's curious, isn't it, that the kid I'm looking for once lived in the same Truxton Circle neighborhood as Luna Ahern."

"That is an interesting connection. How can I have lived in and around DC for almost twenty years and still be hearing neighborhood names for the first time?"

"Truxton Circle is also known as East Shaw. Named for a Navy guy who had a circle dedicated to his memory at Florida Ave and North Capitol Street in 1900 or something before they later removed it because it was causing so many accidents."

"And you just happen to know that?"

"My dad used to tell me stories about where the neighborhoods got their names. He knew them all."

"Wow."

"I think their proximity to each other is a connection worth investigating further. Maybe Brecken Mayfield met Luna Ahern in the neighborhood and became interested. She ignored him, which made him mad enough to want to go after her." Sam flipped through her notes from the night before and called the number for Luna's mother, Court.

"Did you find her?" Court asked when she answered.

"Not yet, but I have a question. You said Luna had trouble with boys who couldn't take no for an answer."

"Yes, it's a constant problem for her, even though she's too young for such things."

"You said the name Brecken Mayfield meant nothing to you. Is that still the case now that you've had time to think about it?"

"I've thought about it constantly since you were here last night, and I can't recall her ever mentioning that name."

"What about a nickname, like B or Breck or BM or—"

"BM," she said. "There was a kid she called Shithead. Could that be him?"

"That's a possible connection," Sam said, feeling the buzz of a potential breakthrough. "What did she say about this Shithead kid?"

"That he was the worst of the worst, so full of himself and relentless in his pursuit of her."

"Did she ever give you particulars about anything he said or did?"

"No, just that he didn't like the fact that she ignored him. He said she was disrespectful and rude, but he couldn't seem to see that his harassment of her was equally so."

"Did you or her father ever report him to anyone?"

"We argued about that. I said we should report it to the police, but Jordy said it seemed extreme to ruin a kid's life over a difference of opinion."

Sam cringed. She'd already heard enough to know it'd gone well beyond *a difference of opinion*. "Had she said anything about this kid recently?"

Court thought about that for a second. "Not in a few weeks, but that doesn't mean she didn't encounter him. It just means that she didn't talk to me about him."

"I have to ask you something that's going to sound super judgmental, but I don't mean it to be anything other than fact-finding. Okay?"

"Trust me, I'm already judging myself for letting her have so much freedom."

"That's what I want to ask about. Why did you allow that, knowing she was being harassed by older boys?"

"Because she assured me she wasn't afraid and could handle them. She has pepper spray with her at all times and knows to use it if she ever feels she's in real danger. I didn't want to keep her locked up at home just because she's pretty, you know?"

"I get it."

"But you wouldn't have allowed it?"

"It wouldn't be fair for me to comment on that. I know things that you'll never know about what goes on in this city, things most people wouldn't want to know. And my kids have world-class security surrounding them at all times. I'll never have to make these decisions for them."

"That's true, and I wish I knew more about the scary stuff. Maybe I wouldn't have been so permissive with her. I hope I get the chance to correct that." Her voice caught on a sob. "I miss her so much. I just want her back home where she belongs. I'll never let her out of my sight again."

"Yes, you will, because it's normal to give your kids freedom as they get older. This information has helped. I'll be back to you with any developments."

"Thank you for all you're doing."

"I wish it could be more, but we're on it, and we're staying on it until we find them. Call me if you think of anything else that might be relevant. Anything at all."

"I will."

Sam ended the call and thought about her next move before she called her parole officer friend, Brendan Sullivan.

"Hey, it's Sam Holland," she said when Brendan answered. "As usual, I need a favor."

"What can I do?"

"I need to talk to one of your juvenile people. I'm looking for a kid in your system. Who should I contact?"

"Tristan McCaffery, the lead juvenile parole officer. He can help you. I'll give you his cell number."

Sam wrote down the phone number he recited. "Thank you, Brendan."

"No problem. Heard about your nephew, and I'm hoping for the best possible outcome."

"Appreciate it. We are, too."

"Let me know if there's anything else I can do."

"Thanks again."

She ended that call and punched in the number for Tristan

McCaffery. Glancing at Nick, she found him watching her intently. "What?"

"Watching you work is sexy."

"Oh for crap's sake."

"What? It is."

She rolled her eyes and listened to the phone ring and ring. *Come on. Pick up.* The only thing that picked up was his voicemail. "This is Lieutenant Sam Holland with the MPD. Please give me a call as soon as possible. It's urgent." She left her number even though he'd already have it on the Caller ID, but whatever. "Thanks."

"Harry texted me. Aubrey and Alden both have strep. Scotty tested negative. He's started the twins on antibiotics. Your mom says they're snuggled up together on the sofa watching a movie."

"Oh man. I hate that we're not there when they're sick."

"They're in very good hands."

She'd no sooner said that than McCaffery called her back. "Hey, this is Lieutenant Holland in Homicide. Thanks for returning my call."

"No problem. What can I do for you?"

"I'm looking for Brecken Mayfield."

"How do you know about him?"

"His name came up in an investigation I'm working on, a missing persons case."

"And his name came up in that?"

"Yes as did your outstanding warrant."

"He's been in our system since he was twelve."

Sam's backbone buzzed with sensation as she homed in on a real thread to pull. "What can you tell me?"

"He's a fucking punk, the type who thinks the rules don't apply to him. He got caught shoplifting hundreds of dollars' worth of merchandise at twelve, spent time in juvie, came out and picked up where he left off. He's escalated to B&E and grand larceny."

"Do you have an address for him?"

"Not at the moment. He's in the wind. We've been looking for him for months. Incidentally, his father is also wanted for parole violations on DV charges."

Domestic violence.

"Sounds like a charming family."

"That's a good word for them. How did he end up on your radar?"

Sam filled him in on her missing nephew and the connection to a kid named Brecken Mayfield.

"It wouldn't surprise me at all if he convinced the younger kids to do some dirty work for him and it possibly went bad."

Sam swallowed hard as she considered the many ways *dirty work* could go bad. "How so?"

"Could be anything with him. He's the ultimate con man."

"We're talking about a kid here, right?"

"Yeah, but he's not your average fifteen-year-old. I'm not a mental health professional and can't make an official diagnosis, but in my opinion, he has sociopathic tendencies."

Her anxiety increased with every new piece of information. "What's the deal with the father?"

"He's a slippery sucker. Manages to get himself out of most jams thanks to his equally sleazy attorney. Do you know Roland Dunning?"

"I've had the displeasure." He'd represented disgraced former Deputy Chief Conklin, who'd sat on evidence that would've solved her father's shooting years earlier while Conklin pretended to be a friend to their family.

"Yeah, well, he's really good at getting Mayfield off on slam-dunk charges. A few things have stuck, though, which is why he's in the parole system. There're warrants out for both him and his son since they've fallen off the radar and missed check-ins."

"Is there anything else you can tell me that might be helpful in finding Brecken?"

"If I had something that would lead to him, he'd be in my

custody. That kid has no business running the streets looking for more trouble."

"Any chance you can send me a photo of him as well as a list of his usual haunts and known associates? I know you're probably checking them all, but maybe we could, too. Who knows what might pop?"

"Sure, I'll send it to your email."

Sam recited the address. "This has been enormously helpful. Thank you so much."

"Wish I could do more. If you pick up a scent, make sure to let me know."

"I'll keep you posted." She closed her phone and glanced at Nick, who looked up from his BlackBerry. "That was productive."

"Sounds like it."

"And also terrifying. If Ethan was hanging out with that kid, then he could be in some big trouble."

"Let's hope he kept his wits about him if he got in over his head. He's a smart, savvy kid. Remember at Christmas when he had all the toys put together before I could even find a screwdriver?"

"Yeah, that was funny. He showed up all the dads."

"He had that Swiss Army knife thing that he got for his birthday, the one with all the tools on it."

"He wanted that so badly. Tracy and Mike gave him a thousand warnings about using it only for good and said it could never go to school with him." Sam smiled at the memory of Ethan using his gadget to conquer Christmas. "Tracy said she frisks him every day on the way out the door to make sure he's not going to school with a weapon."

"Wherever he is, he probably has it with him."

"That's true. God, I hope he does."

When someone knocked on the door, she called for them to come in.

Dr. Trulo poked his head inside. "Is this a good time?"

Sam waved him in. "Always a good time to see you, friend."

He stepped inside and closed the door. "Mr. President."

Nick stood to shake hands with Trulo. "Good to see you, Doc."

"I saw the motorcade outside and suspected we had a VIP visitor."

Nick shook his hand. "Just a husband and uncle today."

Trulo looked to Sam. "Is there any news?"

"Nothing yet. Big meeting at eight with the Feds."

"I spoke to my daughter. She apologized for not getting back to us yesterday. She's had sick kids all weekend. She'll call you this morning."

"That's great, thank you. Sorry to hear about the kids."

"I guess it was a stomach bug kind of weekend."

"Yikes."

"How're you holding up?" he asked.

"I'm freaked out and super anxious, but doing what I do and trying to help where I can. I've been sidelined from the official investigation due to the family connection."

"Ah, I see, well, I suppose that's understandable to everyone but you."

Sam huffed out a laugh. Her friend knew her too well. "I'm on best behavior. Now, anyway. You'd be proud of me."

"I'm always proud of you. Let me know if there's anything at all I can do for you or your family. I'm praying for your nephew's safety and that of the other missing children."

Sam went around her desk to hug him. "Thanks, Doc. You're the best."

"Hang in there, kiddo."

"I'm hanging. Just barely."

After the doctor left, Malone appeared in the doorway. "Avery is here with his team. We're about to get started in the chief's conference room." His was twice the size of the one in her pit.

"Is it okay if Nick sits in with us?"

"Yeah, no problem."

"We'll be right there."

Malone left the door open when he turned to walk away.

As Sam gathered her notebook, pen and an unopened water bottle, Nick stopped her with a hand to her arm. "I want to remind you that you're under no obligation to attend a meeting that's apt to be upsetting to you."

"Everything I do is upsetting. This is just more so than usual."

"This is intensely personal, and no one expects you to digest every awful detail."

"I hear you, and I appreciate the reminder, but this is the one thing I'm good at—digesting the awful details and figuring out what to do about them."

"If the details are too awful in this case, I want you to remove yourself from the mix. There're other people here who can do what you do—not as well, of course..."

"Of course," she said, smiling. "Thank you for looking out for me."

"That's why I'm here, because you never look out for yourself when someone else needs you."

"Love you."

"Love you more."

"I already won that fight." Sam took him by the hand to lead the way to the meeting. As they walked along the corridor, they passed numerous people who did a double take at the sight of the president. "I'm old news around here," Sam said quietly to him, "but you're the shit."

"Gee, thanks. That's what I've always aspired to be."

"I feel guilty making a joke when Ethan is missing."

"You still have to function, and that's how you cope."

"I guess. My coping mechanism seems unsavory at the moment."

"Do whatever it takes to get through it."

Chief Farnsworth was talking to Avery Hill outside the conference room when Sam and Nick approached.

The chief's eyes went wide when he saw that Sam had brought a date. "Sam, Mr. President."

Nick shook hands with both men. "Nice to see you, Joe."

"You as well."

"Avery."

"Mr. President."

"Let's get going," Sam said. "He's been missing since yesterday afternoon, and we're no closer to finding him than we were last night."

"Sorry you and your family are going through this," Avery said. "I hope we can help."

"I hope so, too. Thanks for coming."

Sam and Nick took seats at the far end of the conference table, while Ruiz and Avery took the lead.

Jesse Best came into the room just as Ruiz was about to get started.

"Marshal Best, thank you for joining us," Ruiz said.

Jesse nodded. "Whatever we can do to help."

Sam noticed that he looked tired and strained. One of his closest colleagues had been wounded during the showdown with disgraced Officer Offenbach.

He sat next to her.

"Thank you for being here."

"Any time."

"How's Marshal Costello?"

"Making progress."

"Glad to hear it."

Detectives Green, Carlucci, Dominguez and O'Brien came in and found seats.

Sam sent them a grateful smile. They'd worked all night and had shown up now for her and her family.

When Nick reached for her hand under the table, she held on tight, thankful for his presence.

CHAPTER TWELVE

"Thank you all for being here today." Ruiz went through the information they had so far. "Does anyone have anything to add?"

Sam raised her free hand. "I spoke with Brecken Mayfield's parole officer, which was illuminating." She briefed them on the information McCaffery had provided. "We believe it's possible he became acquainted with Ethan Hogan, Tomas Cambra and Luna Ahern, and could be involved in their disappearance."

"What's your theory, Lieutenant?" the chief asked.

"If I had to venture a guess, Mayfield was interested in Ahern and used Hogan and Cambra to lure her out after Ahern rebuffed his romantic advances. It's a hunch at this point based on the message traffic between them."

"Where do we stand with getting warrants for Mayfield's phone?" Farnsworth asked Malone.

"It's in the works with the court, but we expect the usual pushback with the phone company."

"Let's make sure to emphasize that these are minors who could be in grave danger."

"Yes, sir, that's the plan," Malone said.

"McCaffery said he obviously can't provide a clinical

diagnosis, but he suspects Brecken Mayfield has sociopathic tendencies. There're outstanding parole violation warrants for him and his father, Asher. The father has a long rap sheet that includes numerous domestic violence charges as well as other counts that didn't stick thanks to his sleazy lawyer, Dunning."

"Ah, our old friend," Malone said disdainfully.

"If I may," one of the FBI guys said. "I'm Agent Fuller, from the Domestic Terrorism team, and I'd like to ask who among the various players used the word 'incel.'"

Ruiz handed him printouts of the message traffic in which the boys discussed how Ahern had referred to them as incels.

Fuller scanned the pages. "So the term came from the girl, it seems."

"Yes," Ruiz said.

"The boys would've taken that as a grave insult," Fuller said. "The sort that couldn't go unchallenged."

"How would they know what it means?" Malone asked.

Fuller seemed to choose his words carefully. "Boys and men who have trouble attracting female companionship are well acquainted with the term. When we dig deeper, we're apt to find that at least one of them is active in manosphere spaces."

"Man-o-*what*?" Farnsworth asked, brows furrowed in confusion.

"You should start at the beginning, Agent Fuller," Hill said.

Fuller stood and used a handheld controller to call up a PowerPoint presentation on the screen at the front of the room.

Sam leaned in for a better view, wondering if she needed glasses since she could barely make out the words on the screen.

"The manosphere," Fuller said, "is an online community made up of men and boys who call themselves Pick-Up Artists, Men's Rights Activists, Men Going Their Own Way and incels, all of whom share the common trait of a deep-seated sense of grievance toward women. Incels, which is short for involuntary celibates, believe women have too much of the power in romantic situations. These are usually white men who've failed in their attempts to have meaningful relationships with women. They're deeply resentful of the eighty percent of women, known as Stacys, who show an interest in only twenty percent of men, referred to as Chads, leaving the rest of them out in the cold. Stacys and Chads are their sworn enemies."

"Is this for real?" Farnsworth asked incredulously.

"Unfortunately, yes," Fuller said. "All these types of men have acted on their frustration by sexually assaulting, terrorizing and killing women, and sometimes they harm the men the women are romantically involved with." He went through a long list of cases, dating back to the 1990s when the incel term was first used, through the present. "As recently as three weeks ago, a young couple was kidnapped, tortured, raped and murdered in New Mexico by a man with ties to online manosphere communities."

"Where're these communities located online?" Malone asked.

"YouTube, Reddit, TikTok, X, Facebook, Discord, to name a few of the more commonly known sites," Fuller said. "Many of the incel-related subcommunities on Reddit, called subreddits, have been banned, which leads them to seek out more fringe sites, such as Gab, 4chan and 8chan, that tend to be more permissive than the mainstream sites."

"Does anyone else think this is freaking crazy?" Farnsworth asked. "How have I never even heard of this?"

"Right there with you, Chief," Sam said. "It's all new to me, too."

"It's becoming more mainstream as we document new cases of violent crimes linked to the subculture," Fuller said. "It feeds into the overall discontent that's found among young white men who feel the American dream has passed them by, including the hope of a successful romantic relationship, which they feel is one of their inalienable rights. However, they've learned that they can't make women want them, which compounds the frustration and anger until it boils over."

"Do we have any way to know if the missing kids are active in this so-called subculture?" Green asked.

"Nothing definitive," Ruiz said, "beyond the text messages about the Ahern girl using that word to describe them and Mayfield suggesting they shouldn't let her get away with it."

Archie came into the room and took a seat, his sharp dark-eyed gaze taking in the slides on the screen as he received a printout of the presentation from Avery. "Thank you. Sorry I'm late."

Ruiz introduced him to Agent Fuller and gave him a brief summary of what'd been covered so far.

"I was working on digging into Mayfield," Archie said, "and I found something interesting. His father, Asher Mayfield, is extremely active in the local manosphere groups and leads one of them, called the Dead Chads." Archie handed a stack of stapled documents to the person on either side of him that were passed around.

Sam took one and passed the rest.

The name Asher Mayfield was followed by a list of his affiliations with manosphere groups.

"How were you able to tie him to these groups, Archie?" Sam asked.

"He makes no attempt to hide it. See his social media posts on page three."

Sam read an X post that said, *Who do these bitches think they are, acting like they can have anyone they want while ignoring the rest of us like we're locusts? They think we're the problem when we all know THEY ARE. THEY'RE THE PROBLEM, and that problem needs to be solved.*

The post had thousands of likes and comments in support of the statement.

Bile burned the back of her throat as she read through the horrific public statements. These people were walking around in society, riddled with anger and brimming with violent tendencies that could explode into action at any moment.

She was terrified for Ethan and Tomas, but even more so for Luna. If Brecken and his father had her…

Fuller went through a long glossary of terms used by these men, including Blackpill, hypergamy, mogged, looksmaxxing and truecel, among many other disturbing expressions. Each of them represented some troubling aspect of the manosphere philosophies.

"Holy shit," Nick muttered softly.

Sam squeezed his hand, more thankful than ever that he'd accompanied her today. "How do we use this information to find these missing kids?"

"I think we start with finding Asher Mayfield," Ruiz said. "And his son."

"Agreed," Avery said as Jesse Best nodded.

"There's no way it's a coincidence that Asher's son was spouting off about incels to his younger friends, trying to get them to help lure Ahern out, and then the girl who rejected him goes missing," Jesse said.

"That's my feeling as well," Agent Fuller said. "Locating the Mayfields will be critical to finding these missing kids."

"Then let's get on that," Ruiz said. "Right now."

PLANS WERE MADE and assignments doled out before the officers dispersed to continue the search. Fuller and his team were handling the online forums and Mayfield's social media to look for clues to his whereabouts. Asher Mayfield's parole officer was notified that the MPD would be issuing additional warrants for his arrest on suspicion of aiding his minor son in the kidnapping of three juveniles. They also issued one for Brecken, since he seemed to be the ringleader of whatever had taken place the day before.

"We need to make the case for the arrest warrants," Malone said.

"I could take that if it would help," Sam said.

"Go ahead," Ruiz replied.

"Should we also update the families that we've identified persons of interest?" Sam asked.

"Do you want to take that as well?" Ruiz asked.

Her collegial attitude was a bit jarring, but Sam wasn't about to look the proverbial gift horse in the mouth. "Sure, I'll do that." It occurred to her as she collected her belongings and glanced at Nick to make sure he was with her that he, rather than the story Sam had shared, might be the reason for Ruiz's change in tone. Maybe the captain didn't want to act like a dick in front of the president.

Under any other circumstances, she might take a minute to pick that apart. Under these circumstances, she didn't give a flying fuck why Ruiz was being nice to her as long as Sam was allowed to help find Ethan.

When they returned to her office, Sam fired up her computer and started writing the justification for the Mayfield arrest warrants while Nick took a phone call from his chief of staff, Terry O'Connor, outside the room.

Sam barely blinked as she created a narrative about what they suspected had taken place with Mayfield and his son. She cited the father's active, public embrace of the so-called manosphere and the associated posts, as well as the text messages between the kids, in which the word *incel* had been used.

Based on these facts, it is the conclusion of the MPD, the FBI and the U.S. Marshals that finding Asher Mayfield—and his son Brecken—is a top priority in the effort to locate the three missing minors.

Due to dyslexia, she never trusted herself when it came to reading and writing, but she didn't take the time to dither over that and sent her work right to Malone to get the warrants moving.

Then she began making calls to the families, starting with her sister.

Tracy pounced on the call. "What's up?"

"We had a productive meeting with the FBI and U.S. Marshals and have formed a plan to find Brecken Mayfield and his father, who's well-known to law enforcement, in the hope that he'll lead us to his son and the missing kids."

"That's it? That's all you have after almost twenty-four hours?"

The question stung, even if she knew Tracy didn't mean it as a personal attack. "That's actually a lot when you consider how much data we had to sift through to get to this point. I believe we're on the right track, and our efforts should yield results. It might not happen as fast as we'd like it to, but we're doing everything we can."

"That's easy for you to say when it's not your kid who's missing."

"That's unfair, Tracy. You know how much I love Ethan. We're doing everything in our power to find him and bring him home. I've got to get back to work. I'll call you if there're any developments."

"Mike's out driving around, hoping he'll spot him somewhere. I told him that's a waste of time, but he didn't want to hear it."

"He needs to feel like he's helping."

"I hope he's also looking for a new place to live."

Sam took a deep breath. "I'll be back to you soon."

The line went dead.

Even though she knew exhaustion and emotion were fueling her sister's words, Sam felt beat up after the conversation. As she found the numbers for the other families, she hoped those conversations went better. She detailed the same recitation of facts that she'd presented to Tracy.

Joaquin Cambra was silent when she finished. "Do you think they're still alive?" he asked softly.

"I have every hope they are."

"The longer this goes on, the less hope I have."

"I'll keep you apprised of every development."

"Thank you for your compassion."

"I'll be back in touch."

Luna's mother, Court, wept through the entire conversation. "I'm so scared for her. All I can think about is all the crazy shit boys have said to her and about her. They think it's okay to talk to a child that way. Who's raising them to think that's acceptable?"

In light of the things Sam had learned about incel culture and the manosphere, she chose to evade that question. Court was better off not knowing those details while her daughter was missing.

"Do you have someone there with you?"

"Jordy is here, and my siblings. My parents are on the way from California. It's just a nightmare, Lieutenant."

"Yes, it is. My sister feels the same way you do."

"C-could I maybe speak to her? Mother to mother? It might help us both."

"Of course." Sam recited the landline number at Celia's home. "I'm sure she'd be glad to hear from you."

"Thank you so much for everything you're doing for us."

"I wish it could be more, but we're leaving no stone unturned."

Sam's phone buzzed with an incoming call. "I've got to take another call. I'll be back to you soon." She somehow managed to switch over to take a call from Lieutenant Haggerty from Crime Scene. "Hey, Max, what's up?"

"We're at the Aherns. I thought you'd want to know we found a handwritten note from Ethan to Luna Ahern, telling her he thought she was pretty and would like to get to know her. He included his phone number and told her to call him anytime."

"My niece Brooke had confirmed that Ethan knew Luna and they'd been friendly. She said Ethan really liked her but wasn't sure if it was anything special for Luna."

"I'll pass the info about the note to Ruiz."

"Thanks for the heads-up. I appreciate it."

"We're all hoping your nephew gets home safely, Sam."

"Thank you." She slapped the phone closed. "*Shit, fuck, damn, hell.*"

"What?" Nick asked as he returned to the office in time to hear her outburst.

"Crime Scene detectives found a note at Luna's that can further tie Ethan to her."

"A note doesn't mean anything other than that he wrote her a note."

"I know but... it's another thing that connects him to her. I'm scared of someone making a case that he was involved in her disappearance, as preposterous as that would be." She ran a hand over her face as her eyes watered from exhaustion.

"Babe, you need to get some sleep."

"I couldn't. Not now."

"You won't be any good to Ethan or Tracy if you collapse."

"I'm a long way from collapsing. When I hit the wall, I'll say so. I promise."

He came around the desk. "Come here."

Sam stood and stepped into his outstretched arms, sinking into his embrace and absorbing the special kind of comfort only he could provide. The scent of him—citrus and starch and sexy man, the scent of home—helped to calm and center her. It would've been so easy to close her eyes and nod off, but not as long as Ethan was missing.

"Thank you for this. It's just what I needed."

"I wish there was more I could do for you."

"Having you here with me helps. Is everything okay back at La Casa Blanca?"

"For now. A few things brewing, but Terry and Derek have them handled."

"If you have to go, I understand."

"I'm where I need to be."

"It helps to look up and see your face when I start to feel overwhelmed with fear."

"I'm right here for as long as you need me."

"Gonna be the rest of my life."

"That works out well, because your face is my favorite one in the whole wide world." He caressed her cheek and gave her a soft, sweet kiss. "I'll be watching my favorite face for signs of impending collapse."

"Thanks."

"Love you forever, and I hate to see you suffering."

"I'll be okay. I just need to find him."

"Sam, please tell me you know it's not solely your responsibility to find him and the others."

"I do know that, but if I can fix this for him and Tracy—"

"No, no, no. That's not up to you either. You simply can't take ownership of successfully solving this case. Because if, God forbid, it ends badly, you'd also take the blame, and I won't let you do that."

"We have to find him. We just have to." She pulled back from him, wiped tears from her face and tried to pull herself together. The longer this went on and the more exhausted she became, the harder it was to maintain any semblance of composure.

CHAPTER THIRTEEN

Chief Farnsworth appeared in her open door. "Sorry to interrupt."

"You're not," Sam said as she stepped away from Nick. "Come in."

She returned to her desk chair while the chief took her other visitor chair.

"That meeting has me speechless," he said.

"I know. It's shocking and a lot to process."

"How have we never heard of this?"

"I guess we're lucky that it hadn't factored into a case before."

"Yes, we are, but we'll probably be seeing more of it, based on Agent Fuller's assessment."

"It's terrifying what's happening online that most people know nothing about. I fell into the rabbit hole last night and was as shocked as you are. I'm trying to imagine my sweet nephew caught up in something like this, and it's simply unfathomable."

"I have to think your dad is watching over him wherever he is and will help get him home safely," the chief said.

"That's a comforting thought."

"If there's anything I can do for you or Tracy, please let me know. Marti and I are praying for his safe return."

"Thank you both. That means a lot."

"I'll let you get back to work." He shook hands with Nick and left the office as Sam

picked up her desk phone to call Archie.

"Hey," he said.

"Have you been home?"

"Not yet. I brought the computer from Tracy's house here to continue processing it."

"Thanks for sticking with it. CSU found a note at Luna's house from Ethan in which he tells her he thinks she's pretty and would like to get to know her. He gave her his number."

"Okay, I'll look to see if she ever made that call. Did you tell Ruiz about the note?"

"Haggerty was going to."

"Okay."

"I'm being a team player. Don't worry."

"What? Me worry?"

"Haha, I deserve that."

"Nah, he's one of your kids. It's understandable that you need to be involved. I'll be back to you soon."

"Thanks, Archie. This will never be forgotten."

"You're there for me. I'm there for you. That's how it works."

"Appreciate it," she said softly. After their frequent hookups when she'd been between marriages, things between them could've been awkward, but thankfully, that'd never happened. They'd settled into collegial friendship that was a source of great comfort to her—and to him, too, especially lately as she'd worked on the Offenbach case, which had also involved his new girlfriend, Harlowe.

As Sam tried to think of what she should work on next, her brain went blank. She didn't have a single idea worth pursuing. She sat behind her desk and looked down at the reports that'd been prepared overnight, trying to make sense of words that floated in random order thanks to the fucking dyslexia that kicked in hard when she was overtired.

She stared at the far wall, hoping inspiration would find its way through the fog in her brain to give her some direction.

Her phone rang, and she pounced, hoping for something that would break this thing wide open as the clock inched closer to twenty-four hours without a word from Ethan.

"Holland."

"This is Christi Trulo-Carpenter. I'm so sorry for the delay in reaching out to you. I've had desperately ill children since Friday night."

"I hope they're better now."

"They've stopped actively puking, so that's an improvement. Is there any word on Ethan?"

"Nothing yet."

"I'm so sorry your family is going through this. I've only met with him twice so far, and they were mostly get-to-know-you sessions before the real work begins. So far, I haven't picked up on anything alarming that would lead to him intentionally disappearing. He told me he found the conflict between him and his parents upsetting."

"They'd be glad to hear that. It's upsetting to them, too."

"From what I've seen thus far, he doesn't seem like the kind of kid to do something like this to get back at them or anything like that."

"That'd be my take, too, although I haven't spent enough time with him lately to be able to say that for certain. I've only heard my sister's side of things, which came as a surprise to me. That isn't the Ethan I've known, but he's grown up when I wasn't looking."

"Kids start to chafe at parental confines in middle school, often when friends are allowed to do things they're not. My dad told me when my kids were born that the biggest problem I'd have wouldn't be with other kids. It would be with their parents, who'd have different rules and values than I do. I've already found that to be true, and my kids are in elementary school."

"Your dad is one of the wisest people I've ever known, and

what he said makes a lot of sense. Ethan's friends were allowed to go out, to ride the Metro, to be independent. He wanted what they had."

"Which is entirely normal, if difficult to navigate as a parent whose better judgment might be saying it's too soon for such freedoms."

"That was my sister's position. Her husband disagreed. As she said, when they stopped presenting a united front, Ethan saw an opportunity."

"That's how it often happens. One parent wavers, and the door opens. Of course, once that genie is out of the bottle…"

"Right."

"I remember when I was a freshman in high school on the swim team. We had six a.m. practices on Saturday mornings, so I arranged for one of the older kids to drive me. My parents didn't love that idea, but it was five a.m. on a Saturday, so they allowed it. Then I wanted to go with the same kids to get pizza, and suddenly, they didn't have a leg to stand on with not wanting me riding in cars with other kids. They said later that they failed to think it all the way through and realize that a yes at five a.m. can be seen as a yes to Friday at seven p.m."

"Wow, that's not something I would've thought of either. I'd be all in with getting out of the five a.m. wakeup on a Saturday."

"Most parents would. It's how we lose control of the whole operation and never see it coming."

"This has been very helpful, Christi. I appreciate you taking the time to call when your kids are sick."

"I'm praying for Ethan's safe return."

"Thanks again."

Sam closed the phone and conveyed the gist of what she'd learned to Nick.

"That's something about the kids in cars. I wouldn't have seen that one coming either."

"Another thing we won't have to worry about while our kids

are driven by the Secret Service. Thank you for being president and making that happen."

He grunted out a laugh. "Never expected to hear you say that, and PS, eventually, they'll hate us for not being able to drive like other kids do."

"They'll be able to someday. Just not when their friends can."

"Which is the only time they'll really want to."

"True."

She scrubbed her hands over her face. "I'm taking everything I've learned so far and trying to parse it into action, and nothing is popping for me the way it usually does."

"That's because you're not usually looking for someone who's missing. Usually, you've got a body in your morgue and a routine you follow to figure out what happened. This is an entirely different set of circumstances, so naturally, nothing is working the way you expect it to."

"Wow, you're good at this insightful-husband thing."

"I'm good at *you*. Not so sure about the husband thing."

"Best husband I ever had."

He rolled his eyes. "It was a low bar," he said, as he always did when she said that. While her first marriage had been an unmitigated disaster, this one was as close to perfection as any two people could get. She never should've married Peter in the first place when she was forever in love with Nick Cappuano after only one night together.

Thinking about that was far better than wondering where in the hell her precious nephew could be and whether she'd ever see him again.

THE NOT-KNOWING WAS torturous for Brooke. She tossed and turned all night, waiting and hoping to hear something about Ethan. She was staring up at the ceiling when Nate turned to put an arm around her and draw her in close to him. That he'd slept with her in a bedroom at her grandfather's home with hardly a glance from her parents was a testament to the tension in the house. Her sleeping with her boyfriend with her parents in the same house was the least of their concerns at the moment.

"Did you sleep at all?" he asked.

"I don't think so. I heard my parents up all night, too." Her tired eyes burned with unshed tears. She'd checked her phone a hundred times during the night, hoping for news that'd never come. "What'll we do if he's dead?"

"I know it's really hard not to think the worst, but there're a lot of things that could be happening short of that."

"I just want him back so badly that it's all I can think about, along with every memory I have with him from the day he was born."

He caressed her arm in a soothing pattern. "Tell me about that day."

Brooke smiled as she recalled one of the most momentous days of her life. "I was eight, and before that, I had no idea how long nine months really was. It seemed like it'd taken forever between when my mom and dad told me they were expecting a baby and when he finally showed up. It's really more like ten months, but to me, it was endless. My mom went into labor when she was at the grocery store. She'd left her phone in the car, so we got a call from the store that she was on the way to the hospital and that Dad needed to meet her there."

"That's a fun story."

"My dad was a disaster trying to remember all the things he needed to bring, and he was on his way out the door when he looked back at me and said, 'Shit, I can't leave you here alone.'"

Nate chuckled. "So what did he do?"

"He took me with him, and Grandpa Skip came to get me at the hospital. I came back here with him, and we ate ice cream and watched movies. That was one of my favorite nights ever with Gramps. We were so excited while we waited to hear and finally got the call at around nine that night. I had a baby brother named Ethan Charles, and he was eight pounds, ten ounces, twenty inches long and perfect in every way. His middle name was for Grandpa Skip. That was his real name, but no one ever called him that."

"Ah, that's some family trivia there."

"Yeah. I wanted to go see the baby right then and there, but Gramps said we had to wait until visiting hours the next day. Then my dad called back and asked Gramps to bring me over so I could see Ethan the same day he was born."

"Oh, that's cool."

"Dad said I was a day-one person, and I needed to be there." She wiped away tears. "I've never loved anything the way I loved Ethan from the first second they put him in my arms. My own living, breathing baby doll. I wanted to do everything for him. I fed him and changed him and helped to give him baths. I loved to pick out his outfits every day and to play with him when I was supposed to be doing my homework. Leaving him to go to school was painful. I'd rush home after to find out what I'd missed since I left. I was obsessed."

Nate brushed away the tears on her face.

"Abby was born about two years later," she said, "and it was the same thing all over again. I never resented being asked to babysit them or spend time with them like some of my friends did when their parents asked them to watch younger siblings. I was—and am—crazy about them both."

"I know you are. Their pictures are all over your apartment."

"They're as much my babies as they were my mom and dad's."

"I can totally see that. They love you so much."

"I'm not sure what I'll do if something terrible has happened to him."

Nate hugged her tightly. "I know, honey, but let's try to stay positive."

"I'm trying, but it gets harder the longer we go with no word. The silence is making me crazy."

"Let's go see if anything happened overnight. I'll check in with my office, too, and see if they have anything new."

"Thank you for being here with me. It's the only thing keeping me from losing it."

"Don't you know by now that the only place I want to be is wherever you are?"

"Love you," she whispered tearfully.

He kissed her softly. "Love you, too."

GONZO WALKED into an apartment filled with boxes ahead of their upcoming move to Sam and Nick's home on Ninth Street. It was ten times the size of where he and Christina lived now, and he couldn't wait to be settled there.

Christina came out of the kitchen, dressed for another day as the press secretary to the president. She was so fucking pretty and put together in a sharp navy suit that he was almost afraid to hug her back. "How was the meeting?"

He held her close and nuzzled her neck, breathing her in as he rested a hand on the baby bump under her fuchsia silk blouse. She'd taught him that word—fuchsia. "Good."

She stood back to examine him more closely, placing her hands on his face. No one had ever *seen* him the way she did, but even she hadn't known how bad things had gotten for him with the pain pills before it was almost too late to save him.

"Any news about Ethan?"

"Nothing yet."

"God, what is that about?"

"I don't know, but I hope we find him soon." He looked down at his hand on the curve of her pregnant belly. "How're you feeling?"

"Pretty good today. The nausea didn't last as long as usual." She kissed him. "You look exhausted."

"It was a long night. Where's the boy?"

"If he knows what's good for him, he's getting his shoes on.

He's going to Angela's for a couple of hours to play while I go to work and you get some sleep. Alex? Daddy's home."

An excited scream came from his three-year-old son's room before the boy came bursting out of the hallway, launching himself at Gonzo, who scooped him up into a big hug.

Gonzo kissed his neck and made him giggle. "What's this I hear about shoes?"

"Mommy said to get them, but I can't find them." Alex leaned in to whisper in Gonzo's ear. "I'm in big trouble cuz I didn't put them where they go last night."

It was all Gonzo could do not to laugh. "Well, that sounds like a problem. Maybe I could help you look for them?"

"Yes! Daddy can help!" He squirmed his way out of Gonzo's arms and ran back toward his room, shooting a grin at his mother on the way by.

"See how he does that with the little grin? And then I forget all about why I was annoyed with him." She reached up to cuff Gonzo's chin. "Like father, like son."

"We can't help that we're adorable."

She gave him a playful glare.

"I'd better go help the boy before we're both in trouble."

"That's probably a good idea."

"You're very sexy when you're stern."

She gave him an exasperated look. "Hurry up, Tommy!"

"I'm hurrying."

CHAPTER FOURTEEN

Archie appeared in the doorway to Sam's office. "We got a hit on Ethan's debit card. Ruiz and her team are on the way as we speak. Patrol is backing them up."

Finally, Sam thought as she sat up straighter. They might have a break. "Where?"

"At a convenience store on Connecticut Avenue Northwest."

"Forest Hills," Sam said absently as she refreshed her memory of the neighborhood near Rock Creek Park. "I'm not telling my sister or the other parents until we know more."

Malone appeared behind Archie. "You heard about the debit card?"

"Yeah." Sam wanted to go there so badly that it was all she could do to remain seated and let her colleagues take the lead.

"I'll let you know if I hear anything else," Archie said.

"Thanks for keeping me in the loop."

He nodded and took off for his office on the second floor.

Malone came into Sam's office. "Can I get you guys something to eat?"

Nick looked to Sam.

She shook her head. "I don't think I could get it past the

massive lump in my throat. But you go ahead," she said to Nick. "You must be starving."

"I could eat something. A sandwich maybe?"

"I'll order for all of us and get something for you, too, Sam. Maybe it'll look good to you when it's right in front of you."

"Thanks, Cap."

"We all wish there was more we could do."

"It helps to know that the best of the best are looking for him."

"I'll be back," Malone said as he departed.

Detective Neveah Charles came to the door. "Patrol is reporting they found two young boys running down Connecticut Avenue, wearing no shirts or shoes, with zip ties hanging from their wrists."

Sam shot to her feet. "Oh my God. Is it them?"

"I'm waiting for an update," Neveah said. "Stand by." She turned and left.

Nick came to Sam, put his arms around her and held on tight.

Her heart was racing, her mouth dry and her hands shaking. "Please," she whispered. "Let it be him."

"Lieutenant," Neveah said when she returned.

Sam released Nick and looked to her detective.

Neveah smiled and nodded. "They've got him. He's safe. He and Tomas both are."

Sam broke down as her knees seemed to fail her all at once.

Nick guided her into a chair and held her as she sobbed. "Thank God." He reached for her phone on the desk and handed it to her. "Call your sister."

"I'll call the Cambras," Neveah said.

"What about Luna?" Sam asked.

"No report on her. Just the two boys."

Sam nodded, took a deep breath and called her sister.

"Hello," Tracy said tersely.

"They found him safe, Trace. We've got him—and Tomas."

"*Oh my God!* Thank you so much! Where is he? I want to see him right now."

"I'll call you back as soon as I know where they're taking them."

Neveah looked up from her phone. "They're going to the ER at GW."

Sam conveyed that info to Tracy.

"Are they hurt?"

"They found them running down Connecticut Avenue, so it sounds like they're mostly okay. I'll meet you at GW?"

"Okay. Yes. We're on the way."

"See you there."

TRACY SCREAMED for her husband and daughter. They came bursting into the kitchen, where she'd been sitting by the phone, trying to will it to ring with news. "They found him and Tomas. Sam said they're safe, but they're taking them to the ER at GW. She's going to meet us there."

Mike bent at the waist and started sobbing. "Thank you, thank you, thank you."

Brooke put one hand on his back as she wiped away tears with the other.

Tracy stood and hugged Brooke and then headed for the kitchen door. "Let's get going."

"Trace," Mike said. "Wait."

She glanced at him over her shoulder. "I'm going to see my son. Are you coming?"

"I just want to say..."

Tracy walked away. Nothing would keep her from Ethan now that she knew he was alive and where he was. Besides, there wasn't a single thing Mike could say that would change how she felt about him allowing this nightmare to happen in the first place. In all their years together, she'd never been angrier with him than she was right now, but there'd be time to deal with that situation later.

Right now, she wanted her son. Everything else was second to that.

She went outside to where several MPD officers were standing watch. "I need a ride to the ER at GW. My son has been found and is being taken there."

"Yes, ma'am," one of the young officers said. "I'll take you."

He had the back door to a Patrol car open and waiting for her in a matter of seconds.

She looked to see if Mike was coming, but he was still in the house. "Let's go," she said to the officer. Mike could come with Brooke and Nate.

Tracy appreciated that the officer used the lights and siren to convey her quickly through the District. Having a sister—and a late father—with connections came in handy at a time like this.

She was jonesing for her phone and hoped Sam had called Angela and their mom to update them, but for now, that was also the least of her concerns. They'd find out soon enough if no one had told them yet.

On that quick ride across the District from Capitol Hill to Foggy Bottom, Tracy decided that no matter what'd happened to Ethan, she would love and support him through it, even if he'd committed a crime. Anything could be fixed as long as he was alive.

She wiped at tears that continued to come even when she would've thought there couldn't be any more. Life had thrown her a lot of curveballs, starting with her parents' contentious divorce, her unplanned pregnancy with Brooke at twenty-one, single parenthood, her father's shooting and subsequent quadriplegia, the night Brooke was attacked and nearly killed, her father's death and the subsequent revelations about his shooting, Sam and Nick becoming the FLOTUS and POTUS, and then Spencer's sudden death...

All of it had tried and tested her, but nothing could compare to not knowing where her son was for almost twenty-four of the longest, most agonizing hours she'd ever experienced. She loved her three children with her whole heart and soul, but she'd had a special bond with Ethan from the start. Mothers and sons... As much as she adored her girls, it was different with him, softer, less dramatic. He was her easy kid, and it'd been that way between them from the start. Whereas Brooke and Abby challenged and tested her, Ethan tended to go along to get along.

Until recently, he'd never given her a reason to be annoyed with him, other than not putting his clothes away or leaving his dirty dishes in the sink. The battles over him wanting to run loose with his friends had been an upsetting development and had put the first serious rift in her relationship with Mike. She'd been incredulous when he'd said, in front of Ethan, "Maybe we could try it and see how it goes."

The minute he'd said those words, it was game over for her point of view. Ethan had won the battle and would be allowed to roam free in the city at eleven years old.

Her emotions were a simmering cauldron of relief, gratitude, anger and fear for what would come next. How would this incident change Ethan's life and hers along with it?

"Ma'am," the young officer said. "We're here."

Tracy looked up in surprise to see the signs for the Emergency Department. Suddenly, she was frozen with fear so powerful, it took her breath away. What was waiting for her inside?

The officer came around the cruiser to open the back door for her.

Tracy took the hand he offered her. "Thank you."

"I hope your son is okay."

"Thank you. I do, too." Tracy went into the crowded waiting room and approached the desk. "I'm Tracy Hogan. My son, Ethan, was brought in."

"Right this way, ma'am."

The nurse signaled for Tracy to follow her into the treatment area. She was led to a room in the far back corner on the right side. Police officers stood outside the curtain.

"Mrs. Hogan is here to see her son," the nurse told one of the officers.

"Could I please see some ID?" the officer asked.

"I have nothing on me. I had to leave everything at my house when we were relocated." She summoned every scintilla of calm she could to say, "Please let me see my son."

He held the curtain aside, saving her the need to start screaming.

Tracy rushed into the room where Ethan was asleep in the bed, a blanket pulled up to his chest. He looked exhausted and his hair was standing on end, but it was him, and she'd never been so happy to see anyone. As she leaned over him, her fingers straightening his messy hair, she pressed a kiss to his forehead. "Mommy's here," she whispered. "I'm right here."

His eyes flickered open, and when he saw her there, he let out a cry as he reached for her.

Tracy sobbed as she held him tight. "Ethan…"

"I'm so sorry, Mom. I'm so, so sorry."

She could barely speak over the tsunami of emotion. "As long as you're okay, that's all I care about. Are you hurt?"

"They said I was dehydrated, so they're giving me an IV, and my ribs are bruised."

Tracy hadn't noticed the bag hanging over him until he mentioned it. All she'd seen was his precious face, paler than it should be, but still there. *Still there.*

"Do you have other injuries?"

He brought his arms out from under the covers to show her that his wrists were wrapped in gauze. "They held us with zip ties that cut into my skin. That and the ribs kinda hurt, but otherwise, I'm okay."

"Who held you?"

"Brecken and his father, but his dad was really mad when he found out I'm the president's nephew. He was screaming at

Brecken for being so stupid as to get a kid who's related to the president. He was so mad that I was afraid..."

"Of what, honey?"

"That'd he kill us, so Tomas and me... We used my knife to cut ourselves free, but it took forever because it was dark, we were both tied up, and we couldn't reach. While they were sleeping, we ran away."

"Was Luna there, too?"

"I didn't see her. Is she missing?"

"She is."

"Oh God... Brecken is obsessed with her. This was all about her." His eyes brimmed with tears. "We told him we didn't want to be part of it, but he said we had to do what he told us, or he'd kill our p-parents." The quiver of his chin broke her heart. It'd been years since that'd happened. "She's such a nice girl. I really like her, and she likes me, too. I didn't want to help him get to her."

"Don't say anything to anyone until we talk to Sam. She's on the way over now and so are Dad, Brooke and Nate."

"Brooke is here?"

"She and Nate came home yesterday when we couldn't find you. We've been so upset."

"All I could think about was how mad you were going to be at me—and at Dad."

"I'm not mad at you. I'm just so, so grateful to have you back. Nothing else matters right now except that you're safe and so is Tomas."

A police officer Tracy didn't recognize entered the room. "I'm Captain Ruiz from the MPD, and I'd like to have a word with Ethan if I might."

"He's... he's not ready to talk about it yet. Maybe in a little while."

"We're still looking for Luna Ahern, and as you can imagine, every minute counts."

"I understand." Tracy returned her attention to Ethan. "He'll talk when he's ready."

"Ethan," the captain said, "Luna is counting on you and Tomas to do whatever you can to help her."

"I don't know where she is. I never saw her."

"That's enough for now," Tracy said, resisting the urge to snap at her. Until she saw her sister, he wasn't saying anything to anyone. She was certain that's what her dad would've told her to do if he'd been there. As she held Ethan's hand, she wished more than anything that her dad could walk her through this unprecedented situation. Thank God she had Sam to do it.

A few minutes later, a rustling sound outside the curtain alerted her to people approaching. Tracy sat up, wiped her face and turned to see Sam coming around the curtain. She stood to hug her sister.

Sam released her and went to Ethan, weeping as she hugged him. "Very happy to see you, buddy."

"I'm happy to see you, too."

"A female captain was in here wanting to talk to him, but I waited for you to tell us what he should say."

"I just saw her in the hallway. She's talking to Tomas while I talk to Ethan."

"Oh, okay," Ethan said with a hesitant glance at his mother.

"First of all, are you hurt?" Sam asked.

He ran through the list of injuries he'd already told Tracy about, and Sam made a note of each one in a notebook she pulled out of her back pocket.

"Can you tell me what happened, buddy?" Sam asked as she took a seat on the edge of his bed.

"Tomas and I... We met Brecken a few weeks ago at the Boardwalk arcade down at the Wharf, and he was so nice to us. He and his dad gave us money to play more games when we ran out, and we thought Brecken was really cool. He... he said we were fun to hang with and asked us to come back again this week, so we did. And when we got there, he didn't want to play the games. He wanted us to help him with something else and asked if we could come with him. We liked him, so we said sure, and then he took us to this car—his dad was in the car—and Brecken told us to get in. We were like... We didn't think we should do that, but Brecken shoved us in, and the car took off. Before we knew it, he'd taken our phones, zip-tied our hands, and... we... we were so confused about what was happening."

Tracy was appalled as she tried to imagine how terrified they must've been.

"Where'd they take you?"

"We drove around for a long time. I had to pee really bad, and I told them I was going to wet my pants if I couldn't use the bathroom, but they ignored me. I don't know how long we drove around for, but it was dark when we stopped. They told us to walk up some stairs and be quiet, or they'd shoot us, and then they'd kill our families."

Tracy whimpered.

"What did they want?" Sam asked.

"Our phones. They used them to send texts. I think to Luna. We were kind of friends with her from when we went bowling, and Brecken said if she didn't come out, he would kill us and her, too. I asked him why he was doing this, and he said it was because Luna had disrespected him and needed to be taught a lesson in manners."

Good God, Tracy thought. *What in the world?*

"What happened after they used your phones to send the texts?"

"They left us in a dark room, and we didn't see them again. But we could hear them arguing. Brecken's dad was super mad that he'd involved the nephew of the president. That's when I knew you guys were looking for me, when they found out Nick was my uncle."

"Do you know how long you were in that room?"

"It was a long time. We both peed our pants, and we were starving. We were really, really scared they were going to kill us."

"How did you get free?"

"We used my multitool. They cut our shirts off us and took our shoes but didn't notice it in my pocket. Tomas and I worked together to get it, and he cut me loose, and then I did him. But it took us hours because we couldn't see anything in the dark room, and we didn't want to stab each other by accident. We were careful with the knife, Mom, like you always said."

Tracy wiped away more tears as she smiled. "You did good, pal."

"Do you have any idea where you were held?" Sam asked.

"It was near Connecticut Avenue, because when we got out of the house, we ran toward lights that turned out to be Connecticut."

"Do you know how far you ran before you got to that road?"

"About three blocks. It wasn't far. A police officer saw us and stopped to help. Never been so happy to see the police."

"Did you come from the right side or the left side of Connecticut?"

Ethan thought about that for a second. "It was the right side, and the police officer saw us right near where we came out of the neighborhood, so it's close to that."

"This has been really helpful, Ethan. You and your friend did a great job of getting yourselves out of a bad situation, and the things you've remembered could help us find Luna."

"I'm really scared for her. Brecken was so mad at her for blowing him off."

"Is that what he said? That she blew him off?"

"He said she was super rude to him, and all he did was ask her to hang out, but she wouldn't even look at him. He said she shouldn't be allowed to get away with that."

"Did you ever see her or hear her at the place where you were held?"

He shook his head. "No, but Brecken was mad that she wouldn't answer his texts."

"So tell me about your interactions with his dad before they kidnapped you."

"He bought us pizza at the Wharf a couple of times before this and gave us tokens for the games."

Every cell in Sam's body tingled with sensation the way it did whenever the details of a vexing case came into sharper focus. This guy—and his kid—had targeted and groomed Ethan and Tomas to make them willing to go along with whatever they suggested. The whole thing had been planned with meticulous attention to detail with the ultimate goal of luring Luna to whatever horrors they had in mind for her.

Mike, Brooke and Nate stepped into the cubicle, and Sam stood to give Mike and Brooke room to hug Ethan.

Tracy stayed right where she was, next to her son, where she would remain for every minute he was in the hospital. Then she would take him home and keep him there until he was thirty.

CHAPTER FIFTEEN

Sam had never seen Mike Hogan cry the way he did when he saw Ethan alive and mostly well. As someone who'd always been like a big brother to Sam, seeing him like that hurt her heart. She was deeply concerned about Tracy and Mike's marriage and whether it would survive this incident.

While they talked with Ethan, Sam went to the hallway to compare notes with Ruiz.

"What've you got?" the captain asked.

Sam went through the facts that Ethan had relayed to her. "It sounds as if Mayfield and his son chose them for this mission after buttering them up during previous encounters."

"That's my impression as well."

"Ethan was able to give me fairly specific information about where they were held."

"We've got people canvassing the area now."

"I wonder if they ran once they figured out that Ethan and Tomas had escaped."

"That's possible. I'll pass all the new information on to everyone in the field and update the BOLO to include only Luna. We'll need to update her parents, as well as notifying the media that Ethan and Tomas have been found. Do you want to handle those two things due to the intense public interest in your family connection to this case?"

"Sure, I can do that."

"Thanks."

"Thank you for letting me help."

Ruiz nodded and went to make her calls.

Sam leaned back against the wall, closed her eyes and tried to process the information Ethan had imparted.

That's where Nick found her when he came looking for her. "Hey," he said softly. "Is he okay?"

Sam nodded. "He will be. Eventually. No serious injuries, thank goodness, and the multitool came in handy to cut through zip ties."

"Wow, really?" Nick smiled. "He'll be proud of that."

"As he should be. It got them out of there."

"Can you go home and get some rest now?"

"I have to go back to HQ and update the media."

"You should be able to do that from here. Word is they followed us."

"Oh, well... That's handy." She scrubbed a hand across her face as relief, elation and bone-deep exhaustion sparked a desperate need for sleep. "I have one call to make, and then I can do the briefing. Let me just check in with Tracy, Mike and Ethan first."

"Tell them I'm here and that I love them."

"Come in with me."

"That's okay. They need their space right now."

She patted his arm. "I'll be right back."

"I'll be right here."

Sam went back into the room and gestured for Tracy to come to her. "Nick is here and gives his love to all of you. They're asking me to brief the media, and I want to make sure you have no objections. I'll keep it high-level and say the boys have been found safe and that we're still looking for Luna as well as the perpetrators of this crime."

Tracy had her arms crossed in a protective pose that tugged at Sam's heart. "That's fine. Please thank everyone who helped to look for them."

"I will. Are you... I mean..."

"I don't know what I am other than thankful he's back and seemingly okay, but I'm terrified of what it all means."

"Take it one step at a time. Let's see where the evidence leads. From what he said, it sounds as if he and Tomas were used to perpetrate a scheme that had nothing to do with them."

"I guess that'd be better than people thinking he lured that poor girl to whatever fate was waiting for her."

"Even if he helped to lure her, he had no idea what they had planned."

"So he says."

"He didn't know, Trace."

"I hope you're right."

"Can I hug you?"

"Um, sure."

Sam wrapped her arms around her sister and held on tight for a long moment. "Whatever's next, Nick and I will be right here to get you all through it. I promise."

"Thanks for everything."

"I'll keep you posted."

Tracy nodded and went back to her spot next to Ethan's bed, close enough to stroke his hair. Mike stood on the other side, staring at Ethan as if afraid he might suddenly disappear again. Brooke had her arm around Mike.

Sam left them and stepped into the hallway, where Nick was talking to Nate.

"How is he?" Nate asked.

"He seems okay, all things considered. A lot to unpack, though."

"It's a huge relief they were found alive," Nate said.

That he thought they wouldn't be had Sam's anxiety spiking all over again, until she reminded herself her nephew was alive and mostly well in the room behind her. To Nick, she said, "I need to make a call to update Luna's parents and brief the media. Then we can go home."

"I'm here for whatever you need."

"Stay close. That's what I need."

"Nothing I'd rather do, as you know."

Sam released the clip she'd put in her hair hours ago, ran her fingers through it to bring some order and twisted it up again to keep it out of her way. She was sure her face looked haggard after the ordeal of Ethan's disappearance, but she couldn't be bothered to care about that right now.

Captain Malone was in the waiting room and got up when he saw her coming. "How is he?"

"A little beat up but mostly okay. Ruiz said Tomas is the same."

"Thank goodness they're alive."

Sam nodded as she tried not to break down—again. "Ruiz asked me to brief the media. Nick said they followed us over here."

"Yeah, there's a crowd in the parking lot. Patrol is keeping them contained."

"Let's get it done."

"Do you want me to do it?"

Sam was sorely tempted to turn it over to him. "I'll do it, so I can thank everyone who helped us look for him. I have to call Luna's parents first." She looked around for a quiet spot to make the call and didn't see one.

"This way," Malone said, guiding her toward a hallway that was mostly deserted.

Sam looked up the number and made the call.

"Did you find her?" Court asked.

"Not yet, but we've got Ethan Hogan and Tomas Cambra. They were held in a home in Northwest, and according to Ethan, they didn't see Luna there."

Court's anguished cry broke Sam's heart.

"We've got all the best people looking for her and will continue to work the case from every angle until we have her back."

"I can't bear to think about what she might be going through."

Sam couldn't either. "We're not sharing details, such as the boys not seeing her where they were held, with the public. We need to keep that info close while we look for her, okay?"

"We won't say anything. Do you think it's a good sign for her that they were found alive?"

Sam desperately wanted to reassure her, but she couldn't give her false hope. "I honestly don't know what it means. I can tell you we've got a massive effort under way to find her. I'm about to update the media and will implore people again to be on the lookout for Luna."

"Thank you for all you're doing."

"I'll keep you informed of any developments."

"Okay."

Sam ended the call, feeling shredded by the awful uncertainty Luna's family was still dealing with. "Brutal," she said to Malone.

"It sure is."

"I haven't even asked where we are with the guy murdered at the hotel."

"Cruz is still working with Crime Scene, and Archie's team has the video. It's slow going on both fronts."

"I'll get up to speed on that after I get some sleep."

"This was a tough one after another tough one. Take the time you need. We've got it covered."

"Thanks, Cap." Sam eyed the doors where the media waited to devour her on the other side. She wasn't at all sure she had the fortitude to face them, but Ruiz had asked her to handle it, so that's what she would do. Maintaining the fragile accord with the captain was a priority.

"I'll go out with you. If it's too much, take a step back, and I'll take over."

She nodded, appreciating that he'd given her an out if she ended up needing it.

They walked through the automatic doors out of the Emergency Department into the parking lot where a light mist was falling, just enough to soak the reporters and add to their ire at being made to wait.

Shouted questions started the second they saw Sam coming toward them and continued unabated until she stepped up to the makeshift podium someone had put there. Probably Public Affairs, she thought as she tried to gather herself to tell them what they needed to know.

"Just over an hour ago, two young boys were spotted running on Connecticut Avenue by MPD Patrol officers. The boys, Ethan Hogan and Tomas Cambra, who were reported missing yesterday afternoon, are being treated here at GW for minor injuries that resulted from being held hostage. Our department had issued a be-on-the-lookout alert for them late yesterday after they failed to return home on time. Their cell phones were going to voicemail, and tracking services weren't available, leading their parents to call us for help in finding them. Then we were informed of another missing child, thirteen-year-old Luna Ahern, who has not yet been located. Her disappearance is believed to be related to that of the boys."

"How do you know that?" a reporter asked.

"A connection has been established between the children based on our investigation thus far."

"Hogan is your nephew, is that correct?"

"He is," Sam said. "Needless to say, our family is enormously relieved to have him back safe and mostly sound. We're very thankful to everyone who helped to look for them, including our partners at the FBI and U.S. Marshals, and we ask you to remain vigilant as we continue to look for Luna. If you see her, please contact law enforcement."

"Is this related to you and your husband somehow?"

"Based on what we know so far, we believe it's not related to our positions as president and first lady, but as I said, the investigation is ongoing."

"Where did your sister and her husband think their son was yesterday?"

"They'd given him permission to go get pizza and play video games at the Wharf with Tomas."

"By themselves?" the man asked as a follow-up.

"Yes."

"How did they get there?"

"On the Metro."

"Aren't they young for that at eleven?"

"That's not my decision to make for my sister, her husband or any other parent."

"What do you think as a parent yourself?"

"I don't judge the choices of other parents."

"Ever?"

Sam took a step back, giving Malone the floor.

"Three white kids went missing," a reporter asked, "and we've got the FBI and Marshals working the case. What do you have to say to the parents of missing children of color who seem to get a fraction of that effort?"

"First of all, Tomas Cambra is Hispanic, and second of all, we give our all to every missing-person case we investigate," Malone said. "Some are higher-profile due to a variety of circumstances, but every one of them is important to us. Thank you for your patience tonight. We'll have more for you in the morning."

With his hand on her arm, Malone steered her toward The Beast, which was positioned outside the Emergency Department doors. As he turned her over to Brant, he said, "Get some rest. I'll text you any updates. Come back when you're ready to."

"Thanks, Cap, for everything always."

"You got it."

Brant held the door for her to get into the car, where Nick waited for her with open arms.

He gathered her in close to him and held on as the car began to move toward home. "You did good out there. Most of the networks carried it live."

"I hate that this has blown up into such a big story because of Ethan's connection to us, but I hope all the publicity leads us to Luna." She couldn't bear to think of the potential long-term implications for all three kids.

"I do, too."

"I'm sorry. I shouldn't have said that about it being such a big story. I don't blame you for any of this."

"I know you don't, but it's just another example of the ripple effect. I was relieved to hear the investigation isn't showing any connection to us."

"Ethan said the father of the kid named Brecken was pissed that Brecken didn't know Ethan was our nephew. He said they argued over that. He heard the father say, 'You didn't know he was the president's nephew?'"

"Probably came as a big shock to them after my statement to the media last night."

Sam's phone rang with a call from her stepmother, Celia. "Hi there."

"Sam! I've just heard the news about Ethan. We were on an excursion and hadn't seen any news all day. Is he—"

"He's safe, reunited with Tracy, Mike and Brooke and not in any kind of trouble."

"That's a huge relief. How terrified you all must've been."

"It's been rough. We didn't call you because there was nothing you could do, and we didn't want to ruin the end of your vacation."

"I would've been distraught for sure."

"I'm heading home now to get some sleep. I've lost track of how long I've been up."

"Please give all the Hogans my love and tell them I'm so thankful to hear that Ethan is okay."

"I'll do that. Are you still due home soon? I feel like you've been gone forever."

"Me, too! Yes, we land at five on Monday at Dulles, so I should be home by dinnertime."

"The kids will be thrilled to see you—and I will, too."

"See you then. Love you all."

"Love you, too."

After Sam ended the call, she called GW, identified herself and asked to speak to Tracy in the ER.

A few minutes passed before Tracy came on the line.

"Hey, have you talked to Mom or Angela to update them?"

"Brooke texted them."

"Oh good. Celia called to say she heard the news and is thankful he's ok.

"Glad to hear from Celia."

"How's he doing?"

"He's sleeping right now. Mike, Brooke and Nate are going back to Celia's. I'll stay with him until he's released in the morning."

"Okay, let me know if you need anything."

"I need my phone back."

"I'll see what I can do about that."

"Thanks for all you did to help."

"Love you all."

"Love you, too."

After she texted Archie to ask about returning phones to the Hogans and Cambras, Sam closed her phone and her eyes, resting her head on Nick's shoulder. She couldn't recall the last time she'd been this tired. The days of being single and working around the clock seemed like a long time ago now that they'd been married more than two years and had a family to care for. In the past, she'd regularly pulled all-nighters if the demands of a case called for it. These days, she hardly ever did that, preferring instead to turn things over to the night shift to keep the investigation moving until she returned in the morning.

"We're home, babe," Nick said.

She forced her eyes open and blinked the White House into view.

When the president was in the car, the ushers came outside to greet them rather than waiting inside the door the way they did for her.

"We're relieved to hear your nephew is safe," Harold said as he held the door for them.

"Thank you, Harold," Nick said. "We're relieved as well."

"And he's in good health?"

"He is," Nick said.

"Excellent news."

Sam was thankful that Nick answered the questions and that he helped her out of her coat and steered her toward the elevator, rather than the stairs, to the second floor. In the elevator, she rested her head on his shoulder again. "I want to see the kids."

"In the morning. You've got about three seconds of steam left before you fall over."

"It might be down to one second."

He kept an arm around her as he guided her into their suite and straight to the bedroom, where he helped her get undressed. Somehow, he got a T-shirt over her head before she collapsed onto the pillow and dropped into oblivion.

CHAPTER SIXTEEN

Sam woke much later to darkness and was immediately anxious about Ethan and Tracy and didn't recall for a second that he'd been found.

"Easy, babe," Nick said as he cuddled up to her. "Everyone's safe."

She exhaled as relief flooded her system in a rush of emotions that made her head spin. Ethan was in the hospital. He was safe. He hadn't done anything to contribute to Luna's disappearance. They would do everything they could to find her.

A sob erupted from her chest, taking her by surprise as all the scenarios she'd tried so hard not to consider when he was missing took her breath away. When she pondered the staggering array of horrible things that could've happened to her precious nephew…

Nick caressed her back in small circles. "Let it all out. I've got you, love."

She cried harder than she had since her father died, and all she could think about was what she would've done—what they all would've done—if Ethan had been killed. Somehow, she had to persuade Mike and Tracy to keep him supervised until he was older and more able to trust his own judgment, although no one would have to tell them that after this incident. She'd be surprised if Ethan ever wanted to leave the house again now that he'd experienced some of the evil lurking in the world.

"All the scary shit we learned about men and boys while we were looking for him… I'm haunted by it. The things they're saying and doing and thinking."

"It's terrifying," Nick said. "Kids are being radicalized online while their parents think they're playing video games. They think if they're home, they're safe, but that's not necessarily true anymore."

"We need to do something about this, like sound the alarm and make parents aware of how pervasive it is."

"I want to know if Scotty and Eli have been exposed, and if so, how, when, who."

"Do you think they have been?" Sam asked.

"I'd be shocked if Eli hasn't heard about it. Not sure about Scotty, but I'll find out."

"The whole thing makes me sick, that there's this whole dark underworld online that's fomenting hate and violence. I mean, of course I knew the dark web existed, but learning about this subculture has brought it into sharper focus."

"For me, too. Neither of us spends much time online, so we aren't exposed to it. Not that we'd probably see this kind of stuff."

"It's all very unsettling."

"On another note, I want you to know," he said softly, "I can't stop thinking about what you told Ruiz about Ethan."

"I could've sworn we'd talked about that," she said, sniffling as she wiped away the remaining tears.

"No, you've never told me how the timing of his birth was so consequential for you. I'm glad he arrived when he did and gave you a reason to keep pushing forward so you could eventually collide with me again."

"And, *oh*, how I collided with you."

"Mmm, I love colliding with you. Remember that first time

when we got back together? You weren't supposed to be anywhere near me. It was all so forbidden and so hot."

"Against a wall, as I recall."

"Hey, that's a rhyme."

She snickered and kissed his chest. "You're the only person in the world who could make me laugh when I'm trying to have a serious meltdown."

"I'm sorry to interrupt your meltdown. Please proceed accordingly."

Smiling, she kissed her way to his jaw, which was sprinkled with whiskers. She loved him with a little stubble, but the rest of the world saw him only clean-shaven and put together. "I've lost interest in my meltdown. I'm just so fucking relieved that Ethan is safe."

"Are you planning to talk to Tracy and Mike about making some changes?"

"Not sure I'll have to say anything after this."

"Maybe you should anyway."

"It's a tough spot to be in to be spouting off on what they should do when my own kids are under full-time protection."

"You'd be spouting off as a seasoned law enforcement officer in the city their son wants to run around in unsupervised."

"We'll see if the opportunity presents itself. It's a very fine line for me to walk in light of how protected our kids are."

"I know."

As she yawned, she asked him, "What time is it?"

"Six thirty."

"AM or PM?"

"PM."

"Oh good. I was afraid I'd slept for twelve hours."

"Nah, just about four or so."

"Did you sleep?"

"A little."

"Sorry if I disturbed you."

He pulled her in closer and pushed a leg between hers. "I love when you disturb me, but I hate to see you upset."

"I'm okay now. Thank you for being my soft place to land in the madness. You always make things better."

"Give yourself some time to process everything that's happened in the last couple of weeks. It's been a lot."

"It's always a lot."

"This has been an extra-punishing stretch, even by our standards."

"Yeah, it has."

"Why don't you take a few days off? You have more leave on the books than you could use in a lifetime. Your family has been through an ordeal. You've been through a couple of them. No one would fault you for taking a break."

She tucked her hand under his T-shirt, looking for warm skin. "I might actually do that. I'm mentally and physically exhausted."

"Even Superwoman needs a break every now and then, and you hardly ever take one."

"We just caught a new case that could get complicated with the victim being from Spokane."

"They're all tricky. Your capable team can handle it. Punch out, babe. Take a breather, and P.S., what're you doing?"

"Huh?"

"With the hand?"

Sam snapped out of the relaxed state she'd slipped into to realize her hand was now covering his hard cock. "Whoops. Did I do that?"

"No, it was Millie the housekeeper."

"I knew you had a thing for her."

"She's eighty and insists on still coming to work at the White House."

"God bless her."

"Um, about the hand and the thing you built with it…"

She gave him a squeeze that made him groan. "Is this the thing you're referring to?"

"Yeah," he said, sounding a bit strangled. "That's the one."

"Are there others?"

"Not in this bed if you know what's good for you."

Sam started to laugh and couldn't stop.

"It's not funny! I was minding my own business, and you started doing..."

She stroked him from root to tip over the tight confines of his boxer briefs.

"...*that*, and now..."

"Now what?"

"You'd better think about finishing what you started."

She kept her hand on him but stopped moving it.

"What're you doing?"

"Thinking about whether I want to finish what I started, as directed."

"Samantha..."

"Yes?"

His deep sigh said it all.

She decided to take mercy on him by continuing to stroke him. "You know what?"

"What?" he asked through gritted teeth.

"I love that I'm the only one in the whole world who knows you this way. I know what makes you groan..." She gave him a tight squeeze. "And I know what makes you twitch." She cupped his balls, and sure enough, his whole body reacted. "I know what makes you sigh..."

Then she found out what made him pounce as she found herself on her back with a strong, sexy man on top of her. His hazel eyes were full of fire as he stared down at her. "You know how to drive me crazy."

She smiled. "Do I?"

"You know it."

"Whatever will you do about it?"

He brushed the hair back from her face as he continued to gaze down at her. "You're so tired. You need to sleep."

"I did sleep. Now I need you."

"Are you sure?"

She lifted her hips to press against him, and he groaned. "Any remaining questions?"

"None." He moved quickly to get rid of his briefs and her panties and was inside her in a matter of seconds.

"Oof," she said, smiling. "Tell me how you really feel."

"Thank you," he said as he picked up the pace. "I will, and just remember that you started this."

Sam closed her eyes and held on tight to the love of her life as he took them on a wild ride that was just what she needed to wipe clean the horrors of the last few days.

Then he stopped.

Her eyes flew open to find him grinning as he withdrew from her and kissed a scorching path from her lips to her breasts, biting her nipple through her T-shirt. He pushed up the shirt to get to her and impatiently tugged it over her head.

Sam moaned when she realized he'd decided to pay her back for torturing him. She yawned dramatically. "Can we move things along so I can get back to sleep?"

"Uh-huh."

Rather than speed things up, though, he slowed down even more, giving each nipple a thorough treatment that had her squirming under him and about to beg for relief. "Nick..."

"Yes, dear?"

"Come *on*."

"Where're we going?"

"Ugh. You're so mean."

"How am I mean? I'm making sweet love to my sexy wife. And I believe in doing things right or not doing them at all." This was said as he nibbled on her hip bone, which she hadn't known was sensitive until he showed her. Once he found out that it made her crazy, he made sure to do it as often as he possibly could. When he was in this kind of mood, she'd learned that no amount of pleading would cause him to hurry things along.

So she closed her eyes again and floated in a sea of love and contentment, even if every nerve ending in her body was attuned to him and bracing for release. Here in his arms, there were no murders to contend with or scary shit to process or anything other than peace and love and the kind of desire that made a girl delirious.

With her legs on his shoulders, he set out to drive her mad with slow, easy, sensuous strokes of his tongue. Somehow, he managed to avoid the spot that burned for his attention while he drove her even crazier than she already was. Grasping handfuls of his hair, she tried to direct him, but he only chuckled, refusing to be led.

"Relax," he said. "We'll get there. All in good time."

She wanted to scream, but that might spark a response from the Secret Service, so she bit her lip and tried to find her nonexistent patience.

He peppered kisses on her belly, her inner thighs, the back of her knee and then back up while Sam tried to relax and enjoy the pleasure that had her so hot, she worried she might implode before the big finish.

When he returned to her core, he went right for the gusto, sucking her clit and sending her into orbit in a matter of seconds. Her slow return to reality was interrupted by a deep thrust that immediately had her full attention. She clung to him, holding on as he chased his own release. Right when she thought he was there, he reached between them to coax another from her.

Holy *moly*.

Afterward, she was completely spent. Every muscle had turned to jelly as she vibrated with the aftershocks of explosive desire. "You're wicked good at that, my friend."

"Gee, thanks." His lips moved against her neck, sending goose bumps over her sensitive skin.

"Even when I'm being impatient, I always love you."

"That's good to know, because I always love you, too. It was hard to watch you suffering when Ethan was missing."

"Thank you for staying with me through it all."

"Nowhere else I want to be. Ever."

AFTER SPENDING hours at the hotel reviewing the results of the canvass and speaking to the hotel manager—and what a joy that had been—Freddie was now back at HQ and sitting with Sergeant Walters as they reviewed the video from the lobby and sixth-floor hallway. He'd never given much thought to how tedious it was to sift through hours of video until he offered to help Walters and found out how mind-numbing the process could be.

"How do you guys do this all day, every day?" he asked as he stifled a yawn.

"You get used to it."

"I'm not sure I would. I'm cross-eyed after a couple of hours."

Walters chuckled and then sat up a little straighter. "Cruz, look at this."

Freddie rolled his chair closer to Walters's desk and leaned in for a closer look at a man in a black hoodie with a black knit hat entering the lobby. He was tall, thin, white and had acne on the lower part of his face. Freddie noted that he kept his sunglasses on as he made his way to the elevators.

They lost him when he was inside the elevator but were able to match the time stamp on the sixth-floor footage to see him stepping into the hallway and making his way to Carver's room. He knocked on the door and was admitted.

"That's our guy," Freddie said with the rush of excitement that came with identifying a suspect, even if they were a long way from having what they needed to issue an arrest warrant.

They watched the sixth-floor footage, waiting for something to happen, for close to thirty minutes before Dale Carver emerged from the room, ice bucket in hand, and made his way toward the ice room.

"Wait a minute," Freddie said.

"The guy is still in his room when Dale goes to get the ice?"

"I didn't see him leave."

"So that's not our guy."

They watched Dale walk down the carpeted hallway and enter the ice room.

Freddie stared without blinking, waiting to see someone approach, but that never happened. "The killer was waiting for him inside the ice room."

"That's what I think, too."

"Can we back up the hallway footage to get to where we can see the person go into the room?"

"Yep." Walters reversed the video by ten minutes, looking for the moment when someone entered that room to wait for Dale. When they didn't see anyone, he went back further until they saw a shadowy figure dressed similarly to the other guy emerge from the stairwell and duck into the ice room. At no time could they see his face, which meant he'd been there before and figured out where the cameras were. Shortly after Dale entered the ice room, the man left as efficiently as he'd entered and escaped down the stairwell.

"This was a setup. Two guys working together. Take me back to Dale's room from the time he left to get the ice."

They watched his door until it slowly opened. The guy in the dark clothing took a look up and down the hallway before he left Dale's room and went down the same stairwell the other guy had used.

Freddie rubbed a hand over the stubble on his jaw. "Well, now we know how it went down. What doesn't make sense to me—well, in addition to the murder, which will never make sense—was why did the guy in the room leave the heroin? If this was a drug deal gone south, why wouldn't he take the product?"

"Maybe the whole point was to show what Dale had been up to before he was killed."

"Yeah, that's possible, but who would care enough about a recovering addict to want to set him up that way?"

They glanced at each other.

"What do we know about the wife?" Walters asked.

"Not enough yet, but it's time to find out her deal."

"That's where I'd start. This was a long way from a drug deal gone bad."

"Yeah, it was well planned and executed. Thanks for hanging in there with me."

"No problem. I'll put all the relevant footage on a thumb drive for you."

"Perfect."

"Let me know what you find out. I'm invested."

"Will do."

Freddie headed downstairs to the Homicide pit, which was empty except for Carlucci and Dominguez, who'd arrived for the overnight shift.

"What're you still doing here?" Carlucci asked.

Dani Carlucci was tall, blonde, blue-eyed and fit, while her partner, Gigi Dominguez, was petite and dark-haired with soft brown eyes and light brown skin. They made for a formidable team as detectives, and even though Freddie wanted to dig into the new info himself, he decided to turn it over to them so he could get some sleep.

"You think his wife in Washington state set him up to be bumped off while he was on a business trip to DC?" Dani asked skeptically.

"It's a theory. Maybe she'd discovered he was using again and decided he'd be worth more dead to her than alive. Let's look at their financials and find out if he has life insurance."

"We'll get on it," Dani said.

"I'm going to head home. I'll be back at zero seven hundred."

"See you then."

Eager to get home to his wife after missing all day Sunday together, Freddie headed out to the used pickup truck he'd bought from a friend to hold him over until he found something worthy of replacing his beloved old Mustang that had finally died. He missed that stupid car and was thinking about the Nova he'd seen online that he wanted to check out when someone stepped out of the shadows created by the parking lot lights.

Freddie's hand immediately went to his weapon.

CHAPTER SEVENTEEN

The man held up his hands to show he was unarmed. "I mean you no harm."

"What do you want?"

"You're the first lady's partner, right?"

"So what?"

"You need to tell her... This thing with her nephew... It's a big deal. Mayfield is a big-time trafficker. He uses his kid to get to others. Check other missing-persons cases, the less-high-profile ones. You can tie some of them back to Mayfield and his organization."

"Can you come inside and talk?"

He shook his head. "I've risked my neck by coming here. Dig deep into Mayfield. That's all I can say."

"What's your name?"

"Nah, doesn't matter. The info is solid."

He took off as fast as he'd appeared, disappearing into the ether as Freddie stood there for a second, processing what he'd said. He thought about calling Sam but decided against it because he hoped she was getting some much-needed sleep. Instead, he called Malone.

"Yeah."

Freddie conveyed the gist of what he'd been told by the mystery guy.

"He wouldn't give you his name?"

"No, he said it didn't matter who he was, that we need to look closely at Mayfield, who he called 'a big-time trafficker.'"

"I'm out near Connecticut Ave with Ruiz and the Feds. They're about to go into a house where we believe he and the son are. We're hoping to find Luna Ahern there as well."

"Let me know how it goes, will you?"

"Yeah, I will."

The line went dead, and Freddie said a silent prayer for the colleagues who'd be putting themselves in harm's way to capture the Mayfields and hopefully save Luna Ahern. The scourge of human trafficking was the one thing Freddie considered to be as bad as murder, with people being stolen from their lives and forced into a nightmare of sexual servitude and other horrors.

When he thought about innocent kids being taken hostage and sold to the highest bidders, it made him question whether he wanted children. Was it fair to bring them into this screwed-up world?

That question weighed heavily on him as he drove home to Wardman Park, where his gorgeous wife waited for him. She was like a tonic that washed away the filth of what he dealt with every day on the job. When he was with her, he wasn't thinking about the staggering number of ways people found to harm one another.

He recalled Sam telling him that he couldn't internalize the things they experienced on the job and project them onto his own life. The longer he spent on the job, however, the harder it became not to internalize the horrors. He worried he'd never be able to handle having children he couldn't protect at all times.

If Sam's nephew could be snatched, what would keep something like that from happening to his kid? How would he do anything other than worry about them every second they were out of his sight? How would he raise them to be independent while he hovered over them like a Black Hawk helicopter on a mission? He wasn't sure how anyone could bear having kids when everything was so dangerous and scary.

After finding a parking space three blocks from their building, Freddie jogged toward home, staying vigilant as he went. Having that guy refer to him as the first lady's partner had been unsettling. Her high profile had raised his, too, making them both less safe than they'd been before Nick became president. Not that he'd ever say that to her. She certainly understood the reality of their situation better than he ever could.

He used his key to get into the building and went up the stairs toward home. In a couple of weeks, they'd be moving to Celia's house on Ninth Street, which would give them four times the space they had now. They'd have room for a baby, if that was meant to be for them. He'd been devastated by Elin's miscarriage earlier in the year and had been hopeful that they might conceive again.

But now... The horrific tension that'd gripped everyone who loved Ethan while he was missing would stay with Freddie forever.

One thing he was fairly sure of was that he'd never survive one of his kids going missing—or worse. It would ruin him.

Elin, sitting up in bed with her Kindle, smiled when he came into the bedroom, making a beeline for her. She wrapped her arms around him. "I was so relieved to hear Ethan had been found."

"Me, too."

"And he's all right?"

"Physically, a little banged up. I'm not sure about the emotional fallout."

"Did they get the guys who had him?"

"They're raiding the house now. I haven't heard how it went."

"Is the girl still missing?"

"Yeah, they're hoping they'll find her at the house."

"How's Sam doing?"

"I haven't seen her all day. I was working on another case, but I heard she went home to get some sleep."

"That's good. She looked exhausted at the press briefing. It's all so terrifying."

And she didn't know the half of it.

"Did you take a nap?" he asked.

"For a while, but then I saw your text that you were coming home."

He rested his head on her chest while she ran her fingers through his hair. Nothing could soothe him the way she did. "I was thinking on the way home how I'd lose it if something like this ever happened to our kid, so let's just not have any."

She grunted out a half laugh. "You'd never let our kid out on the town alone at eleven."

"I'd like to think I wouldn't, but who knows how I'll feel about it by then? Maybe it'll be easier to let them than fight with them."

"Nah, you won't fall for that."

"I wish I could be sure."

"I'm sure enough for both of us. You'll be a great dad. They'll adore you and do what you ask because you'll show them that you know what you're talking about."

"If you'd asked me if Mike would let Ethan go out at eleven, I would've said no way."

"After you told me that earlier, I was thinking that he and Tracy have been parents for a long time. Brooke is eight years older than Ethan. Maybe they've run out of steam with being strict parents."

"But after what happened to Brooke, I'd think he'd keep Ethan and Abby under lock and key."

"Which isn't sustainable. Eventually, they'll be old enough for some independence, which every parent has to acknowledge long before they're ready to."

"I had a lot of independence as a kid. My mom was a single

parent, and my grandparents had me a lot, but they were easy to fool. Not that I ever did anything terrible, but I was out and about long before I should've been. My mother would've killed me if she'd known where I was and who I was with."

Elin smiled. "Was my very good boy naughty sometimes?"

"Hardly. I was the one saying, 'I don't think that's a good idea,' while the rest of them were telling me to shut up and quit being a dad."

"I can so see that," she said with a giggle. "You're such a nerd."

"Hey! That's mean."

"It's only mean if it's not the truth."

"How did a nerd like me end up with a goddess like you?"

"That's one of life's greatest mysteries."

Smiling, he raised his head to kiss her. "I'm the luckiest nerd who ever lived."

"Yes, you are, and you're about to be even luckier."

"Is that right? Do tell."

"Well, I know you're determined to remain childless after what happened to Ethan, but alas, that's not going to happen."

His heart stopped. "It isn't?"

She shook her head as her eyes brimmed with tears. "I'm terrified."

"Aw, honey... It's going to be fine this time. I know it."

"How do you know?"

"What happened the first time was a sign that that baby wasn't meant to be. This one will be different."

"And you'll not dress our children in Bubble Wrap and forbid them from leaving the house until they're thirty?"

"Twenty—and that's my final offer." He rested his forehead on hers. "I love you so, so much, and I know every day how lucky I am that you love me, too."

"Oh, Freddie, please. I'm the one who hit the jackpot here with the nicest, kindest, smartest, sexiest husband there is. All my friends are jealous that I got one of the good ones."

"They are?"

Laughing, she said, "Is that the only thing you heard?"

"Nah, I heard the rest, too, and I loved every word of it. We're both lucky, and it's about to get so much better with a new home and new baby. So much to look forward to."

"You came in saying you were never having kids."

"That was before I knew I was having one. Now, I guess I'll have to find a way to cope with the fear. You'll be there to keep me from turning them into anxiety-ridden little people, right?"

"I'll do my best to keep you from succumbing to fear. That's no way to live, my love."

"No, it isn't, and I know that."

"Maybe you should talk to Dr. Trulo about this at some point. He raised his daughters while working for the department and hearing the worst of the worst."

"That's a good idea. I'll see if I can find some time with him."

"Please do that. I want you to enjoy every second of this incredible adventure, so let's do what it takes to get you ready for it."

"I will. I promise."

"Good, now come to bed. Your wife is feeling lonely."

"Is that code for..."

Her smile took his breath away. "Come to bed and find out."

JAKE MALONE STOOD next to Michelle Ruiz, Jesse Best and Avery Hill, waiting for FBI and MPD SWAT officers to give the signal that they were ready to go into the home where Mayfield and his son were believed to be hiding out. They'd followed a tip from an informant to the house that Mayfield had apparently rented under his real name, which made it easy to confirm. Thermal-imaging devices had been used to determine two people were inside the home. They'd been hoping for three.

"My people are ready," Hill said.

Jake asked for a status check from Captain Nickleson, the SWAT commander.

"Ready," Nickleson said.

He listened as Nickleson coordinated with the FBI commander to go in together.

Within seconds, the sounds of windows smashing and doors being battered turned the quiet, residential neighborhood into an active crime scene. Jake noticed lights coming on at nearby houses. Patrol officers had been positioned to keep residents in their homes while the raid went down.

"We have Mayfield and his son," Nickleson reported.

"What about the girl?" Malone asked.

"Nothing yet."

Wearing sweats and T-shirts, the Mayfields were marched out in cuffs and loaded into separate MPD cruisers while the officers inside turned the house upside down in their search for Luna.

"Let's get everyone out and redo the FLIR," Hill said, referring to the thermal imaging that would detect body heat in the house.

Both teams recalled their people so the FLIR could be rerun.

After a couple of minutes, Hill shook his head. "Nothing."

"Goddamn it," Jake muttered. "Let's get them back to HQ and into interrogation."

He sent texts to the chief, deputy chief and Sam, letting them know they had the Mayfields in custody, but Luna had not been found at the house.

"We'll continue the search," Jessie Best said as they reached their vehicles. "We won't give up until we find her."

Malone shook the marshal's hand. "Thank you for the support."

"Of course. I'll have people on this around the clock until we locate her. I'll check in tomorrow."

"Talk to you then."

. . .

As Jesse walked toward his car, he called one of his deputies, David Rinner, who was working on the case overnight.

"Hey," David said. "How'd the raid go?"

"Got the father and son. No sign of the girl. MPD is taking them back to their house for interrogation."

"We're working on following up on tips and checking train and bus stations as well as the airports."

"I'm going home to catch a few hours of sleep."

"I'll have an update for you by zero seven hundred."

"Thanks."

Jesse pressed a button on the wheel of his Dodge Charger to end the call. He pressed the accelerator, eager to get to the hospital to check on another of his deputies, Memphis Rose Costello, after having been gone for hours.

Her mother and grandmother had arrived with all the chaos Memphis had warned him they would bring and had quickly driven him batshit crazy with their nonstop chatter, questions, anxiety, nosiness and intrusiveness. Because they were with Memphis, Jesse had gone to help find Sam Holland's nephew, even though he was technically on leave after the showdown with Offenbach that'd led to Memphis being shot in the leg.

With her mom and grandmother around, Jesse could've gone straight home to get some sleep, but he headed for the hospital anyway. He needed to be with her, to see that she was still there. He'd come far too close to losing her, which had opened his eyes to a few things that made him exquisitely uncomfortable. The first of those things was that she mattered to him much more than he'd previously acknowledged.

At some point, their highly inappropriate, casual sex-buddies-who-worked-together relationship had become serious, and he hadn't realized that until he'd almost lost her. By now, word was out that Jesse had barely left her bedside since she'd arrived by helicopter at GW Trauma in critical condition. His command would be asking questions, and he'd need to come up with the answers—quickly—or risk endangering both their careers.

The thing was... He had no answers. All he knew was that he needed to be there for her until she recovered from her injury and things could get back to normal. If that meant taking a leave of absence from work so he could care for her without anyone knowing about it, then that's what he'd do. Whatever it took to keep her with him where she belonged.

Wait... He wasn't saying she *belonged* with him. It was just that he wanted to keep her close while she recovered. After that, they could go back to the way things had been before he'd thought he might lose her forever. And why that possibility had completely upended his entire existence was something he was still trying to process days later.

There'd been so much blood. How could a person lose that much blood and still be alive? For a time, he'd been certain she would die. He'd felt the foundation under him crack and splinter at the thought of not having her by his side at work and in life. He, who'd been a rule follower all his life, didn't give a flying fuck if anyone found out he was in a relationship—if that's what it was called—with one of his subordinates.

Technically, she answered to him at work. In reality, she was the one who kept him on track and focused. She was the only thing keeping the wheels on the bus of his entire life, and the possibility of losing her had been one of the most terrifying things that'd ever happened.

It was a crazy thing to realize someone was the most important person in your life when you were on the precipice of losing them forever. The sick, queasy sensation in his stomach had stayed with him since that tense chopper ride from Shenandoah to UVA Health, the closest level-one trauma center.

Jesse broke into a cold sweat as he recalled the frantic efforts of the paramedics to keep her alive during the fifteen-minute flight. As someone trained to catalog details, he'd remember every one of those endless minutes spent in agonizing fear. How was it possible that the endlessly aggravating chatterbox known as Memphis Rose could've been silenced by something so pedestrian as a bullet?

Before then, Jesse would've thought a bullet would bounce off her tough outer shell, not puncture her soft skin and nick an artery, putting her life in peril. Finding out she was actually human had been humbling for someone who went through his life trying not to form attachments to people who could disappear with no warning, never to return—the way his sister had.

He couldn't think about Jordan. Not when he was trying so hard to keep it together. He'd asked his friend Sam Holland to look at the files he'd compiled during the decades-long search for his missing sister. Hopefully, she'd get a chance to think more about that since her nephew had been found alive. Her partner, Detective Cruz, had suggested some true-crime podcasts that might be interested in the story of the U.S. marshal who found people for a living and the one person he'd never been able to find, the most important one of all.

Even though everything in him recoiled at the idea of making his private pain public for all the world to chew on, he planned to pursue that idea as soon as Memphis was recovered.

It didn't take a shrink to tell him that Jordan was the reason he didn't let himself form attachments to people. The first person he'd ever truly loved—the only one—had disappeared without a trace, never to be seen or heard from again. He'd learned early not to give his heart to anyone. That way, he could never be shattered when they left. With Memphis Rose, he'd broken all his own rules and formed an attachment, as much as he might've denied that before she was wounded.

Now, though… As he made his way into George Washington University Hospital, where she'd been transferred after being stabilized at UVA, so she'd be closer to home, he had no idea what he was going to do about that attachment he'd never wanted in the first place.

Exhaustion clung to him as he took the elevator to the fifth floor, where she was in the ICU. That she was still in the ICU was further cause for anxiety. Wasn't she much better? Couldn't she be transferred to a regular room? He'd get some answers to those questions while he was there. Outside her room, he was relieved to see her alone and resting. He didn't have the bandwidth to deal with her mother and grandmother tonight.

"She's doing better," a nurse he recognized said.

He'd been so intent on studying Memphis that he hadn't heard the nurse approach. He was losing it in more ways than one. "Why is she still in ICU?"

Memphis had given them permission to speak to him, so the nurse said, "Her blood pressure is still lower than we'd like it to be, so we're monitoring her until it improves. She's also still getting transfusions."

"Can't they do that stuff on the regular floor?"

"They can, but we watch her much more closely up here." She put her hand on his arm. "Try not to worry. She's doing well, considering what she's been through."

Considering what she's been through...

Meaning that she'd nearly bled to death after taking a bullet that should've hit him instead of her. If only he'd stayed closer to her while they'd hunted Offenbach, maybe he'd be in that bed rather than her. He'd much prefer that.

"I'm sure she'd like to see you. She lights up when you're around."

What the hell did that mean? "Oh, um, okay. How long has she been asleep?"

"About an hour."

"Is it normal for her to be so terribly pale?"

"After what she's endured, it's entirely normal. She'll be back to her usual self in a few weeks."

That last part was the only thing he wanted to hear. "Thank you."

"Of course."

After she went to check on other patients, Jesse continued to stand outside the room, gazing through the window at the tiny firebrand in the bed and breaking into a cold sweat for the hundredth time since she'd been wounded. He fucking loved her, and that was the last goddamned thing he'd intended to let happen.

He was about to walk away, to go home where she couldn't get to him, at least not while she was still attached to machines that were making her better. But then she opened her eyes, saw him there and smiled. As she crooked her finger at him, he understood what the nurse had meant when she'd said Memphis lit up when he was there. He saw the light in her eyes and was humbled to know he'd put it there.

CHAPTER EIGHTEEN

As Jesse pushed open the door to Memphis's room, he couldn't deny the powerful need she invoked in him. He'd prided himself on not needing anyone or anything to get by, but this one... She'd worked her way under his skin so deep, it would take ten men and a team of mules to get her out, and even then, she'd probably kick their asses before she'd let them take her away from him.

She held out her hand to him. The back of it was bruised from IVs, but the softness of her skin flooded him with comfort only she could provide. Why her? Why not any one of a dozen other meaningless hookups that'd passed through his life like ships in the night? Why was she the one who'd anchored herself to his soul, refusing to let go no matter how hard he tried to push her away?

"How was your day, dear?"

"Ethan and Tomas are back with their families. Got the father and son who kidnapped them. Still looking for the girl."

She winced at that last part, having spent more than five years working on the Marshals' Missing Child Program team, tracking down children who'd been endangered or victims of crime or human trafficking. That assignment had led her to declare she was never having kids of her own.

"What can I do to help?" she asked.

"Nothing. You're supposed to be resting and relaxing and growing new blood."

Her smile was less dazzling than usual, but still a welcome sight, even if her paleness freaked him out. "How does one grow new blood?"

"Who the fuck knows? Just hurry up and get it done so we can get you out of here."

She released his hand to run her fingers through his hair, straightening it as she went. "You look terrible."

"You look worse."

"Mama said I should find me a man who says sweet things to me."

"You should listen to your mama."

"You need to cross-check WIN and NCIC," she said, referring to the Warrant Information Network and the National Crime Information Center. "Look for suspected traffickers who might've been in the area at the time the kids went missing. Identify all the father's known associates. Do the kid's, too. Who knows what he's gotten himself into with that dirtbag as his father?"

"Stop," Jesse said. "You're not on this case."

"I want you to find that girl before it's too late. Follow the money. Check to see if the father received any big payments— and make sure to look at the son, too. Maybe the father had the money sent to the kid, thinking we wouldn't check a minor's accounts."

"Deputy U.S. Marshal Costello, you've been ordered to stand down by your commanding officer."

"Whatever."

"This is why we can't keep on like we've been. You say 'whatever' when I give you a direct order."

"I'm on medical leave, so I don't have to take orders from you,

Chief Marshal Best, and if you're smart, you'll do the things I suggested and find that kid before she's lost forever to a nightmare."

"It's all being done, so you can rest easy. But thank you for the help."

"Are you sure they're checking the kid's financials, too? They might not think to do that."

"I'll make sure."

"Do it now."

Exasperated, Best pulled out his phone to send a text to Rinner about checking the Mayfield kid's financials. "Done. Now get back to resting and recovering so you can get out of here."

"They said I might have to do a stint in rehab to get my leg working again."

"Can you do that at home? They could come in or something."

"They said I can't be home alone."

He stared at her, unblinking, until she said, "What?"

"What the hell do you think? That I'd let you go home alone after this?"

"I don't expect anything from you. It's no problem if I have to go to a facility."

"You're not going anywhere but home with me, where you belong. That's it."

She raised her right eyebrow. "Another order, Chief Marshal?"

Jesse crossed his arms as he sat back in his seat, agitated and annoyed. "Call it whatever you want."

"I'll let you know what I decide to do."

"There's no decision. You'll come home with me, we'll get you therapists or whatever, and I'll take care of you until you're back on your feet."

"What if I don't want to go home with you? And besides, weren't you the one who said we had to keep it below the radar at work? How we gonna do that if you take leave at the same time I'm out? You don't think that'll get them talking?"

"I don't care if they're talking. I'm taking care of you, and that's the end of it."

"You know you can't actually tell me what to do when we're not at work, right?"

"This is work! You're in that bed because of work."

"I'm on full medical leave and not under your direction."

"So we're going to fight about semantics when you could just say, 'Thank you, Jesse, that sounds like a good plan'?"

"Now you're telling me what to say, too? Last week, you were keeping me at arm's length, and now you want me staying with you for who knows how long."

"Last week, I was an idiot, and now I'm not."

"And what brought about this miraculous transformation?"

Keeping his arms tight around himself, he crossed his legs and tried to find a way to say it without revealing too much. "I didn't like seeing you bleeding all over the place."

Memphis fanned her face. "Aw, is that your romantic way of saying you care?"

She was so goddamned annoying sometimes. "What if it is?"

"I'm not sure I'd know what to do with that information."

"Don't act like I haven't always cared about you, because I have, and you know it. It's just, you know... more so now."

"Ah, because I almost kicked it. I see how it is."

"You don't see anything," he said more sharply than he'd intended. "You were unconscious for most of it."

She held out her hand.

He stared at it for a long moment, wanting to keep his distance while he still could.

"Take my hand, Jesse."

With great reluctance, he did as she asked.

"I'm sorry for what you went through after I was wounded. I'm sure it was awful for you."

"You have no idea."

"Tell me."

"I don't want to talk about it."

"I do. I want to know how it was."

"It was fucking terrifying, okay? Is that what you want to know?"

"How so?"

Jesse blew out a deep breath, full of aggravation that she'd make him relive it. "I'd never seen anyone lose that much blood and survive. I was sure you weren't going to make it. And the urgency of the first responders didn't do shit to calm my nerves. They thought you were going to die, too, even as they did everything they could to save you. We had to get you out of there fast and find a place where the chopper could land... Took fucking forever."

He wasn't going to fucking *cry* in front of her.

As he stood abruptly, he released her hand. "I've got to go."

"Please don't leave me, Jesse."

If he didn't get the hell out of there, he might never leave her side again. He stood, frozen with indecision, until she spoke again, more softly this time, as if her burst of energy was fading.

"Please."

Exhaling loudly, he sat back down and took the hand she extended to him once again. When was she going to decide he wasn't worth the bother? Probably any time now.

As she gave his hand a squeeze, he was glad it wouldn't happen tonight. He'd bought himself a reprieve. Tomorrow, he'd remind her that she was coming home with him.

ARCHIE COULDN'T REMEMBER the last time he'd gone so long without sleep. He arrived at home completely tapped out, but so excited to see Harlowe that sleep was the last thing on his mind as he used his key in the door.

Inside, he was hit with the smell of something cooking.

He found her in the kitchen, standing at the stove, spatula in hand, her auburn hair twisted into a bun that made her look smart and sexy. "What're you doing up? It's four thirty in the morning."

"I know what time it is, thank you. I got your text that you were on the way home, and I figured you might be hungry."

He was starving and had planned to grab a PowerBar before he hit the sack. "I only texted so I wouldn't startle you." She was still unsettled after Offenbach had kidnapped and assaulted her during his reign of terror. Thankfully, she didn't remember much of what'd happened because he'd also drugged her.

"Which I appreciate, but I was awake, so I decided to make you an omelet and toast."

His stomach growled loudly, making them both laugh. "That's very nice of you, and it smells delicious."

"When was the last time you ate something?"

Archie thought about that. "I have no idea."

"You need to take better care of yourself."

"Normally, I do, but when there're kids missing, and one of them is the nephew of a close friend..." He shrugged. "None of the normal rules apply."

"I'm so glad Sam's nephew and the other boy were found safe."

"Me, too."

"Have they found the missing girl?"

Archie shook his head.

"I'm so worried about her."

"I know. We all are. I didn't want to leave while she's still missing, but I was out of gas."

She turned to him and put her hands on his chest, looking up at him with gorgeous brown eyes full of compassion. "I can't imagine how hard it must be to leave when there's a child still missing, but you're only human. You have to take care of yourself so you can continue to help find her."

"It sucked to leave, but I left things in good hands so I could get some rest."

"This is ready, so have a seat."

He glanced over her shoulder at the omelet that included some of the broccoli and peppers he'd gotten at the grocery store Friday night after work. "That looks good. Thank you for getting up to cook for me."

"Oh please, it's the least I can do after everything you've done for me, plus it helped to have something to do. Hearing about the missing girl has been a bit... triggering."

When she would've stepped away from him, he stopped her with an arm around her waist. He was still careful about how and when he touched her, not wanting to hurt her healing ribs. "Although I hate the reason you needed my help, I've loved every second of having you here with me. In fact, if you want to just stay, that'd be okay with me."

She blinked twice in rapid succession. "Oh, um, you want me to stay?"

He drew her in closer to him and stared down at her gorgeous face. The bruises had faded from a dark purple to light yellow, but he still wanted to murder Offenbach for daring to harm her. That he'd hurt her to get back at Archie was something he'd suffer over for the rest of his life.

"What're you thinking? Your whole expression changed."

"That I probably have no right to ask you for anything after you were hurt because of me."

"It wasn't because of you."

"Yes, it was, Harlowe. He had a beef with me because I helped to prove he was having an affair that torched his whole life."

"It was because of him and only him. He did this. You did your job."

"Still..."

"No, Archie. I need you to hear me on this. I don't blame you. Not for one second do I think you'd ever let anyone hurt me intentionally. In fact, I've started to think you might step in front of a bullet that was coming for me."

"I would. I absolutely would."

"Don't do that. It would break my heart to lose you."

"It would?"

She smiled, which was a thing of beauty, even with the bruises. "Of course it would. You're not the only one who's developed... feelings... here."

"You have feelings? For me?"

She surprised the living shit out of him when she placed her hands over the scratchy whiskers on his face and went up on tiptoes to press a soft, sweet kiss to his lips that nearly made his knees buckle. "Yes, you silly man. I have feelings for you. Big ones."

"I... um... Mine are big, too. Like, really, really big."

Her smile warmed him on the inside, where he'd gone cold with fear and outrage while searching for three missing kids.

She laid her head on his chest and sighed. "You're supposed to be eating your breakfast."

He wondered if she could feel and hear his heart pounding. "I will, but I'm not ready to let you go yet."

"I'll still be here after you eat."

"Promise?"

Laughing, she nodded. "I promise."

"In that case, I'll let you go, but only temporarily."

"Got it."

Archie felt like he'd been through an earthquake or something equally dramatic in the last few minutes. The gorgeous, sexy, smart, funny, adorable Harlowe St. John had *big feelings* for him. That was the best news he'd ever gotten, because his feelings for her were immense.

He took a seat on one of the barstools and watched her every move as she got out a plate and served him the omelet, buttered toast and a bowl of fruit on the side. Then she went back to pour him a glass of orange juice.

"I figured you wouldn't want coffee if you're planning to sleep."

"You figured right." He took a bite of delicious egg, cheese and vegetables. "This is amazing. Thank you again for getting up to cook for me."

She brought a second glass of juice for herself and sat next to him. "It felt good to do something for you after everything you've done for me."

"You don't have to thank me, Harlowe."

"Oh, yes, I really do. I'm not sure what I would've done without your TLC while I was recovering. You've made me feel safe and cared for and... I'll never forget this time with you."

He paused in midbite. "That sounds like an ending rather than a beginning."

"I didn't mean it that way."

His heart started beating again as soon as she said that. "Oh. Good. You scared me for a second there."

"God, I suck at this."

"No, you don't."

"I really do. The only guy I've ever really dated was one I grew up with, and we know how that turned out." She'd married the guy, and he'd abused her, which her parents hadn't believed because they'd known him all his life.

"I can't even think about him or Offenbach without wanting to commit murder."

"Don't do that. You'd look terrible in prison orange."

He gave her a withering look. "I'm not kidding. I want to track down your ex. I don't like not knowing where he is."

"I'm sure he's long gone, making a new life somewhere where no one knows who he is or what he did."

"Guys like him don't forget about the women who allegedly wronged them. That very thing is factoring into this case with the kids."

"How so?"

"I'd rather not talk about that, if it's okay with you. It's disturbing and upsetting, and you've had more than enough of that shit lately. But I do want to know where your ex-husband is hanging his hat these days, just to be on the safe side, okay?"

"That's fine, if you think it's necessary."

"I really do."

"Thank you for caring."

He looked over at her. "I really do."

As she smiled, he leaned in, hoping she'd meet him halfway. When she did, his heart stopped again, for entirely different reasons this time, as her lips brushed against his.

"Harlowe…"

"Yes, Archie?"

"I love kissing you."

"I love kissing you, too."

"I want to do much, much more of that."

"Not until you get some rest."

He groaned. "Come on. You can't give me an appetizer and not follow up."

"I gave you a whole meal!"

"Metaphorically speaking, sweetheart."

She sighed.

"What?"

"I like that you called me that."

He took her hand and brought it to his lips. "You'd better put me down for a nap before I forget I'm tired."

She gave him a tug, and he stood.

"I'll do the dishes," he said.

"No way. I'll do them later. Don't worry about it."

With her hands on his hips, she steered him toward the bedroom.

"Are you going to undress me, too?" he asked hopefully.

"Not this time."

"Don't get me all hopeful that there'll be a next time."

Her reply was a gentle shove toward the bathroom.

So this was what it was like, he thought as he took a leak and brushed his teeth. To be truly in love. He'd had a few girlfriends here and there, had fancied himself in love with one or two of them, but that'd been nothing compared to this.

This... this was everything, and now that he knew she felt the same way he did, he was going to make sure they had forever together. He would also figure out where the fuck her ex-husband was and keep him far, far away from Harlowe, no matter what it took.

CHAPTER NINETEEN

Back at HQ, Jake Malone and Avery Hill prepared to interrogate Asher and Brecken Mayfield. They'd start with the son, while the father sat in the cooler, hopefully worrying about what the kid might tell them.

Phillips, the officer who'd taken them to Central Booking, appeared in the doorway to Malone's office. "Asher is downstairs in lockup. Brecken is in interview one."

"Anyone asking for a lawyer?" Jake asked.

"Not to me."

"And they've been read their rights?"

"Twice."

"Excellent, thanks, Phillips."

"No problem, sir."

"Any word from the USA's Office?" Malone asked.

"AUSA Charity Miller is here."

"Let's go have a chat with Brecken," Malone said to Hill. "I'll take the lead."

"I'm with you, Cap."

Though it went against everything his team believed in to "enjoy" working with Feds, Jake liked Agent Hill and appreciated that he knew when to defer to them. He found AUSA Miller in the hallway by the interrogation rooms, checking her phone.

She looked up when she saw them coming. "I heard one is a juvenile."

"Yes, he's fifteen, but we believe he was an integral player in whatever game his father is playing."

"Proceed with caution," she said. "Read him his rights again and make sure he understands them."

"Will do," Jake said, while he bit back the urge to remind her that he'd been doing this since before she was born.

They burst into the room, scaring the shit out of the kid. Good. He should be scared, Jake thought as he activated the recording device.

"I'm Captain Jake Malone, and FBI Special Agent-in-Charge Avery Hill is also here with Brecken Mayfield."

Brecken Mayfield was a handsome kid with wavy dark hair and brown eyes that should have attracted a lot of female attention. He had broad shoulders and the muscular chest of an athlete.

"Wh-why is the FBI here?"

"Because when kids go missing, it's all hands on deck," Jake said.

"I didn't... I didn't do anything."

"Let's start at the beginning, Brecken." Jake recited the Miranda rights, outlining Brecken's right to remain silent and to request counsel. "Do you understand your rights in this matter?"

"Yes, I already told the other officer that I understand, but like I told him, I didn't do anything. I don't know why I'm here."

"Where's Luna Ahern?" Avery asked.

"Who?"

Jake put printouts of the texts between Brecken, Ethan and Tomas on the table that showed Brecken knew exactly who she was.

Brecken's Adam's apple bobbed in his throat.

"Do you want to try that again?" Avery asked.

"I don't know her or those other kids."

They said nothing, simply staring at him until he began to sweat.

Jake slapped his hand on the table, startling Brecken. "*Where is she, Brecken?*"

"I don't know!"

"So now you're admitting you know her?" Avery asked.

"I know *of* her."

"Why did you lie when I asked you about her before?"

"I'm scared! I don't know what to say! I've never been arrested before."

"You can drop the act. We've seen your record."

"How's that possible? Juvenile records are supposed to be sealed."

Interesting that he knew that and had been perhaps counting on that info remaining inaccessible, Jake thought. "When you're involved in adult-level crimes, adult-level access applies."

"That doesn't seem fair."

"Did your dad tell you what to do if you were taken into custody?"

Brecken seemed incredulous as he shook his head. "He's never been arrested."

Jake pushed Asher's rap sheet across the table for his son to see. "He's been arrested more than twenty times."

Brecken scanned the pages that detailed Asher Mayfield's criminal history. "I... I didn't know."

"Why do I smell bullshit in the air, Agent Hill?"

"Maybe because the air is thick with it."

"Do you know what an incel is?"

He looked up, eyes big, mouth agape. "What about it?"

"Are you an incel, Brecken?" Avery asked.

"What? No. I'm not involved with that stuff."

Which meant he knew what it was since he didn't ask what it meant. "Your devices are being examined by our IT detectives as we speak," Jake said. "Do you want to think about your answer to Agent Hill's question?"

"D-don't you have to have a warrant or something for that?"

"We've got one. How do you know about warrants?"

"From TV. *Law & Order*."

"You're a fan of that show?" Jake asked.

He shrugged. "I've seen some of it."

"Then you know you're in a shit-ton of trouble here, Brecken," Jake said. "The way we see it, you used phones belonging to Ethan Hogan and Tomas Cambra to lure Luna Ahern to you. What did you do to her when you got her there?"

"I never saw her. Ethan and Tomas were with her."

"That's not what they told us."

"Wait, where are they?"

"In the hospital."

He clearly hadn't been expecting that news. Interesting to note that Brecken hadn't known the boys had escaped from the home where they'd been held.

"That's right," Hill said with a little grin. "They managed to escape. I can tell that's news to you. Were you hoping they'd never get out of wherever you two put them?"

"I... I haven't seen them in a couple of weeks."

"That's not what they said."

His eyes bugged as it seemed to set in with him that this wasn't a *Law & Order* episode, but a real police station with real officers sitting before him, accusing him of serious crimes.

"The girls must *love* you." Avery took Brecken by surprise with the shift in tone. "A handsome kid like you... They must be knocking down your door."

Jake sat back to let Avery take the lead on this line of questioning.

"Hardly," Brecken said with a hard edge to his voice. "They don't like me."

"Why not?"

"Who the fuck knows? They like Ethan and Tomas, but they won't even talk to me."

"That must make you mad."

"It's ridiculous. Look at them and look at me. If you were a girl, who would you rather be seen with?"

"Looks are important to them?"

"Looks are *everything*. I'm better-looking than both of them, so why do girls like them and not me? They're a couple of Chads."

"I'm not familiar with that term. Can you tell me what it means?"

Brecken sighed, as if this was a huge waste of his time. "A Chad is a guy who gets all the girls without doing much of anything besides being a douchebag. The Stacys, those are the girls who love the Chads and ignore the rest of us."

Even though he knew all this, Avery still took notes as if he were hearing the information for the first time.

"How do you know about Chads and Stacys?"

"My dad and his friends talk about them. My mom is a Stacy. She's with a Chad now."

Bingo, Jake thought. That could've been the inciting incident that'd led to him and his father becoming active in incel culture.

"Do you see your mom?" Avery asked.

"Fuck no. I want nothing to do with her. She's part of the problem."

"When was the last time you saw her?"

"When I was, like, ten or something."

"Do you know where she lives?"

"I think in Potomac. She married the Chad." He rolled his eyes. "That guy is the *biggest* douchebag ever."

"So you've met him?"

"Once. A long time ago." He shrugged. "They're nothing to us. My dad and I have been a team for years. We don't need anyone else."

"Why'd you want Ethan and Tomas to invite Luna out, then?"

"I didn't. They did that."

"Brecken, the text messages show you encouraging them to invite her and them resisting. The messages from them to her are from after they stopped responding to their parents. That means you knew her, and you used their phones to get her to come out so you could see her. Is that right? Was that the reason you bothered to kidnap Ethan and Tomas? Because she'd respond to them in a way she never would to you?"

Brecken's eyes narrowed, indicating his displeasure with the question. "I'd seen her around. She's nothing special. Just another bitch who thinks her shit doesn't stink."

"How do you know that about her if you've never spent time with her?"

"I know her type. They're all the same. They walk around like they're something important and people need to pay attention to them. But I see through that bullshit."

"Does your dad have a girlfriend?"

"Hell no. He says they aren't worth the bother."

"Has he had any girlfriends since your mom left him?"

"She didn't leave him. He kicked her out when he found out she was cheating on him. He made sure she got nothing but the clothes on her back, that lying cunt."

"Whoa," Avery said. "That's a nasty word to call your mother."

"Nasty people deserve nasty words."

The kid's eyes were so cold and devoid of emotion that Jake felt a chill go down his spine.

"Has your dad had any girlfriends since then?" Avery asked again.

"Nah, he says he's better off alone than dealing with their crap."

Neither one of them could attract female attention, so they'd become bitter toward all women, Jake concluded. He was sure Avery was thinking the same thing—that they needed to talk to Brecken's mother right away.

"Did your parents fight over you in court?"

"Yeah, she tried to take me away from him, but I wasn't having that. I didn't want to live with her and her asshole lover."

"What's her name?" Avery asked.

"Why does that matter?"

"Because I'm asking, and when the FBI asks you a question, it's a good idea to answer it."

"Her name is Melanie. She took Chad's last name. I don't remember it."

Jake got up and left the interrogation room to find Ruiz, who was still in her office after having pulled an all-nighter. "Brecken Mayfield's mother is named Melanie, and she's married to a guy in Potomac. There was a custody dispute over Brecken between her and his father, Asher. We need to find her and talk to her ASAP."

"I'm on it."

"Can you assign it to one of your people and go home to get some rest?"

"I'm invested. I want to find Luna."

"Thanks for sticking with it."

"No problem. I'll let you know what I find."

Jake nodded and returned to the interrogation room, where Avery was talking to Brecken about why he'd wanted to speak to Luna.

He shrugged. "I wanted to know why she was being such a bitch when I was nothing but nice to her."

"So that means you did talk to her?"

"I tried to. She took one look at me, made a disgusted face and wouldn't have anything to do with me after that. She didn't even know me, and she was, like, nah. You see why I hate girls like her?"

"How much do you hate girls like her?"

"A lot."

"Enough to kill one of them?"

His nonchalant position sent another chill down Jake's spine. "I didn't kill her, but if someone did, she probably had it coming."

"Is Luna dead?"

"How the fuck would I know? I just told you she won't have anything to do with me."

"When you used Ethan's and Tomas's phones to try to get her to come hang out, what happened?"

"She never showed up."

"Did you go looking for her?"

"Why would I waste my time on a cunt like her?"

"Why do you call women and girls that word?"

"My dad says that's the only way to describe them when they act like they own the world."

"Did he tell you that women find that word offensive?"

"What do we care if it hurts their delicate sensibilities?"

"Delicate sensibilities," Avery said incredulously. "Who taught you that phrase? Your father?"

Brecken shrugged as he shifted his weight in the seat.

"Does it ever occur to you that women can sense you hate them, and that might be why they stay away from you?"

"They can't tell that."

Avery gave him a skeptical look. "You don't think so?"

"Nah, they're too fucking stupid. The only thing they're good for is spreading their legs and spitting out babies."

"Did your dad teach you that, too?"

"It's the truth. I figured that out for myself."

"Where's Luna?" Jake asked.

"I got no fucking clue. I'd be the last person who'd know where that bitch is. You should ask Ethan and Tomas. They probably did something to her because she blew them off, too."

"How could they have harmed her when they were being held by you and your father, with zip ties on their wrists?"

"You can't prove we did anything to them."

"Actually, we can. We've got Crime Scene detectives at your house right now, combing through every inch of the place. When they find Ethan's and Tomas's DNA in your house, that'll tie them to you and your father."

"I'm sure it's easy enough for the cops to plant something to make us look guilty."

"When we review the video at the Wharf, we'll see them leaving with you two. And when we add that evidence to the DNA we're sure to find at your house after they sawed themselves loose using a pocketknife, that'll look pretty bad for you and your dad. You'll be charged as an adult. Do you know what that means?"

He gave them a blank look.

"You'll serve hard time with adult prisoners. They don't take too kindly to boys like you who mistreat women and girls. You're looking at a rough stretch when they find out what you did to Luna."

"I didn't do anything to her!"

"Did your dad do anything to her?"

"He doesn't even know her."

"Did you tell him she ignored you? Would that have made him mad on your behalf?"

"He knows she's another Stacy and that she's a nasty bitch, but he doesn't know her."

"Until you used Ethan and Tomas to lead him to her, right?"

"You'd have to ask him about that," he said, some of his bravado fading as it became clear they were building a solid case against him and his father.

"We'll do that," Jake said, "but before we do, you might want to think about helping us out. Tell us where Luna is and what happened to her, and we'll help you in return. Once we talk to your dad, he can tell us it was all you, that you killed her, and he found out about it after the fact. You'll go down for the whole thing."

A vein in Brecken's forehead began to pulse. "That's not how it happened!"

Jake sat back in his chair, feeling a sense of dread over Luna's fate. "How did it happen?"

Brecken crossed his arms defiantly. "I don't know."

"Then I guess it's time to talk to your dad," Jake said.

Both men stood to leave the room.

"Wait."

They turned back to him.

Jake noticed that he seemed more like a scared kid than an arrogant young man now that shit was getting real.

"If I tell you what you want to know, what happens to me?"

"That depends on what you tell us, if it leads to Luna and whether you harmed her in any way."

"I never touched her."

"Did your dad?"

His jaw set in an obstinate position, and that quickly, the angry young man had returned. "You'd have to ask him that."

Jake returned to the table, laid his hands flat on the surface and leaned in close to Brecken. "Where is she?"

When the kid hesitated, Jake slapped the table. "*Where the fuck is she?*"

"Th-there's a storage unit on Florida Ave. She might be there."

"Is she alive?"

"I... I don't know."

Jake put a pen and notepad on the table. "Write down the name of it and the unit number. Be quick about it."

He was satisfied to see Brecken's hand tremble as he wrote the information.

Jake snatched the pad off the table and made for the door, jogging straight to Ruiz's office.

"I was just coming to find you," she said.

"The son gave us the location of a storage unit on Florida Ave. Let's go."

"Let me know," Avery called after them.

"Will do."

CHAPTER TWENTY

Jake waited while Ruiz grabbed a pair of bolt cutters from the corner of her office, and then she followed him to his SUV. On the way to Florida Avenue, she called in the Emergency Response Team for backup and requested EMS at the scene.

"You keep bolt cutters in your office?"

"I've needed them before, and it's easier to have my own than to find some when I need them."

He was almost afraid to ask, "When have you needed them in the past?"

"Similar situation to this. A few times." She looked over at him. "What'd the kid say about Luna?"

"After he claimed he knew nothing about her or her whereabouts, we told him he'd be charged as an adult and was looking at a long stretch in prison with men who wouldn't take kindly to him harming a young girl. That seemed to get his attention, but he says he had nothing to do with anything that might've happened to her."

"Sure, he didn't."

"The kid gave me the creeps. Said the nastiest stuff about

women, raised by an incel father who was done dirty by a Stacy who married her douchebag Chad."

"The custody battle between them was intense," Ruiz said. "A search of our database brought up numerous calls for assistance from the mother, which led to a restraining order against the father that he regularly violated."

"Why didn't this come up when we did a search for him earlier?"

"It was filed under domestic incidents, which don't show up during a routine search. He was held for three weeks at one point and told to stay away from her and his son, but he refused to."

"How'd he end up with custody, then?"

"The kid kept running away from home and turning up with the father, so the courts finally gave the kid what he wanted."

"That's crazy."

"The mother agreed. She filed numerous lawsuits against the District and the courts that never went anywhere because the kid was old enough to say he didn't want to live with her. The father demanded that all the charges against him be dropped because he was acting in his son's best interests. The court dropped the charges with warnings for him to stay away from his ex-wife and her new husband or face new charges."

"She might've been better off losing custody of that kid. He's a real prize."

"Who knows what he would've been like if he'd been raised by his mother instead of his incel father?"

"True.

"She was done dirty in this case."

"I want to talk to her."

"Yeah, me, too."

"He says he hasn't seen her since he was ten, but I spent thirty minutes with him, which was just enough time to see who he's grown up to be under his father's misogynistic tutelage. It's truly horrifying."

"Yes, it is."

"Did you know about this incel culture stuff before this case?" Jake asked.

"Unfortunately, yes. I've read about it. I believe it's factored into some SVU cases where men took what they felt they deserved from the women who'd disdained them. There was a double murder in Baltimore that was tied to an incel punishing the woman who rejected him. He also murdered her new boyfriend."

"It's so sick. They feel like they have a right to these women, regardless of whether they're wanted or not."

"They're never wanted, which becomes the problem. Rather than look internally to figure out what would make them more attractive to women, they blame the women for all of it and often lash out with violence or doxing or other forms of harassment."

"I can't wrap my head around this."

"It's one of the many ways the internet has been a curse. It's given people with these sorts of grievances a place to find others who agree with them. When they're in an echo chamber with everyone on the same page, there's no one to say, 'Hey, what you're saying is sick and twisted, and you might be the problem.'"

"People say stuff online they'd never say out loud."

"Right, and when everyone they're saying it to agrees with them, it gives them permission to pursue these dark thoughts." Ruiz's phone buzzed with a text. "Emergency Response is in place and ready to assist."

Jake's stomach twisted with anxiety. "I'm so scared of what we're going to find in that storage unit."

"Me, too."

After having dinner with the kids and going to bed early, Sam slept fitfully during the night. At five a.m., she checked her phone to see if there were any developments in the search for

Luna. She'd received a text from Captain Malone an hour ago, saying they had a lead on her whereabouts and were following up, but nothing since then.

Thinking about what Luna might be going through had Sam wide awake and wanting to help if she could. Moving carefully so she wouldn't disturb Nick, she got out of bed and went into the adjoining bathroom, closing the door behind her. She called the number she'd been given to arrange Secret Service escorts after hours.

"Good morning, Mrs. Cappuano. This is Agent Quigley. How may I help you?"

"They've got you working the overnight shift, Q?"

"Yes, ma'am."

"I need to go into work. Would you please arrange that?"

"Absolutely, ma'am. I'll meet you in the lobby in ten minutes?"

"Perfect, thank you."

"My pleasure, ma'am."

That was a lot of *ma'am* in one conversation, she thought as she rushed through a shower and got dressed in jeans and a pullover sweatshirt. He probably had supervisors listening to him. She put her hair up in a clip, applied some moisturizer and mascara and declared herself fit for public consumption.

She was tiptoeing out of their bedroom when Nick called to her.

"Where're you going?" He'd pushed himself up on one elbow.

"Into work for a bit. There've been some developments, and I'm awake. May as well help out if I can."

"I thought you were taking a break."

"I will, after we find Luna. I can't bear knowing she's out there somewhere... dealing with God knows what. I'll be home as soon as I can."

"Be safe out there."

Sam returned to the bed to kiss him. "I always am. Agent Q is taking me."

"I wasn't going to ask."

"Look at us, making progress all over the place."

His smile sent her off with a warm feeling inside. No matter what might be upside down in her life, he was always the one who kept her right side up with his unwavering love and devotion. She'd never forget him calling out to work as president of the United States to spend the day supporting her while Ethan was missing.

Thank God her nephew was back with his family and recovering from his ordeal. She still couldn't think about the many possible outcomes without her knees feeling weak. So as she went down the stairs to meet Agent Q, she didn't think about that so she wouldn't fall. The last thing she needed was another injury when her fractured hip had finally healed.

She felt out of sorts, off her game and emotionally exhausted, but she still wanted to be at work to help out if she could. Doing something about whatever was causing her anxiety always made her feel better.

"Good morning, ma'am," Q said when he greeted her in the lobby. Even though she'd told him to call her Sam, he'd never do that when the ushers were around.

"Morning, Agent Q, and thank you, Harold."

The older man helped her into her coat. "My pleasure, ma'am."

At some point in the last few months, she'd become accustomed to the routine at the White House, having people help her into her coat and hold doors for her. What would it be like, she wondered, to go back to real life without ushers and butlers and room service? She'd miss the ushers, the room service and the other perks, and the kids would probably be ruined forever by these three years in the White House.

But what a way to go, she thought as she slid into the back seat of the warm SUV while Q held the door for her.

"Did you have to ask Vernon's permission to drive me?" she asked when they were on the way.

He laughed. "No, ma'am. But I'm sure he's being told as we speak that we're on a rogue mission without him. This is Agent Lewis, by the way."

Sam leaned forward to make eye contact with the young agent. She had dark hair and eyes and a serious look to her. "Nice to meet you, Agent Lewis."

"Likewise, ma'am."

"Do we need to tell Agent Lewis the rules of the SUV and refresh your memory as well?"

"No, ma'am. I mean, Sam. I told her we're on a first-name basis in the SUV."

"Excellent."

"What's your first name, Agent Lewis?"

"Vivian, ma'am."

"Ah, I love that name. I might've named a daughter that if I'd had one the old-fashioned way."

"It was my grandmother's name."

"It's a lovely name. Do you go by Viv?"

"That's what my family calls me. You should feel free to do so as well."

"Thank you."

"I can't believe we're supposed to call you Sam," Lewis said, smiling back at her.

"Well, you're not *supposed* to, but I like to keep it real when it's just us LEOs on the job, you know?"

"It's an honor to work on your detail. I respect what you're doing, keeping your job while serving as first lady."

"Am I serving as first lady, or do I have an amazing staff that makes it seem as if I am? Hmm..."

The agents laughed.

"The new photos of you and the kids are really nice," Q said.

"Mr. Fenty did an amazing job of making us look good," Sam said of the White House photographer.

As they chatted, Sam sent a text to Malone. *Couldn't sleep so coming in. Any news?*

He didn't reply right away, so she hoped that meant they were in the midst of rescuing Luna. She was on pins and needles as they drove through the start of rush hour in the capital city.

ON THE WAY to the storage facility, Ruiz had tracked down the owner, called to wake him up and told him what they needed. He was waiting for them when they arrived and shook hands with Jake and Ruiz as they introduced themselves.

"Normally, I'd want a warrant, but I'm not going to require that in this case."

Jake wanted to tell him about exigent circumstances and how his requirements didn't matter when someone's life might be on the line, but he held his tongue since the guy was cooperating.

"Thank you for the cooperation," Ruiz said. "We appreciate it."

"Right this way."

Ruiz signaled for her Emergency Response Team to follow them into the cavernous building.

Jake's eyes adjusted to the bright fluorescent lighting as they were led down a winding series of corridors that led to Mayfield's unit.

"It's that one," the owner said, pointing.

"Thank you very much." On a hunch, Jake added, "While you wait for us, will you please look to see if the owner of this unit has others here?"

The realization that he couldn't stay to watch what happened next clearly disappointed the man, but Jake didn't have time to care. He stared him down.

"Yeah, I'll do that."

"Thank you."

Watching him walk away, Jake wondered why anyone would want to be part of this nightmare if they didn't have to be.

Ruiz used her bolt cutters to remove the padlock on the unit.

As she raised the garage-like door, Jake held his breath, trying to prepare himself for what they might find.

A rank smell greeted them as Ruiz shone a flashlight into the unit, landing on a huddled form in the corner.

Ruiz signaled for the others to stay back as she went in for a closer look. "It's Luna," she called back to them. "Pulse is faint. Let's get EMS in here, stat."

Jake made the call for EMS and ordered the rest of Ruiz's team to stand down.

As the paramedics rushed in, Ruiz stepped out. She had tears in her eyes as she shook her head. "Who does that to a child?"

"A fucking monster. That's who."

"I... I need to call her parents."

"Want me to do it?" he asked, noting the hard-charging captain was seriously undone by what she'd seen.

"No, I've got it. I just need a second."

He watched as she pulled herself together to call Luna's mother to tell her they'd found her daughter, and she was being taken to GW's ER.

Jake could hear the woman's screams coming through the phone.

"She's in rough shape, ma'am," Ruiz added. "Please prepare yourselves..." After a pause, she said, "Yes, we'll meet you there."

"I want to call in Erica Lucas from SVU," Jake said.

Ruiz nodded. "Good idea."

Jake made the call to Lucas, apologized for waking her up and explained the situation with Luna.

"I'll meet you at GW."

"Thanks, Erica."

"No problem."

Of course, it was a huge problem to be called out of bed at the crack of dawn when you weren't due to work for a couple more hours, but Erica was the best when it came to sensitive situations that might include sexual assault. This child deserved the best.

When the paramedics brought Luna out, her bruised, lifeless face made Jake want to kill someone. The paramedics' urgency indicated that her condition was critical.

On the way out of the storage facility, Jake called Joe Farnsworth.

"Yeah, what's up?" the chief asked, accustomed to middle-of-the-night and early-morning phone calls.

"We've got Luna Ahern. She was in a storage unit on Florida Ave and is in rough shape."

"Good God. She was in a storage unit?"

"Yeah, the Mayfield kid told us we might find her there."

"Is she... Was she..."

"We don't know anything yet. She's on the way to GW. We've notified the parents and called in Lucas."

"Keep me posted, will you?"

"You got it."

"Are you okay?"

"I guess so. I just hope we found her in time."

"I'll say a prayer."

"She needs all the prayers she can get. I'll be back to you when I know more."

"Thanks."

The owner of the facility chased after Jake. "He has three more units."

Jake gestured to members of Ruiz's team, and a sergeant stepped forward. "The guy who did this has three more units here. Take the bolt cutters and check them. Call in Crime Scene if needed and let me know what you find."

"Yes, sir," the sergeant said.

Ruiz was on another call as they got into Jake's SUV to head for GW.

While Ruiz finished her call, Jake focused on the road as he sped through the start of rush hour with his lights flashing, filled with dread over what they would learn about Luna's ordeal—and what might be found in the other storage units. Considering the info that they'd gotten from the informant who'd approached Cruz, anything was possible. Jake had seen a lot of awful shit during his decades on the job, but anything involving kids was always the worst.

Cases from more than twenty years ago still haunted him. While he sometimes forgot the details of a case, the youngest victims always stayed with him. They became his, and he honored them by remembering them.

His phone rang with a call from Sam. "Hey."

"Heard you found Luna."

"Yeah, she's on the way to GW. We're right behind them."

"What's your next move?"

"After I stop at the hospital, I'm going back to HQ to have a word with Asher Mayfield."

"I'm there now. You want me to take it?"

"Wait for me, and we'll talk to him together since Ruiz will be going home to get some sleep. I need someone to keep me from killing him."

"I'll be here, Cap."

CHAPTER TWENTY-ONE

While she waited for Malone to arrive, Sam read the reports on the murder of Dale Carver. Gonzo and Freddie had outlined what they'd learned during the canvass of the hotel guests and their discussions with hotel management.

Archie's team was still reviewing the film, and Freddie had spent most of the previous day assisting with that laborious task. He and Walters had put together the sequence of events around Carver's room, indicating two men had been involved and had slipped in and out of the sixth-floor area without showing their faces on camera.

Malone had requested warrants for Carver's cell phone and the data, and they were awaiting that so they could sift through the data.

Freddie had made a note about wanting to request warrants for the wife's phone, too. *Working a hunch here,* he'd noted. *Understand we need more to request this one. Will work on that tomorrow.*

Sam got on her computer and looked up the Carver family from Spokane, Washington. She searched for Dale and Trisha Carver and was led to a Facebook account for Trisha, who had posted photos of their young children, a boy and a girl who were adorable blonds with big blue eyes. Their mother had documented their activities and posted about being a busy mom. The most recent photos showed a newborn with Dale and Trisha, as well as a photo with the three siblings.

So pleased to announce the arrival of Zachery Paul, born on March 23, weighing in at seven pounds, eight ounces and twenty inches in length. Mom and baby are both doing great. Big sister, Reagan, and big brother, Cody, are thrilled to meet baby Zach. We are blessed.

Sam hurt for a woman she'd never met and might never know. To have three young children, including a newborn, and get the call that her husband had been murdered—it was an unimaginable tragedy. She wondered why Freddie wanted a look at Trisha's phone and made a note to ask him.

Detectives Dani Carlucci and Gigi Dominguez came into the pit, stopping short outside her open door.

"What're you doing here, Lieutenant?" Carlucci asked.

"Couldn't sleep, so I figured I'd come in and make myself useful."

"Did you hear that Luna Ahern has been located?" Dominguez asked.

"I did. I just talked to Captain Malone."

"We heard she's in bad shape," Carlucci said, frowning. "They aren't sure she's going to make it. You'd have to be a fucking animal to leave a child locked in a storage unit, not to mention what else she may have endured."

Dominguez shuddered.

Her taller partner put an arm around her. "Sorry."

"I'm fine."

Gigi had been attacked and sexually assaulted in her home by the ex-girlfriend of Detective Cameron Green, who was now involved with Gigi.

Understanding that Gigi didn't want to be treated differently, Sam said, "Anything new on the Carver case?"

"The financials are interesting," Gigi said. "Everything is in the wife's name. Dale didn't have so much as a bank account to call his own."

"What did he do for work?"

"He was in sales with an agricultural company and was here for meetings with USDA."

"The wife's sister told Gonzo that he was a recovering addict, so that might be why everything is in her name."

"I saw that Freddie made a note about getting warrants for her phone," Sam said. "What's the thinking there?"

"His theory was that if Dale had started using again, maybe she hired someone to deal with him while he was out of town so she could be rid of him once and for all," Dani said.

"They both have life insurance policies worth two-point-five million dollars each," Gigi said.

Sam let out a low whistle. "That's a hefty amount."

"They were issued more than ten years ago," Gigi said. "I dug a little deeper and found that Trisha Carver's father owns a huge insurance company in the Spokane area. It might've been something he set up for them."

Sam mulled over the new information. "So it's not like she just got this huge policy for him and then bumped him off. She's known all along that she'd cash in if he died."

"They both knew that, which is a hell of a piece of information to walk through life with as a married couple," Dani said. Affecting a darker tone, she added, "'Don't piss me off. You're worth more to me dead than alive.'"

"How often do you suppose one of them trotted that out during a fight?" Gigi asked.

"Right?" Dani said.

"I want to know more about his addiction and recovery," Sam said.

"We can talk to the sister in the morning," Dani said. "She could fill in some more of the blanks."

"I have her info here in the report," Sam said. "I'll call her."

"Remember, they're three hours behind us," Dani said. "Not

that I think they're getting much sleep with this going on and a new baby to care for."

"Thanks for the reminder," Sam said. "I probably wouldn't have thought of the time difference."

"How's Ethan?" Gigi asked.

"Last I heard, he was resting comfortably."

"And Tracy?" Dani asked.

"Trying to recover her nervous system."

"I can't imagine," Gigi said. "What a terrible thing. Did Ethan say anything about what happened?"

"Just that Brecken Mayfield befriended them, and the dad gave them a ride. They were pushed into Asher's car, zip-tied and their phones apparently used to lure Luna before they were shut off. Ethan said he hadn't texted Luna, so the texts must've come from the Mayfields."

"It's so sick," Dani said. "All because Luna wasn't interested in Brecken?"

"We believe that was the primary reason."

"This is why I stay away from all men," Dani said. "How do you know which ones you can trust?"

"You trust the one who never wavers in his devotion to you," Gigi said quietly, speaking from some experience. "You choose the one who'd push you out of the way of a speeding car and take the hit so you aren't hurt. You choose the one who shows up, every day, with the same exact intentions he had the day before. That's the one you choose."

"Well said," Sam said softly. "And I'll add that you choose the one you couldn't possibly live without once you know he's in the world."

"Yes," Gigi said. "That, too. For sure."

"You guys got lucky. Not everyone does."

"That's very true," Gigi said, "but just because you haven't met him yet doesn't mean he's not out there waiting to find you."

"If you say so," Dani said with a grin for her partner. "For now, I'm all about avoidance."

. . .

At seven, Dani and Gigi handed off to the day shift and went home to get some rest. On the way out of the pit, Sam saw Gigi squeeze Cameron's arm before they parted company. She loved the two of them together and had encouraged their relationship. They rarely worked on the same shift, and neither of them supervised the other, so it was no big deal to her.

She enjoyed seeing them happy, especially after what they'd been through with exes who'd refused to take "no more" for an answer. Gigi had been badly beaten by her ex-boyfriend, and then they'd both faced a nightmare at the hands of Cameron's ex-girlfriend Jaycee.

They were still facing a wrongful death lawsuit from Jaycee's family, which claimed she and her mother had died because of Cameron and Gigi. That was false. Sam was convinced the lawsuit would go nowhere, but it was still stressful for her detectives—and friends—to have to deal with that on top of the emotional fallout from the trauma.

When the day team was gathered in the conference room, Sam updated them on the developments from overnight. "I'm still waiting to hear something about Luna's condition. I heard from Tracy that they all got some sleep overnight, and they expect Ethan and Tomas to be discharged later today."

The others expressed relief that both boys had been found safe.

"Moving on to the Carver case, Gonzo and Freddie, can you please provide an update on what we know so far?"

Gonzo began with a recitation of the facts of the case thus far and the canvass he'd overseen at the hotel. Freddie picked it up with the review he'd done with Sergeant Walters from IT and how that part of the investigation was ongoing.

He'd no sooner said that than Walters came to the door, holding up a thumb drive. "Cruz asked me to bring this down and walk you through it."

Walters went to the computer terminal at the front of the room and projected video onto the screen that showed a man in a black hoodie strolling confidently through the lobby toward the elevators. "We picked him up getting off the elevator on the sixth floor about twenty minutes before the time of death assigned by the ME. He goes into the ice room and doesn't come out. But what's interesting is that another guy, dressed similarly, entered the sixth floor from the stairwell. Here he comes now. He knocks on the door to Carver's room, and he's admitted as if he'd been expected.

"Both men ensured their faces weren't picked up on video, which means they knew where the cameras were."

Which spoke to premeditation, Sam thought.

"Keep watching," Walter said.

A few minutes after the guy was admitted to the room, Carver came out, carrying the ice bucket.

"Wait for it," Walters said.

Another minute passed before the other guy ducked out of the ice room and exited the hallway at the stairwell.

"Total setup," Gonzo said.

"I was thinking professional job," Cameron added.

"Well done, Sergeant Walters and Detective Cruz," Sam said. "Thank you for your hard work on this case."

"Glad to help." Walters ejected the thumb drive and handed it to Gonzo, who was seated closest to him. "We'll continue to work on reviewing on the outside cameras in the area to see if we can find anything else that might help. We'll keep you posted."

"Thanks again, Sarge," Gonzo said. "Great job."

Walters was smiling as he left the room.

"Well," Detective Neveah Charles said, "now we know how it went down. What's our next move?"

"When considering motive," Gonzo said, "I keep coming back to the wife."

"What would be her motive in having her husband killed

when she's got three little kids at home?" Detective Matt O'Brien asked.

"Two things," Sam said. "It would remove her drug-addict husband from her life, and she'd get a two-point-five-million-dollar life insurance payout."

O'Brien released a low whistle. "Wow. That's a serious policy."

"They each had one," Sam said. "Carlucci and Dominguez found them overnight. Apparently, Trisha Carver's father is a big insurance broker. They've had the policies for years."

"Possibly a wedding gift?" Cameron asked.

"Maybe," Sam said.

"Is that a weird gift?" Freddie asked. "I mean, who's thinking about death when they're getting married?"

"That'd literally be the dad's job, though," Charles said. "To think about worst-case scenarios."

"I was talking about that with Carlucci and Dominiguez overnight, and Carlucci made a good point. Wouldn't you remind your spouse, during every fight and rough patch, that they were worth more to you dead than alive?"

"I mean, I wouldn't say that to Elin," Freddie said, "but I can picture people doing that if they weren't happily married."

"The sister-in-law said the drug problem was intense for years before he got clean," Gonzo said.

"Roll with me here," Sam said. "Say he got clean after a long, difficult struggle and was doing well. Things were good again, and they decided to have that third baby to celebrate having survived something that could've ruined everything. And then, after the baby arrives, or maybe even before, she finds out he's using again. The anger would've been epic, right?"

"Totally," Gonzo said. "She probably wanted to strangle him with her own hands. I was continuously surprised—and thankful—that Christina never did that to me."

"But would a mother of young kids go so far as to hire professionals to deal with him?" Charles asked. "And if so, why do it in a place that's teeming with cameras? Why not jump him on the street?"

"Because," Sam said slowly as the pieces fell together, "she wanted it to look like a drug deal gone wrong. She wanted that to be the story she could tell people afterward, that she'd done all she could to help him, but in the end, it just wasn't enough. She'd rather live fat on the insurance money without him around to ruin everything."

The others were silent as they pondered that.

"In a way," Gonzo said, "I wouldn't blame her for wanting him gone, but she could've divorced him."

"But that two-point-five mil would make all the difference to her as a single mom," Freddie said. "She could be a full-time mother and pay everything, including college, for all three kids without breaking a sweat."

"We're not going to entertain the possibility that it really was a drug deal gone bad?" O'Brien asked.

"We'll entertain all possibilities," Sam said, "but I need someone to get to Spokane today to get her phone—and let's do the sister's while we're at it. Any volunteers?"

A moment of silence followed the question.

"I'll go," Charles finally said.

"Thank you, Detective Charles. Let's get to work on those warrants while you get yourself to Washington state and work out backup with the Spokane Police Department."

"I'll handle the warrants," Gonzo said.

"Is there a procedure for handling travel?" Charles asked. "I haven't had to know before now."

"I'll help you with that," Sam said. "In the meantime, Cam and Matt, I want you to look into the drug-deal-gone-bad angle. We should be getting the warrants for Carver's phone any minute and see what you can find out about his movements since he arrived in town."

"On it," Green said for himself and his partner.

"Let's get to work." Sam gestured for Charles to come into

her office to arrange travel. "Thank you for volunteering. I appreciate it."

"No problem."

"What do we know about Spokane?" Sam asked as she logged on to the department's travel portal to look for same-day flights.

"It's located on the eastern side of the state."

"Did you remember that from high school geography?"

Charles grinned. "Nah, I checked online during the meeting."

"Ah, okay. That's better than you being so smart you remember everything you ever learned."

"I remember most of it."

"Don't gloat." While she waited for the results of the search, Sam glanced at Charles, who was twisting her hands as she stood next to the desk. "Everything okay?"

"Yes, of course, it's just that... Well, I've never flown before."

"*Never?*"

The young woman shook her head. "Haven't really had the opportunity."

"This is a long, involved trip for your first time. I can send someone else."

"No, it's fine. I want to do it."

"You're sure?"

She gave a brave nod. "Someone has to go. It may as well be me."

"I appreciate you, Detective. You're always willing to do whatever needs to be done, and that'll go a long way toward ensuring a successful career."

"That's my only goal."

"Do you think you'd want to sit on the aisle or next to a window?"

"What do you suggest?"

"Well, if you have to pee every five seconds like I do, you'd want the aisle. If you want to be able to see outside, you'll want the window. It's pretty cool to look at the clouds and see the mountains and stuff."

"I think I'd like the window."

"Got it. You'll leave here at four forty-eight this afternoon, connect through Minneapolis/Saint Paul and arrive in Spokane around nine local time. We'll get you a hotel by the airport, and you can see Mrs. Carver in the morning. We'll set the return for two twenty tomorrow afternoon and connect through MSP again. You'll land here around midnight local time. All of this can be shifted around if need be. Sound good?"

"Yep," she said.

Sam rolled her chair toward the file cabinet, opened a drawer and produced two hard-plastic boxes. "One for your weapon and the other for the ammunition. You have to put them in your checked luggage and disclose to the gate agent that they're in your bag. You can only carry onboard with advance planning that we don't have time to do now."

"Got it. One more question—how do you want me to get from the hotel to Mrs. Carver's house? I could do a cab or Uber. Whatever is best."

"A rental car would be easier. This is a lot for your first time, Neveah. Are you sure you don't want me to ask someone else?"

"I'll figure it out like everyone else does."

"All right, come sit over here and type in your birthday and the other info they need for the plane ticket. Make sure you spell everything correctly, or they'll stop you at security. You have a Real ID, right?"

"Yes, I do."

"Excellent."

Sam got up to cede her chair to Neveah and sat in one of her visitor chairs to check her phone. When she looked up, Neveah was smiling. "What?"

"Just checking out the view from the catbird seat."

Sam laughed. "Don't get too comfortable over there."

"Oh, I never would. This seat is all yours."

"I can see it being yours someday."

The young woman's eyes went wide. "You can? Really?"

"Hell yes. You remind me a lot of myself as a young officer."

"That's a huge compliment."

"Don't suck up."

"Then don't say stuff like that!"

They shared a laugh.

"You have to know what it means to me to be mentored by you," Neveah said.

"I do know, and I'm excited to see the places you'll go. But right now, I need you to go to Spokane."

"Should I click on 'purchase' if everything is in?"

"Go for it."

"It's more than a thousand dollars! What the heck?"

"Welcome to last-minute air travel, my friend. Now let's do the hotel and rental car."

CHAPTER TWENTY-TWO

After Sam had sent Neveah home to pack for her overnight trip, she went out to the pit to see what the others were doing. Matt and Cam were huddled around Cameron's computer. Gonzo was working on the warrants, and Freddie was writing updates to the reports on the Carver case.

"What can I do, peeps?"

"We got the warrant, and Walters did the dump on Carver's phone," Cameron said. "We're dividing the data to track down the contacts, starting with the local ones."

"I can do some, if you want."

"We've got it, but we'll let you know if we need help."

"Sounds good."

As she turned to return to her office, Captain Malone came in from the hallway that led to the morgue.

Sam met his gaze.

He shook his head.

Her heart dropped into her stomach. "No."

"I'm going to fucking murder that son of a bitch Mayfield."

Sam had never seen the captain look more furious or heartbroken.

"What he did to that little girl…"

As her mind raced with a million thoughts—primarily that she'd have to tell Tracy this news, and Tracy would have to tell Ethan—Sam took the captain by the arm and led him into her office, closing the door and nudging him toward one of her visitor chairs. She sat next to him, keeping a hand on his arm.

He exhaled and dropped his head into his hands, his shoulders shaking with quiet sobs.

Tears rolled silently down her face as she absorbed the news as well as the captain's emotional reaction, which broke her heart all over again. Thinking of Luna's parents and everyone who'd loved her was almost more than she could bear.

"She was just a baby," Malone said many minutes later. "A baby with her whole life ahead of her." He wiped the tears from his face and made a visible effort to pull himself together. "There were three more storage units with kids in them," Malone said. "Thirty-two girls waiting to be sent who knows where."

"Good God. Are they okay?"

"From what Emergency Response reported, they're mostly in decent condition, but of course they're terrified after being held for who knows how long in dark storage units with no food, water or toilets. They said the smell was unholy."

"This tracks with what the informant told Freddie, about Asher Mayfield being a major trafficker."

"Yeah." Malone took a deep breath and blew it out.

"What do you need?"

"SVU and Crime Scene have taken the lead at the storage units. They're working on getting medical care for the girls and reuniting them with their parents. They've also arrested the owner of the facility as he would've had access to the cameras and had to have known what those units were being used for." He sat up straighter, took another breath and said, "Let's get Asher Mayfield in a room."

"Take another minute, Cap."

"We need to put that fucking monster in a cage for the rest of his life."

"I understand, but we have to do this right, as you certainly know. And before we can do that, we have to get our emotions in check."

He took a deep, shuddering breath and released it slowly. "You're right."

"Maybe it shouldn't be us with Mayfield. We're too close to it."

The look he gave her was full of rage and heartbreak. "We need the A team on this one. We can't leave anything to chance." After another cleansing breath, he added, "I requested warrants for father-and-son DNA last night, and they came through this morning. Lindsey will take care of that after she returns from picking up Luna."

"Should we confirm the DNA is a match before we talk to him?"

"I don't think we need to wait for that. We've got enough to start with." He ran his fingers through his wiry gray hair as he tried to find his composure. "Sorry about the outburst."

"Please don't be. It's horrible."

"How's Ethan?"

"Tracy said they all got some rest."

"Good to hear. I'm going to grab a shower, put on some clean clothes and get my head together."

"Do you want me to get Charity back here?"

"Yeah, give me an hour."

"I'll take care of it."

Sam stayed seated after he left, undone by her friend and mentor's despair. He was someone she counted on to always hold it together. To see him broken by a case was rare, if not unprecedented.

Freddie came in and stopped short when he found her in one of the visitor chairs. "What's going on?"

"Luna Ahern is dead, and they found thirty-two more kids in various conditions in the other storage units."

"Oh God, no."

"Malone took Luna's death hard. He just left to shower and change before we talk to Asher Mayfield."

Freddie took the chair recently vacated by Malone. "Are you okay?"

"I'm devastated for her, her family and everyone else who loved her, as well as all the other kids and families who've suffered at their hands."

"Wouldn't we have heard about thirty-two missing kids?" Freddie asked.

"Not if they were plucked from all over the place. I honestly cannot believe the details of this entire nightmare case. I'm not going to lie—I'm shook by it."

"I know. I am, too. Just when we think we've seen everything…"

"Yeah, exactly." Sam stood, feeling weary after the lack of sleep and overload of emotions. "I need to check in with Tracy and tell her we found Luna."

"I came to tell you that IT reported there was no other activity around Carver's room at the time of death. We've been through every minute of the sixth-floor film twice, and there was nothing else. They're looking outside the hotel now and will let us know if they find anything related."

"Thanks for closing that loop. O'Brien's point was well taken earlier that we can't assume it was the wife, but all my instincts are pointing in that direction."

"As are mine. Is Charles good to go get the phones?"

"Yeah, she's booked and will hopefully be back late tomorrow night. She'll be flying for the first time."

"Oh wow. Is she okay with that?"

"She says she is."

"You want me to go with her?"

"I appreciate that, but I'm going to let her do it. She says she can handle it, and I need to give her the chance."

"Okay, but if you change your mind, I'll go with her."

"Thanks, Freddie." She went to sit behind her desk to call

Tracy while he went to the pit to report the new information to the others.

Tracy answered on the third ring. "Hey."

"How's it going?'

"Pretty good. The boys are being discharged this morning."

"That's great news."

"Have you heard anything about Luna?"

Sam didn't want to tell Tracy that news. "Are you with Ethan?"

"He's in the bathroom."

"Trace…"

"Oh God. Don't tell me she's dead."

"I'm so sorry to have to tell you that."

Tracy let out a wail full of pure distress. "Oh, Sam. What in the world? These kids are *babies*. She was *thirteen*."

"I know. It's horrifying."

"Her poor mother. I talked to her last night and saw her on the news pleading for her daughter's safe return…"

Tracy's sobs echoed through the phone, bringing new tears to Sam's eyes.

"Other missing kids were found, too," Sam said as Tracy gasped, "which is the one good thing to come out of this, that they'll be reunited with their families."

"What does all this mean for Ethan and Tomas?" Tracy asked hesitantly. "Are they in trouble?"

"Not that I know of. From what they told us, they were used as pawns in a much larger scheme."

"It's unbearable. Every bit of this is truly unbearable."

"I know, and I'm so sorry."

"I'm *enraged*, Sam. I can't imagine how I'll stay with Mike after this."

"Don't say that when everything is so raw. Take some time."

"What time do I need to recognize that he allowed something that ended up changing our lives forever, and not in a good way? If only he'd listened to me, our son would've had nothing to do with any of this. Now his name is permanently linked to the murder of a young girl. It's beyond horrifying."

"It is, but, Trace, don't do anything you might regret later."

"I won't regret it. I've got another child to think about, too. His judgment is whacked, and it led to this. I can't stay with him."

Sam couldn't picture her sister without the brother-in-law who'd been in their lives since Sam was in high school.

"I know you love him," Tracy said.

"We all do. When I think of him, the first thing I remember is how he came into your life and Brooke's and never blinked an eye about becoming her father."

Tracy was crying too hard to speak for a moment. "I'll always love him for that and a million other things... But this... I can't live with this. I told him it was a huge mistake, and he said I was being dramatic. He wouldn't even listen to my point of view. How do I go forward with him after that?"

"Consider this... Even if you're not with him, he can still allow them to do things you wouldn't approve of."

"Not if I sue him for full custody of Ethan and Abby."

"Tracy..."

"I have to go. The doctor is coming to talk to us."

The line went dead. Sam held the phone in her hand for a long moment as she processed what Tracy had said. Not only did she plan to leave Mike, but she was going to sue him for full custody of the kids. What would've been unfathomable to her days ago was now her sister's reality.

Freddie returned to the office. "What's wrong?"

"I talked to Tracy just now."

"Is Ethan okay?"

"He's doing as well as can be expected, but Tracy... She said she's leaving Mike and suing for custody of the kids."

"*What?*"

"My feelings exactly. I can't imagine a world without them as a couple. He's been in my life since I was a freshman in high school. He's... Well, he's the big brother I never had, you know?"

Freddie closed the office door and took a seat. "I know he is. Do you think she'll go through with it?"

"She's so angry. I've never seen her like this. Apparently, Mike totally blew her off when she expressed concerns about letting Ethan go out with his friends. She said he was too young for that kind of responsibility, but Mike was okay with it. And once Ethan knew that, there wasn't much Tracy could say."

"Their united front was breached."

"Yes, exactly. And now everyone in their lives knows Ethan was missing, and his name will forever be tied to Luna's death, even though he had no direct role in it. How does she not blame Mike for all of it?"

"Playing devil's advocate here... Someone else is responsible for Luna's death, not Mike."

"But if Ethan hadn't been allowed out unsupervised, he never would've met Brecken or his father and wouldn't be tied to this whole nightmare."

"That's true, but Mike didn't kidnap them or murder Luna. I hope Tracy is able to see that forest for the trees."

"It was a crime of opportunity, Freddie. Mike gave Ethan the opportunity to be caught up in something like this, which was exactly what Tracy was afraid of when she objected to him having that kind of freedom at eleven."

After a long moment of quiet, Freddie said, "Elin is pregnant."

Sam gasped. "That's amazing news! Congratulations."

"I'm terrified. I was on my way home to tell her I thought we shouldn't have kids after everything we've learned during this case. And then... she told me..." His chin wobbled ever so slightly.

Sam got up, walked around the desk and leaned over to hug him tightly. "You'll be an amazing father, and Elin will be an awesome mother."

"What'll we do when our eleven-year-old wants the same freedom all his friends have?"

"You'll say, 'Hell no, mister, you're far too young for that.'"

"I'll want to say that when he's sixteen, seventeen, eighteen…"

Sam pulled back from the hug and sat in the other chair. "The best thing you can do is educate him or her about the reasons you're saying no without terrifying them about the world we live in."

"How exactly does one walk that fine line?"

"Carefully. I have no doubt whatsoever that by the time that happens, you'll be more than up to the task."

"I wish I were as confident."

"I'll be there to help you through it. I promise."

"You'd better be, because I'm going to need all the help I can get."

"Let's not dwell on the future. Let's celebrate the baby on the way who'll make all our lives so much sweeter just by existing. I can't wait to meet my little niece or nephew."

"His aunt and uncle, the first couple," Freddie said with a laugh.

"Nah, we're just Aunt Sam and Uncle Nick to him—or her."

"I'm gonna be a dad," he said with a look of pure wonder.

"I couldn't be happier for you and Elin."

"Thanks. We're pretty happy, too."

"Stay in that place for as long as you can, and don't worry about the future. You'll be ready for it when the time comes. We'll make sure of it."

"Thank you for always being there for me."

"Likewise. If Mike's the big brother I never had, you're the little brother, and you're stuck with me forever."

"That's fine by me. What's our next move on the case?"

"Malone and I are going to talk to Asher Mayfield."

"Make sure he never walks free again," Freddie said fiercely.

"That's the plan."

. . .

Holding hands, Brooke and Nate walked toward Ethan's room, where Tracy was outside the door, sobbing.

"Mom, what's wrong?"

"Luna Ahern is dead."

"No," Brooke said. "*No.*"

"She is, and now your brother's name—and Tomas's—will always be linked to the murder of a young girl. That's where we're at."

"But he had nothing to do with her being killed," Brooke said as a sense of panic overtook her. That couldn't be Ethan's fate. They couldn't let that happen.

"Do you think the court of public opinion will care that he had nothing to do with it when they have text messages from his phone, luring her to her death?"

"But he said he didn't send those texts. Brecken or his father did it."

"And how do we prove that?"

"They'll dust the phones for prints, Mrs. Hogan," Nate said. "If Brecken or his father sent those texts, their prints will be on the phones."

"Unless they wiped them away." As the daughter and sister of cops, Tracy knew the deal. "And if they did, Ethan and Tomas will own those texts."

"There're other ways they can determine who sent them," Nate said. "There'll be an examination of the video from where the boys were taken by the Mayfields. When they can prove the texts were sent after the boys were abducted, that'll prove the boys didn't send them. We're a long way from knowing the full story of what went down. Ethan and Tomas say they never texted Luna on Saturday. They'd met her before, and Ethan said he really liked her, but they hadn't spent much time together. If Brecken knew Ethan liked her and that maybe Luna liked Ethan, too, that might've been enough for Brecken to see an in with her through Ethan. With both boys telling the same story, that'll matter."

Nate's words had calmed Tracy somewhat. "I guess we'll see, won't we?"

Mike came down the hallway toward Ethan's room, carrying a cup of coffee. He shook hands with Nate and kissed Brooke's cheek before going into Ethan's room.

He knew Tracy wanted to strangle him, which was why he never so much as glanced at her.

"What can I do?" Brooke asked.

"You should get back to school," Tracy said. "You need to be there with your semester ending so soon."

"I can't leave you guys like this. How do I think about anything else?"

"You have to," Tracy said. "Your acceptance to Princeton is on the line. Go back to school, finish strong and come home for the summer. That's what I need you to do, honey." Tracy hugged her eldest child. She'd been so young when she had Brooke that, in many ways, they'd grown up together. "I so appreciate you coming. Having you here made all the difference, but you have to go back and finish."

"I don't want to," Brooke said, weeping. "I want to be here with you guys."

"I know, but there's nothing you can do here that's more important than finishing your school year."

Brooke pulled back from the hug. "Will you be okay?"

Tracy wiped the tears off her daughter's lovely face. "Of course I will." She told Brooke what she needed to hear, but after the past forty-eight hours, she wasn't sure she'd ever be okay again. "I'll feel much better if you're where you need to be."

"What about Abby? Should I go pick her up from Nana?"

"I'll ask Nana to bring her home later today, after we get Ethan settled." Tracy smoothed her hands over Brooke's silky long dark hair. "I'll never forget you guys coming home to be with us when we needed you." Her glance took in the tall, handsome Secret Service agent who was in love with her daughter. "We appreciate it more than you'll ever know."

Brooke hugged her again. "I love you so much, Mommy."

She hadn't called Tracy that in years.

"I love you, too. Go see Ethan and then get on the road. I'll be waiting to hear you're home safely."

"I'll make sure she gets home safe," Nate said.

Tracy released Brooke to hug him. "I know you will. Thank you for your steady presence these last couple of days. It's meant a lot."

"If there's anything I can do, you have my number," Nate said. "Feel free to call if you have questions or just need to talk."

"Thank you," Tracy said. "That's very kind of you."

While they went in to say goodbye for now to Ethan and Mike, Tracy stayed in the hallway, her head back against the concrete wall. It was all she could do not to bash her head against that hard surface until she lost consciousness. That would be better than having to think about what might be ahead for her son and their family.

Mike walked out with Brooke and Nate. Tracy hugged them both again before they left.

As Brooke walked down the long corridor that led to the elevators, she cast a tearful look back at her parents.

They waved to her.

"I'm glad she's going back," Mike said.

Tracy walked around him and went in to see to Ethan.

She had nothing to say to her husband.

CHAPTER TWENTY-THREE

Brooke took a sense of dread with her when she walked away from her parents. She'd never seen them like this, even after her terrible ordeal, and never wanted to see it again. From the minute her dad had come into their lives when Brooke was still very young, her parents' relationship had been solid, loving and steady. They'd inspired her to want what they had, and now...

Would they be able to come back from this nightmare with their marriage intact? She was beginning to fear not.

"What's wrong?" Nate asked when they were in the elevator on the way to the lobby. "You're all tense again."

Thank God for him. He'd barely left her side while they'd waited for word of Ethan's fate, or after they'd heard he was safe. "My parents. I've never seen them as far apart as they are now. They're barely speaking. I don't think my mom will ever be able to forgive him for caving to Ethan and letting him go out with his friends."

"I can see why she's angry. Can you?"

"Of course, but my dad feels terrible, and she doesn't want to hear it. She goes silent when she's furious, but I've never seen her quite like this. She'll blame him forever for allowing Ethan to end up in a mess like this."

"It's a tough situation."

"Can I be honest?"

He took her hand for the walk to his car. "Always."

"I'm mad at my dad, too. I mean, after what happened to me, I'd have expected him to be extra careful with Ethan and Abby. I'm shocked he allowed this. He was super overprotective of me until I was in high school. Then he finally started letting me go out more, but before then, no way."

"Sometimes parents are different with their daughters, which I understand. But boys can find their share of trouble, too."

She glanced at him. "Did you?"

"I had my moments. Nothing terrible or life-changing, but certainly things my parents wouldn't have wanted me doing."

"Like what?"

He held the car door for her, smiling. "You want, like, details?"

"Details would be good."

"Hmmm." With a coy look, he closed the door and went around to the driver's side. As soon as they had left the parking lot, he reached for her hand again. "I'm trying to think of what I can tell you that won't get me in trouble."

"Haha. I'm not your mother."

"Believe me, I know." He gave her hand a squeeze. "It was mostly drinking, smoking and some fun with girls."

"They must've *loved* you."

"I did all right."

"He says with pretend modesty." As she looked over at him, she noticed a slight flush to his cheeks. "Oh. My. God. Are you *blushing*?"

"Secret Service agents don't blush. It's in the manual. We're not allowed."

For the first time in days, Brooke laughed. "Oh, this must've been something. Remind me to discuss your dating history with your mother the next time I see her."

"There's absolutely no need for that."

"Oh, there's every need. I needed that laugh, so thanks a lot."

"Happy to be of service."

"You've been an incredible support to us. I never would've gotten through these last couple of days without you by my side."

"Yes, you would have, because you're the strongest person I've ever known."

"That can't possibly be true."

"Brooke, come on. A lot of people who know what you've been through think that. Look at you now... I mean, some people understandably never recover from what happened to you. But you... You've not only recovered as much as a person can, but you've been determined to thrive in spite of the trauma. You're on the dean's list. You got into Princeton..."

"I have you, a man *all* the girls wanted."

He rolled his eyes at that last part. "And you have me and everything that goes with me, which was certainly never guaranteed after what happened. I'm so proud of you, sweetheart, and everyone who knows you is, too."

"Thanks. That's nice to hear."

"I'm not just saying words. It's true. You're an inspiration."

"Before everything happened with Ethan, Sam texted me about a woman she recently met who'd been through a similar thing. Attacked and sexually assaulted. Like me, she doesn't remember the assault but has to live with the aftermath of realizing it happened. Sam asked me if I might be willing to speak to her at some point."

"What'd you say?"

"I told her I would. If I can help her, why wouldn't I?"

"Are you sure that's the right thing for you, though? To reopen that wound?"

"That wound is never really far from the surface, and I've

come to accept that it'll always be a part of who I am. In fact, I've been thinking about adding a psychology minor when I get to Princeton and possibly pursuing counseling for victims of sexual and domestic assault."

"Wow, that'd be amazing, if you can handle dwelling in that space every day."

"That's my one hesitation, but I figure I can try it and see how it goes. Maybe helping others would help me, too, you know?"

"See why I'm amazed by you?"

"Oh stop. It's all just talk at this point."

"But the fact that you want to give back says a lot about who you are, and I love who you are."

"I hope you know how much your love and support means to me. It gives me strength I didn't have before I had you in my life."

He brought her hand to his lips. "And I hope you know that works both ways. I hate every minute we spend apart, and I can't wait to live in the same town with you."

"Two more weeks until no more long distance. I can't wait either."

They settled into companionable silence flavored with his classic rock playlist. Brooke dozed for a time and woke up as they arrived in Charlottesville. "I can't believe we're here already."

"Time goes by fast when you sleep for hours."

"Was it hours?"

"Hours and hours. I missed you."

"I'm sorry. You've been doing nothing but driving on your days off."

"I've gotten to be with you, which was my only goal for my days off. We have one more night together. What do you feel like doing?"

She needed to get back to work on the paper that was due this coming week and study for her last final exam, but that would keep until tomorrow, when she was back to living without him again for a couple of weeks.

"I want to be with you."

"I'm here all night, babe."

She reached over to place her hand on his thigh, giving a suggestive squeeze. "I want to be *with* you."

"Why didn't you just say so?"

She laughed. "I thought I did."

"Men are dense sometimes. You have to be clearer."

"In that case, you want to go to bed, Agent Zimmerman?"

"Um, yes, I do. I want that more than anything."

They walked into her apartment ten minutes later, dropping their bags inside the door and turning toward each other in a move that would've seemed choreographed if anyone else had seen it. But with both her roommates at work, they had the place to themselves.

"Hi," he said, smiling as he kissed her.

"How's it going?"

"Much better now that we know my love's baby brother is safe."

"Thank you for being my rock."

"I was where I always want to be—with you." As he kissed her, he hooked an arm around her waist to lift her and walk toward her bedroom. With her still suspended, he kicked the door closed and lowered her to the bed, coming down on top of her without missing a beat in the kiss of all kisses.

She'd been too distracted and upset to do more than hold hands with him for days, and they had time to make up for now that the crisis had passed.

"That was very sexy," she whispered against his lips.

"What was?"

"The lift, the carry, the door kick, the bed landing. Smoothly executed. A ten out of ten."

"You liked that, huh?"

"I like *you*. So, so, so much."

"That's a whole lotta like, baby."

"So much like and even more love."

"Right back at you."

He multitasked kissing and undressing them both while she helped where she could, tugging his shirt over his head and running her hands over his smooth, warm skin and making him tremble. She loved the way he reacted to her, how he never made her feel anything other than well and truly loved.

So many of her friends were dating guys who had them constantly in distress as they tried to interpret the unsavory word or action of the moment. Brooke never felt that way with Nate, probably because he was a grown-ass man and not a boy pretending to be a man like so many of the guys they knew at college.

He also knew what he was doing in bed, which she'd heard was another thing her friends found lacking. That certainly wasn't a problem with Nate.

With her breasts pressed to the soft hair on his chest, she shuddered with the desire that still took her by surprise despite the many times they'd done this since the first time. Once she'd had a taste of the pleasure she found with him, she couldn't get enough. And after she'd feared she might never be able to enjoy sex after being violently attacked, it'd been such a relief to discover otherwise. But only with Nate, the love of her life. As he kissed her breasts and teased her nipples until she was wriggling under him, she couldn't imagine sharing this kind of intimacy with anyone else.

"I'm obsessed with your soft skin, your sweet breasts, your curves, your face, your silky dark hair and stunning blue eyes, your freckles." He dabbed his tongue against a mole next to her belly button. "I love everything about you."

Brooke grasped handfuls of his thick hair as he moved down to part her thighs and love her with his tongue as his fingers slid inside her. The combination always did it for her, and this time was no different. He was also really good at keeping it going until she was almost begging him to let her take a breath.

When he'd reduced her to a quivering mess, he kissed his way back up her body, stopping to give each breast the full treatment as he sank into her, filling her in one deep thrust that sparked a second wave of ecstasy. There was simply no other word for what she felt when she was with him this way.

"Mmm, hottest thing I've ever felt is you squeezing me so tightly from inside," he whispered. "It's all I can do not to explode when that happens."

"Don't let me stop you from exploding," she said with a smile.

"Not yet. I want one more from you first."

Brooke groaned dramatically as he pushed himself up on muscular arms and began to move, giving her deep thrusts that hit all the right spots and had her climbing toward another peak in no time at all. Making her senseless with desire was his superpower, or so it seemed to her as they clung to each other in a moment of perfection that never ceased to leave her stupefied in the aftermath. Until him, she hadn't known such things were even possible. Now she couldn't imagine living without him or the special kind of magic he brought to her life.

"I can't wait until next fall when we get to sleep together every night," she whispered.

"I can't wait until this summer when you can sleep at my place every night. In fact, you should just plan to stay with me rather than moving home. You can still be with your family all the time."

She hadn't considered that possibility. "We wouldn't have to wait months to be together every day."

"What do you think your parents would say about it?"

"They know we're planning to live together in the fall. I can't imagine they'd object to us spending the summer together, too. They love you almost as much as I do."

"If there's tension between them, it might be better for you not to be on the front lines of that."

"But I'd hate to leave Abby and Ethan to deal with it on their own."

"They won't have to deal with it. Your folks won't fight in front of them."

"No, they won't, but the silence can also be deafening, you know?"

"You'd be right there in town if the kids needed you."

"True. The thought of being with you like this every day, with no school to deal with for a few months, makes me feel breathless with excitement."

"I like when you're happy. All I want is to make you happy every day."

"You do. Even when we're not together. But when we are…"

"That's the best thing ever."

"It sure is."

Brooke felt guilty for feeling as if she was on top of the world when her parents and Ethan were struggling with so many challenges. But even as she stood ready to support them through whatever came next, she took a little moment to enjoy the sheer joy of being completely in love with the most wonderful man.

CHAPTER TWENTY-FOUR

When Malone returned to Sam's office almost an hour after he'd left, he looked much better than he had earlier. He'd showered, shaved and changed into a navy pullover and khakis. He wore his gold badge on his belt, and his normally amiable eyes had taken on a hard edge that was so unlike him that it startled her.

"Are you ready to talk to Mayfield?" he asked. "Lindsey has done the DNA swabs."

"I'm ready when you are, and Charity Miller is standing by, too. How do you want to play this?"

"My plan is to trap him with his own hubris."

"I'm down with that. I'll let you take the lead and step in if needed?"

"Sounds good. I'm very determined not to get emotional."

"Are you sure you don't want me to take it so you don't have to?"

"I thought about handing it off, but I decided the emotion will make me more effective if I can just keep it in check."

"You will. You'll find your zone and get it done."

"If I falter…"

"I'll be right there and ready to take over."

He nodded. "Thank you."

"Of course."

Sam texted Charity that they were ready to proceed with the Mayfield interrogation that she would witness from an adjoining observation room.

"After this, we'll have to brief the media," Malone said. "We need to announce Luna's murder and that we have suspects in custody. We're not announcing that other kids have been found in units rented by Mayfield until we have time to figure out who they are and who they belong to. We can announce that additional charges are expected."

"I'll be right there through the whole thing."

"Let's get this done. I want justice for that sweet little girl and the other kids he's harmed."

Sam knew he was thinking of his own daughter, Mel, and his young granddaughter as he walked toward the room where Asher Mayfield was being guarded by Officer Montgomery.

The young patrolman nodded to Malone and Sam.

"Nice to see you, Officer Montgomery," Sam said. "It's been a minute." He'd been first on the scene when she and Nick had been chased into a rollover car crash early in their relationship. She'd been knocked unconscious, but Nick had later told her that Montgomery had been critical to their survival.

"Yes, ma'am. Good to see you as well." He tipped his head toward the interrogation room. "This guy's a piece of work. Full of himself."

"He's a fucking monster," Malone said.

Charity Miller joined them in the hallway. "I just read the preliminary report. Tell me we've got this guy nailed."

"Not completely, but hopefully we will after this."

"What about the son?"

"Let's see what the DNA shows, and then we'll figure out what to do about him," Malone said. "It's possible he didn't participate in what was done to Luna."

"What's your gut on that?" Charity asked.

"I honestly don't know if the dad acted alone once he got what he needed from Brecken, Ethan and Tomas," Malone said. "Or if Brecken was involved in the whole plan and execution. That's part of what I aim to find out."

Lindsey McNamara came down the hallway, carrying two manila folders that she handed to Malone and Charity. "Preliminary photos."

Sam swallowed hard. She so did not want to look at those photos.

Lindsey's expression conveyed the empathy that made her so good at her job. "You may want to prepare yourselves."

With justice for Luna front of mind, Sam forced herself to look at the images that depicted a brutal physical and sexual assault. Bile burned her throat as she tried to remain professional and focused on the task at hand. Inside, however, she broke for Luna and her devoted parents.

"Good God," Charity whispered as she closed the file.

Her face looked like it had been bleached of all color.

Sam reached out a hand to her.

Charity took her hand and gave it a squeeze.

Then they shook it off as best they could, determined to make sure that the man, or men, who'd tortured and killed Luna never saw the light of day outside prison again.

They burst into the room, as they often did, but this guy... Oh, he was a cool customer. He wasn't rattled by the sudden entrance of detectives, but he did cast a smarmy little grin Sam's way.

"Oh wow, I'm honored. I get the first lady."

"Shut the fuck up, Mayfield." Malone turned on the recording device and recited the names of those present in the room and in observation. Then he recited the Miranda warning. "Do you understand these rights as they've been presented to you?"

"Yep. Nothing I haven't heard before." Asher had the same wavy dark hair as his son with hard hazel eyes that were the same shade as Nick's, but with none of the warmth that his had.

"You must be so proud of your extensive criminal history," Malone said.

He shrugged. "What can you do? Shit happens."

Malone put a printout on the table that detailed Mayfield's long rap sheet. "Shit seems to happen to you more often than most."

"I'm misunderstood."

"Are you, though?"

"What can I say? People piss me off."

Malone put a school photo of Luna on the table. "What'd she do to piss you off?"

"Who's that?"

"Oh please. Like you don't recognize the girl who disrespected your son and sent you into a murderous rage."

"I've never seen her before in my life."

Malone laughed. "That's not what your son said."

Mayfield's entire disposition changed. He sat up straighter, his smile fading. "He never told you anything about me."

"Is that what you think?" Malone put the photos of Luna's battered body on the table. "How do you think we found her? And what do you think the DNA will tell us?"

Mayfield glanced down at the photos, seeming incredulous as a muscle twitched in his cheek. "I'd like an attorney."

"I'll bet you would. Who should we call?"

"It's not like I've got someone on retainer."

"Oh, funny. I would've thought a guy like you would have an attorney on speed dial. Or did you not pay the last guy?" Without giving him the chance to reply, Malone said, "I'll call the public defender. Will probably be a day or two before they send someone over." Malone pressed the recorder to end the interview and headed for the door with Sam.

"I can't wait to tell all my friends I met the first lady. They think you're a hot piece, but you're probably a bitch like all the others."

Sam couldn't resist turning back to him. "Oh, I am a hot piece, and like *all* the others, I want *nothing* to do with you."

The look of pure hatred he gave her made it worth dignifying his comment with a reply.

"Well said," Malone muttered when they were in the hallway.

"Sorry you had to hear that about, you know... the hotness of my piece."

He barked out a laugh, which was a welcome sound after a grim few hours.

Charity joined them in the hallway. "I'll be looking for the DNA and autopsy reports while I prepare to file charges."

"Are you including the son?" Sam asked.

"At least for participating in the kidnapping of Ethan and Tomas, with possibly more charges coming depending on what the DNA says."

"We'll get Lindsey's report to you as soon as we have it," Malone said.

"I'll be back in touch."

After Charity walked away, Malone leaned back against the tan concrete wall, closed his eyes and exhaled.

Sam stood next to him, providing silent support to someone who was always there for her.

"I'm never going to forget this one."

"Is it weird that I want to go see her mother?"

"It'd probably mean a lot to her."

"Normally, I'd run from something like that, but I feel this overwhelming need to see her."

"Because you're a mother yourself now, and you feel for what she's lost."

"Yeah, I guess that's it. I'll go after I do the briefing."

"I'll come with you," Malone said.

"You don't have to."

"It's okay. I'll see it through, and then I'm going home."

"Will you come back?" Sam asked, going for a moment of levity.

"I'll let you know."

"Please do."

"Sometimes it's just far too fucking much."

"Almost all the time, it is."

"Yeah."

"You know what's encouraging?" she asked.

"There's something encouraging?"

"It's that you've been doing this job for decades, and you still care so much that you're devasted by the loss of this young girl. At times, I've worried about becoming numb to it, but you're showing me that we never become entirely numb."

"It'd be nice if we could, right?"

"Definitely. Will you see Dr. Trulo after you get some rest?"

"We'll see."

"Will you do it for me?"

He gave her a side-eyed look full of exasperation. "That's low, Holland. I expect better from you."

She shrugged. "Friends take care of friends."

"I'll talk to him."

"And you won't get mad at me if I make sure you do it?" They'd become experts at avoidance of the kind of help Trulo provided. However, after he'd saved her sanity and her career—more than once—Sam had become a fan of his way of helping.

"Who's the boss around here, anyway?"

"Is that a rhetorical question?"

His grunt of laughter was his only answer. "Let's get this shit finished so I can get the hell out of here."

She walked with him into the pit, where they used her office to pound out a statement about finding Luna Ahern's body. "I'll update on the Carver case, too."

When they were ready, they walked to the lobby, where they

encountered Chief Farnsworth in a discussion with Deputy Chief Jeannie McBride.

"What's up, guys?"

"I was coming to tell you we're getting pushback from the judge on the warrant for the phones of Carver's wife and sister-in-law," McBride said.

"We've got Detective Charles on the way to retrieve them," Sam said.

"We have to make a stronger case to the judge to get the warrants," McBride replied. "Who wants to take that?"

"I'll ask Gonzo to do it after I do the briefing," Sam said.

"While you do the briefing, I'll talk to Gonzo so Charles's trip isn't in vain."

"Great, thanks, Jeannie."

"Where do we stand on the Ahern case?" Farnsworth asked.

Malone brought him up to speed on what they'd learned from their brief interview with Asher Mayfield. He also added how they believed the entire thing stemmed from Luna refusing to engage with Brecken.

The chief was incredulous. "She was murdered because she wouldn't give his son the time of day?"

"We believe that was the reason, but it's part of a bigger issue," Sam said, "which we'll touch on in our briefing."

The chief shook his head, aghast over the disturbing details of the case. "We see a lot of crazy crap around here, but this..."

"It's crazier than most," Sam said.

Sam glanced at Malone, who nodded to indicate he was ready to accompany her outside, where a much-larger-than-usual press corps awaited an update. They'd decided she would give the briefing since they were still ravenous for info about her nephew's condition.

Reporters started shouting at her the minute she came through the door and didn't stop until they realized she wasn't going to say anything until they shut up. You'd think they'd have figured that out by now, but it was a lesson they had to relearn every day.

"I have a lot to share today, so I'd appreciate the chance to fully brief you before I answer questions. As you know, three local children were recently reported missing—Luna Ahern, age thirteen, Tomas Cambra, age eleven, and Ethan Hogan, also age eleven. As you know by now, Ethan Hogan is my nephew. He's the son of my sister Tracy and her husband, Mike. Needless to say, our entire family is relieved and thankful for the safe return of both him and Tomas. We wish we had the same news about Luna."

A ripple of gasps sounded.

"Thanks to the efforts of Captains Jake Malone and Michelle Ruiz, we were able to locate Luna in a storage unit on Florida Avenue."

Another series of gasps went through the gathering.

"She was in critical condition when located and was transported to GW Trauma, where she passed away from her extensive injuries. Our hearts are with her parents, family and friends as they process this unfathomable loss. I use the word 'unfathomable' intentionally, as the motive behind this crime is the very definition of that word. We believe Luna was murdered because she rebuffed the advances of a fifteen-year-old boy."

More sounds of disbelief as the reporters took frantic notes.

"But it goes deeper than the rebuff to an entire 'manosphere' built around male grievance toward the women who reject them. An entirely new vernacular has entered our lexicon during this investigation. We learned about incel culture. Incel stands for involuntary celibate, which speaks to men who are unable to achieve romantic success with women and, in turn, blame the women for their failures. They believe that eighty percent of women are interested in only twenty percent of men, and the other eighty percent of men are left out in the cold. This is part of a larger movement of disaffected men who share their grievances in online forums where they find like-minded individuals to validate their positions. Some of these people go so far as to act out against the women who've rejected them, as well as their romantic partners.

"We've arrested Asher Mayfield and his son, a juvenile we're not naming at this time, for suspicion of kidnapping all three children. We expect further charges to be forthcoming. We believe Luna rejected Mayfield's son. Driven by a long history of personal failures with women himself, the senior Mayfield decided to exact revenge on his son's behalf. Father and son befriended Ethan and Tomas over a period of weeks and then kidnapped the boys and used their phones to lure Luna, who was friendly with Ethan and Tomas, to meet Mayfield and his son. The boys were able to escape from where they were being held. They received medical treatment at the hospital and are recovering at home with their families."

"What injuries did they sustain?" a reporter asked.

"They were dehydrated and had cuts and abrasions from the zip ties that were used to restrain them. Ethan had bruised ribs as well."

"How were they able to escape?"

"Ethan had an all-purpose pocketknife that they used. Because of how they were bound, however, it took many hours for the boys to get free. Asher Mayfield is an active leader in the manosphere scene and is president of a local organization called the Dead Chads, which is the name they give to men who are successful with women. Women who choose these men are referred to as Stacys."

"Is this shit for real?" Darren Tabor from the *Washington Star* asked.

"Unfortunately, yes," Sam said. "It's all too real and has led to other murders." She went through the list of well-documented incel-related murders that'd occurred around the country as well as some of the history behind the movement. "Mayfield and his son will initially be charged with three counts of kidnapping. We expect additional charges to be forthcoming after the medical examiner completes her work. I'll take a few more questions."

"Had you heard of incel culture or the mano... whatever it's called... before this case?"

"It's called the manosphere, and no, most of us had never heard of any of this, and we wish we hadn't heard of it now. I think it's important to note that for the many, many ways the internet has made life easier and more efficient, it also has a dark side where like-minded individuals with serious grievances can find community and in some cases can organize to perpetrate violence upon their perceived enemies."

"This sounds like a pretty sophisticated society, if you will, with common vernacular and terminology. Is this something regular people, and women in particular, need to be afraid of?"

"I wouldn't advise wide-scale fear, but more of an awareness that this mindset exists. We've all known of cases in which a woman rejects a man's advances and is served with violent retribution of some kind. It can be everything from stalking to intimidation to assault to murder. Many of those cases are not directly tied to incel culture or the manosphere, but in this case, there's a direct tie."

"How did Mayfield and his son make contact with Tomas and Ethan?"

"The boys met at a video arcade at the Wharf some time ago and became friendly, meeting up several times after that initial contact. Once, Asher Mayfield accompanied his son and met the boys. He treated them to more games and pizza. They said the son was, as they put it, obsessed with Luna. Ethan and Tomas had met her a couple of times. At one point, Ethan passed her a note that said he thought she was very pretty and he'd like to talk more. He gave her his phone number. To our knowledge, she never reached out to him, nor do we believe the younger Mayfield ever knew about the note from Ethan to Luna."

"How do you know about the note?"

"It was found in Luna's room when our detectives searched

it. We believe the Mayfields targeted Ethan and Tomas and encouraged their friendship with her so they could use the boys' phones to get her to come out to meet them. Except she didn't know it wasn't them waiting for her."

"I know one of these kids is your nephew, Lieutenant, but aren't they young to be running around the city unsupervised?" The question came from a male TV reporter, who she guessed to be in his early forties. "I have middle school kids who don't go anywhere without an adult with them."

"I hear you, and I understand that parents will be questioning their decisions on these things in light of this case. I want to be clear that I'm not standing in judgment of any parents, especially my sister and brother-in-law, who have to confront these challenges with their tweens and teens. As I told my sister, I'm the last person in the world who'd ever judge the choices of other parents, especially with my kids under Secret Service protection. That said, as a police officer, I was surprised that Ethan was allowed to go out with only his friends at age eleven."

"So you were unaware he was allowed to do that?"

"I was. In this high-tech age, I think parents are possibly lulled into a false sense of security because of cell phones and the ability to track their child's location. They have the numbers of the friends their children will be with and parameters set on where the kids are allowed to go—and where they're not allowed to go. In the case of my nephew, my sister and brother-in-law first became alarmed when they realized Ethan's phone had been shut off. They were no longer able to see his location, their calls were going to voicemail, and texts weren't being delivered."

"Lieutenant, with this case involving a family member, were you permitted to work on it?"

"I wasn't formally assigned to the case, but I did help out behind the scenes where I could without compromising the investigation in any way. I was sent out here today to talk to you because there've been a lot of specific questions about my nephew and my family, and they wanted me to share with you that he's home safe and that everyone involved is heartbroken over the senseless murder of Luna Ahern." She took a beat before she continued. "I'd like to also brief you on a second case, that of Dale Carver, who was fatally stabbed at the Vacation Inn and Suites on 10th Street Northwest. He was in town from Spokane, Washington, for meetings at USDA."

"Was he stabbed in his room?"

"No, it happened in the room where guests go to get ice. We're pursuing a number of leads in that case and will have updates for you as they become available. That's all I have for now."

"Lieutenant, were you and the president concerned that your nephew's disappearance might somehow be tied to your roles as POTUS and FLOTUS?"

Sam debated whether she should answer and decided to address it to hopefully shut down that line of questioning. "Of course it crossed our minds before the evidence led in other directions."

"Was the federal response to his disappearance due to his proximity to you and the president?"

"The FBI and U.S. Marshals regularly assist us, and that was no different in this case."

"Who called them in?"

"Thanks, everyone."

Sam ducked inside, ignoring the shouted follow-up questions.

Malone followed her. "You did good."

"Is that question about the Feds going to haunt me?"

"Maybe a little, but who cares who we asked for help? We have the culprits in custody."

"We'll get a lot of follow-up questions about this case."

"We'll let Public Affairs take them. I'll make sure they're fully briefed."

"Let me do that so you can go home and get some rest."

"Are you sure?"

"I am. Go ahead."

"Thanks. I won't say no to that."

"Do you want me to wait to see Luna's mother until you can come, too?"

"No, go ahead and do that. I think it'd mean a lot to her if you stopped by."

"You did everything you could for Luna. Tell me you know that."

"I know it, but my everything wasn't enough, and that'll haunt me for the rest of my life."

With that, he walked away.

CHAPTER TWENTY-FIVE

S am watched him go, worried about him and everyone who'd worked on this case. Then she went upstairs to find Captain Norris of Public Affairs so she could educate him and his team on the manosphere and incel culture.

Thirty minutes later, the faces of the PA team were blank with shock, even though most of them had seen her briefing. She'd given them many more details than she'd provided to the media.

"Is this for real?" Norris asked.

"Unfortunately, yes, and as our case will show, these beefs and the resulting thirst for vengeance led to the murder of Luna Ahern. You should expect to receive follow-up questions from the media."

"We already are," one of the younger officers said. She held up her phone. "Multiple emails and texts asking for clarification."

"What're we supposed to say," Norris asked, "when we've never heard of any of this until now?"

"You could say we'll release more information when we have it."

"That's a good plan," Norris said. "That's what we'll do. Thanks for the briefing, Lieutenant."

"Of course. No problem."

"We're getting a lot of questions about your nephew, your sister's family, your involvement in the investigation and whether your nephew will be charged," another of the younger officers said.

Sam experienced a flash of anger that had her considering some choice words for the media. But since that would only make everything worse, she said, "You can say Ethan Hogan and Tomas Cambra were kidnapped and are victims in this crime. Their families are handling the aftermath privately and will have nothing further to say to the media about Ethan, nor will Lieutenant Holland."

One of the officers wrote down the statement.

"Please don't deviate from that or give them any openings for further exposition."

"Yes, ma'am."

"Thank you." To Norris, she added, "You have my number if you need any more information."

"I do. Thanks for coming up."

Sam nodded and left their offices, heading downstairs to hers, but taking an odd vibe from Norris with her. After the Ramsey/Offenbach nightmare, she was hypersensitive to such vibes, but she was also determined not to be sidetracked by them. Whatever issues people had with her were their problem, not hers.

On the first floor, she hung a right to see if Dr. Trulo was still in his office. His door was closed, so she started to leave. A second later, he called out to her.

Sam turned back. "Hey, I thought you were in a session."

"I was on the phone, but I'm done now. You want to come in?"

She followed him into his office and took a seat. "I want to talk to you about Captain Malone."

"What about him?"

"He was on the Ahern case and took it hard. I've never seen him so upset. I suggested he check in with you, and he said he would, but…"

"I'll reach out to him."

"Thank you."

"How are you? And how's your nephew?"

"He's safe, thankfully. I'm not sure if there'll be long-term effects, but for now, we're very grateful to have him back at home where he belongs."

"I was very saddened to hear about Luna."

"We all were. It's unbearable. What do you know about this incel culture stuff?"

"I've read a lot about it and how it's tied into cases over the years."

"One more thing for women to be afraid of."

"Is there anything I can do for you, friend? It's been a rougher-than-usual couple of weeks for you."

"Thank you, but I'm okay. I need to get back to work on our other case."

"Don't be afraid to take a break if you need one."

"I won't."

"Check in with me."

"Yes, Doc," she said with pretend exasperation.

"I mean it, Sam. You just had two now ex-colleagues plot to kill you and a nephew kidnapped in a case that involved the murder of a young girl. Please don't act like either of those things is normal."

"I hear you, and I appreciate you. I'll keep in touch."

"See that you do."

Sam would keep her promise to be in contact with him. There was a time, not that long ago, when she would've resented his insistence—and his interference. But he'd helped her too much in the past to discount the impact of his involvement in her life and career.

Back in the pit, she found Gonzo consulting with Lindsey McNamara. "What's up, guys?"

"We have DNA matches for both Mayfields," Lindsey reported.

"Despite his criminal history, I'd really hoped the kid was just another of his dad's victims and not as much of a monster as his father is," Sam said with a sigh.

"I said the same thing," Gonzo replied.

Lindsey handed Sam a copy of the printed report.

"I'll get with Charity about updating the charges against both of them. Thanks for the quick work, Doc."

"No problem." Lindsey glanced at Sam, her green eyes brimming with tears. "They made her suffer before they killed her. I hope they rot in prison for the rest of their miserable lives."

"We'll see to it," Sam said.

Lindsey nodded and walked away.

"I so don't want to read this report," Sam said.

"Me either," Gonzo said.

Sam had to remind herself that she was the commanding officer in the Homicide division, and it was her job to know the details of what'd happened to Luna Ahern so she could ensure justice for the girl and her family.

She took a deep breath and turned toward her office, determined to do whatever was necessary to put the Mayfields away for life, even though she had to absorb details that would haunt her forever.

She'd do it for Luna.

And then she'd go see Luna's mother.

TRACY DREADED HAVING to tell Ethan that Luna was dead. He'd been quiet and withdrawn since they'd brought him home from the hospital as he seemed to be processing the events of the past forty-eight hours. She'd been in touch with his therapist, Dr. Christi Trulo-Carpenter, the daughter of Sam's colleague. Christi had offered to come to the house in the morning, and Tracy had gratefully accepted.

Ethan was in no condition to go anywhere. Not now, anyway.

She carried a tray upstairs to Ethan's room, which Brooke and Nate had put back to rights after the house had been searched for evidence. Though she'd understood the necessity, Tracy felt further violated having their things rifled through by strangers. She told herself the only thing that mattered was that her son was home safe, but after having been through the aftermath of Brooke's assault, she knew the healing wouldn't happen overnight. When the dust settled, she'd be left to wonder who she'd pissed off in a previous life that had led to two of her three children being the victims of traumatic crimes.

Ethan was sitting up in bed, a pile of pillows behind him, covered by the Capitals' team blanket she'd bought him for Christmas.

"I made you some of that chicken noodle soup you like," she said as she placed the tray on his lap. "With oyster crackers, of course."

They were his favorite.

"Thanks."

She'd also made him a cup of hot chocolate with marshmallows and had put yellow sandwich cookies in a bowl, hoping that seeing his favorites would get him to eat something.

But he only stared down at the tray, unseeing.

"Have a bite, honey. You need to keep up your strength." Tracy picked up the spoon to feed him like she had when he was a baby.

Thankfully, he opened his mouth to take the bite she offered.

They kept that up for several quiet minutes while he ate most of the soup and a handful of the crackers.

"You want some hot chocolate? It's got the marshmallows you love." She handed him the mug, and he took a sip.

"Thank you."

He'd taken the bandages off the wounds on his wrists, which were red and raw.

"Is there any news about Luna?" he asked for the hundredth time.

Tracy hesitated, only for a second, but it was enough to alert him to something he didn't want to hear.

"No."

"I'm so sorry, honey."

"Oh my God. She's *dead*? She's really dead?"

"She is."

He let out an anguished cry that was so loud, Mike came running from wherever he was to see what was wrong.

Tracy took the mug, removed the tray, put it on the floor and crawled into bed to wrap her arms around Ethan as he sobbed.

His heartbroken wails wrecked her.

"What happened?" Mike asked.

Tracy ignored him to keep her focus on Ethan. He didn't need to hear the news again. She hadn't seen Ethan cry like this since he'd broken his wrist as a six-year-old, and it killed her to see him suffering. He also hadn't clung to her in years the way he was now.

"Shhh, honey. Take a breath."

He was on the verge of hyperventilating.

Mike sat on the other side of the bed and put his hand on Ethan's back.

Thankfully, Mike didn't ask any other questions. Maybe he'd figured out what'd happened.

Over the next half hour, Ethan cried himself to sleep, hiccupping with sobs long after he was asleep.

Tracy carefully extricated herself, hoping he'd sleep for a while. She put the bowl of cookies on his bedside table, picked up the tray and tiptoed out of the room, aware of Mike following her downstairs to the kitchen.

As she put dishes in the dishwasher and wiped the counter, she felt him hovering in the background.

"Are you going to tell me what's going on?"

"Luna is dead."

He gasped. "Oh God. Oh my God."

Tracy turned to him as he sat at the kitchen table, hands over his face as his shoulders shook with sobs.

Excluding the men who'd been involved in her father's shooting and eventual murder, Tracy had never been angrier at anyone than she was at him. She could see no possible way forward for their marriage after this.

After a long silence, Mike raised his head and looked at her, as if seeking answers or insight into how they might cope with this horrible tragedy.

She had nothing for him. Her entire focus was on Ethan—and Abby, who'd also want an explanation for what'd occurred. She'd barely thought of her younger daughter in hours as she'd cared for Ethan and tried not to fall apart. Knowing Abby was with her mother and had been able to go to the party she'd looked forward to made Tracy feel better.

"Will Ethan and Tomas be implicated in her murder?"

"They had nothing to do with her kidnapping or murder."

"I can't believe she was murdered."

"Really? You can't?"

"Yes, I really can't! What kind of monster murders a thirteen-year-old girl?"

"The same one who kidnapped our eleven-year-old son because he was running around the city unsupervised. I mean, what could possibly go wrong there?"

He sat back, giving her a hard look. "So this is all my fault, right?"

"Well, it's not my fault! I said he was too young for that kind of freedom, but you told me to lighten up and let him be independent. Look where that got us."

"He was in the wrong place at the wrong time."

"No, he was exactly where people like this go to find kids to prey on, which is what I said could happen if he was given this kind of freedom."

"So you were right. Is that what you want to hear?"

"No, Mike, that's not what I want to hear. I couldn't care less about being right! I care about how I'm going to get my son through this trauma without him blaming himself for an innocent girl being murdered. I'm focused on making sure he's treated as a victim of this crime and not a perpetrator. That's *all* I care about."

"Your son. Not *our* son."

"I think you should move out." The fact that she felt nothing at all as she said those words should've terrified her.

"Are you serious?"

"I'm dead serious."

"Come on, Tracy. This isn't the time—"

"It's exactly the time. Don't pretend like this is some kind of shock to you. We've been out of sync for a long time, and that nearly cost us our son. I don't want you here."

"You sure as fuck wanted me here when you were a single mother."

"That was a long time ago, wasn't it? Back when you would've killed to protect our kids. That guy would've never allowed an eleven-year-old to run around this city on his own. Now... I don't even know who you are anymore."

"That is so not fair."

"It isn't? Really? When I told you it was wrong to let him go out with his friends at eleven, you said I was overreacting, that I was hysterical, that I was hovering and turning him into a mama's boy. Remember all that disrespectful shit you said to me when I sounded the alarm about our *child* being too young for that kind of freedom? Remember how you told me I've been a helicopter mother since Brooke was assaulted? Is that ringing any bells?"

"I shouldn't have said that stuff. I'm sorry."

"Fuck you and your Monday-morning-quarterback apology. I want you out of here. I can't bear to look at you."

"You can't be serious. You're going to throw away twenty years of marriage over a mistake?"

"*A mistake?* Is that how you see an egregious lack of judgment? I can't take the chance that you'll allow something like this again, against my wishes. You made me completely powerless in this situation by agreeing with what he wanted. How could I say no after you'd said yes? What happened to our united front that we always said was so critical? You opened the door, and Ethan walked right through it like I hadn't said no. I have two children to protect, and we're not at all on the same page about how to do that, so I want you to go."

"And not see my kids anymore?"

"I never said that, but you're not making any more big decisions for them. That much is for certain."

"And how do you propose to eliminate me from decision-making for them?"

"By getting a lawyer, divorcing you and suing for full custody, with visitation for you."

He stared at her, incredulous. "You can't be serious."

"I am as serious as I have ever been about anything. Our marriage is over. I no longer trust your judgment, and I no longer love you the way I once did."

"Do you honestly think I don't feel sick about what's happened?"

"I'm sure you do. Too bad you didn't listen to me when I told you what *could* happen. No, I was overwrought, hysterical, overprotective. And I was fucking *right*, so please, do us all a big favor and get the fuck out of here before I have you thrown out."

"With what army?"

She gave him a look that she hoped reminded him of who her sister was and what she did for a living.

"Sam won't force me out of my own home."

"You don't think so? If I ask her to, she'll do it. Don't mistake her affection for you as greater than her loyalty toward me and the kids. If I call her and tell her I want you out of here and you're refusing to go, she'll do something about it. Let's not go there. Our family has already had enough negative attention thanks to you. Do the right thing and go quietly."

She stared him down as he waited for her to change her mind, to soften her directive, to take back what she'd said. None of that was going to happen. This wasn't about being right. It was about keeping their kids safe.

"I can't believe you're so quick to throw away more than twenty years together and the family we've built because I made a mistake."

"If that's how you see it, then I'm definitely doing the right thing. I've said everything I have to say to you. My next move will be to call Sam and ask for her help."

They were engaged in another stare-down when Ethan came into the kitchen.

His pale face and haunted eyes only added to her fury. Her child had been changed forever by this incident, and his father was calling it a "mistake."

"What's going on?" he asked, glancing between them.

"Nothing, honey," Tracy said as she went to him. "Let's get you back to bed. You need to be resting."

"Why are you fighting?"

"You may as well tell him, Tracy. He'll find out soon enough."

She glared at him, wondering when he'd become such an asshole. "Dad and I are separating."

"What? Why?"

"Because it's what I need right now."

"Are you getting divorced?"

"We're taking a break."

"Joey's parents took a break, and then they got divorced."

"I don't want you to worry about that right now. We need you focused on getting some rest and recovering from your injuries."

"Mom's right, buddy. That's all you need to be thinking about."

Ethan's eyes filled with tears. "I don't want you to get divorced because of me."

"Oh, baby, it wouldn't be because of you," Tracy said. "I swear." She took him by the arm and escorted him back upstairs to his room. As she tucked him in, she said, "Please don't worry about me and Dad. We just need a break from each other. That's all it is."

"Will you tell me if it's more than that?"

"Yeah, sweetie. I will." She ran her fingers through his thick hair and tried to bring some order to it, beyond thankful to have him back where he belonged, safe and mostly sound.

"What if people think I hurt her?"

"The police will say who did it when they announce the charges against the Mayfields."

"Do you think Brecken will be charged, too?"

"He'll be charged for the role he played in you and Tomas being kidnapped. I don't know if he was involved in what happened to Luna."

"I don't think he wanted to hurt her. His dad told him what to do."

"You'll have to tell Sam everything you know at some point."

"I don't know much."

"Still, you might have information that'll make a difference in getting justice for Luna."

"I want to help if I can."

"And you'll get the chance. For now, you need to rest." She stood to leave him, even though she really didn't want to.

"Mom?"

She turned back to him. "Yes, honey?"

"Will it always hurt this bad?"

His devastation only added to her fury, as unreasonable as it might seem to Mike. "No, honey. Eventually, the agony will fade, but you'll always carry the ache for someone who was denied the chance to have a long and happy life."

"Will I always feel responsible?"

"You're *not* responsible. You didn't do anything wrong."

"Why does it feel like I did?"

"Because something terrible happened, and we're all sick over it. It's perfectly normal to feel the way you do."

"I've never felt this bad in my life. I only met Luna twice, but she seemed like a nice girl, and she was so pretty."

"It's really important that you understand none of this was your fault. Brecken and his father set up this entire thing. They used you and Tomas to get to her."

"Why?"

"I don't know, honey, but the story will come out. It always does." Tracy hated that her little boy would be forced to grow up far sooner than he should've had to. That was another thing to blame on Mike and his shit judgment. "The most important thing to remember is you were a victim of this crime, too, but because of your quick thinking, you and Tomas survived. And I'm so proud of you for keeping your wits about you and getting yourself and your friend out of there."

"I wish I could've saved Luna, too."

"I know, buddy, but you did what you could, and by coming home, you saved me and Dad and Brooke and Abby, too."

"Will you stay here with me for a while?"

"Of course." Tracy snuggled up and put her arm around him. "I'll stay for as long as you want me to."

CHAPTER TWENTY-SIX

Neveah had told Sam she could handle the mission to pick up the cell phones in Spokane, Washington, but truth be told, she was scared out of her mind to get on an airplane and jet through the night sky to the other side of the country.

By herself.

As she waited in line at security, she hoped she'd done everything right after viewing several YouTube videos on the rules of what was allowed and what wasn't. While she waited, she watched what the people ahead of her did when they got to the front of the line and took mental notes so she could move quickly and not irritate the travelers behind her.

Getting through security with nothing confiscated counted as her first victory.

Finding the gate, buying food for the flight and being where she needed to be when they started boarding the plane counted as her second victory.

She texted Sam. *Getting on the plane. Will text when I land in Spokane.*

Safe travels, Sam replied a few minutes later.

Neveah knew that was something people said when

someone was traveling, but it made her nervous to think about what an unsafe flight would be like.

Her phone rang with a call from her dad. "Hey," she said. "Did you get my message?"

"I did. You're really flying to Spokane tonight?"

"I really am."

"What's there?"

"The cell phones of our murder victim's wife and her sister. My job is to bring them back for analysis."

"Do they know you've never flown before?"

"I told Sam that, and she offered me an out, but I didn't take it."

"I'll never get over you working with the first lady or calling her Sam."

"That's her name, and if I called her anything else, she'd be pissed."

"So you say, but still... Are you scared?"

"Terrified!"

"Aw, it'll be fine. Find someone to talk to, and the flight will go by in a blink."

"No one wants to talk on planes. I saw that on YouTube."

"You might get lucky."

"I have to go. They're boarding."

"Text me when you land. Both times."

"I will. Love you."

"Love you, too, baby girl. Be safe, and don't be scared. It's safer to fly than to drive in a car."

"Great, now I'll be scared the next time I'm driving."

"You should be scared every time you're in a car."

"Bye, Daddy."

"Bye, baby."

He was her best friend in the world, her port in a storm, the one who'd raised her on his own after her mother was murdered. If asked, he would say he'd had tons of help from his parents and siblings as well as her mother's sisters, but it had mostly been the two of them, and despite what he said, he'd done the majority of the work required to successfully raise a child.

As she presented her boarding pass to the gate agent, she thought of all the things the two of them had been through together, from kindergarten to middle school to her first period and getting her ears pierced, to high school, college and then the police academy, which had been the source of their one major disagreement.

Her father had been vehemently opposed to her becoming a police officer.

They'd argued for days about it, but Neveah had refused to back down. In the back of her mind, always, was the hope that maybe one day she might be able to work on her mother's unsolved case, but she never told him that.

He knew, though. Of course he did. He seemed to know everything where she was concerned. "They'll never let you anywhere near that case, so if that's your plan, find another one."

They hadn't talked for days after that argument, which was a first. She'd suffered in that silence and knew he had, too.

Pulling her suitcase behind her, she stepped aboard an airplane for the first time in her life, nodded to the flight attendant, and made her way past first class, where some of the passengers already had cocktails. She watched people stowing luggage in the overhead bins and followed suit when she reached row fifteen.

Neveah was settled in her window seat, watching the activity on the tarmac below when a young man settled into the middle seat.

She looked over at him, startled by the most extravagant eyelashes she'd ever seen on a man, framing golden-brown eyes.

He smiled. "Hey. How's it going?"

"Not bad. You?"

"Eh, middle seat. Not my favorite thing."

She didn't know what to say to that, having never experienced sitting in the middle seat on a plane.

"You headed to Minnesota or just connecting there?" he asked.

"Flying on to Spokane."

"It's pretty there. My cousins lived there when we were growing up. Spent some summers out there."

"It'll be my first time. Looking forward to seeing it. What about you?"

"Going to Seattle for a work conference."

"What do you do?"

"IT. How about you?"

"I'm a DC police officer."

"Oh, that's cool. Do you know the first lady?"

"She's my boss."

"No shit! What's she like?"

"She's an inspirational leader, although she'd hate me saying that. She doesn't like anyone fawning over her or treating her differently. She's a cop's cop in every possible way. I'm honored to work with her and learn from her. And P.S., she wouldn't like me saying that either."

"She sounds like a fun boss."

"She is, but she's also very focused and always looking for justice on behalf of our victims."

"That's cool. I'm Jeremy, by the way."

"Neveah."

"That's heaven spelled backward, right?"

"It's supposed to be, but my mother didn't spell it correctly."

"That's funny."

"She didn't think so when it was too late to change the birth certificate without a major hassle."

His low chuckle brought out a dimple on the right side of his face. "So if the first lady is your boss, then you're a homicide detective?"

"I am."

"Aren't you, like, kinda young for that job?"

"I've been a police officer for nine years."

"And you're already a homicide detective?"

"I am." She didn't mention the hundreds of extra hours she'd worked at every rank to move toward the next one, or how she always gave one thousand percent to everything she did, which had been noticed by people who mattered.

"That's hella impressive. Congratulations."

"Thanks, although working the murder beat isn't as much fun as it seems on TV."

"I can't imagine."

"Most people can't and are better off if they don't."

"I saw in the news that your boss's nephew was one of the missing kids. I was glad to hear they were found safe."

"Two of them were, including her nephew. The young girl is dead, though."

"What? No way. I hadn't heard that."

"Yeah, it's terrible."

"Did you work that case?"

"I helped out where I could, but a different case is taking me to Spokane."

"Oh, so it's a work trip?"

"Yes."

When the plane began to back away from the gate, Neveah grasped the armrests as her anxiety spiked into the red zone.

"Are you okay?"

"Can I tell you something silly?"

"Sure."

"I've never flown before."

"Never?"

"Nope."

"Are you scared?"

"Terrified."

"Don't be. It's not bad at all. You'll see."

As they taxied toward the runway, Neveah wished she hadn't

volunteered for this mission or been so confident in her assurances that she could handle it. At the moment, she felt like she was about to implode from anxiety.

"Hey, are you okay? It's really nothing to worry about. It's super safe."

"I'm okay," she said through gritted teeth as the pilot announced that their flight had been cleared for takeoff.

Jeremy extended his hand. "You want to hold on?"

She did. More than anything. "My hands are sweaty. They get like that when I'm nervous."

"That's no problem. Hold on. I've got you."

Neveah wiped her palm on her jeans and then took the hand he offered to hold on for takeoff, which was one of the most exhilarating and terrifying experiences of her life. The whirs of machinery and thumps and bumps as the plane ascended caused her anxiety to skyrocket.

"That's the landing gear being put away, the flaps adjusting for altitude and a few bumps from the clouds that don't appreciate us disturbing them."

With her eyes tightly closed and her focus on breathing, Neveah didn't want to smile at his commentary, but the cloud thing was cute.

"Open your eyes. Check it out. It's like looking at heaven, spelled correctly."

She chuckled and forced her eyes open so she could look out, and sure enough, if there was such a thing as heaven, it must look just like that.

"Nice, right?"

"Yeah." She realized she was still gripping his hand tightly and released him. "Sorry about that." Her father would have something to say about her holding hands with a white guy, which didn't matter at all to her. As she regularly told her dad, people were people, and she'd spend time with anyone she wanted to.

"No worries. I'm here for the whole flight if you need a hand to hold."

"Thank you so much. That's very nice of you."

"Not a problem. What do you do for fun when you're not working?"

"I work a lot."

"You know what they say about all work and no play..."

"I'm a very dull girl."

"I don't think so at all. You're a homicide detective. That's baller."

"Not sure about that, but if you say so."

"Tell me about the gnarliest murder you've ever worked on."

"You don't want to hear about that."

"Oh, I really do."

"Well, there was this one guy who was abducted by aliens, and when they returned him to Earth... they'd taken his most important parts, if you know what I mean."

He stared at her as if trying to decide if she was for real.

Then she smiled, and he laughed.

"You got me for a second there."

"What could've been the giveaway that I was messing with you? Was it the aliens?"

"You're funny."

"Nothing funny about murder, though." When she thought of the many ways her mother's murder had ruined her life and her father's, she wanted to talk about something else. "So," she said, "where're you from?"

"Grew up in Springfield, Virginia, but I live in Arlington now. What about you?"

"Born and raised in the District and still live there."

They chatted the rest of the way to Minneapolis, which made her almost forget she was on a plane. As the pilot announced their final approach into the Twin Cities, Jeremy held out his hand again. "You want to hold on for the landing?" After a beat, he added, "Since it's your first time and all."

"Sure, thanks," she said as she accepted his offer.

Holding his hand felt different this time after spending a couple of hours getting to know him.

"Will you give me your number so we can get together when we're back at home?"

"You want to get together?"

"Yeah, I do. Don't you?"

After being intensely focused on her career for years, she had about as much experience with men as she had with airplanes.

"Don't answer too quickly. You wouldn't want me to think you like me or anything."

She laughed. "I do like you, and yes, I'll give you my number."

He smiled, revealing that cute dimple again. "Great, now hold on tight for landing."

CHAPTER TWENTY-SEVEN

Nick returned to the residence to check on the twins, who were feeling much better, thankfully. As he walked toward the family kitchen, he heard chatter that had him smiling.

Alden saw him first. "Nick! Did you hear we're not sick anymore?"

"I did, and I'm so glad to see you looking much better." Their cheeks were a little rosier than usual, but otherwise, they seemed to be in good spirits.

"Dr. Harry said we still need a lot of ice cream," Aubrey said as she delicately dabbed a French toast stick in syrup. "And Nana said we could have French toast sticks anytime we want because they're soft on our throats."

"Nana is very wise." Nick kissed each of them on the top of their blond heads and gave his mother-in-law a smile. "And Dr. Harry is the boss. If he prescribes ice cream, then that's what we'll have. How's Nana holding up?"

"We're doing much better all around," Brenda said, "especially since... you know."

"I do know." While he, too, was so thankful that Ethan was home safe, he couldn't think about the murdered young girl without feeling a murderous rage toward the men who'd harmed her.

Brenda's eyes brimmed with tears that told him she felt the same way, but neither of them wanted the twins to hear about what'd happened to Ethan or Luna, so they forced themselves to move on.

"Is Scotty still at baseball practice?" Nick asked.

"Yep," Aubrey said. "But he'll be home soon."

"Is Sam home?" Alden asked.

"Not right now, but she should be back soon."

"Can we stay home tomorrow, too?" Alden asked

"You should be all better in time for school."

"Not fair," Alden said.

Nick made himself a glass of ice water. "What's this? You love school."

"I also love a good sick day."

Nick laughed and tousled his hair. "Nothing fun about being sick, though."

"That's true," Aubrey said. "My throat hurt *bad.*"

"How's Nana feeling?"

Brenda grimaced. "So far, so good. Fingers crossed."

"Thanks for taking one for the team."

"I'm very happy to have this time with them."

"We appreciate it so much, especially after these last couple of weeks."

"How's Sam doing?" Brenda asked.

"She's exhausted. I'm hoping she'll take some time off as soon as she can get a break in the action."

"*If* she gets a break in the action."

"Right. That's always a big if."

"Do you have to work tonight, Nick?" Alden asked.

"For a little while, but not until later."

"Okay," Alden said.

"Guess what?" Nick said. "Celia will be home soon."

That news was greeted with cheers and excitement.

"I've missed her *so* much," Aubrey said.

"Make sure you tell her that," Brenda said. "It'll mean a lot to her."

"I will."

Scotty came into the kitchen and went straight for the fridge to grab a bottle of the red Gatorade they kept on hand for him. He wore baseball pants with dirty knees and his team ballcap on backward. "You two are looking better. Did the cooties clear up?"

"We didn't have cooties," Aubrey said indignantly. "We had strep."

"Same thing," Scotty said, making a grossed-out face.

"Are you still feeling okay, buddy?" Nick asked.

"I'm fine, but if I timed my exposure right, I should be in line for a sick day tomorrow."

Nick and Brenda laughed. "Nice try."

"Strep is highly contagious, you know."

"And you're robustly healthy, according to Harry."

"You're raising a con man, Nick," Brenda said.

"I'm beginning to think you're right."

"If a guy isn't smart enough, he's a loser. If he's too smart, he's a con man. You can't win in this world."

"Take a walk with me," Nick said.

"Uh-oh. That sounds ominous."

"Nothing like that."

Scotty glanced at Brenda. "Send help if I don't come back."

"Will do."

He brought the Gatorade with him when he joined Nick in the hallway. "What's up? Is Ethan okay?"

"He's resting at home. I'm sure he's processing everything that's happened. Did you hear the news about Luna?"

"I did. It's so horrible. Do they know who killed her?"

"I think so, and Mom's team is working on making sure they're charged."

"All my friends are talking about it."

"What're they saying?"

"Just that no one's safe anymore, even kids. They know Ethan is my cousin, so they've had questions. But don't worry, I haven't said anything private. I wouldn't do that to them."

"Thank you for being protective of them."

"They're our family."

"That's right." Nick led him into the suite he shared with Sam, shut the door and sat next to him on the sofa. "I wanted to ask you if you've ever heard of an incel."

"Oh yeah. Those are guys that can't get girls."

Nick was shocked to hear Scotty knew the term and what it meant. "And that's something kids talk about?"

"It's one of the things they like to say when they're talking shit about their friends. No one takes it seriously, though. None of us can get girls at our age."

Nick didn't want to laugh, but a chuckle escaped nonetheless. Scotty was just so freaking cute.

"Why do you want to know about that?" Scotty asked.

"I heard that word for the first time recently, and I found out there's a lot of unsavory things attached to it. Most of it happens on the internet, and I wondered if you've seen stuff about it online or heard about something called the manosphere."

"I haven't heard of that, but I've seen people talking about incels. Girls like to toss that word around when they're rejecting us. According to them, me and all my friends are incels."

Alarmed by their use of a word fraught with violence and hatred, Nick said, "You know I always try to keep it real with you, right?"

"Yeah, why?"

"No one should be tossing that word around casually. There's an entire subculture devoted to it online, full of rejected men sharing their grievances toward women and plotting ways to exact revenge."

"Really?"

"Unfortunately, yes. It's a dangerous word to throw around."

"Okay. Should I tell the other guys that?"

"You could possibly suggest another word to tease each other with besides that one."

"Should I tell them you said it's not a good word to use?"

"You could say, 'My dad doesn't like me using that word casually. He said it has dangerous undertones.'"

He knit his brows. "Do I have to say 'undertones'? The guys will have no idea what that means."

Nick laughed. "Just say it's a dangerous word to throw around casually."

"I can do that."

"Do me a favor?"

"Sure."

"Stay away from the dark corners of the web where they talk about stuff like this."

"I have no interest in dark corners."

"I know you don't, but I need you to promise me that if we continue to give you full access to the internet, you'll handle it responsibly."

"I promise. I mostly follow my friends and my favorite teams and athletes."

"If you stumble upon something that scares you, or someone tries to get you to do something you know is wrong, will you come to me with that?"

"I will. Does this have something to do with what happened to Ethan?"

Nick hesitated, but only for a second. At fourteen, Scotty was old enough to know the truth about what'd happened—and Nick wanted that info to come from him, not online sources or friends. "It does. The man who took him and the other kids is well-known in the incel culture. Mom and the police believe he used Ethan and Tomas to lure Luna out so they could hurt her for rejecting the man's son."

Scotty's eyes got bigger with every word Nick said. "So they killed her because she didn't want to date his son?"

"That's the theory."

"But she was thirteen! She probably didn't want to date anyone. I'm a year older than her, and I'm not into that stuff yet. I mean…" His eyes filled. "We're still kids."

Nick reached for him and pulled him into a tight hug.

"We're just kids."

"I know, buddy. It's horrifying, and I hate that you have to be aware of this kind of stuff when you're just a kid. But unfortunately, we live in a world where people prey on kids, and I want you to keep you safe. That means staying away from anything that reeks of toxic masculinity. Do you know what that means?"

"Guys who hate women?"

"That's part of it, but it goes much deeper than that. Women owe us nothing, but not every guy thinks that way, and they become dangerous when they start to feel entitled to things they have no right to. Do you understand what I mean?"

Scotty pulled back. "We're talking about sex here, right?"

His facial expressions were priceless. "Among other things."

"You don't need to worry about me growing up to be the kind of guy who thinks women—or the world—owe him anything. I know I have to work for anything I want, because that's what you and Mom had to do. Just because you ended up in the Oval Office doesn't mean you think you deserve it or anything."

"That's right. No one 'deserves' anything. It's all about hard work and dedication, and with girls and women, it's about treating them with kindness and respect, never with a sense of entitlement."

"I get it."

"I know you do, and I'm enormously proud of the young man you're growing up to be."

"That means a lot to me. That you're proud of me."

"Oh, buddy, I'm *so* proud. I look at you every day and can't believe I got lucky enough to have such an amazing son."

"I'm the lucky one. I still think about that day we met, when you came to where I was living in Virginia... That was the best day of my life up to then. It's only gotten better since."

"Same goes, pal. That was right up there as one of the best days of my life, too. And I'm glad you think it's gotten better despite being under Secret Service protection and having to live in the White House."

"Are you kidding? I'm the coolest kid in school because my dad is the president and my mom is the butt-kicking FLOTUS cop. Everyone wants to be me cuz their parents are boring compared to mine."

"Is that right?" Nick asked, endlessly amused by him.

"Oh yeah. There are a lot of advantages to being the president's kid. For one thing, everyone thinks I'm smart because you are."

"I hadn't thought of that."

"It's true. I just have to fake it till I make it because people already think I'm going places just because you went to all the places."

Laughing, Nick gave him a one-armed hug and kissed the top of his head. "You're a dope."

"I know! But *they* don't know that."

Ah, this kid... What a treasure he was. "You're too much."

"I only speak the truth."

"And you promise you'll come to me if you ever have questions about anything—good, bad, ugly, disturbing. No matter what it is, come to me."

"I will. Always."

"Love you."

"Love you, too. Now about that sick day tomorrow..."

"Dream on."

AFTER LEAVING Scotty to finish his homework and the twins snuggled up to watch a movie with Celia, who'd been greeted like returning royalty with gifts for everyone, Nick went into the residence for a video meeting with his senior advisers. Terry had requested the late meeting after they'd tried all day to find time to fit it into an already-packed schedule.

Nick's conversation with Scotty had been the highlight of his day. He truly was the luckiest dad to have Scotty, the twins and Eli as his kids, and was looking forward to soon finalizing the adoption of Eli and the twins.

He felt better after discussing the disturbing meaning behind the word *incel* with Scotty and making the deal to keep the lines of communication open as his son grew into adulthood. That was happening much faster than Nick would like, but he wanted to enjoy every minute they had together before Scotty left for college.

He couldn't even think about that day without wanting to wail. Life would be so boring without him around to entertain them every day. Thankfully, they had four years of high school to look forward to before that happened.

He was reviewing the documents for the meeting when his BlackBerry rang with a call from Elijah.

"Hey, what's up?"

"Just wondering how Ethan and the family are doing."

"They took him home early this morning, but I haven't heard anything more today."

"It's such a sad story. I can't believe the girl is dead."

"I know. None of us can."

"I saw Sam's briefing about incel culture. That's some fucked-up shit."

"It sure is. Were you familiar with the term before this?"

"Yeah, I've heard about it, and we discussed it in one of my classes last year. Hard to believe there're men out there who think that way about women, but I suppose we shouldn't be surprised."

"It's very disturbing. All of it. And that it led to the murder of an innocent child..."

"Candace and I have been really upset about that," he said, referring to his wife, "and worried about how it'll affect Ethan."

"I know. Same here. We'll do everything we can to support them through this."

"If it wouldn't be weird, I'd like to spend some time with Ethan when I get home. Maybe some big brother-cousin support would help."

"I'm sure they'd appreciate that a lot, Eli. Thanks for offering."

"I wish there was more I could do. How's Scotty handling it all?"

"We had a good talk this afternoon, and he's processing it the same way we all are. And in other news, the twins are feeling much better."

"That was the other reason I called. Glad to hear it. I'll be home next Friday for the court date and then home for the summer a week after that."

"We can't wait to see you both times."

"Same. Have the kiddos FaceTime me at bedtime, will you?"

"Will do. Thanks for calling."

Before his meeting, Nick took a minute to text Sam to let her know the twins were feeling better, that he'd talked to Scotty about incel culture and he'd heard from Eli, who'd called to check on Ethan and the family.

Hope you're able to come home soon and get some rest. Love you.

She wrote back a few minutes later. *Going to see Luna's family, and then I'll be home. Glad to hear the twins are feeling better. What did Scotty have to say?*

He's heard the term and knows what it means, but not all the dark elements. We had a good talk, and he promised to come to me if he ever has questions about things like that. Eli has also heard of it. Said it came up in a class last year. He offered to spend some time with Ethan when he gets home for the summer.

That's so sweet of him. Thanks for talking to them about it. I can't wait to see the kids. I feel like it's been a month.

Tough couple of days. Going into a meeting, but I'll see you when you get home.

Will look forward to that. Love you, too.

He put down the BlackBerry as his team came online, led by Chief of Staff Terry O'Connor and including Deputy Chief of Staff Derek Kavanaugh, Communications Director Trevor Donnelly, Press Secretary Christina Billings-Gonzales and Medical Director Dr. Harry Flynn.

"Thanks for hopping on, everyone," Terry said. "How's Ethan and the family?"

"He was released this morning and is resting at home," Nick said.

"I can't believe they murdered Luna Ahern," Christina said. "Tommy says the details are hideous."

"It's horrific," Nick said. "Everyone involved in the case is heartbroken."

Vice President Gretchen Henderson came online from her home office. "So sorry I'm late. I had a kid struggling with algebra problems that I was unable to solve. Imagine that."

"No problem," Nick said, smiling at the face she made. "We're just getting started."

"I was so relieved to hear the first lady's nephew is safe," Gretchen said.

"Thank you." Nick was eager to get down to business, so he'd be free by the time Sam got home. "What's up, Terry?"

"As you know, this promises to be a big week as we roll out the first initiative from our gun violence task force. We worked this weekend to finalize the plans and wanted to update you, Mr. President."

"Thank you all for keeping things moving while I was out of the loop."

"Harry," Terry said, "you've been instrumental in the drafting of the plan, so if you'd like to brief us on the final details..."

"Happy to," Harry said. "As you know, Mr. President, this week, we'll introduce our mental health reporting mechanism through the Department of Health and Human Services, which is charged with receiving notifications from concerned family members. The idea is that a team of mental health professionals will follow up on these reports in an effort to intervene medically rather than a law enforcement response to hopefully de-escalate situations that could lead to gun violence."

As he listened to Harry and the others discuss the details, Nick was thrilled with the program they'd put together, which included teams in all fifty states and the District that were ready to respond to concerns from family members. And as he listened to his top advisers iron out the plans for how it would be introduced to the public, Nick couldn't wait to see his first major program in action.

CHAPTER TWENTY-EIGHT

Before she left to see the Aherns and then take a much-needed break after a dreadful couple of weeks, Sam called Brecken Mayfield's mother, Melanie, who'd been located by Ruiz's team after a somewhat exhaustive search. From what Ruiz had reported, Melanie had clearly not wanted to be found and had gone to some effort to stay off the grid. Despite that, Ruiz's detectives had gotten a phone number for her that she'd texted to Sam, asking her to follow up.

Sam placed the call, hoping Melanie would answer a call from an unknown number, so Sam didn't have to go to Potomac to see her in person. That'd take hours she didn't feel like spending at work when she was eager to see her family.

Melanie's voicemail picked up.

"This is Lieutenant Holland from the DC Metropolitan Police Department. I'd appreciate it if you could call me back as soon as possible."

A few minutes later, her phone chimed with a text from Melanie. *I have nothing to say about my son or ex-husband. I haven't seen either of them in years. Whatever they've done now, it does not involve me. Please leave me out of it.*

Freddie came into Sam's office. "Hey, are you going to see the Aherns? I'll go with you."

"You don't have to."

"I know."

He wouldn't let her go alone, and she loved him for that.

"I reached out to Brecken Mayfield's mother, and she wants nothing to do with us or them." She read the woman's text to him.

"Will you leave it at that?"

"I guess I'll have to. What can she tell us when she hasn't seen either of them in years?"

"Right, and there's no sense further traumatizing her by dragging her into it."

"Besides, if there're trials, she'll probably be subpoenaed eventually."

"True."

Recognizing a dead end when she encountered one, Sam replied by text to thank Melanie for her response.

"Walters has written up the warrant request for tower pings on the Mayfields' cell phones," Freddie said. "We hope to be able to put them in the vicinity of where the kids were when they went missing. That has to go to the cell phone company, though, so after we get the warrant, it's apt to take a few days."

"Right, but that'll be helpful in cementing our case against them."

Gonzo came to the door. "Brecken Mayfield is asking to speak to us."

Sam desperately wanted to leave so she could see Luna's family and then go home to her own.

"We can take it," Gonzo said, sensing her hesitation.

"No, I want to hear what he has to say. Let's get him into interrogation and ask Charity to come in, too."

Waiting for her to get there would require another delay, but it was important for the prosecutor to witness whatever the kid had to say.

She sat in her desk chair, exhaustion tugging at every cell in her body.

"You should let Gonzo take over," Freddie said. "He can fully brief you afterward. Cam's here, too. The two of them can handle it."

"I know they can, but I want to be there."

"I'm afraid you're going to keel over on me."

"I won't. I promise but do me a favor if you would."

"What's that?"

"Will you see about getting phones back to Tracy, Mike and the other families?"

"Yeah, I'll take care of that right away."

"Thank you." While she waited for all the players to arrive, she tipped her head back and closed her eyes.

"Sam."

Freddie's voice roused her.

She opened her eyes. "Did I fall asleep?"

"Yeah, for half an hour. Charity's here, and Brecken is in interrogation."

"Don't tell anyone I corked off."

He gave her a look that said, *What do you take me for?* "I'm going to watch from observation, and I'll be here when you're ready to go see the Aherns. Also, phones are on the way back to the families with Patrol."

"Thank you."

Sam and Freddie found Charity and Gonzo outside the door to interview two. "Are we ready?"

"Let's see what he wants," Gonzo said.

Sam and Gonzo went into the room, where a noticeably rattled Brecken Mayfield awaited them.

He lunged to his feet.

"Sit down," Gonzo said.

He collapsed into the chair and buried his face in his hands as his composure seemed to break.

They waited him out.

When Brecken finally looked up at them, Gonzo turned on the recording device, noted who was in the room and that AUSA Charity Miller was in observation and said, "You have the right to remain silent. Anything you say can and will be used against you in a court of law. You have the right to an attorney. If you can't afford one, a court-appointed attorney will be provided at no cost to you. Do you understand these rights as I've stated them?"

Mayfield nodded.

"I need you to say the words out loud."

"I understand."

"Do you wish to proceed with this discussion?"

"I do."

"You requested this meeting. What can we do for you?"

"I... I wanted to say... I never meant for anything to happen to Luna. I... just wanted to talk to her."

"If that's the case, why was your DNA found on her during the autopsy?" Sam asked.

He ran trembling fingers through his hair, seeming to think about what he wanted to say. "You have to understand that my dad... He's not someone you mess around with. If he tells you to do something, you do it."

"And that includes attacking and sexually assaulting a thirteen-year-old girl?" Sam asked.

"You don't know how he is... Nothing is ever enough for him. He said he wanted me to find a way to talk to Luna, so that's what I did, and then... when I realized what he really wanted, I told him no. I said I wasn't doing it, but then..." He shook his head. "I didn't want to hurt her."

"So tell me how it works when you say you want nothing to do with what he had planned for her, but your semen is found on her."

"He made me," he said on a low sob. "He told me he'd disown me if I wimped out on him and that he wanted a son he could be proud of, not a sniveling baby who couldn't follow through when he had the chance to get revenge. It's been me and him... My whole life, it's been us."

"And for all that time, he's been feeding you a toxic diet of hostility toward women, right?" Gonzo asked. "Beginning with your own mother."

The kid's eyes flashed with hatred. "She deserved to be disrespected."

"No, she didn't," Sam said. "She tried to save you from the exact predicament you find yourself in now, but your dad poisoned your mind toward her so he could exert full influence over you."

"That's not how it happened."

"Isn't it?" Sam asked. "Did she try to take you away from him when you were still young enough to be saved?"

"I didn't need her to save me! I was fine with him!"

"Until he told you to rape and murder a child."

"I didn't want to do that! I told him! I cared about her... All I wanted was for her to notice me and be nice to me."

"You made sure she noticed you when you raped her, right?" Sam asked.

He broke down into sobs, hands fisted against his eyes. "I didn't want to hurt her."

"Then why did you? Why didn't you tell your father no? Why didn't you defend her against him?"

Brecken dropped his hands from his face and stared at her with cold, unseeing eyes. "Because that's not how it works. She disrespected me. She had to be made to pay for that."

"With her life?" Sam asked, incredulous.

Brecken shrugged. "If that's what it took."

His swing from heartbroken to psychotic was truly jarring to witness.

"Is there anything else you wanted to say?" Gonzo asked.

"No, that's it. When can I get out of here?"

That he thought he had any prayer of being released was hard to believe.

"Never," Sam said.

Gonzo turned off the recording device as they stood to leave the room.

"Wait! What do you mean 'never'? My dad made me do it! I didn't want to."

That quickly, he was back to being a bewildered little boy.

They ignored him and left the room.

Charity and Freddie met them in the hallway.

"Are you guys thinking what I am?" Sam asked.

"Multiple personality disorder?" Gonzo said.

"It's called something else now," Sam said, trying to remember the current terminology.

"Dissociative identity disorder." Charity rubbed her arms as if to contend with goose bumps. "I'll request a full psych eval."

Cameron Green came down the corridor toward them. "Got the warrants for the wife's and sister-in-law's phones in the Carver case."

"Great, thanks," Gonzo said to his partner.

"Why do you guys look so spooked?"

"Take a look at the video for the conversation we just had with Brecken Mayfield," Sam said. "We're having a full psych eval done. Possible dissociative identity disorder."

"Oh wow. I've never seen that before in person."

"Be thankful for that," Sam said. "I'll never forget it."

"Same," Gonzo said as Charity and Freddie nodded.

"Will you get him back to lockup?" Sam asked Gonzo. "We're headed to see the Aherns."

"Yeah, I'll take care of it."

"I'll work on arranging the psych eval," Charity said before she left.

While Gonzo and Cam took care of moving Brecken back to lockup, Sam and Freddie headed for the morgue exit.

"I've never wanted out of here more than I do right now," Sam said.

"Right there with you. That was unreal."

"Is it weird that I started to feel empathy for him as it became clear he's seriously unwell?"

"No, it's not, because I did, too. This is all on the father who molded his son into a monster in his own image."

"I feel for the mom who tried to stop it."

"I know. If only she'd been able to get him away from the father."

"It was too late by the time she tried. The son was old enough to say where he wanted to be."

"I don't get why Asher Mayfield didn't lose custody after he was charged with multiple crimes, though."

"It seemed like he was good at disappearing when things got hot," Sam said.

They stepped out into the chilly April air and were greeted by Vernon, who held the back door of the SUV for her. She was happy to see him after such a difficult day.

"Heard about the Ahern girl. How're you doing?"

"Terrible, but I'm determined to see her parents on the way home."

"Do you have to do that?"

"I feel compelled."

"Let's get it done, then."

When they were on the way to the Aherns' home, Sam called Tristan McCaffery, the juvenile parole officer.

"McCaffery."

"It's Lieutenant Holland with the MPD."

"I heard you found Brecken Mayfield."

"We did, and I have questions."

"I'm sure you do."

"First and foremost, we're wondering how Brecken remained in his father's custody when both of them were committing multiple crimes and the son wasn't attending school."

"We brought CPS in multiple times. The kid refused to be relocated. He was physically and verbally abusive to anyone and everyone who tried to take him from his father. After the last time we tried to get CPS involved, the Mayfields took off. We had officers trying to find them, but their trail went cold. Eventually, we quit actively looking for them because we had so many other cases to deal with. The disappearance was reported to the court and school district, and warrants were issued for them."

"Would you be surprised to learn they were living just off Connecticut Avenue, and that's where they held two young boys hostage and used their phones to lure a young girl to her death?"

After a long pause, McCaffery said, "I'm not surprised."

"I hate to be a pain in your ass, but you do realize there'll be fallout over this, right? Brecken was in our system, but we lost track of him and stopped looking for him."

"I've known for a long time that kid could be the one who ends my career prematurely."

"And yet, no alarm was sounded. No one said, 'Hey, we've got a pretty dangerous kid on the loose in this city and people need to be aware'?"

"He's a juvenile. We don't put them on blast."

"Who was responsible for the father?"

"That'd be the adult division. I can give you the number for their director."

"Thank you." Sam wrote down the name and number he recited.

"Can you tell me what Brecken will be charged with?"

"First degree murder and sexual assault, to start."

"Jesus."

"Take care, Mr. McCaffery." She closed the phone, feeling outraged. "They don't put dangerous juveniles on blast, you see."

"I caught the gist," Freddie said. "And he's right. Juvenile criminals are protected by the system."

"We need a new system."

"Do you think?"

Sam rolled her eyes at him as she made the call to Matteo Ramos, director of adult probation in the U.S. Probation Office's DC division, which fell under the jurisdiction of the U.S. Courts.

Because the District's cases were handled by the U.S. Attorney for the District of Columbia, the probation unit landed at the federal level.

When Ramos's voicemail picked up, Sam left a message. "Please call me back on an urgent matter involving one of your parolees."

As they pulled onto the Aherns' street, her entire system was in an uproar of nerves and emotion as she contemplated this dreadful meeting. As the commander of the Homicide division, she tried to see the families of all their victims and to make herself available as their cases wound their way through the courts.

That was often a multiyear process that required a tremendous amount of support for the families.

Vernon brought the SUV to a stop a block from the Ahern home. "Give us a couple of minutes to clear the way," he said.

"Okay." She hoped they were quick, because exhaustion was winning the war.

CHAPTER TWENTY-NINE

Agent Q stayed with them while Vernon consulted with other agents who must've been summoned to support them as they took her into a home that was overrun with people.

"Have you heard anything from Jimmy?" Sam asked Q, wanting to take her mind off what she was about to do.

"I talked to him yesterday. He's up and about and itching to come back to work—literally, he said. The wound is itchy, and it's making him crazy."

"Glad to hear he's on the mend, but sorry to hear about the itching. When will he be able to come back?"

"In about three weeks. You're stuck with me until then."

"Happy to have you, but I wish Jimmy hadn't gotten hurt protecting me."

"I shouldn't say this, and Vernon would have my head for it, but... In our line of work, saving a protectee leads to a certain amount of, shall we call it... swagger?"

Freddie chuckled. "In other words, Jimmy will always be the guy who saved the first lady."

"That," Q said. "Exactly."

"Thank you for elaborating, Detective Cruz," Sam said

sarcastically. "I doubt I could've ascertained his meaning without your help."

"Please. You're about to fall over. It would've taken you two days to piece that together."

"Don't tell Vernon I said that, okay?" Q said. "I'd never want to be quoted as saying getting injured on the job is a good thing."

"What happens in the SUV stays in the SUV," Sam reminded him. "But I'm glad to know that saving my ass might've given Agent McFarland some bragging rights."

"For the rest of his life," Q said.

Sam would've been amused by that at any other time, but a visit with the parents of a murdered child cast a pall over everything. By the time Vernon came to retrieve them, she'd worked herself into an anxious mess.

"Sorry it took so long," Vernon said. "We asked the visitors in the house to wait outside while we bring you in."

"I don't like disrupting them that way."

"I understand, but it was too many people, and they were fine with it. They said the parents want to see you."

She walked with Vernon and Freddie to the Aherns' front door, where they were let in by a woman with dark hair and red, swollen eyes. It took a second for Sam to recognize her as the woman on the porch who'd freaked out the first time they met.

"I'm Court's sister, Janelle. Thank you for coming by."

"Of course. I'm so sorry for your loss."

"Thank you. This way."

She led Sam to the same room where she'd met Court and Jordy the first time she'd been there. Like then, they sat close to each other, hands tightly grasped.

Sam ached for them as Janelle told them she was there.

When they looked up at her, they barely resembled the people they'd been only a couple of days ago.

Court broke down.

Sam went to sit beside her, putting her arms around the grieving mother. "I'm so, so sorry."

"I don't know why anyone would want to hurt my little girl," Court said between sobs. "She's... she's my whole world. What do I do now? No one can tell me what to do."

"I don't have the answers you need, but I want you to know I'll be right here by your side through this entire process."

Though she was fully focused on Court, Sam saw Freddie wiping tears from his face as he stood in the doorway.

"It means a lot to us that you stopped by," Jordy said.

"I so wish we'd been able to bring about a different outcome. Everyone who worked on this case is devastated by the loss of Luna. We've all come to love her as we tried to find her."

"We appreciate what everyone did for her and for us," he said. "Please let them know."

"I will. When the time is right, I'll tell you more about the grief group we run at MPD headquarters for victims of violent crime."

He nodded to let her know he'd heard her.

"I won't take any more of your time, but you have my number, and if you'd like, I can keep you informed about developments in the case."

"We'd like to know that," he said as Court nodded.

"I'll take care of that personally. You and your family are in our thoughts and prayers."

"Thank you again for coming by."

Sam hugged them both before she got up to leave.

"Lieutenant."

She turned back to face Court.

"They... they made her suffer before they killed her. Make sure they pay for that."

"I will. I promise."

Sam hooked her arm through Freddie's and let him lead her to the door since she was blinded by tears. No matter how many years she spent in the Homicide division, the senselessness of murder never got easier to comprehend. That people could be so cruel to each other, that one person could steal another's life... She'd never become accustomed to how often that happened.

And when a child was murdered...

Nothing was worse than that.

OUTSIDE, Freddie wrapped her up in a tight hug. Normally, Sam would tell him she was fine, but she wasn't. Not this time. That beautiful child hadn't deserved to die this way, and when she thought of the many opportunities there'd been to put the Mayfields away for life, she became enraged on behalf of Luna and her parents, as well as Ethan, Tomas and their families.

The boys had thankfully survived, but would have to live with the horror and trauma of this incident for the rest of their lives.

After a few minutes, she pulled back from Freddie, wiped her face and tried to get herself together while he did the same.

Vernon handed them tissues, which they gratefully accepted.

"I'd ask how they're doing..." Vernon said.

Sam shook her head and found there were no words, even for him.

"I'll go to the Metro, Vernon," Freddie said when they were settled in the back seat of the SUV.

"Got it."

As they pulled away from the curb, Freddie put his hand on top of Sam's.

She turned her hand to clasp his, thankful for his steadfast support through the few ups and many downs of this difficult career. On days like this, she wondered if she could bear to go back for more tomorrow.

They rode in silence until Vernon pulled up to the Shaw-Howard University Metro station.

Freddie looked over at her. "Will you be okay?"

"Of course I will. What choice do I have? We have to be okay so that we can make things okay for them. Not that they'll ever be okay again, but we can help get justice for them. If you need to take some time tomorrow, go ahead."

"Thanks. I'll let you know, and you do the same. After these last couple of weeks, no one would blame you if you took a month off."

"Don't tempt me."

He released her hand with a final squeeze and got out of the SUV. "Call if you need me during the night."

"I will."

He shut the door and took off at a jog toward the station, always eager to get home to his wife.

As Vernon drove her home, she caught him taking occasional glances at her in the mirror, checking to make sure she was all right.

"It's always so much worse when it's kids," she said after a long silence.

"I know."

"And to find out that their parole officers lost track of them. I fear that's going to haunt us all."

"It might," Vernon said, "but maybe it should."

"Yeah, I guess, but it's just another hit on top of all the others."

"I know it's almost impossible but try to leave it all behind and get some rest tonight."

"I'll try."

He pulled up to the door at the White House a short time later, and when George, one of the ushers, came out to greet her, she wondered if Vernon had called ahead to say she was in rough shape. Her suspicions were confirmed when Nick followed George out the door.

"I've got this, George," Nick said as he helped her out of the car. He put his arm around her and took her inside and straight up the stairs to the residence.

"I really need to see my kids."

"They're asleep. They all conked out early."

"That's okay. I can still kiss them good night." She stopped first at the twins' room, adjusted their covers and kissed their soft, sweet heads and whispered that she loved them. Then she went to Scotty's room and did the same with him, giving Skippy, the dog, a pat on the head before she left them to sleep.

They went into their room and closed the door, sealing off the outside world for a few precious hours.

"I hate that I haven't seen them in two days and missed a whole weekend with them. What kind of mother does that make me?"

"A working mother who was sucked into a particularly difficult situation and handled it as well as she could, as she always does. Ethan needed you this weekend more than our kids did."

"In the meantime, my kids are at home sick with strep, and I'm nowhere to be found."

"They're fine, your mom took great care of them, and I was with them most of this afternoon and evening. They're much better and will be able to go to school tomorrow."

Sam sat on the bed, too tired to even get undressed. "That's good news."

Nick sat next to her, took her hand and said, "What do you need, love?"

"I don't even know. I'm all over the place tonight. I've just come from seeing Luna Ahern's parents."

"I know. I heard."

"Did Vernon call ahead?"

"Maybe, but I'm glad he did."

"Me, too. It was a tough one. I also found out that Probation had been looking for them for a long time and had lost track of them while Asher Mayfield was trafficking girls through his storage units." She shuddered as she said those words. "If only they'd sounded the alarm or said something or tried a little harder or asked for help looking for them, who knows what could've been avoided here?"

"So now, on top of everything else, you're feeling guilty because you weren't able to prevent this from happening?"

"I'm sad that there're so many of them and so few of us and that there're always going be some who slip through the cracks, which allows things like this to happen. I'm not blaming the Probation team. I'm sure they did what they could to find people who knew how to stay missing, but I wish more could've been done."

"The odds are stacked against you, babe, with far more bad guys outnumbering the good guys. You'll never win them all. That's just how it works."

"I don't like how it works. I don't like that so many of them slide through the gaps in the system and keep committing crimes that ruin people's lives forever. Those poor parents... Life as they know it is over, and it's so senseless."

"Murder is always senseless."

"That sounds like something I would say, and it's probably trademarked."

He smiled and rested his head against hers. "How about I draw you a bath?"

"That'd be awesome."

She rested her head against a pillow, processing the events of the day until he returned.

"Bath is ready, love," Nick said.

Sam walked into the bathroom, dropping clothes as she went, and slipped into the tub a minute later, sighing from the pleasure of the hot water and bath oil. "This was just what I needed."

"Don't fall asleep. Not sure I could get you out of there." He left the room for a few minutes and returned with a glass of wine that he handed to her as he took a seat next to the tub, holding a short glass of bourbon for himself.

He touched his glass to hers, and while she soaked, he silently provided his love and support, giving her space to cope with a difficult day.

"Scotty must be in his feelings about Ethan."

"He is, and he's eager to see him. I told him we need to give Ethan a little space right now."

"Maybe we can arrange a phone call for them tomorrow. I'll ask Tracy about it."

"How are things with her and Mike?"

"Not good at all. She's talking about divorcing him and asking for full custody."

"No way."

"Yeah," Sam said with a sigh. "It's bad. I'm not sure they'll be able to come back from this."

"Wow, I can't imagine the two of them not together."

"Me either. They've been a couple since I was still a kid. And you know I consider him a brother."

"Hell, I do, too."

"As much as I love Mike, though, I totally see where Tracy's coming from. Apparently, he told her she was being overprotective and hysterical, among other things he never should've said."

"Yeah, that's not necessary."

"The minute he seemed to side with Ethan, she lost the fight, and I'm not sure she'll forgive him for that. Especially now that Ethan has to live with having been involved in something that led to the violent death of another kid. How does he even begin to cope with that?"

"I don't know, but hopefully, with time and patience and therapy, he'll get back on track."

"I hope so, but I hate that this'll always be tied to him, and that's the part Tracy is the most upset about, too. In addition to his own ordeal, of course."

"I'm sure Mike is just as upset about all of it."

"Of course he is, but he made a huge mistake in judgment that led to this. It makes no sense when you consider what they went through with Brooke."

"I've been grappling with that myself, like how does he not become a *more* protective parent after that?"

"Exactly. But as much as I see Tracy's point, I sure as hell feel for him, too. He certainly never wanted anything like this to happen."

"No, he didn't. What do you think will happen now?"

"I have no idea, but I'm really worried about them all."

"I am, too."

CHAPTER THIRTY

Mike Hogan was in a state of disbelief as he packed a bag, checked on his sleeping son and daughter, then walked down the stairs and out of the house he'd called home for more than twenty years without a word to the woman he'd loved for all that time.

Almost everything that mattered to him was inside those four walls. He'd cried like a baby earlier when Brenda had brought Abby home. She'd run into the house, crying as she'd hugged him and Tracy, and then raced upstairs to see her brother.

Those two kids adored each other, even if they bickered like typical siblings. Seeing them back together had helped to soothe some of the agony he'd been living in since they'd realized Ethan was missing.

And yes, he knew it was all his fault. That was why he'd left the house the way Tracy asked him to, even though that was the last thing he wanted to do. He wanted to stay with his family and repair the damage that'd been done by his mistake in judgment. Every parent made mistakes, but some were bigger than others, and his had ruined everything.

Hearing that Luna Ahern was dead had been like a knife to the gut. And it was clear that Ethan's name would be tied to that horrible crime, even though he, too, had been a victim of the men who'd killed Luna. Would people remember that? Or would they think his son had helped to murder a young girl?

The implications were so horrifying, he could barely breathe.

He sat in his car for a long time, trying to figure out where he should go before he turned on the engine, put the car in Drive and left his family for who knew how long.

Tears slid down his face as he drove aimlessly through familiar, deserted streets late on a Monday night. Usually, by this time, he'd be watching TV with Tracy after the kids had gone to bed. With the kids getting older, he felt like he barely saw them during the week because they were so busy with after-school activities, friends and other things that kept them away from home.

He loved their weekends together, but even those were different now that their younger kids weren't little anymore. He prided himself on trying to grow along with his children, giving them the space they needed to become the people they were meant to be. But he'd fucked this up badly, and it was beginning to dawn on him that he'd pay for that mistake for the rest of his life. He regretted the things he'd said to Tracy when they'd fought about giving Ethan more independence. He never should've said she was being overprotective or hysterical, or any of the other stupid shit that'd come out of his mouth in the heat of battle. He'd regretted saying those things even before Ethan had gone missing.

Things had been different between him and Tracy in recent years. The stress of raising two younger children after their eldest had survived an attack in which other kids had died had put a strain between them that hadn't been there before. He knew they weren't unique in having parenthood take a toll on their marriage. It happened all the time, but it was unique to him to feel so disconnected from the woman he'd loved with all his heart for most of his adult life.

Things had been going wrong between them since Brooke had been attacked. Tracy had distanced herself from him as she'd helped their daughter through the traumatic aftermath. Once Brooke had recovered as much as she could from such a thing and left for college, he'd hoped he and Tracy might bridge the gap.

But it had only gotten wider.

Over the last couple of days, while Ethan had been missing, he'd had far too much time to ponder the many mistakes he'd made that'd led to this disastrous episode. It would be easy to say that all he cared about was having Ethan home safe, and of course, that was his prevailing emotion. However, he also cared about the damage that'd been done to his marriage and their family as a whole.

Would the children he loved with all his heart hate him someday for the mistakes he'd made that had allowed this horrible thing to happen to Ethan? Would Tracy turn them against him if they split up? Would she really sue him for sole custody of Ethan and Abby? Questions that would've been unfathomable three short days ago now hung over him with no easy answers.

In all their years together, Tracy had never been as angry at him as she was now. They'd never been separated or talked about splitting up or anything like that. Until now.

His phone rang with a call from his sister-in-law Angela. Even though he didn't feel like talking to anyone, he took her call because he knew how worried she'd been about Ethan.

"Hey, Ang."

"Oh, hi, Mike. I've been trying to call Tracy, but she's not picking up, so I figured I'd try you. How's Ethan? And how are you guys?"

"Ethan is sleeping finally, which is a relief. He's been super upset all day since we got the news about Luna."

"I can't believe she's dead. It's unbelievable."

"Yes, it certainly is."

"How are you guys doing?"

"Honestly, not so great. Tracy asked me to leave."

"Wait. What?"

"She's very angry and is blaming me for what happened because I allowed him to go out with his friends. She was adamantly opposed to that, but I felt he was ready for a little independence. Clearly, I was wrong, and she'll blame me forever."

"Where are you now?"

"Driving around, trying to figure out what to do."

"Come over here, Mike. Come to my house."

"Tracy won't appreciate you putting me up."

"We'll worry about that tomorrow. You can stay in the guest room. You shouldn't be alone right now."

"Are you sure you don't mind risking the wrath of your sister?"

"Don't worry about that. I can handle her. I just now put the porch light on for you. You've got the code."

"Thanks, Ang."

"See you soon."

At the next light, he hung a left to go back toward Capitol Hill, where Angela lived a few blocks from them. After Spencer died earlier in the year, Mike had made a point of stopping by regularly after work to spend time with the kids. He was there a lot. Hopefully, it wouldn't seem odd to them to wake up and find Uncle Mike there first thing in the morning.

He pulled onto Angela's street a few minutes later and found a parking space three doors down. After grabbing his bag from the back seat, he made his way to her house, recalling the door code the family had been given so they could get into the

Radcliffe house if necessary. Tracy worried endlessly about her younger sister being alone with two little ones and a baby on the way. She wondered how Angela would possibly handle it all on her own.

No one had been more there for Angela than Tracy had been since Spencer died. Under normal circumstances, Sam would've been there just as much, but her life had become even more complicated than it already was after Nick became president.

It wasn't lost on Mike that the strain of helping to care for Angela's family had contributed to some of the distance between him and Tracy, not that he blamed Tracy or Angela for that. Tracy was doing exactly what anyone would for a newly widowed sister. Anyone who knew Tracy well understood how much her younger sisters meant to her. There was nothing she wouldn't do for them, as she'd proven time and again over the years, especially in recent months when both her sisters had faced extraordinary challenges.

He went up the stairs to the front porch, put in the code and pushed open the door.

Angela was right there to greet him with a tight hug as he dropped his bag inside the door.

Mike was mortified to break down into deep sobs, which was the last thing Angela needed when she had more than enough on her own plate.

"It's okay," she said. "Everything will be okay. Emotions are running high after this stressful weekend. As soon as things calm down, Tracy will be willing to talk to you about what's gone wrong. She'll see that all that matters is Ethan being home safe."

"I don't know," Mike said. "I've never seen her like this."

"Her son has never gone missing before, thank God."

"This was all my fault, Ang."

"It was the fault of the men who took him."

"They wouldn't have had access to him if I hadn't let him run around with his friends."

"What were you supposed to do? Keep him under lock and key until he's twenty?"

"That's what we would've done if Tracy had had her way. At least until he was fifteen, maybe. I'm telling you... She won't forgive me."

"It all looks terrible right now, but after everyone gets some rest and calms down, maybe you can try to talk it out."

"Sure," he said. "Anything is possible." That was what she wanted to hear, but he knew for certain that it wouldn't be fixed that easily.

"Do you want to talk some more?" she asked.

He shook his head. "I'm all talked out after these last few days."

Angela led him upstairs to the guest room. "Make yourself at home. There're towels in the bathroom closet. Help yourself to anything you need."

"You got any booze?"

"You know where it is, in the cabinet over the fridge. I think Spencer still had some of the good bourbon in there. He'd want you to have it."

He hugged her and kissed her cheek. "Thanks for having me."

"Oh, Mike," she said tearfully. "I love you so much. I wouldn't have survived these last few months without you and Tracy. I'll do whatever I can for either of you any time."

"Love you, too, sis."

After she walked away, he teared up again at the thought of losing her and her kids from his life if Tracy succeeded in excommunicating him. He couldn't imagine living without the Holland family. They were as much his as they were Tracy's at this point.

Mike changed into sweats and a T-shirt and went downstairs to help himself to some of Spencer's good bourbon. He agreed with Angela that his brother-in-law would want him to have it. They'd been friends from the start, and his death had left a hole in Mike's life, too. Sure, the guy could be insufferable at times, but Mike had loved him, and his sudden, tragic death had been among the worst things to ever happen in Mike's life.

He downed the bourbon, had a second glass and then went upstairs to try to get some sleep. Before he shut the light off, he accessed the location services setting on his phone and turned it off in case Tracy decided to check where he'd ended up.

She didn't need to know he was at her sister's house.

AFTER A TURBULENT FLIGHT from Minneapolis without Jeremy there to reassure her, Neveah landed in Spokane. They'd exchanged phone numbers before parting company in the Minneapolis airport, and she wondered if she would hear from him.

At the Spokane airport, which was tiny compared to the intimidating massiveness of MSP, she followed the signs to the rental car area and discovered the counter for the company she needed was closed.

"Great, what do I do now?"

As she looked around, trying to figure out her next move, another traveler approached. "Are they closed?" the woman asked. "Sometimes they leave the keys for us if we're coming in late. Let's see if we can find them."

The woman went around to the back side of the desk like she worked there and located envelopes with names on them and keys inside. The envelopes were also marked with the numbers of parking spaces.

Neveah spotted the one with her name on it and said, "That's me."

The woman handed it over.

"Thanks, I never would've thought to check there," Neveah said.

"I fly in and out of here a lot," the woman said. "I've had to do this before."

"Well, I appreciate you showing me the ropes."

"Come with me. I'll also show you where the cars are."

"That'd be great. Thanks." Neveah dragged her suitcase along as she followed the woman into a parking garage, where the parking spaces were marked with letters and numbers.

"This one is mine. Thanks again for your help."

"No problem. Hope you have a good time in Spokane."

"You, too." Neveah didn't expect to have a good time, but she was proud of getting herself there, with a little help from some new friends.

In the rental car, she reached for her phone to put the hotel address into the GPS and found a text from Jeremy.

Holy moly, my flight to Seattle was rough. I hope yours was better than mine. I was worried about whether you were scared. Let me know how you are.

It was so nice of him to check on her. Though it was late and she was exhausted, Neveah replied to his kind text. *Mine was rough, too, and I sure did miss having your hand to hold when the plane was bouncing through the sky. Thanks for checking on me.*

She also texted her dad to let him know she'd landed in Spokane. He replied immediately. *Duh, I always know where my baby girl is.*

She kept threatening to take away his tracking capabilities, but she couldn't bring herself to actually do it

Thank goodness for GPS, she thought as she followed the directions from the airport to the hotel and checked in. Once she was in her room, she released a deep sigh of relief that she'd made it without any catastrophes. Then she checked her email to find a note from Gonzo that included the warrants for the phones of Trisha Carver and her sister.

After she changed into her pajamas, she checked the distance from her hotel to the Carver home so she could plan for the morning. It would take about half an hour to get there at this hour, but probably longer in the morning. Then she took yet another look at Trisha Carver's social media. She'd been waiting to see if the mom who posted about every detail of her life had mentioned her husband's murder in DC. There hadn't been anything the last time she'd checked, but it was there this time.

Heartbroken to announce that my sweet husband, Dale, passed away while on a business trip to Washington, DC. As many of you know, Dale has fought a valiant battle with addiction over the last few years, and while we thought we'd finally won the battle, it wasn't to be. Please pray for my children and for me as we face the rest of our lives without our beloved husband and father. Dale, we love you so much, and we'll miss you forever.

The post included photos of Dale and group shots of the family. The comments contained an outpouring of love and support for the family.

Neveah found it strange that Trisha didn't say Dale had been murdered but instead had made it seem like he'd lost his battle with addiction. Why would she do that when he'd fought so hard to get clean?

She took a screenshot of the post and texted it to Sam and Gonzo, asking if they found it as bizarre as she did. *Why doesn't Trisha say he was murdered? Why is she letting people think he died of a drug overdose when he didn't? Does this give us probable cause to arrest her? Please advise on what you think my next move should be.*

Gonzo wrote back right away, agreeing that it was odd and that the wife seemed to have created a new timeline of events rather than reporting what'd actually happened

Then she received a text from Sam. *I see probable cause all over the place here. Let's issue arrest warrants for her and the sister in the morning so we're ready if needed. We'll also need a governor's warrant for extradition, which can be issued by the chief judge of the DC Superior Court. Spokane has to make the arrest since it's out of our jurisdiction. The suspects can then either waive extradition or contest it. If they contest it, there's a hearing, and the judge has to approve the extradition, then we'd have to arrange transport, which we can arrange with the U.S. Marshals. It's really important that we follow this procedure to the letter, so we don't leave any opportunity for them to contest the process. We should also ask Spokane if they can dump the phones for us, so we'll know if we have grounds for an arrest while you're still there.*

Thank you so much for that information, Lieutenant. It's very helpful. My first move in the morning is to coordinate with Spokane police and outline our plan to them. We'll go from there, and I'll keep you posted.

Thank you, Neveah.

I'll handle all the warrants, Gonzo added. *I'll get that rolling tonight so we're ready. I imagine the Superior Court warrant will take a minute.*

You imagine correctly, Sam said. *Neveah, we might need you to stay out there for a couple of days to get this taken care of.*

Whatever it takes, Neveah said.

You're the best, thanks again.

While she was basking in the glow of her boss's praise, Neveah's phone chimed with another text from Jeremy. *Sorry to hear your flight was rough, too, but hey, now you can say you've survived a turbulent flight all on your own, which probably wasn't on your bucket list. Lol. I really enjoyed meeting you, and I hope you'll text me when you get back to DC. Let's grab dinner or a drink soon.*

The message had her grinning like a fool, but he was so sweet, or at least that's how he seemed. They were all nice at the beginning, weren't they? For the first time in a long time, Neveah wished she was the kind of woman who had girlfriends she could tell about meeting a nice guy on a plane who took the time to check on her after they'd gone their separate ways.

But she didn't have girlfriends because she'd spent all her time focused on the goal of ending up exactly where she was now, as a detective with the Metropolitan Police Department. Never in her wildest dreams had she imagined she would one day work for her idol, Sam Holland, but her years of hard work and dedication had paid off when Sam had invited her to join her team in Homicide.

That had been one of the best days of her life, and every day since then had been a new adventure, even if working the murder beat could be difficult and devastating. Her dad worried endlessly that it was too much for her, especially since she'd witnessed her mother's murder as a child, but Neveah told him she was exactly where she wanted to be, and she hoped her mother would be pleased to see her living her best life. She was fairly certain she would, because her mother's favorite show had been *Law & Order*, and they'd watched it together when Neveah was far too young for such things.

Losing her at six had been the most devastating thing to ever happen, especially since she'd been the lone witness to a murder that remained unsolved twenty years later.

While she waited to hear from Gonzo, she replied to Jeremy's text. *I really enjoyed meeting you, too. Will be in touch when I get back to DC.*

Her phone rang with a call from Gonzo.

"Hey, what's up, Sarge?"

"I wanted to make sure you were okay after your first flights."

While she was touched by the concern, she wondered if they all thought she was a bumpkin because she'd never flown before. "The first one wasn't bad, but the second was really bumpy. I didn't care for that."

Gonzo laughed. "Most of us hate that."

"I can see why."

"Thanks again for making the trip."

"Sure, no problem. Is there anything new in the Ahern investigation?"

"Sam and Freddie went to see the parents. It was rough."

"Ugh, I'm sure it was terrible."

"We had another chat with the Mayfield kid, and based on his behavior, we suspect there could be a personality disorder or something. Charity is requesting a psych eval."

"Oh wow, that's interesting."

"It was fucking creepy. Anyway, get some rest and check in after you see Mrs. Carver."

"Will do."

Neveah plugged her phone into the charger, got into bed, shut off the lights and stared up at the dark ceiling, thinking about her mother, *Law & Order*, the mission she'd undertake tomorrow, and a sweet, handsome guy named Jeremy who'd held her hand on her first-ever flight.

CHAPTER THIRTY-ONE

Archie arrived home after another long day and went looking for Harlowe. She was seated on the floor of his bedroom, folding a huge pile of laundry. He'd texted her to say he was on his way home, as he was still concerned about startling her as she recovered from her ordeal with Offenbach.

"Hey."

She smiled up at him. "There you are. Another long day."

"They all are lately."

"I did the laundry."

"Oh, thanks. I was planning to do that when I got home."

"Now you don't have to. I liked having something to do."

Archie dropped to his knees next to her and kissed her cheek. "Thank you."

"Welcome. Are you hungry? I used Instacart and got some stuff to make soup. It's on the stove."

"I could smell it when I came in." He kept his head on her shoulder, breathing in the sweet scent that was all her. No enhancements needed. "I like coming home to you."

"I was wondering if I'm outstaying my welcome."

"What? No. That's not possible. If I had my way, you'd stay forever. If you want to, that is."

"Forever is a long time."

"I have a feeling it won't be long enough."

"You should think about it when you're not exhausted after working so many extra hours."

"I'm perfectly clearheaded, and I don't need to think about anything. I'd love to have you living with me all the time, not just temporarily. But only if you're comfortable with it."

She bit her lip as she studied him in a way that made his heart flutter, which had never happened before he'd met her. "The fact that you care about me being comfortable means a lot to me. I've been... remembering more about being married to Evan and how miserable I was, and then later how afraid I was of him." Her memory had been spotty since her ordeal with Offenbach.

"I hate that you had to live like that."

"He showed me what to avoid—men who make it all about them, who need to be the center of everything, and when they don't get the attention they feel they deserve, they lash out." She shuddered. "I wish those memories had stayed buried with the other bad stuff."

Archie put his arm around her and held her close. He lived in desperate fear of her remembering being assaulted by Offenbach, especially when she'd seemed so much more like herself again in the last few days. The attack had left her with badly bruised ribs that had caused her no end of agony until a day or two ago, when she'd seemed to start moving more easily again.

"You never have to worry about any of that with me. I hope you know that."

"I do, and that means so much to me."

"Can I tell you something?"

"Anything you want."

He took a second to choose his words carefully. They were the most important words he'd ever say to anyone. "From the first minute I saw you across the room at Joe and Deb's, I had this incredibly strong feeling that you were going to change my life. It was the strangest thing... I'd never experienced anything like the absolute certainty that came over me, and I hadn't yet exchanged a single word with you."

"Archie," she said on a sigh.

"You were—and are—the most beautiful person I've ever met. You're beautiful inside and out, and after seeing you only a few times, I was already completely obsessed and wanted to spend every minute I could with you. I was leaving work on time! My whole team was asking me what was wrong. 'Nothing,' I said. 'Everything is finally just right.'"

She chuckled and dabbed at tears with a washcloth from the folded laundry. "You're making a mess of me."

"When I heard you'd been hurt... I honestly felt like I could kill the person who'd dared to harm you, and then, when I found out that it was tied to me and my work..." He shook his head. "I wanted to walk away from you and never look back because I was absolutely sick at the thought of someone hurting you like that because of me."

"We've already had this argument, and I won, remember? You would never hurt me, and I'll never blame you for what happened."

"That's more than I deserve."

She shook her head and gazed at him like no one else ever had. "You deserve all the good things, and after this, I want you to never say again that it was your fault, okay? I don't blame you, so you shouldn't either."

That was easier said than done for him, but if it was what she wanted, he could give her that. "It might take me a minute or two to get past feeling responsible, but I promise not to bring it up with you again." He took her hand and brought it to his lips. "What I'm trying to say in the most roundabout way possible is that I love you. I'm in love with you, and I have been from that first second I saw you."

He tucked a strand of gorgeous auburn hair behind her ear.

"So if you're wondering if you're outstaying your welcome, please believe me when I say the only thing I want in this entire world is you right here with me. I want to come home to you every night. I want to sleep with you in my arms. I want to wake up with you every morning and do everything else with you. Please don't go. You'd ruin me if you did."

She pressed the washcloth to her eyes, and when she pulled it back, she was smiling. "I love you, too. How could I not? My fierce protector, my guardian angel, my everything." She put her hand on his face and ran her thumb over the late-day stubble on his jaw. "Not to mention, the handsomest, sexiest, sweetest man I've ever known. You're the one I pictured when I was a little girl, thinking about the man of my dreams and what he'd be like. He's you."

"Harlowe," he whispered as he leaned in to kiss her. "She's the one I've been waiting for, and her name is Harlowe."

The kiss went from soft and sweet to fiery in a matter of seconds. Moving carefully, he eased her back until they were stretched out on the floor next to the piles of folded clothes as one kiss became another. Her arms circled his neck as she kept him anchored to her when he would've pulled back to slow things down. When he tried, she whimpered.

"Don't stop."

"You're not ready for this."

"I am."

"No, honey, you're really not, and rushing it would be the worst thing we could do right now when you're feeling so much better." He sprinkled soft kisses on her cheeks, the tip of her nose and on each eyelid. "I'll be right here when the time comes, but for now, you need to rest and continue to recover."

"What about what I want?"

"That's all that matters to me."

"Then you should definitely keep kissing me, because that's what I want."

"Harlowe…"

"Archie..."

"Kissing only."

"We'll see."

"I'm serious."

"As am I, and if you treat me like I'm made of fragile glass, this will never work between us."

"I intend to treat you as if you're the most precious thing in my life, which you are." He caressed her face and buried his fingers in her soft, silky hair. "Two days ago, you were still having trouble moving around. Everything you want will be waiting for you to be fully recovered from your injuries."

Her bottom lip pressed forward in a pout for the ages.

Smiling, he nibbled on it, which was a mistake because she pounced on the opportunity to lure him into another tongue-twisting kiss that had him forgetting everything he'd just said in a matter of seconds.

"You're very pleased with yourself, aren't you?" he asked when he finally recovered his wits and came up for air.

"I am indeed."

"I love seeing you like this."

"Like what?"

"Happy, smiling, disobedient."

She laughed. "That last one might be a problem for a law-and-order guy like you."

"That'll never be a problem for me. I like you just the way you are."

"How will you react when I truly make you mad?"

"I can't imagine ever being truly mad with you."

Her brows knit in frustration. Even that was adorable on her. "Be so for real right now, will you please?"

"If, and that's a very big if, you ever make me truly mad, you can expect maybe a little silence and moodiness."

"Hmm, how long should I expect that to last?"

"A day or two, maybe. But that was in the past. With you, I probably won't be able to sustain it for that long."

She ran her fingers through his hair, triggering goose bumps on his arms and back. "Maybe instead of going silent on me, you could talk to me about whatever is bugging you."

"I could do that, but like I said, I'll be surprised if that happens."

"You're being for real, remember? You haven't seen me bitchy or cranky yet."

"I can't wait to experience all the moods you wish to have. I'm here for it all."

"It wasn't like that for me in the past."

"That was then. This is now. If I ever do anything that scares you, I want you to tell me the second it happens so I can make sure I never do it again."

"You could never scare me."

"We're being so for real, right?"

"That only applied to you, not me."

He laughed. "I see how it is. I can be intense sometimes, and if that ever worries you, all you have to do is say so."

"I will. Thank you for saying that."

"Let's get you off the floor."

"But I was having so much fun down here until you got all adult on me."

He kissed her once more, softly and sweetly and with all the love he felt for her. "There'll be much more fun to come when you're fully recovered."

"I'm going to hold you to it."

"I can't wait for that."

After Mike left, Tracy walked through the house, checking doors and windows to make sure everything was locked and no one could get in to harm her or her children. She wished they'd put in a security system years ago, because she'd really like to have it on a night like this, when she was home alone with her babies and raw after the trauma of the last few days.

She couldn't recall the last time she'd spent the night alone with the kids. Mike used to travel a lot for work, but a series of promotions had made it so he rarely left the DC area these days. It'd been years since she'd spent a night without him.

It was strange to know that he was gone, even though it'd been necessary to her that he leave. She couldn't bear to look at him and realize how close they'd come to utter catastrophe, so it was good to take some time apart and figure out the next steps without the pressure of having to deal with each other.

Upstairs, she stood in the doorway to Ethan's room, watching him sleep, bathed in the glow of a nightlight that hadn't been used in years. She was swamped with relief and gratitude that he was home where he belonged, but overwhelmed with grief for Luna's family.

Tracy could've stood there all night, keeping watch over him, but she was exhausted and desperately hoping she could sleep —for a little while, anyway. After she checked on Abby, she went into the room she shared with Mike, which felt lonely and bereft tonight without him.

Not that she regretted asking him to leave, because she didn't. She didn't have the bandwidth to contend with him and the rage at the same time she was tending to Ethan. He was the only thing that mattered right now, and he would have her full attention, as would Abby, who'd have questions in the bright light of day that she'd been too tired to ask tonight.

Tracy could only hope she would have the answers that Abby needed, because she couldn't explain a lot of it to herself quite yet. She'd also have to deal with the kids asking where Mike was, a thought that made her even more exhausted than she already was.

In bed, she checked her phone for the first time in hours and found more than a hundred messages from family and friends. She didn't have the fortitude to scroll through them tonight, but the outpouring made her feel loved and supported, until she read a message from Nick.

Sam is asleep, but she'd want me to tell you that in the morning, we'll be all over making sure Ethan's name isn't tied to Luna's murder. Don't go online. Don't read what people are saying. They're only saying that shit because he's my nephew, and I will fix this for him—and for your family. Once they hear the full story, we have to believe everything will be fine. We love you, and we'll take care of you.

A sob ripped from Tracy's chest as the dam finally broke. People were talking about them. They were talking about her precious, innocent child and tying his name to the murder of a beautiful young girl. Now she wondered how many of those hundred text messages waiting on her phone were actually supportive.

Whatever was blowing up online had to be terrible for Nick to reach out about it with all he had to do. He had to be distraught that the higher profile their entire family had as a result of him being president was causing people to be extra interested in Ethan's disappearance in the first place.

She'd take his advice, and she wouldn't look at anything online so she'd have a prayer of getting some rest. She shut off the light and closed her eyes, trying to clear her mind of the horrors of the last few days, already knowing she'd never forget any of it.

Despite the rage, despite the directive for him to leave, all she wanted at a time like this was Mike, and that she couldn't turn to him for comfort was unbelievable. That she might never have him to turn to again broke her once again. She hadn't cried like this since her dad died. Even Spencer's untimely death and all the associated grief hadn't hit her this hard.

"Mommy."

Abby's soft voice from the doorway had Tracy trying to get herself under control so she wouldn't scare her baby.

"Can I come in?"

"Of course. Come here, honey."

Abby crawled up on the bed and into Tracy's arms.

"Did something else happen?"

"No, sweetie. I'm sorry if I scared you."

"I thought you'd feel better now that Ethan is home safe."

"I do feel better, I'm so, so relieved he's home and he's safe."

"Then why are you crying?"

"It's all catching up to me, I suppose. What happened, what could've happened, what happened to Luna... All of it."

"Where's Daddy?"

"He's... He went out for a while."

"Why?"

"We needed a little time to ourselves."

"Will he come back tomorrow?"

"I don't know yet. Sometimes mommies and daddies need a little break from each other. It's nothing to worry about."

"I am worried. You've never needed a break from each other before."

"I don't want you to be upset. We both love you very much, and we always will. If it's okay with you, maybe we could just snuggle and talk more in the morning. Tomorrow will be another day, and we can talk about anything on your mind then. Okay?"

Abby nodded and burrowed deeper into Tracy's embrace.

"I'm glad you're here with me. You're still the best snuggle bug ever."

"Better than Brooke and Ethan?"

"Better than anyone, but let's make that our little secret."

Her soft giggle was just what Tracy needed as she closed her eyes, took a deep breath and tried to sleep.

CHAPTER THIRTY-TWO

Jesse hadn't expected to spend the night and had awakened with the most unholy crick in his neck from sleeping in the chair next to Memphis's bed. When he tried to move his head, a sharp pain stabbed his upper back.

His gasp woke her and had her turning toward him to see what was up.

"Slept wrong," he said as he rubbed at the ache in his neck.

"I told you to go home."

"You're not the boss of me."

"Maybe I should be. If you'd listened to me, you wouldn't have a crick in your neck."

He scowled at her as he tried to stretch the kinks out and succeeded only in making it worse. "Son of a bitch."

"You're getting too old to spend the night in a crappy hospital recliner."

"Who are you calling old?" At thirty-seven, he'd never felt older than he had lately, but he was allowed to think that of himself. She didn't get to say it.

"Which one of us is moaning and groaning because he can't move his own head?"

A snappy comeback died on his lips as another sharp pain

required his full attention. Cripes, he'd be walking crooked for a week at this rate.

"Hey, Jesse?"

The soft, uncertain-sounding question put him immediately on alert. His Memphis didn't ever sound vulnerable, so what was up with that? "Yeah?"

"What're we going to do?"

"About what?"

"This. You, me, work, all of it."

"Why do we have to do anything about it? We've gotten away with it for this long."

"You want me to go home with you after I get out of here."

"That's right, and that's what we're doing."

"People will have questions."

"Fuck them. It's none of their business."

"It's not Lafferty's business?" she asked, referring to their boss.

He'd spent the better part of a year praying that Lafferty would never catch wind of his... whatever it was... with a subordinate. "It's no one's business what we do on our own time."

"You know that's not true. You've conveniently forgotten that you're my boss, and we're not allowed to be together outside of work."

"We've been together outside work for a long time, and it's never affected anything. Why should it now?"

A deep sigh was her only response.

"Why don't you just say what's on your mind?" he said in a snappier-than-intended tone.

"I'm trying to, but you're being obtuse."

Jesse stood and immediately regretted the movement when the pain had him trying not to cry like a baby. "How am I being obtuse?"

She stared at him in that way of hers that made him anxious from her ability to see right through him and his bullshit. "You said things to me… after I was shot that made me think you maybe see me as more than just a fuck buddy."

He stared back at her. "I don't think of you that way."

"How do you think of me?"

Before he could answer that burning question, her mother and grandmother came breezing into the room, bringing their traveling circus with them.

"How is our darling girl today?" her mother, Alberta, asked in a singsong voice that grated on his last nerve as she swooped in to hug and kiss Memphis like she hadn't seen her in a year.

Judging by her perturbed expression, Memphis wasn't pleased to have their conversation interrupted, whereas Jesse felt like he'd been thrown a life ring.

He knew it was a temporary reprieve and that he'd better have some answers for her the next time they had a minute alone. What those answers would be, he couldn't say. "I, uh, I'm going to run home to shower and change. I'll be back."

The three women ignored him as he moved carefully to leave the room, his head tilted at a fifteen-degree angle to keep the agony under control.

MEMPHIS WANTED to scream from frustration and annoyance. Her mother and grandmother's timing was exquisite, as always.

"What's the matter with you?" her grandmother, Beatrice, asked.

"Nothing. I was talking to Jesse."

"That man…" Alberta plumped Memphis's pillows. "He's a strange one."

The comment made Memphis want to defend him when she'd wanted to stab him a few minutes ago. He gave a little and then took it away again so fast that she existed in a constant state of whiplash. And he thought *his* neck hurt. Ha! "He's not strange." Yes, he was, but her mother wasn't allowed to say that.

"Does he speak?" Beatrice asked. "Or only grunt?"

"He speaks." *And when he does, he ties me up in knots,* she thought, not that she would ever say that to them.

"What're you doing with him?" Alberta asked.

"We're friends. And colleagues."

"He's your boss, right?"

"Technically."

Beatrice snorted. "Is he or is he not your boss?"

"He is." She'd sucked at lying to them all her life, so there was no point in trying to get away with it now.

Alberta crossed her arms and gave Memphis the stare-down from the right side, while Beatrice armed the left flank. Did they care that she was still in the ICU?

"So what's he doing sleeping in your room?" Alberta asked.

"He came to check on me last night and fell asleep. He's been looking for the first lady's missing nephew and had been up for two days."

"What would his boss have to say about him spending the night in your hospital room?" Alberta asked.

"Good question," Beatrice said.

As always, they were the ultimate tag team.

"Can we save this inquisition for another time? I'm not feeling great."

"You look much better," Alberta said.

"Great, but my leg hurts like a bitch."

"Language," Beatrice said with a frown.

What would she say if Memphis said *fuck this shit* at the top of her lungs, the way she wanted to?

"What's his story?" Alberta asked, never one to give up the proverbial bone once she had a taste of it.

"He's a marshal, like me."

"What's the rest of his story? Why's he so weird?"

"He's not weird, Mom! Stop saying that!"

Maybe she shouldn't have responded so vehemently, because their curiosity was even more piqued than it'd been before.

"No need to be defensive. He's just a guy you work with, right?"

"Yeah."

"You know what I always say, Mama?" Alberta asked her mother.

"What's that, sugar?"

"You can lie to some people, but your mama and your grandmama can see right through your nonsense."

"You do say that—a lot."

Memphis wished she could glare at them both at the same time. "Are you two done?"

"Nah, baby, we're just getting started," Alberta said, "and we aren't leaving until we're sure our girl is making good decisions for herself—and the career she worked so hard to have."

"Thanks for the warning," Memphis said under her breath.

"What was that?"

"Nothing."

"That's what I thought you said."

She wanted to remind them that she was thirty-three years old and a fully grown adult in charge of her own life and could decide who was important to her. But she'd never say that out loud. They'd raised her to respect them, and she did. Most of the time, anyway. When they weren't trying to run her life the way they had when she'd lived at home. Leaving for college had been the best thing to ever happen to her, even if she'd missed them fiercely.

How long would Jesse be gone this time, she wondered, and what would he have to say when he returned? And could they go back in time to when she first woke up from surgery, when he called her baby and was about to cry with gratitude because she hadn't gone and died on him? That'd be nice.

"BABE."

Nick's whispered word and the soft kiss to her cheek roused Sam from the deepest of deep sleeps.

"Mmm. Not yet."

"You've got to wake up. Social media is on fire over Ethan and the murder of Luna Ahern."

Sam's eyes flew open so fast, it was a wonder she didn't sprain her eyelids. "What?"

"People are speculating about what happened, saying he was probably involved, but we're covering it up to preserve his reputation or some such nonsense."

Groaning, she said, "Come on. We already said he was a victim, not a perp."

"You have to say it again—and soon. It's already spinning out of control."

Her phone rang with a call from Malone.

"Wonder what he's calling about," she said as she reached for the phone. "Hey."

"Are you seeing the stuff online?"

"Not yet, but Nick just told me about it. What's the plan?"

"We need to issue an update ASAP to put a stop to the speculation. We're prepared to announce we're charging Asher and Brecken Mayfield with kidnapping, first-degree sexual assault, unlawful imprisonment and felony murder. Brecken will be charged as an adult, even though he's only fifteen. The statement will also reiterate that neither Ethan Hogan nor Tomas Cambra was involved in the kidnapping, sexual assault or murder of Luna Ahern. Does that work for you?"

"Yes, that's fine. Thank you for handling it."

"We'll get it right out and put a stop to this shit."

"I hope that does it." She glanced at Nick. "Do you mind if Nick's team puts out a statement after yours?"

"Do whatever it takes to shut this shit down."

"Thanks, Cap. If it's okay with you, I think I'll take a personal day today."

"It's fine with me. Take tomorrow, too."

"Tell Gonzo to call me as needed on the Carver case."

"We've got it. Take a much-needed break and be with your family."

"Call me if you need me for anything."

"Will do."

Sam slapped her phone closed. "I've got the next two days off."

"Oh boy, what's your plan?"

"More than anything, I want to be with the kids, and I want to see Tracy and her kids."

"Technically, even though Harry cleared them to return to school, the twins could probably use one more day to recover, and Scotty would lose his mind if we let him take a sick day."

"Tell me the truth."

Her serious tone had his brows knitting with confusion. "About?"

"Did the apocalypse happen while I was asleep?"

"Huh?"

"Are you, the ultimate nerd rule follower, actually suggesting we give our kids a fake sick day?"

He attempted to look sinister—and failed miserably. "Did you just call me a nerd?"

"Does the shoe fit, Mr. President?"

"Here I am, trying to give my precious wife the thing she said she most needs today, and what do I get for my trouble but name-calling and disdain."

"You're very cute when you're being indignant."

He leaned over her to nuzzle her neck. "You're cute all the time, even when you're calling your husband the president a nerd."

Sam giggled as much from the words as the ticklish feel of his lips on her neck. "Why do you smell so ridiculously good at the ass crack of dawn?"

"Because I've already been up for two hours, showered,

shaved, had two cups of coffee and am about to leave for my briefing."

Sam put her arms around him. "They can't start without you, right?"

"Usually, I'm the main event."

"Tell me everything will be okay with Ethan."

"We've got all the right people on it, and I also think keeping Scotty out of school and away from the questions today is the right move."

"That's a very good point."

"I'll have Christina release the statement we prepared. It reiterates that Ethan and his friend were victims of a senseless, violent crime, and thanks to their own ingenuity, they were able to escape. Anyone who says otherwise is peddling lies and conspiracy theories and could be opening themselves up to legal action. The statement also says that while we're thankful and relieved to have Ethan and Tomas home safe, the first couple's hearts are broken for the Ahern family."

"You're good at this. You might want to consider a career in politics."

"Do you think I could go all the way?"

She gave him a lascivious smile as she ran her fingers over his silk tie. "Any time you want, sailor."

"That's commander in chief to you, ma'am."

"Look at you, acting all presidential and shit. It's not going to your head, is it?"

"Maybe a little. After all, they break into a special song just for me any time I enter the room."

"My heart breaks into a special song just for you every time you enter the room."

He kissed her. "That's the only song that matters."

HE LEFT the room after promising to call the kids out of school, have Trevor issue the statement as soon as the MPD got theirs out and try to come back for breakfast with the kids.

Sam sent Tracy a message to let her know that her people and Nick's were all over the situation online.

As she contemplated whether she might go back to sleep for a little while, her phone chimed with a text from Tracy.

Thank you both. I'm not looking.

Me either, and from what Nick said, that's for the best. We know the truth, and we'll never deviate from it. Did you sleep at all?

I think so. But it was fitful. Mike left last night.

Sam called her sister. "Where'd he go?"

"I don't know."

"Trace... He feels terrible."

"Hang on."

Sam heard rustling in the background before a door clicked shut.

"I had to go into the bathroom. Abby's sleeping in my bed. I'm keeping her home today since the whole world is apparently accusing her brother of murder. I thought she probably shouldn't be in school with that going on."

"I'm so sorry about all this."

"Me, too, and as much as you might want to defend Mike—"

"Wait! I'm not defending him. I'm only saying he's devastated."

"I know he is, but that doesn't change the fact that the only reason we're all devastated is because he allowed our son to do something I said was unsafe. So I'm sorry if I just can't be around him right now, but I simply cannot."

"I get it, and I'm always on your side, even if I love him, too."

"I'm not asking you or Angela or anyone to pick sides."

"We'd always choose you and your kids. You know that."

"I don't want him kicked out of the family. I just need to find a way to deal with this without him sulking in the background."

"What can I do?"

"Nothing. I'm fine. Any time I start to think I can't handle it, I consider what Luna's mother is going through, and I stop my whining. My son is home safe. Did he have a horrifying ordeal? Yes. Is the fallout from that ordeal going to last the rest of his life and mine? Probably. But all that matters is that he's okay. When I think about how this could've ended for him and Tomas…"

"Don't go there."

"It's hard not to when these men were capable of torturing and killing a young girl. Imagine what they had planned for Ethan and Tomas."

"I'd rather not. Can I come see you later?"

"Don't you have work?"

"The kids and I are taking a personal day."

"I think some cousin time might be just what Ethan and Abby need—and I could use some sister time."

"We'll be over after lunch."

"See you then."

CHAPTER THIRTY-THREE

S am was coming out of the shower an hour later when her phone rang with a call from Faith Miller.

"Hey."

"Heard you were taking a personal day, and I'm sorry to bother you."

"No worries. What's up?"

"First of all, how's your nephew and your family?"

"We're hanging in there, avoiding the internet and doing what we can to stem the damage."

"It's outrageous. People with no information whatsoever are speculating wildly about eleven-year-old boys being complicit in murder, all because one of them is related to the first couple. Absolute madness."

"Yes, it is. I heard you're charging the Mayfields."

"Charity is at their arraignment now. We've all seen a lot, but that case is seriously disturbing."

"It certainly is."

"So, I'm calling to remind you of two upcoming court dates. You said you wanted to be notified of anything having to do with Thomas O'Connor, right?"

"Yes, that's right." Not only had he murdered his father and

Nick's former boss, Senator John O'Connor, but Thomas had also killed several of the women his father had dated—and the husband of one of them—while pretending to be faithful to Thomas's mother.

"There's a hearing next week to discuss next steps. His defense is still aiming for an insanity defense, but I have to tell you, we're not on board with that recommendation. We think it's possible he's faking it to try to avoid prison."

"What makes you say that?"

"The fact that the doctors at the psych hospital haven't witnessed a single thing that would lead them to believe he's insane or in any way diminished mentally. If anything, they've found him to be a well-spoken, articulate young man who gets along well with the other patients and participates in individual and group therapy while seeming to enjoy the interactions. Most of our younger defendants tend to be deeply hostile toward therapy. Thomas loves it. Other than the murders he committed, there's simply no evidence to support an insanity defense."

"I see. Thank you for explaining that. Have you been in touch with Senator and Mrs. O'Connor?"

"They're my next call."

"I assume it's okay to tell my husband the hearing is coming up?"

"Yes, of course. Secondly, as you're certainly aware, the Christopher Nelson trial begins a week from Monday. I wanted to check in to make sure you're set to testify the first day."

"That's the plan." The son of the late president had conspired to discredit Nick, his father's popular vice president, to further his own political aspirations. Among other things, Christopher had tortured and killed Sam's ex-husband, Peter Gibson, who'd refused to give up dirt that could be used against Sam and Nick.

"Do you have any questions or concerns for me?"

"No questions. Many concerns about reopening the wound

of my ex-husband's murder, as well as the countless reasons he was my ex-husband."

"I'm sorry to put you through it."

"It's fine. Goes with the territory. And in case you were wondering, I do hate how often this stuff strikes too close to home for me."

"I give you credit for rolling with it all."

"What choice do I have? I can't give up. I've got kids watching me."

"Not just your own either."

"I forget about that."

Faith sputtered with laughter. "Only you, Sam."

"I wish I had a buck for every time someone says that to me."

"Let me guess... You'd be a millionaire."

"Possibly a billionaire."

"Thanks for the laugh. I'll send you the details of the O'Connor hearing."

"Thanks for calling, Faith."

"Have a good break and call me if you need anything."

Sam closed her phone and reached for the secure BlackBerry to update Nick about the O'Connor hearing. *Faith told me they're fighting the insanity defense.*

She couldn't hear the name Thomas O'Connor without being transported right back to the first time she saw Nick, six years after the night they first met and connected. If you could call what happened between them that night "connecting." It was more like nuclear fusion that was followed by a series of misunderstandings—and manipulation—that'd cost them six years together.

As she dried her hair, she recalled the thrill of seeing him again, even if it was at Senator John O'Connor's murder scene. Everything had been so fraught then. She'd still been reeling after an undercover assignment had resulted in the death of a young child. Two and a half years later, she still couldn't think of

Quentin Johnson and the series of events that'd led to his death without wanting to wail.

She'd gone into the O'Connor investigation determined to get her career back on track and had smacked headfirst into the one man she'd never forgotten—O'Connor's chief of staff and a witness in her case. That had put him firmly off-limits, which only made him all the more enticing.

Nick returned her text. *Interesting about the insanity defense.*

Faith said it's a nonstarter. Speaking of the O'Connor case, I was thinking about that first week back together, and I want to pretend we haven't seen each other in six years and everything between us is forbidden...

What the hell, babe? I have a meeting in two minutes. I'm going to have to stay behind the Resolute Desk.

Picturing his shocked and outraged expression, Sam laughed so hard, she had tears in her eyes. *Hahahahahaha.*

NOT FUNNY.

HAHAHAHAHAHAHA. So can we?

Why, hello, Ms. Secretary of State...

Oooph

Have a seat by my desk because... wood.

Hahahahaha. Love you.

Grrrrrr.

While she was messing around with him, she got a text from Neveah that also went to Gonzo.

I've been awake for two hours already, and it's only four a.m. here. This time change is no joke. I've been in touch with Spokane police, and they're set to go with me to the Carver home at nine. Gonzo was able to get the governor's warrant from the court, so we're good to go if we decide to take the women into custody.

Great job, Neveah. Please borrow a vest from Spokane if you go back to arrest them.

Will do, and I'll keep you posted.

Scotty appeared in the open bathroom door. "Did you forget something, Mother?"

Sam smiled at his grumpy face and went to hug him. "Did you actually get yourself up?"

"Someone had to do it. My parents are asleep at the wheel."

"Your parents are giving you a fake sick day."

He tipped his head as his brow lifted. "You *both* are?"

"We are."

"Is Dad under the influence or something?"

"Nope. I told him what I want more than anything today is some time with you and the twins, who are still recovering from being sick, and he suggested we take a mental health day."

"*He* suggested it? Am I still asleep and dreaming? If so, I don't want to wake up."

"You're wide awake and off for the day. Dad is going to call you out."

"Can you imagine the office ladies at school getting a call from the man himself? They'll probably wet their pants."

Sam laughed at his delighted expression as he did a happy dance into the bedroom, where he flopped onto the bed.

"Best day of my life!"

The twins came in, shrieking when they saw Scotty on the bed. They launched themselves at him and landed on top of him.

He wrapped his arms around them and held them tightly, ramping up the screaming exponentially. "I've got 'em, Mom. Come and get them."

Sam jogged toward the bed and landed right next to them, tickling Aubrey while Scotty got Alden. They were the rare kids who loved being tickled. She'd hated it—and still did.

"We're not sick anymore!" Aubrey announced at the top of her lungs.

"I'm so glad and very sorry I missed the whole thing." She gathered Aubrey into her arms while the boys wrestled. "I wanted to be here with you."

"It's okay. We had Grandma Brenda, and Nick was here.

Shelby and the kids came by, too. Maisie farted!" She dissolved into helpless giggles. "It was stinky!"

"So stinky!" Alden said.

"She's just a baby," Scotty said. "She doesn't stink as bad as you guys do."

"I don't stink!" Aubrey said.

"You farted right on me the other night," Scotty said. "Trust me, you do stink."

Aubrey giggled. "That was funny."

"Hysterical."

As Sam snuggled with them and talked about stupid things like farts and French toast sticks, she was the happiest mother in the whole world.

"Guess what, you guys?" Scotty said.

"What?"

"Mom said we can stay home today."

The twins looked at her for confirmation.

"But Dr. Harry—"

Aubrey put her hand over Alden's mouth and shook her head, giving Sam a glimpse of the teenager she'd be someday.

"Is it true, Sam?" Alden asked. "Do we get to stay home?"

"We're all staying home. We've got the whole day to do whatever we want. What should we do?"

"Can we go to the Feds game?" Scotty asked.

"No!" Aubrey said. "No baseball. It's so boring."

"Those are fighting words, little sister."

She stuck her tongue out at him. "No baseball."

"Laser tag!" Alden said.

"Build-a-Bear!" Aubrey said.

"No bears," Scotty and Alden said.

"This is a challenge, citizens," Sam said. "What else?"

"How about ice skating?" Scotty asked. "I could give you guys another lesson."

Aubrey glanced at Alden, who shrugged.

"We'll do that," Aubrey said for both of them. She was often their spokesperson. "This would be the best day ever if Elijah was here, too."

"We can FaceTime him at breakfast," Sam said. "I also want to go see Tracy and the kids. They're home today, too."

Scotty glanced at her, seeming to connect the dots to his own day off.

When the twins ran off to tell their Secret Service agents they were staying home, Scotty looked to Sam. "Is this because of Ethan?"

"In part. Mostly, it's because I want to spend time with you guys. But we also don't want you having to answer questions."

"About what?"

"You'll see when you look at your social media, but people are trying to tie Ethan to Luna's murder."

"What? How? He had nothing to do with that."

"It's what people do. They make shit up, especially due to his connection to us and the chance to make us look bad. Who knows why they do it?"

"It's sick that anyone would say such a thing about a child who was abducted."

"I agree, honey. Remember that the twins don't know what happened, and we're trying to keep it that way."

"I won't say anything. I don't want them to know that things like that can happen. They've already seen enough horrible stuff."

"Yes, they have. Thank you for always thinking about what's best for them."

"After you and Dad, they're the best thing to ever happen to me. Eli, too. I love having siblings."

"I love that for you, too."

"You know what I love more than anything in the whole world?"

"What's that?"

"A fake sick day approved by my dad, the POTUS."

"He's going to live to regret this, isn't he?"

"If he doesn't already, he should."

Sam collapsed into laughter with him.

"It's so rare that he makes such a huge strategic mistake like this," Scotty said. "We have to enjoy every second of it."

"Oh, we will, my friend. Don't you worry."

"Can I still go to practice this afternoon?"

"You'll be feeling much better by then."

His big grin, directed at his mother and coconspirator, was the best thing ever.

CHAPTER THIRTY-FOUR

Neveah left her hotel at eight thirty to drive to the address where the Spokane police would meet her before they went to the Carvers' home. One of their detectives would be going in with her for the initial meeting while other officers provided backup outside.

Her stomach was in knots, but no one would know that. She was determined to be cool, competent and professional as she completed her mission. The meeting place was the parking lot of a hardware store. When she drove in, she spotted the officers in unmarked cars and pulled up next to one of them.

"Detective Charles?" a man with a buzz cut and hard blue eyes asked.

"That's me."

He studied her for a second, and she wondered if he was surprised that she was young or that she was Black. Could be either—or both. Not that she cared what he was thinking.

"I'm Detective Anthony. We spoke on the phone."

"Right. Thank you for your help."

"No problem. We'll follow you. The Patrol cars will remain out of sight, as we discussed."

"Great. See you there." Neveah led the way to the Carvers'

well-kept raised ranch home in a neighborhood of similar houses. On the way in, she'd spotted swing sets, bikes and other indications of many young children nearby.

A red Dodge minivan was in the driveway at the Carvers' home, along with a black Jeep Cherokee.

With the printed copy of the warrant for the phones tucked into her pocket, she met Anthony on the sidewalk and headed for the front door to ring the bell.

A woman with dark hair and eyes answered the door. Neveah recognized her as Trisha Carver's sister Mercy from Trisha's social media posts. "May I help you?"

Neveah showed her badge. "I'm Detective Neveah Charles from the DC Metropolitan Police Department, and this is Detective Anthony from the Spokane Police Department. We'd like to see Trisha Carver, please."

Mercy's gaze darted between Neveah and Anthony before landing back on her. "She's not seeing anyone right now. I'm sure you can imagine that she's not doing well at all."

"I understand, and I'm sorry to intrude at such a difficult time, but I'm afraid this isn't a social call. We're investigating her husband's homicide, and we need to speak to her."

Mercy stared at her for a long moment before she finally blinked. "Come in."

Neveah and Anthony entered the home. Shoes littered the entryway, and toys were scattered about. A baby was crying in another room.

"I'll go get her," Mercy said.

"Thank you."

While they waited, Neveah walked toward the sliding glass door to look out at a backyard that contained a wooden swing set, more toys and two tricycles on a concrete patio. She turned back toward the living room as Trisha came into the room, carrying the baby, Mercy trailing behind her.

Trisha's hair was a lighter shade of brown than her sister's, and she had clear, cool blue eyes. Neveah noted immediately that, unlike most grieving people she encountered, the woman's eyes weren't red or swollen from crying. In fact, she looked remarkably well-rested, given that her husband had recently been murdered.

"Thank you for seeing us, Mrs. Carver." She showed her badge again while Anthony did the same. "I'm Detective Neveah Charles with the DC Metropolitan Police Department, and this is Detective Anthony with the Spokane police."

"You came all this way from DC?"

"I did."

"Have you found the person who murdered my husband?"

"Not yet, ma'am, but we're following a number of leads. Could we have a seat and talk with you and your sister for a minute?"

"Um, I guess. I'm not sure what we can do to help."

"We have a few routine questions for you," Neveah said.

"Okay."

"Why do you need to talk to me?" Mercy asked.

"Have a seat," Neveah said, hoping to convey the message that she wasn't asking.

The two women sat together on the sofa while Neveah and Anthony sat in upholstered chairs that faced the sofa.

"Sorry for the mess," Trisha said. "I haven't been cleaning up after the kids the way I normally do."

"Are your older children at home?"

"No, they're at the sitter's house. I needed a little break. It's been..." She teared up. "I still can't believe this has happened to Dale."

"I was wondering why your social media post didn't indicate that he was murdered. Rather, you made it sound like he died due to a drug overdose."

"I didn't make it sound like that."

"You did, ma'am. It seemed like an effort to ensure that's what people would think when, in fact, he was stabbed in the chest."

"Is this really necessary?" Mercy asked. "My sister just lost her husband. She has three young children and isn't thinking clearly. Would you be after that happened to you?"

"I hope I never find out what that is like," Neveah said, "but it strikes me as odd that after he fought such a valiant battle with addiction that you'd want him to be remembered for dying from an overdose."

"A valiant battle," Trisha said with a huff of sarcasm. "Is that what it was? To me, it was more of a never-ending nightmare that took over my entire life and left me constantly wondering when something like this would happen."

"Something like him being stabbed in the chest?"

"*Something!* It could've been anything with the way he was living!"

"How was he living?"

"He was back to all his old habits. Disappearing for days at a time. Coming home looking like a skid-row bum and smelling like death." Her chin wobbled. "After the last trip to rehab, he promised me he was done with all of it. He talked me into having another baby to celebrate that we'd survived. We'd won. It was all lies. He built a house of cards under us, and I'm left to pick up the pieces. I knew it was only a matter of time before someone killed him."

"At least you'll have the insurance money. That'll make a big difference for you and your kids."

The comment obviously shocked them. They hadn't expected her to know about that.

"Wh-what insurance money?"

"The two-point-five-million-dollar policy your father gave you as a wedding gift. Surely you remember that. If I check, will I find that you've already reached out about the payout?"

Trisha's grief-stricken expression shifted to something much harder in a flash. "What're you implying?"

"I'm asking you if you've already taken steps to redeem your husband's hefty life insurance policy. The one you just said you didn't know about."

"Is this how your department treats widows?" Mercy asked. "You harass them over the kind of details anyone would be dealing with after something like this?"

"Most of the widows I meet aren't sitting on multimillion-dollar life insurance policies."

"That's enough," Mercy said. "You need to leave. My sister is in mourning and doesn't deserve this."

"Did Dale deserve a knife to the chest?"

"Yes!" Trisha said.

"Trisha."

Ignoring her sister, Trisha said, "He deserved anything he got after the way he lied to me and disrespected our marriage and family for the entire time we were together. He was an addict when we met and hid it from me until it was too late. By the time I found out, we had two children, a mortgage, car payments and stacks of debt from his recklessness. We spent more than a hundred thousand dollars on rehab, and none of it worked. After the last time, he swore to me that everything would be different. He begged me not to leave him and to give him one more chance to show me who he could be when he was clean. Except he was never clean. It was more lies, and look at me now, with another child to care for on my own. So yes, if someone stabbed him in the chest, he probably deserved it."

"Did you have anything to do with him being stabbed?"

Her face lost all color in an instant. "What?" She glanced at her sister. "What is she saying?"

"I asked if you had anything to do with your husband being stabbed."

"Get out of here," Mercy said. "How dare you come into her home and accuse her of such a thing?"

"Did you have anything to do with it?" Neveah asked Mercy.

"Fuck you."

Neveah reached into her coat pocket, withdrew the warrant

and handed it to Mercy. "This is a warrant for both of your phones. I'll need you to turn them over to me. Now."

"You can't take our phones!" Trisha said. "This is outrageous. We haven't done anything."

"If that's the case, they'll be returned to you as soon as they're processed."

"I want a lawyer," Trisha said.

"You're free to engage with counsel, but the phones are still coming with us. You can either retrieve them immediately, or we'll bring in officers to search the house for them."

"You can't do this!" Trisha cried.

"That piece of paper says I can. Now, what's it going to be? I'm giving you two minutes to produce the phones before we call in backup."

"What're we supposed to do without our phones?" Mercy asked.

"That's not my problem, ma'am."

She engaged in a stare-down with Mercy that ended when the other woman blinked.

Neveah noticed that Mercy's hands were trembling.

After a long silence, Neveah turned to Anthony. "Detective Anthony, will you ask your colleagues to come in to look for the phones?"

"I'll take care of that right away."

"Wait," Trisha said. "We have nothing to hide. You can have them."

"Trisha—"

"Be quiet, Mercy, and get the phones."

With a furious look for her sister, Mercy got up to retrieve both phones from chargers in the kitchen.

Neveah watched her without blinking so she wouldn't miss it if Mercy did anything to either phone.

Mercy dropped them on the coffee table.

Neveah put on gloves to place them into separate evidence bags. "Which one is which?"

"The blue one is Trisha's."

"What are the codes?"

She wrote down the numbers the women recited. "Thank you."

When the detectives got up to leave, Mercy said, "That's it? You come in here, harass my widowed sister, take our phones and leave?"

"That's it for now. If we find anything interesting on the phones, we'll be back."

"What does that mean? What would be interesting?"

"I won't know until I see it."

"Are you accusing us of a crime?" Trisha asked.

"Not at the moment. Did you commit a crime?"

"No! I'm a wife and a mother, not a criminal."

"Then you should have nothing to worry about. We'll show ourselves out."

When they were outside, Anthony said, "That was well done, Detective."

That he sounded surprised should've been no surprise to her, but it smarted just the same. "Thank you."

"You think they were involved."

"We're almost sure they hired it done."

"Wow. What's the next step?"

"Would it be possible to have your IT people take a look at the phones?"

"Sure, we can do that. I'll set you up with one of our detectives."

"Great, thanks. In the meantime, I think we should have eyes on them."

"I agree. I'll keep our Patrol officers on them. Follow me to our house, and we'll get those phones processed."

"Excellent, thanks again."

.   .   .

SAM WAS at the rink watching Scotty patiently assist the twins on the ice when she received an update from Neveah.

After seeing Trisha and her sister, I'm more convinced they were involved. I'm working with a Spokane IT detective to dump the phones now while their Patrol officers watch the house. I'll keep you posted.

Excellent work, Sam replied.

"Sam!" Alden called to her as he went by, pushing an orange cone around on the ice. "Look at me! I'm doing it. I'm skating!"

"You sure are."

"Me, too, Sam," Aubrey said as she followed her brother.

Scotty skated circles around them, showing off and making them laugh as they scooted around.

Using Scotty's phone, she took the ton of pictures Nick had requested when he'd heard their plans for the day.

"Ten more minutes, and then it's time for lunch," she told them.

Before they'd left the White House, they'd made a full itinerary for their day, which would include pizza before a visit with Tracy, Angela and the kids at Tracy's. Her sister had assured her that Ethan wanted to see them and that Abby couldn't wait for cousin time.

"They're doing great," Vernon said when he joined her at the boards.

"They really are."

"Scotty is so patient with them."

"He's thrilled to be a big brother."

"Are we ready to move to pizza?"

"Just about."

Sam and Scotty helped the twins change out of their skates and back into sneakers. Their cheeks were red from the cold, which made her wonder if she'd been wise to let them get heated up in the cold after being sick. That hadn't even occurred to her until it was too late. Oh well. She would never be Mother of the Year, that was for sure.

The Secret Service moved them from one thing to the next

with a minimum of fuss and only three SUVs in the motorcade, which wasn't bad considering four members of the first family were in the middle vehicle.

Sam loved being in the car with them, taking them to do fun things on a school day and hearing their adorable conversations about why Scotty was such a good skater and why they weren't.

"It took me years to get this good. You guys will get there, too. And you're old enough to play hockey this fall if you want to."

"I want to!" Aubrey said. "Can girls play?"

"Girls can do anything boys can do," Scotty told her. "And often far better than we can."

"That's right." Sam gave Aubrey a fist bump. "Girl power."

Her little giggle was so, so cute.

"Guys, can I tell you something?" Sam asked.

"You don't have to ask," Scotty said with teenager disdain. "You're the mom."

"Gee, thank you, son."

He gave a snort of laughter. "Well, it's true."

With a smile for him, she said, "I just want you to know that I wish I could spend every day like this with you guys."

"No one is making you send us to school," Scotty said with that devilish little grin that reminded her so much of Nick. "That's a personal choice."

"Wait," Aubrey said. "We don't have to go to school?"

"Yes, you do," Sam said with a mom look for Scotty. "That's how you grow up to be smart, educated, productive citizens of the world."

"I don't want to live in the whole world," Alden said.

"You don't have to," Sam said, continuously amused by their literal interpretations. "But we're all citizens of the world and hopefully making contributions that make things better for others."

"Like how you catch bad guys," Aubrey said.

"Just like that. But as I was saying, I wish we could hang out like this every day. It makes me so sad that you guys were sick this weekend and I couldn't be there."

"It's okay, Sam," Alden said. "We know you have an important job."

"That's nice of you to say, buddy, but I hope you know that nothing is more important to me than you are, and even if I'm not there with you, you're always the most important people to me."

Aubrey, who was seated in a booster seat next to Sam, reached for her hand. "Don't be sad, Sam. We're not. Well... we are sometimes because we miss our mommy and daddy, and Scotty misses his mom and grandpa, but most of the time, we're happy. And we love our family and having another big brother."

"The kids at school think we're cool," Alden said, "because our new dad is the president, and our new mom is the first lady and a detective who chases bad guys."

Hearing them refer to her and Nick as their new dad and new mom made Sam teary-eyed.

"Uh-oh," Scotty said. "Now you've done it. She's gonna cry."

"No, I'm not," Sam said. "Hush your mouth." They giggled at the face she made at Scotty. "I love you guys. So, so much."

"We love you, too, Sam," Aubrey said.

"Don't worry about us," Scotty said. "We're all good. Keep doing what you gotta do and making us proud."

The twins nodded.

"Thanks, guys," Sam said, incredibly moved by their kindness and love.

"Pizza!" Alden said as the car came to a stop outside the restaurant they'd turn into a circus with their presence.

CHAPTER THIRTY-FIVE

After pizza, ice cream and posing for photos with the delightful staff, they took two pizzas to-go for Tracy, Angela and the kids and headed to Tracy's house.

Sam was looking forward to spending some time with her sisters, nieces and nephews and getting a sense for how they could best support Tracy and Ethan through this difficult time.

The sisters had exchanged texts earlier, about reminding the older kids that the younger ones didn't know about what'd happened to Ethan and agreed they wanted to keep it that way.

Their arrival with pizza was heralded with much excitement from the kids and their moms. Even Ethan, who'd been resting on the sofa, sat up to greet them.

"Now I don't have to worry about dinner tonight," Angela said. "Yay for Auntie Sam!"

Scotty gave Tracy a long hug and said something to her that had Sam's sister smiling and teary-eyed.

"You're the sweetest boy," Tracy said.

"I'm a man, and I ain't sweet."

"You are if we say you are."

"And we say you are," Sam and Angela said together.

"That sister thing is creepy," he said as he went to find Jack and Ethan.

"How's Ethan?" Sam asked when it was just the three sisters in the kitchen.

"He's been quiet today, but he's up, and he ate, and… I guess he's okay. His therapist, Christi, came by earlier, and they talked for a bit, but he didn't have much to say. She said he's still processing it and will probably have more to say going forward. Finding out he's the subject of online conspiracies didn't help."

"How'd he hear about that?" Sam asked.

"One of his friends stopped by to see how he was doing, and when I let him talk to Ethan, he mentioned it. I forgot to ask him not to."

"We forget that their whole lives are online these days," Sam said.

"I'm not thinking straight, or I would've thought to ask him not to say anything."

"Of course you would have," Angela said.

"I hate that he knows people are talking about him that way."

"He would've heard about it the minute he returned to school," Sam said, "so maybe it's better he knows now and can process all of it at the same time."

"You guys don't have any cigarettes, do you?" Tracy asked.

"Ah, no," Sam said. "I haven't had one since the last time I smoked with you guys." That, too, had happened the week she'd reconnected with Nick after John O'Connor's murder.

"Kinda pregnant over here," Angela said. "None for me."

"I might go buy some."

"Don't start that up again, Trace," Sam said.

"If it helps my anxiety, why not?"

"Have you talked to Mike?"

"He called to ask how Ethan is doing, but that was it."

"You'll let him see the kids, won't you?" Ang asked tentatively.

"He can come by sometime, but he can't stay."

"Trace..." The single word from Angela conveyed a world of agony. "You can't mean to freeze him out entirely."

"That's exactly what I mean to do. He's proven I can't trust him to make sound decisions for our children. We got lucky this time." She made air quotes around the word *lucky*. "Our son is only traumatized, not dead. I'm not giving him another chance to decide what Ethan and Abby are allowed to do."

"That's reasonable," Sam said. "If he comes back, you're in charge of the kids. Nonnegotiable."

"It's not that simple. Imagine if Nick or Spencer allowed your children to do something that nearly got one of them killed, after you tried to tell him it was unwise. Add to it that he was condescending and dismissive of your concerns. Would you be so quick to forgive?"

"Probably not," Sam said, even as she couldn't imagine a scenario where she'd feel that way about Nick. Often, he was the voice of reason when it came to their kids, while she advocated a looser approach, which was kind of funny since she was the cop.

"Yeah, it wouldn't be simple," Angela said. "That's for sure."

"I know you guys love Mike. *I* love Mike. But I'm very, very angry about his role in allowing something like this to happen, and it won't be fixed overnight, if ever."

"Fair enough," Sam said. "You'll tell us what we can do to help?"

"The statements the MPD and Nick's team issued seem to have helped. From what I'm hearing, a lot of people are telling the conspiracy peddlers to stand down and stop preying on innocent kids. I just hope it's not too little too late to preserve his reputation."

"He had nothing to do with what happened to Luna," Sam said. "The case is being made against the men who did, and Ethan won't be charged with anything. He's a victim of a crime."

"You know that, and I know that, but it's what everyone else thinks that matters. Will the stuff that was said about him in the last twelve hours keep him out of college someday or make it so he can't get a job?"

"I hope not," Sam said.

"We all know it's possible this'll haunt him for the rest of his life—and that's why I'll be hard-pressed to forgive Mike."

"Don't think we don't understand, because we do," Sam said. "It's just that we love you both, and it's hard for us to imagine a world where you're not together and happy."

"We haven't been happy in a while," Tracy confessed, taking her sisters by surprise.

"Since when?" Angela said.

"Probably around the time Brooke was attacked. Things changed between us after that. I was consumed with her, and he was often critical of how I was handling things."

"How were you supposed to handle such a thing?" Sam asked.

"Who knows? It's not like there's a handbook on what to do when your daughter is drugged and gang-raped at a party where other kids were murdered. I handled it the best way I knew how, by loving her through it. Apparently, I didn't save enough love for him."

Angela crossed her arms and looked down at the floor. "That doesn't sound like him."

"You don't live with him. He's quick with the critique and to tell me how he would've done something differently. When he started saying I was being overprotective of Ethan because of what'd happened to Brooke, and how it wasn't fair to Ethan… After a while, I started doubting my own judgment. Like, maybe he was right, and I was wrong."

"He wasn't right," Sam said. "You were."

"And I *knew* that. I absolutely knew it, but he'd already given an inch, and that was just enough space in the parental unity for Ethan to walk right through the door into freedom." Tracy wiped away a tear. "Mike never intended for something like this to happen. I know that, and I feel for him. I really do. But I'm so fucking angry."

"You have every right to be, Trace," Sam said.

"I must've pissed someone off in a past life to have this stuff happen to two of my kids."

"You're a great mom, and you've never done anything to anyone that would make it so you deserve this." Sam glanced at Angela, who was still looking at the floor. "Right, Ang?"

"Definitely."

"Are you okay?" Sam asked Angela.

She nodded and then just as quickly shook her head. "I feel so guilty." She glanced at Tracy. "I let Mike stay at my house last night, and I'm scared you're going to hate me for that."

"How'd that happen?"

"When I couldn't reach you, I called him to see how Ethan was doing. He told me you'd asked him to leave, and I said he should stay with us. I'm sorry if that adds to your anger, Trace, but I felt so bad for him."

"It's fine. I'd rather he stay with you than run up the credit card at a hotel."

"Really? You're not mad?"

"I'm sad and worried and anxious and devastated, but I'm not mad at you. I get that you guys love him like a brother, and I've always wanted that. I'd never ask you to turn your backs on him. But please... Don't push me when it comes to him. If and when I talk to him, it'll be when I'm ready and not one second before."

Sam hugged her. "Whatever you need." After she released her sister, she went to look in on the kids in the living room. Scotty, Jack and Alden were sitting with Ethan on the sofa while Abby braided Aubrey's hair as Ella looked on. Sam signaled to her sisters. "Come see our babies."

They peeked through the door together.

"It's good for him to have the kids around," Tracy said. "Especially Scotty. He looks up to him."

"He has been so concerned about Ethan. He asked to see him today."

"Tell me he's going to be okay."

"He will be," Angela said.

"It might not happen overnight," Sam said, "but he'll get through this, and so will you."

"I sure hope you're right, because right now, it feels like I'm staring up yet another mountain that has to be climbed to get my child back on track."

Sam put her arm around Tracy. "If anyone is capable of climbing that mountain, it's you."

AT LUNCHTIME ON THAT TUESDAY, Archie bought Chinese takeout for his team since they'd been working overtime on the missing children and Carver cases. After the food arrived, the group gathered in the conference room to eat like the ravenous wildebeests they were when free food was put in front of them.

Archie sat with them for a few minutes before taking his box of rice and chicken, along with a set of chopsticks, with him when he went down two flights of stairs to the city jail. He nodded to the sergeant on duty and made his way to the last cell on the right, where he took a seat on the floor across from the cell to eat his lunch.

He'd waited to do this until he was almost certain he'd be able to maintain the upper hand and never let on how utterly devastated he'd been by what his ex-colleague had done to the woman Archie loved. He still wasn't completely sure that he wouldn't be tempted to murder the guy.

Dylan Offenbach noticed him right away but stayed seated on the bed inside the cell while Archie silently ate his lunch.

"What do you want?" Offenbach finally asked.

"I wanted to see you inside a cell. I have to say it's every bit as satisfying as I'd hoped it would be."

"Fuck off, Archie. You brought this on yourself."

"How's that?"

"You didn't have to tell Holland where I was when you tracked my phone. You could've kept that to yourself."

"I can see how you'd feel that way, what with you off having an affair while your wife was expecting your fifth—or was it your sixth—kid. Not to mention you were supposed to be at a conference in Philadelphia, not cavorting on the Jersey Shore with your side piece."

"A real man would've had the back of a colleague."

"A real man doesn't drug women, beat and sexually assault them. I guess our definition of manhood differs a bit."

"I bet you're looking rather paltry to her after she's had me."

Archie had to remind himself he wasn't allowed to kill the son of a bitch. But, oh, how he wanted to, and it was the first time in his life he'd ever felt the desire to commit murder.

"She's doing great. Doesn't remember a thing about her time with you, thankfully, so all those extra charges were for naught. You're nothing to her. But let me tell you what... I'll never forget what you did to her, and you can bet your ass that I'll be calling my lengthy list of contacts to make sure your time in prison is as miserable as it can possibly be. Every time someone gives you a taste of your own medicine, I want you thinking of Harlowe's beautiful face and how she doesn't even remember you."

Archie got up from the floor. "I've got to get back to work now. You have a good day, Dylan. Maybe I'll give your wife a call to see what's up. She must be getting lonely by now."

He leaped from the bed and came to the bars, grasping them. "Stay the fuck away from my wife."

"You'd like that, wouldn't you? Heard there's a girlfriend, too. You're a busy guy. Or, well, you *were* a busy guy. Not getting much action now, are you? I bet they'd love a little attention from someone who isn't about to spend the rest of his life in the can."

"If you go near them, I'll have you killed."

"Is that a threat, Offenbach? Aren't you in enough trouble without threatening the life of a law enforcement officer? Luckily, I've got cameras all over this place, so I'll be making a copy of that comment to send off to the USA as soon as I get back upstairs. I wonder how long it'll be before they're filing even more charges against you. Watch your back, Dylan. You'll never know when someone might be coming for you. I'll make sure they let you know that Harlowe sent them, and I'll tell your girlfriend you said hi."

"Stay the fuck away from her, you motherfucking asshole!"

Archie laughed as he walked away.

Offenbach was still screaming obscenities at him as Archie took the stairs two at a time, letting out a belch in the stairwell that echoed so loudly, it cracked him up. He went straight back to his office to make a copy of Offenbach's threat for the U.S. Attorney.

All in all, it'd been a rather satisfying lunch break.

Neveah received a text message from Detective Williams with the Spokane Police IT department.

Hit pay dirt with an encrypted app on the sister's phone where they orchestrated the plan. You've got what you need to execute arrest warrants. Come on in to take a look and plan next steps. I emailed the info about the guys they hired to you to pass on to your team at home.

Thank you very much. Will be there in an hour.

Neveah texted the update to Gonzo, telling him she'd forwarded the message about the hired hit men to his email.

Excellent. Let us know when you have them in custody.

What happens to the kids?

Spokane will have a contact with local CPS.

Got it.

I'll arrange transport and send you the details.

She felt a little sick thinking of the kids losing both parents so suddenly, but that wasn't her fault or her problem. Or so she tried to tell herself. As someone who'd lost a parent suddenly, she could attest to the lifelong fallout ahead for the Carver kids.

As she left the hotel room, she took everything with her so she could head right to the airport with her prisoners.

When she was en route to the police station, she received a call from Williams.

"Your targets are packing up the minivan and not even trying to be coy about it. We suggest you go right there to make the arrests. We'll back you up."

"Got it. On the way."

Adrenaline zipped through her veins as she navigated workday traffic in the scenic city on her way to the Carver home. She crossed a suspension bridge over the Spokane River, noting signs for an upcoming Lilac Festival. As she entered the Carvers' neighborhood, she spotted Patrol cars parked a few blocks from the house and parked behind them. Before she got out of the car, she pulled two sets of handcuffs from her backpack and strapped on her service weapon.

Detective Williams saw her coming and waved her over, handing her a bulletproof vest.

"Thank you." Neveah put on the vest and tightened the Velcro straps.

"Our SWAT team is surrounding the house. We're waiting for word that they're ready. When they give us the go-ahead, we'll drive you over there to make the arrest."

"Appreciate all the great support."

"Wait until you read the messages between the sister and the professional hit men she hired to take out the brother-in-law on her sister's behalf and how they wanted it to look like a drug deal gone wrong. They weren't even careful about what they said because they never expected to be caught."

"They wanted us to see the drugs and jump to that conclusion," Neveah said.

"The thing is, if they'd killed him in the room with the drugs all around, you might not have investigated further."

"Exactly."

"SWAT is good to go, Detective," one of the Patrol officers said to Williams.

"Let's roll," Williams said. "You can ride with us."

CHAPTER THIRTY-SIX

Neveah got into the back seat of an unmarked car for the short ride to the Carver home, which was abuzz with activity. The hatchback of the red Dodge minivan was open as Mercy attempted to load another suitcase into a space already tightly packed with luggage and baby equipment.

"Detective Charles, it's all yours."

She swallowed hard and nodded as she got out of the car.

"Going somewhere?" she asked Mercy, taking the other woman by surprise.

"We're going to Coeur d'Alene to see our parents."

"Seems like you're taking a lot of stuff for a visit."

"Do you know how much equipment is needed for babies and young kids?"

"I can't say that I do, but the thing is... You're under arrest for planning the murder-for-hire of your brother-in-law Dale Carver." Before the words had registered, Neveah had the woman cuffed with her arms behind her back.

A Spokane officer took the screaming woman to a Patrol car. Accompanied by SWAT team members, Neveah and Williams approached the open door, weapons drawn, looking for Trisha.

"Hold up." Williams leaned in to gauge the situation inside since he had the better view from his side. "Clear."

They entered the house and fanned out, looking for Trisha and her children.

With her heart pounding like a bass drum in her ears, Neveah pointed toward the hallway that led to the bedrooms. Williams nodded and indicated that he'd follow her. She passed two empty bedrooms decorated for children and stopped at the doorway to the main bedroom, where an unmade king-sized bed took up most of the available space.

She moved quietly into the room and used her right foot to open a closet door.

The first thing she saw was Trisha with a handgun pointed at the head of her son while her daughter and the baby slept on the floor next to her.

Neveah immediately suspected they'd been drugged.

Trisha eyes had a wild, unhinged look to them. "I don't want to kill him."

Cody's blue eyes were huge with fright and possibly shock.

"There's no need to kill anyone," Neveah said.

"You're not taking me away from my kids." She tightened the arm she had around Cody's neck. "I'll kill us all before that'll happen."

"Your kids are counting on you to do the right thing for them," Neveah said.

"I did the right thing for my kids! He was going to drag us all down with him—*again*. I couldn't let that happen. You don't know what it was like! We survived a *nightmare*. A freaking nightmare, and he was using again." She began to cry. "He promised me that was all behind us. He said we should have another baby to celebrate his recovery. Two days after Zach was born, I found out the truth. He'd never stopped. What would you have done?"

Neveah empathized with her, but there were a lot of things Trisha could've done short of plotting her husband's murder.

"Put down the gun, Trisha. Let your son go. He hasn't done anything to deserve being hurt, and I'm worried about Reagan and Zach. It doesn't look like they're breathing."

"They're fine. They're just sleeping."

"They're not fine. You're their mom. They're counting on you to get help for them. Can we help them?"

She cast a nervous glance at Reagan and the baby, who were preternaturally still.

Neveah acted before she fully thought through the plan, diving toward Trisha while she was briefly distracted, knocking the gun from Trisha's hand as Neveah screamed at Cody to run.

He bolted from the closet and into the arms of Detective Williams.

Neveah knelt on Trisha's back to cuff her. "Get EMS for the kids."

"They're coming in now," Williams said. "That was impressive, Detective. Did you play football in high school?"

She released a nervous laugh as she pulled Trisha to her feet to get her out of the way of the paramedics.

"*You can't take me from my babies!*" Trisha said on a scream.

Neveah wanted to tell her she should've thought of her kids when she and her sister were plotting her husband's murder, but she decided it wasn't worth wasting her breath. She'd figure that out soon enough on her own.

Gonzo had arranged transport through the U.S. Marshals Service's Justice Prisoner Air Transportation System, known as JPATS. As soon as Neveah notified him that the women were in custody, he told her two marshals were standing by to help get them back to DC. They met her outside the Carver home, where the women were being held in separate Patrol vehicles.

"Let's get them loaded up," said Deputy Marshal Getty, a man of about forty with buzz-cut gray hair and steely blue eyes.

His partner, a Black woman with pretty brown eyes named Deputy Marshal Singer, nodded to Neveah.

"Heard you made a hell of an arrest in there, Detective," Singer said. "Congratulations."

"Thanks and for the assistance in getting them home."

"That's what we do," Getty said. "We've got a plane standing by at the airport."

When Neveah opened the back door of the cruiser where Trisha was being held, she began screaming for her children. *"Where are they? What've you done with them?"*

Neveah ignored her shrieks, as well as Mercy's, as she helped transfer them to the marshals' vehicle.

All three officers ignored their vociferous protests as they buckled them in for the ride to the airport.

"Where are you taking us? I want to see my children! I have rights. Get me a lawyer!"

Neveah closed the door in her face. "I need to return the rental, and then where should I meet you?"

"We'll follow you to the drop-off and deliver you to the tarmac."

"Excellent, thanks."

Back in her rental car, she headed to Spokane International Airport. On the way, she called Gonzo to let him know the women were in custody and they were headed to the airport. "Trisha is screaming for her kids."

"Oh well," Gonzo said.

"What a mess. That poor little boy will never forget his mother holding a gun to his head."

"How'd it go down?"

"I think she'd drugged the other two, because they were asleep on the floor next to her. I said I wasn't sure they were breathing, and when she looked over at them, I jumped on her, knocked the gun out of her hand and got the boy out of there."

"Whoa, look at you go. Nice job."

"I didn't think too much. I just went for it."

"I'm glad you're okay."

"How's it going finding the guys they hired to do the job?"

"We've got Jesse Best's team helping to track them down. I'll keep you posted and will have your flight met at Reagan when you land."

"Thanks for all the support."

"We didn't do much. You're the one who got it done out there. We'll wait to brief the media until you can do it."

"Oh, um... Really?"

"Hell yes, this is your arrest, Detective."

"Okay, thanks for the warning. I'll need a good five or six hours to mentally prepare for that."

Gonzo laughed. "You just tackled a woman with a gun. Handling the press will be nothing after that."

"If you say so."

"See you soon. Safe travels."

After she returned the rental car, she was picked up by the marshals and driven to a special gate that led to a private jet on the tarmac.

Both women were still screaming and crying and threatening their jobs with the lawsuit they planned to file.

Neveah's favorite was when Trisha said, "I'm a breastfeeding mother! This is an outrage. I have rights!"

She wanted to remind Trisha that her husband had had rights, too, which had been taken from him by her and her sister's craven desire to be rid of him and cash in on the insurance money.

Neveah was usually empathetic toward others, almost to a fault, at times looking past obvious red flags to try to see the best in people. This time, she saw two women who were about to get everything they deserved after taking Dale's life in such a depraved fashion.

They were belted in for takeoff when her phone chimed with a text from Jeremy. *How's it going? Did you get your case wrapped up?*

She replied with a brief summary of events. *We're on a flight with the U.S. Marshals now, escorting the suspects back to DC for arraignment. The guy's wife is wailing because she's been taken from her kids. I'm trying to feel bad for her, but after she held a gun to the head of her son and drugged the other two, I'm glad she's out of their lives.*

Holy crap! You went head-to-head with a woman and a gun? You're a badass! Hope the flight is smooth, and text me when you land. Can't wait to get home and hear all about it in person.

After she gave his message a heart reply, she powered down her phone for takeoff, smiling as she thought of him and wondered how long it would be before she could see him.

JESSE HAD WALKED around like a crooked arrow all day and was in one hell of a mood by the time he returned to the hospital and took the elevator to the ICU. As he approached Memphis's room, he saw one of the nurses he recognized and would've nodded to her if his freaking head weren't frozen at a tilt.

Christ have mercy, he thought. Nothing was helping, not four ibuprofens, nor the muscle balm he'd bought at the pharmacy. As the day had gone on, he'd become surlier with every passing hour without relief from the pain in his neck—or the one in his heart as it'd become clear that he needed to do *something* about Memphis Rose.

He still wasn't sure what he would say to her as he approached her room—and found it empty. Spinning around to chase after the nurse, he asked where she was. Surely if something had happened, they would've called him, right? Someone would've called him... Or would they? Who was he to her besides her boss and friend? Did he even qualify as a friend?

The thoughts, arriving one after the other like machine-gun fire, had him bending at the waist to process the sickening realization that he would've had no right to a phone call if the worst had happened. He'd never allowed himself to fully commit, so why would he be her point of contact?

"Are you all right?"

He forced himself to stand upright, and fuck, that hurt. "Where's Memphis Rose Costello?"

"She was moved to a regular room earlier today."

"Oh."

"No one told you?"

When he tried to shake his head, he immediately regretted it.

She eyed him. "What's wrong with you?"

"Slept wrong in the chair last night. Woke up crooked."

"Ouch. Come to the desk. I'll write down an over-the-counter med you can get that should help."

"Thanks."

At the desk, she produced a slip of paper with the name of the med and the number 471.

"That's the room she was moved to."

"Thank you."

"She's a special person," the nurse added.

"Yes."

"And her mother and grandmother are a couple of characters. We all enjoyed getting to know them."

"Thanks for taking good care of her."

"Are you two…"

"Yeah, we are," he said with a deep sigh as the reality of the situation settled with unflinching certainty. "We are."

"I was going to ask if you wanted to grab a drink sometime, but instead, I'll hope for all the best for you and Memphis."

"Thanks again for everything. Tell the others, too."

"I will. Good luck to you."

She had no way to know that he'd need all the luck he could get. On the fourth floor, he followed the noise to room 471, where Beatrice and Alberta held court. The three of them were laughing like they were at a party rather than in a hospital room after Memphis had been nearly killed.

Jesse stood in the doorway, looking at her in the bed, her eyes dancing with amusement at whatever her mother and grandmother were talking about, and he was struck dumb by how fucking beautiful she was. Ever since he'd lost Jordan so suddenly, he'd resisted caring about anyone else, knowing all too well how gut-wrenching it was to lose someone who couldn't be replaced.

In those clarifying seconds, he understood that he'd come to a fork in the road. He could either push her away and learn to live without her, too, or he could acknowledge that she'd changed his life forever, for better or worse, and break all his personal rules for self-preservation to let her all the way in.

"Ladies."

They all noticed him at the same time and went silent. He'd spent enough time with them to know how unusual silence was for them.

"I was about to text to tell you they moved me," Memphis said.

Jesse gazed at her, unblinking, drinking in the sight of her sweet face, relieved to see some of the rosiness returning to her cheeks. "I just came from the ICU, where I got the word."

He was slightly aware of Beatrice nudging Alberta, and then the two of them kissed Memphis and told her they'd be back in a while before they left the room, leaving a cloud of perfume in their wake as they brushed by Jesse.

"Was it something I said?" he asked as he moved closer to her, unable to resist the undeniable pull.

"It's more what you *don't* say. They think you're a glowering lunkhead who doesn't speak unless he has to."

"They figured me out kinda quick."

She snorted out a laugh. "You're not hard to figure out, Best."

He could tell he surprised her when he went around to the

left side of her bed, away from her injured leg, perched on the edge of the mattress and took her hand.

"Why are you still crooked?"

"Really effed up my neck. The ICU nurse told me what to get for it."

"You should go get what you need."

"I will, but first..." He glanced down at their joined hands. "I want to tell you..."

She put her other hand on top of his. "What do you want to tell me?"

"You know how I lost my sister."

"Yes, and I ache for you. We all do."

"We had... It was a rough childhood. Our grandparents took our mother to court to get custody. It was ugly. Both parents were drug addicts. We only saw them sporadically, and the grandparents were okay, but bitter about having to raise another generation of kids. Jordan was the only person in my entire life that I've ever truly loved, and when she disappeared... It was like something vital inside me ceased to function."

"Jesse," she whispered tearfully. "I'm so sorry you've been missing her for all this time. I... I've tried to find her."

He looked up at her so quickly that he winced from the pain that shot through his neck. "You have?"

She nodded. "It's what we do. We find people, and I figured maybe a fresh look would help. But there's just... There's nothing."

"Believe me, I know, but it means a lot that you tried."

"I'd give anything to fix this for you."

Hearing her say that, knowing she'd been looking for Jordan, he realized his path forward had become crystal clear. "I said Jordan was the only person I've ever truly loved, and that was true for most of my life. Until recently."

She seemed to hold her breath, waiting to hear what else he would say.

"I love you, Memphis Rose, and I'll be honest… I didn't want to."

Laughing as tears slid down her cheeks, she said, "No kidding. Really?"

"This is no time for sarcasm. I'm being serious."

She made a comical effort to stop laughing, but her gorgeous eyes still danced with delight as she let him twist in the wind. "As you were saying…"

"Often, when one person says they love someone, the other person is required to say it back."

She raised a brow. "*Required* to?"

"It's the polite thing to do, but if you're intent on making me suffer the way I've made you suffer…" He moved to get up and instantly regretted it.

"Sit your ass down and give me a second, will you? I was unprepared for you to come in here and say these things. I thought…"

"What did you think?"

"That maybe it was never going to happen between us. That you were too sealed off to ever let anyone else in."

"I tried to be, but despite my best efforts, you managed to break the seal."

"How does it feel?"

"Terrifying."

"Why?"

"Look at how close I came to losing you, too. How am I supposed to move around in the world feeling this way about someone I can't protect for every minute of every day?"

"Come here."

"I'm here."

"Come all the way."

"I don't want to hurt your leg."

"You won't if you move carefully."

"That's the only way I can move today, thanks to that godforsaken chair. And don't laugh. It's not funny."

"It's a little funny how the Tin Man—before the oilcan—told me he loves me."

He kicked off his boots and got on the bed, moving slowly so he wouldn't hurt either of them.

"Why'd I have to fall for a smartass like you, anyway?"

"Because you would've been bored with anyone else."

With his head next to hers on the pillow, he rested his hand on her face and moved his thumb over the softest skin he'd ever felt. "I'm not sure I would've survived losing you, too, so thanks for not dying."

"You're welcome."

"Is there anything else you want to say to me?"

She seemed to give that some considerable thought. "That's about it."

"Memphis Rose..."

Laughing, she said, "I love you, too, you big idiot. I have for a long time, and I think you knew that, which is why you kept me at arm's length."

"I was also worried about messing up your very promising career."

"What're we going to do about that?"

"I'll come clean to Lafferty, but I'll say it's a recent development. No need to confess to sneaking around behind his back for a year."

"I've sort of wondered if he's known all along but turned a blind eye because having me around made you more tolerable."

His scowl made her laugh again. He loved when she laughed, even when she was laughing at him.

"If you tell him," she added, "you'll force him to do something about it when we could leave well enough alone and hope for the best."

"It would kill me if I caused trouble in your career."

"It's a chance I'm willing to take to keep from being separated from you right when things are getting interesting."

He raised himself up as much as he could without wanting to

howl from the pain and pressed a soft kiss to her lips. "I'm sorry for what I've put you through. You deserve someone easier to deal with."

"I suppose I could continue to look around for that guy while I hang out with you."

He stared at her, momentarily stunned.

Her smile lit up her entire gorgeous face. "I wish I'd had a camera ready to take a picture of your face when I said that."

"Stop fucking with me. It's not funny."

"It *is* funny, and, Jesse, my love, I've only just begun to fuck with you."

CHAPTER THIRTY-SEVEN

"Do you want to play NHL?" Scotty asked Ethan when the other kids went to play in Tracy's small backyard while the moms had coffee in the kitchen. He and Ethan often played their favorite videogame when they were together.

"Nah."

"It might be fun to do something normal, you know?"

"Not sure anything will ever be normal again."

"Remember how I used to live in a home for kids in Richmond, before Sam and Nick adopted me?"

"Yeah."

"Mrs. Littlefield was my guardian then, and she used to talk to us about how there's a new normal after something bad happens, and the good news about the new normal is we get to figure out for ourselves what that looks like."

"Did she say how to do that?"

"First, she'd say, you have to figure out what you need to be happy and healthy. Then you have to figure out how to get it."

"I don't think I'll ever be happy again. They *killed* Luna." Ethan's eyes went bright with tears. "They actually killed her, all because she didn't like Brecken."

"That'll never make sense to you as someone who cares about other people. Not everyone does, you know."

"I know that now. I wish I didn't know that."

"You knew it before now. Remember what happened to Grandpa Skip and Uncle Spencer? Those things happened because people who don't care about others did bad things that harmed them. You and me... We're not like that. We care about what happens to others, which is why you'll be happy again someday. Caring about other people will make you happy."

"I can't stop thinking about Luna and how nice she was to me. And that she thought she was coming to meet me. Did she die thinking I betrayed her?"

"She was probably smart enough to figure out who betrayed her—and it wasn't you. You were nowhere to be found when she was harmed. You didn't do it. They did."

"I hope she doesn't think I'd ever try to hurt her."

"She doesn't, and wherever she is now, she knows the truth."

"How can you be so sure?"

"Well, obviously, I don't know for certain, but if you believe there's an afterlife, then you have to also believe it's where everyone knows the truth about what happened in this life. It's where they set the record straight."

"You really think that's what happens?"

"Would be nice if it did, right?"

"Yeah, that'd be cool."

"Look, what happened to you and your friends was horrible. But it wasn't your fault. An adult man who's been a waste of space his whole life and his equally useless son were responsible for it. The way I see it, you've got a choice about what you do now."

"I do?"

"Uh-huh. You can let those assholes ruin your life, too, or you can decide not to let them win. You can decide to survive it and to do good in the world. My dad says all the time that we get to choose our destinies, and yours could have something to do with protecting kids from people like those Mayfield guys."

"How do you do it, though? Every time I think of her... I want to die myself."

"When I first went to live with Mrs. Littlefield, it was right after my mom and grandfather died really close together. I was left with no one, and it was super scary. I didn't know what was going to happen to me. I asked her if I'd always feel so sad and scared, and she promised me I wouldn't. She said there was a great big, beautiful life waiting for me to find it. She said my mom and grandfather would always be with me, and they wouldn't want me to suffer forever because they were gone. I bet Luna wouldn't want that for you either."

"I didn't know her well enough to be sure of that."

"I'm pretty sure she was probably a good kid who'd want the best for you."

"Why'd this have to happen?"

"I don't know, bud. I really don't get why bad things have to happen to good people. But one thing I know for sure is that you've got a lot of people who care about you, and if you let us, we'll get you through it."

"Thanks for talking to me."

"I'm here any time you need me. And I mean that."

"I know. My mom is really mad with my dad because he let me go out with my friends. She said it was too soon. I wish I'd listened to her."

"I'm sure they'll figure it out, but that's not your fault either. That's between them."

Ethan cracked the first hint of a grin. "How'd you get so smart, anyway?"

"Life, man. It does that to ya."

S AM RETREATED from the doorway back into the kitchen, where her sisters were talking at the kitchen table. She'd wanted to check on the boys and had overheard their conversation. "You guys… I just heard Scotty talking to Ethan, and… my heart can't handle it."

She returned to her seat at the table, reaching for a napkin to dab at her eyes.

"What were they saying?" Tracy asked.

"Scotty was giving him advice about how to handle bad things, and it was just so… It was lovely."

"That's just what Ethan needs right now."

"Sometimes I forget what Scotty went through before we knew him," Sam said. "He's so well adjusted to his new life, but the trauma is always there."

"And now Ethan has trauma to carry as well."

"Scotty gave him some good advice on how to handle it, and Ethan seemed really open to it."

"It's nice of Scotty to try."

Sam checked her watch. "We need to head home to get him ready for baseball practice."

"Thanks for coming, you guys. It means a lot to us."

"We'll come any time you need us," Angela said.

"Always," Sam said.

AT HOME, Sam went to Scotty's room to make sure he was ready to leave for practice with his detail. "It's fun to be around to see you off."

"It's fun to have you around. And the fake sick day was *epic*."

"We'll do it once in a while."

"Good luck getting that past the POTUS."

"He might be mellowing in his old age."

Scotty cracked up. "Right. I think that could be wishful thinking."

"Hey, bud?"

He glanced at her. "What's up?"

"I heard some of what you said to Ethan. I just wanted to say thank you. He thinks the world of you, and he needed to hear what you had to say."

"I hope it helps."

"You're a very special young man, Scott Cappuano, and I couldn't be prouder to be your mom."

With his baseball bag hooked over one shoulder, he came over to hug her. "I'm pretty proud of you, too."

"I can't begin to tell you how you've made my entire life complete."

"Same goes, Mama."

They hugged until a throat clearing in the hallway alerted them to the arrival of Debra, the lead agent on his detail.

"Love you," Sam whispered.

"Love you, too."

As she watched him go down the hall with Debra, she understood the concept of her heart walking around outside her body, often used to describe motherhood. Just as Scotty reached the stairway, Nick appeared in time for a fist bump before practice.

"See you when you get back," Nick said.

He smiled when he saw her leaning against the wall, arms crossed, watching him come toward her.

"Is this what it's like to be home when you finish work for the day, dear?" she asked when he swept her up in a hug.

"I think it might be."

"I'm digging it. Need to do it more often."

He buried his face in her neck, sending a cascade of goose bumps down her back. "Where're the Littles?"

"Upstairs with Celia, looking at her pictures and videos from Alaska."

"Will they be up there for a while?"

"Celia said she took more than a thousand photos."

Nick grasped her hand and walked them swiftly into their room, kicking the door closed behind him. "Text her to tell her you're taking a little nap and ask if she can keep them up there until dinnertime."

"She might be tired after traveling."

"Ask her anyway."

Sam rolled her eyes at his shamelessness and sent the text.

Celia replied right away that there was nothing she'd rather do than hang out with the twins after missing them so much.

Sam read the response to Nick.

"*Yes.* Thank goodness for grandmothers."

"Wait! Before you go feral on me, I have to watch Neveah give a statement to the press about the resolution of the Carver case."

Nick moaned. Loudly.

"Put it on ice for a minute, Mr. President."

"There'll be no putting anything on ice," he said with a pout as he sat next to her to watch the press briefing.

"I'm so proud of her!" Sam said as Neveah walked through the main doors at headquarters with Captain Malone accompanying her. "She's got to be freaking out on the inside."

"I'm Detective Neveah Charles with the Homicide division, and I'm here to brief you on the arrests of four people in connection to the murder of Dale Carver of Spokane, Washington, at the Vacation Inn and Suites on 10th Street Northwest." She detailed the facts of the case and the investigation that'd led to the arrest of Dale's wife and sister-in-law in Spokane, as well as the two men they'd hired to commit the crime, who were apprehended by the U.S. Marshals in Baltimore.

"How does a wife and mother arrange for murder on the other side of the country?" a reporter asked.

"They did their research and used an encrypted app to reach out to the men they hired. We're in debt to the fine work of the Spokane Police Department as well as the U.S. Marshals, both of which were instrumental in closing this case."

She answered several other routine questions before concluding the gaggle.

Nick had Sam naked and spread out under him in a matter of seconds after Neveah left the podium, or that's how it seemed to Sam.

She looped her arms around his neck. "I have more good news for you, in addition to my protégé bringing home the prisoners from Spokane."

"Better than having you naked in bed when it's still daylight on a weekday?"

"Even better than that. Asher and Brecken Mayfield have been charged with enough felonies to keep them locked up forever. Thirty-two little girls have been reunited with their grateful parents, and Captain Malone is in line for a commendation for thinking to ask if the Mayfields had other storage units. He's getting the rightful credit for finding those girls."

"That's all very good news indeed."

"But I saved the best for last. I'm taking a week off to be a mom and first lady."

"And a wife?"

"That, too."

He kissed her. "I love Vacation Sam. She's all... *uninhibited.*"

"We've still got two kids in the house, so don't get too crazy, Mr. President."

"I'll try not to but just remember what you started earlier with those texts."

"Who, me?"

As he joined their bodies, she sighed from the bone-deep pleasure she could find only with him.

"This week," he said, "we'll roll out our mental health initiative, officially welcome Elijah and the twins to the family and then finally have that spa getaway you got me for Christmas."

"It's already the best week ever, and it's only just begun."

EPILOGUE

On Friday morning at ten o'clock, the Cappuano and Armstrong families appeared before Family Court Judge Denton Seawall to officially complete the adoptions of Elijah, Aubrey and Alden.

While Scotty was thrilled to have a second day off that week, he was more thrilled to have siblings he got to keep forever.

"Mr. President, Mrs. Cappuano and Scotty," Judge Seawall said, "it is my great honor to finalize the adoptions of Elijah, Aubrey and Alden Armstrong into your loving family. I hope you all will have many years of great happiness together as you go forward." He brought down his gavel. "This matter is concluded."

Sam hadn't expected to cry, but after the heartbreaking infertility battles of the past, she couldn't contain the emotional reaction to becoming a mother to four beautiful kids who could never be taken away from them. As she hugged each of them, she said a silent prayer of thanks to whatever higher power had decided she was good enough to be their mother and vowed to love and protect them for the rest of her life.

"Congratulations," her daughter-in-law, Candace, said. "Elijah is thrilled to have this done."

"We're thrilled, too."

Nick's communications team had prepared a release to announce the news of the adoptions that would go live as soon as he gave the go-ahead. "Are we good to release the statement?" he asked after they'd posed for photos with the judge.

Elijah had been tasked with sending one of the photos to Christina to accompany the news.

"Good to go," Eli said after he sent the text.

Nick then sent a text to Christina to release the statement as he and Sam exhaled a collective sigh of relief that nothing had happened at the last minute to derail their plans. They'd been fending off efforts by the twins' maternal grandparents, aunt and uncle to get at their money through the kids for as long as they'd lived together. To know that was now over was a huge load off their minds.

They returned to the White House for a celebratory lunch in the East Room with their extended family, including Tracy, Ethan, Abby, Angela, Jack, Ella, Celia, Brenda, Shelby, Noah and Maisie as well as Nick's dad, Leo, his wife, Stacy, and their sons, Brock and Brayden. Mike had been invited but hadn't come. Tracy said she hadn't talked to him in days, and Angela said he hadn't had much to say to her either.

They'd let the twins choose the menu, which was how they'd ended up dining on chicken tenders, grilled cheese, french fries and milkshakes.

It was the best lunch Sam and Nick had ever had.

They were enjoying ice cream sundaes for dessert when Christina ducked into the room to whisper in Nick's ear. He went completely rigid, which put Sam on alert for trouble.

"What's wrong?"

"The twins' grandparents are reacting—badly—to the news of their adoption. They're accusing us of a craven effort to control the billions of dollars their parents left them."

"What?" Elijah said. "Did I just hear you say..."

"You heard me right," Nick said.

"Could I make a statement to put a stop to this once and for all?" Eli asked.

Sam had never seen the young man look so furious. She placed a hand on Nick's arm. "Let him. It needs to come from him."

"Are you sure?" Nick asked Eli.

"Never been surer in my life."

"We'll go with you," Sam said.

She whispered to Tracy and Angela to tell them what was going on and asked them to take the twins back to the residence when they were done with their ice cream.

"We've got them," Tracy said.

Sam, Nick, Eli and Candace told the kids they'd meet them upstairs in a few minutes and walked to the briefing room, where Christina waited for them with the press, who'd been told the president would be making a statement.

"Elijah will handle the statement," Nick told her.

"Do you want me to introduce him, Mr. President?"

"I'll do it," Nick said, "but thank you."

"Of course."

She stepped aside to allow Nick to move toward the podium.

"Today has been one of the happiest days of my life and Sam's," Nick said. "With the formal adoptions of Elijah, Alden and Aubrey, our family is now complete in a way we never dreamed possible. We're well aware that two extraordinary people had to die in the most horrific, senseless crime to make this day possible for us. Jameson and Cleo Armstrong are very present in all our lives and will remain so going forward. Sam and I are delighted to stand by Elijah's side as he completes his education at Princeton and begins married life with his wife, Candace, and to be given the huge honor of helping to raise Aubrey and Alden. We love them with all our hearts and are the proudest parents in the world today to have four extraordinary children and an exceptional daughter-in-law to love for the rest of our lives. I'm pleased to introduce for the first time as my son, Elijah Armstrong-Cappuano."

Sam's heart had never felt bigger in her chest than it did as she heard Nick introduce Eli as his son.

Elijah stepped before the ravenous White House press corps, showing none of the nerves that must've been raging inside him. His composure made her so proud.

"Today, my brother, sister and I officially became members of the family that has wrapped their loving arms around us for every minute of the last six months since our parents were senselessly murdered. From that first horrible night, Sam and Nick and their extraordinary son, Scotty, stepped up for my precious brother and sister, opening their home and their hearts to two traumatized young children at the worst moment of their lives.

"All that love and support was extended to me, as well, and when it came time to make the most important decision of my life about who would be charged with helping me raise the twins while I finished college and started my career, I never hesitated to leave them exactly where they were, surrounded by the love of an extended family who've made it possible for the three of us to survive the unthinkable loss of parents we adored.

"I'm lucky to still have my mother in my life, in addition to my Cappuano family, and while I would've preferred to keep the twins' maternal family in their lives, they very quickly showed me their true motivations. As they waged a public battle to upend the clear wishes of our parents that I serve as the twins' legal guardian, they've never once inquired about the children's well-being. It's no secret that my father, Jameson Armstrong, was an incredibly successful businessman or that my siblings and I inherited an extensive estate after our parents' deaths. The motives of the twins' maternal relatives have always been clear. They're after one thing and one thing only with this relentless desire to gain custody of my brother and sister—they want to get their hands on the money, especially since their once-profitable business enterprises have failed.

"I would ask them at this juncture to consider the trauma their grandchildren have endured following the loss of our parents and to leave us alone going forward. We've made our choice, and we're honored and delighted to be official members of the Cappuano family as of today. We'll have nothing else to say about this matter now or ever. Thank you."

The reporters shouted questions at Eli as he left the room with Sam, Nick and Candace.

His wife embraced him the second they were behind a closed door. "That was perfect," she said.

"Yes, it was," Nick said.

"I can't believe you came up with that on the fly," Sam said.

"In a way, I've been preparing to say that for six months now. I was ready."

"You did great," Sam said.

"Shall we rejoin the celebration already in progress?" Nick asked.

"Let's go," Eli said with a smile. "That ice cream won't eat itself."

THE NEXT MORNING, Sam and Nick left the twins and Scotty in the capable hands of Eli and Candace for the night and were conveyed by motorcade to Nick's cabin in Virginia, where they'd be treated to facials and a couple's massage. The Secret Service had suggested the cabin as the easiest way to achieve the goal of a "spa weekend" without having to shut down an entire facility.

The aestheticians and massage therapists had been hired by Sam's chief of staff, Lilia Van Nostrand, and had signed iron-clad NDAs to protect their privacy.

"I've never had a facial," Sam told the woman who'd been assigned to her.

"Neither have I," Nick said.

"You're in for a treat."

"This is delightful," Sam said an hour later. "We need to do this more often."

"We need to do a lot of things more often," her husband said from the chair next to hers.

The two women giggled at his comment.

"Don't forget those NDAs," Sam said.

"We'd never say a word, ma'am. Don't worry."

"She's trained to be suspicious by nature," Nick said, making all of them laugh.

After the facials, they moved to massage tables that'd been set up next to the fireplace, where Nick had built a nice fire earlier. They were experiencing an April cold snap that had the region on edge about the impact on the cherry blossoms that were set to bloom soon.

"I've never been more relaxed," Sam said as the therapists kneaded the tension from her muscles while working around Sam and Nick's joined hands across the gap between their tables.

"Same. This was the best idea you've ever had."

At the end of the massages, they waited for the therapists to depart.

Nick waggled his brows at her and whispered, "I want you when you're all greasy."

"Stop."

"Never."

The door to the cabin closed, and they got up slowly, stretching muscles that'd been reduced to jelly. "God, that felt good."

"*So* good. We need to invite them over again soon." He sat on the edge of the massage table in all his glory. "Get over here to see me. I've missed you terribly."

"I was right here!"

"Too far from me."

"You're ridiculous, Mr. President."

"So you like to tell me."

She stepped between his spread legs.

He wrapped her up in his fragrant embrace. "You're all naked and slippery."

She ran her hands over his slick back. "So are you."

"Do you think one of these tables can hold both of us?"

"Do we want to find out the hard way if they can't?"

"Probably not. Come with me, love."

"Where're we going?"

"Not far at all." He grabbed the sheet off his bed, spread it on the rug next to the fireplace and then helped her down next to him. Then he tugged the blanket off his bed over them. "Warm enough?"

She snuggled into his cozy embrace. "Mmm. Perfect."

He ran his hand over her slippery skin. "You're the sexiest mom of four I've ever met."

She laughed. They'd worked their four kids into almost every conversation they'd had in the last eventful week as his new mental health awareness program had gone public with great fanfare and had helped to change the conversation that'd blown up after Eli's statement to the press.

The grandparents weren't going quietly, but they'd all agreed to ignore them going forward.

"A mom of four," Sam said, still incredulous at the twists and turns that'd led them to their destiny.

"Thank you for our beautiful family."

"Thank *you*. None of it happens without you."

"None of it happens without *us*."

"Remember the first time we ever spent a night here, and we were supposed to keep our distance from each other?"

"That was torturous. I wanted you so bad."

"I wanted you just as much. I still do."

He effortlessly arranged her on top of him and his impressive erection.

"What've I told you about handling me like a side of beef?" she asked with a huff of exasperation.

"That you love it and want me to do it more?"

She slapped his shoulder. "That's not what I've said."

He laughed as he held her in place while he pressed against her. "Let's not waste valuable time fighting, babe."

"We're not fighting. We're discussing your propensity to treat me like a side of beef."

"Sexiest side of beef I've ever handled."

"That's not helping your cause."

"How about this, then?" He lifted her just enough to enter her in one deep thrust that had her head falling back in surrender. "Does that help?"

"Yes," she said on a gasp. "Let's talk about that instead."

"My favorite subject."

Sam took control, loving the way his gorgeous hazel eyes heated at the sight of her, shiny with massage oil and lit by the glow of the fire.

"My very own goddess."

"Yes, that's me."

He let his arms fall over his head. "Have your way with me."

"Don't mind if I do."

"I won't mind at all."

THE NEXT AFTERNOON, they were on their way home after a blissful, relaxing getaway when Sam received a call from Gonzo.

"Hey," he said, "sorry to bug you when you're off, but I thought you'd want to know that Mike Hogan has been arrested."

ACK, there it is! The baby cliffhanger I like to leave you with to get us revved up for the next First Family book, *State of Unrest!* Get your copy at *marieforce.com/stateofunrest.*

I'm not going to lie. This one almost killed me as I was plagued with a crazy arm cramp that slowed me way down. HUGE thanks to my editors Joyce Lamb and Linda Ingmanson for editing in chunks while I tried to get to THE END. I'm thrilled with this complex story that brought to light some disturbing topics.

I first became aware of incel culture when I watched the astounding series *Adolescence* on Netflix earlier this year. I'd never heard of it before and fell into a deep rabbit hole reading about it. If you haven't seen the show, I highly recommend it. Among its many other astonishing achievements, each of the four episodes was filmed in one continuous take, which is amazing considering how much content is covered.

Obviously, there's much more to the subculture than I was able to convey here, so I intentionally kept it "high-level" so I wouldn't bog down an already-dense plot with more details than needed to tell this story.

Thank you to my primary beta readers, Kara Conrad and Tracey Suppo, for your many contributions. Gwen Neff reads for continuity, which is a huge help as this series has gotten ridiculously long! Keeping track becomes a tougher job all the time, so I'm thankful for all the help that Gwen and the other Fatal/First Family betas provide, including: Karina, Maricar, Jennifer, Irene, Ellen, Kelley, Sarah, Gina, Phuong, Kelly, Jennifer and Amy.

Thank you also to Captain Russ Hayes, (retired) Newport, RI Police Department, for his assistance in reviewing the police work in this book. I'm so thankful for his contributions over twenty-six Sam and Nick books.

As always, a huge thank you to the amazing team that supports me behind the scenes, including my husband, Dan, and my tremendous HTJB crew: Julie Cupp, Lisa Cafferty, Jean

Mello, Nikki Haley and Ashley Lopez, as well as my daughter and sidekick, Emily Force.

Discuss STATE OF PRESERVATION with spoilers allowed here: *www.facebook.com/groups/stateofpreservation/* and make sure you're a member of the Fatal/First Family Group (no spoilers please) *here: www.facebook.com/groups/FatalSeries*. If you're not receiving weekly emails from me, please join my list at *https://marieforce.com/subscribe* and make sure you indicate where you prefer to get your books, so we can keep you informed of books coming and going from your favorite retailer.

And finally, to the readers who've supported this series for fifteen years, I love how you think of Sam and Nick as real people, just like I do. Thank you for your love and support of me and my books.

Xoxo

Marie

ALSO BY MARIE FORCE

Romantic Suspense Novels Available from Marie Force

The First Family Series

Book 1: State of Affairs

Book 2: State of Grace

Book 3: State of the Union

Book 4: State of Shock

Book 5: State of Denial

Book 6: State of Bliss

Book 7: State of Suspense

Book 8: State of Alert

Book 9: State of Retribution

Book 10: State of Preservation

Book 11: State of Unrest

Book 12: State of Mind *(2026)*

Read Sam and Nick's earlier stories in the Fatal Series!

*The Fatal Series**

One Night With You, *A Fatal Series Prequel Novella*

Book 1: Fatal Affair

Book 2: Fatal Justice

Book 3: Fatal Consequences

Book 3.5: Fatal Destiny, *the Wedding Novella*

Book 4: Fatal Flaw

Book 5: Fatal Deception

Book 6: Fatal Mistake

Book 7: Fatal Jeopardy

Book 8: Fatal Scandal

Book 9: Fatal Frenzy

Book 10: Fatal Identity

Book 11: Fatal Threat

Book 12: Fatal Chaos

Book 13: Fatal Invasion

Book 14: Fatal Reckoning

Book 15: Fatal Accusation

Book 16: Fatal Fraud

Fatal Series Compendium

Contemporary Romances Available from Marie Force

The Wild Widows Series—a Fatal Series Spin-Off

Book 1: Someone Like You *(Roni & Derek)*

Book 2: Someone to Hold *(Iris & Gage)*

Book 3: Someone to Love *(Wynter & Adrian)*

Book 4: Someone to Watch Over Me *(Lexi & Tom)*

Book 5: Someone to Remember *(All Cast)*

Book 6: Someone to Save *(2027)*

*The Gansett Island Series**

Book 1: Maid for Love *(Mac & Maddie)*

Book 2: Fool for Love *(Joe & Janey)*

Book 3: Ready for Love *(Luke & Sydney)*

Book 4: Falling for Love *(Grant & Stephanie)*

Book 5: Hoping for Love *(Evan & Grace)*

Book 6: Season for Love *(Owen & Laura)*

Book 7: Longing for Love *(Blaine & Tiffany)*

Book 8: Waiting for Love *(Adam & Abby)*

Book 9: Time for Love *(David & Daisy)*

Book 10: Meant for Love *(Jenny & Alex)*

Book 10.5: Chance for Love, *A Gansett Island Novella (Jared & Lizzie)*

Book 11: Gansett After Dark *(Owen & Laura)*

Book 12: Kisses After Dark *(Shane & Katie)*

Book 13: Love After Dark *(Paul & Hope)*

Book 14: Celebration After Dark *(Big Mac & Linda)*

Book 15: Desire After Dark *(Slim & Erin)*

Book 16: Light After Dark *(Mallory & Quinn)*

Book 17: Victoria & Shannon (Episode 1)

Book 18: Kevin & Chelsea (Episode 2)

A Gansett Island Christmas Novella *(Appears in Mine After Dark)*

Book 19: Mine After Dark *(Riley & Nikki)*

Book 20: Yours After Dark *(Finn & Chloe)*

Book 21: Trouble After Dark *(Deacon & Julia)*

Book 22: Rescue After Dark *(Mason & Jordan)*

Book 23: Blackout After Dark *(Full Cast)*

Book 24: Temptation After Dark *(Gigi & Cooper)*

Book 25: Resilience After Dark *(Jace & Cindy)*

Book 26: Hurricane After Dark *(Full Cast)*

Book 27: Renewal After Dark *(Duke & McKenzie)*

Book 28: Delivery After Dark *(Full Cast)*

Gansett Island Compendium, Volume 1, Books 1-14

Gansett Island Compendium, Volume 2, Books 15-28

Downeast

Dan & Kara: A Downeast Prequel

Homecoming: A Downeast Novel

The Quantum Series

Book 1: Virtuous *(Flynn & Natalie)*

Book 2: Valorous *(Flynn & Natalie)*

Book 3: Victorious *(Flynn & Natalie)*

Book 4: Rapturous *(Addie & Hayden)*

Book 5: Ravenous *(Jasper & Ellie)*

Book 6: Delirious *(Kristian & Aileen)*

Book 7: Outrageous *(Emmett & Leah)*

Book 8: Famous *(Marlowe & Sebastian)*

Book 9: Illustrious *(Max & Stella)*

Book 10: Momentous *(Olivia's story, coming 2026)*

Remington Family Law Series—A Quantum Series Spin-Off

Book 1: Acrimonious

Book 2: Contentious *(Sept. 2026)*

Book 3: Ferocious *(2027)*

The Green Mountain Series*

Book 1: All You Need Is Love *(Will & Cameron)*

Book 2: I Want to Hold Your Hand *(Nolan & Hannah)*

Book 3: I Saw Her Standing There *(Colton & Lucy)*

Book 4: And I Love Her *(Hunter & Megan)*

Novella: You'll Be Mine *(Will & Cam's Wedding)*

Book 5: It's Only Love *(Gavin & Ella)*

Book 6: Ain't She Sweet *(Tyler & Charlotte)*

The Butler, Vermont Series*

(Continuation of Green Mountain)

Book 1: Every Little Thing *(Grayson & Emma)*

Book 2: Can't Buy Me Love *(Mary & Patrick)*

Book 3: Here Comes the Sun *(Wade & Mia)*

Book 4: Till There Was You *(Lucas & Dani)*

Book 5: All My Loving *(Landon & Amanda)*

Book 6: Let It Be *(Lincoln & Molly)*

Book 7: Come Together *(Noah & Brianna)*

Book 8: Here, There & Everywhere *(Izzy & Cabot)*

Book 9: The Long and Winding Road *(Max & Lexi)*

*The Miami Nights Series**

Book 1: How Much I Feel *(Carmen & Jason)*

Book 2: How Much I Care *(Maria & Austin)*

Book 3: How Much I Love *(Dee's story)*

Nochebuena, A Miami Nights Novella

Book 4: How Much I Want *(Nico & Sofia)*

Book 5: How Much I Need *(Milo & Gianna)*

*The Treading Water Series**

Book 1: Treading Water *(Jack & Andy)*

Book 2: Marking Time *(Clare & Aidan)*

Book 3: Starting Over *(Brandon & Daphne)*

Book 4: Coming Home *(Reid & Kate)*

Book 5: Finding Forever *(Maggie & Brayden)*

Single Titles

In the Air Tonight

Five Years Gone

One Year Home

Sex Machine

Sex God

Georgia on My Mind

True North

The Fall

The Wreck

Love at First Flight

Everyone Loves a Hero

Line of Scrimmage

Historical Romance Available from Marie Force

*The Gilded Series**

Book 1: Duchess by Deception

Book 2: Deceived by Desire

** Completed Series*

ABOUT THE AUTHOR

Marie Force is the *New York Times* best-selling author of 120 contemporary romance, romantic suspense and erotic romance novels. Her series include Remington Family Law, Fatal, First Family, Gansett Island, Butler Vermont, Quantum, Treading Water, Miami Nights and Wild Widows. She has also written 12 single titles. 

Her books have sold more than 15 million copies worldwide, have been translated into more than a dozen languages and have appeared on the *New York Times* bestseller list more than 30 times. She is also a *USA Today* and #1 *Wall Street Journal* bestseller, as well as a Spiegel bestseller in Germany.

Her goals in life are simple—to spend as much time as possible with her adult children, to keep writing books for as long as she possibly can and to never be on a flight that makes the news.

Join Marie's mailing list on her website at *marieforce.com* for news about new books and upcoming appearances in your area. Follow her on Facebook, at *www.Facebook.com/MarieForceAuthor* and Instagram *@marieforceauthor*. Contact Marie at *marie@marieforce.com*.

9 781966 871187